UPTOWN GIRL

Olivia Goldsmith is the bestselling author of *The First Wives Club*, *Flavour of the Month*, *Bestseller*, *The Switch*, *Young Wives*, *Bad Boy* and most recently, *Insiders*. She has contributed to *The New York Times*, *Cosmopolitan*, *In Style*, and the *Observer*, among other publications. She lives in Manhattan. For more about Olivia Goldsmith, visit her website at www.olivia-goldsmith.com.

Acclaim for Olivia Goldsmith:

'Full of wisecracks and gossip . . . Olivia Goldsmith can keep you reading'
Cosmopolitan

'A bubbly, fizzy story'
Daily Mail

'Olivia Goldsmith's forte has always been the writing of revenge novels with great good humor'
Washington Post

'Goldsmith hands out her characters' rewards and come-uppances like Jane Austen dealing blackjack . . . You keep licking your fingers and reaching for the next page as if it were another potato chip'
Newsweek

'Fizzing with acerbic dialogue and high-level sexual slapstick'
Good Housekeeping

OLIVIA GOLDSMITH

Uptown Girl

BCA

This edition published 2003
by BCA
by arrangement with HarperCollins*Publishers*

CN 114082

Typeset in Meridien by Palimpsest Book Production Limited,
Polmont, Stirlingshire

Printed and bound in Great Britain by
Mackays of Chatham Ltd, Chatham, Kent

To Nina
and to
Ethel Esther Brandsfronbrener Schutz
A lover of books, mangos, oranges and me

Acknowledgements

Perhaps belatedly, as this is my tenth novel, I would like to most sincerely thank those of you who have read my books. I hope they have given you much enjoyment and diversion. It is difficult to make one's way as a writer, and the reception I have gotten in the UK has always touched and delighted me. I am obviously American, more deeply a New Yorker, but my great grandmother and grandfather emigrated to the States from Liverpool and I have always been an Anglophile. From the time I began writing on the top of London buses to the day when my first novel was accepted for publication in London and I walked out of the doors and down Fulham Road telling myself over and over that 'I am an author', I have met with fairness, encouragement, intelligence and humor, all of which have delighted me. I thank you all, and only hope that I have, at times, delighted you.

Almost as importantly, I would like to thank the people at HarperCollins UK. I have been very, very lucky, and I know it is largely due to your efforts. While editors, sales staff, publicists and publishers have shifted and moved on, I would like to thank HarperCollins past and present. Special thanks to Lynne Drew, who both 'gets' me and expertly guides me, Nick Sayers, who has bet on me again and again, the legendary Rachel Hore and her gentle but brilliant proddings, Jennifer Parr for her humor, encouragement and attention to detail (not to mention a few great shout lines), Karen Duffy, certainly the best publicity manager in all the world, Jane Harris for her tireless effort on my books' behalf, Lee Motley for her inspired artistry, Martin Palmer and James Prichard for their unflagging enthusiasm and, of course, to Amanda Ridout, who makes all things possible.

I'd also like to acknowledge the help and support of Val Hudson, Philip Gwyn Jones, David Young, Malcolm Edwards, Imogen Taylor, and my very dear friend Adrian Bourne.

I am sure I have inadvertently left out others who have been wonderfully kind. Your omission is not for lack of appreciation but for lack of functioning brain cells. Please forgive me and know that, despite my momentary lapse, you have my thanks.

1

Katherine Sean Jameson sat behind her desk and looked at her client. Although she was a published psychologist with a doctorate and had even completed some post-doc work, her office was simply furnished. It didn't feature Freud's classic psychiatric couch. That was because Kate Jameson wasn't a Freudian, and certainly didn't need an office full of relics and pottery shards to look at. To look at her what you'd see was rather a mildly pretty twenty-four-year-old (though she was actually thirty-one) with long curls of wild red hair. Now, as she looked at Brian Conroy, she unconsciously twisted those curls into an impromptu bun at the nape of her neck and pushed a pencil through it to hold it in place, a practiced motion.

It was warm. Her office was not air-conditioned and the breeze from the open window felt good on the back of her neck. Brian, looking intently at her, was sweating, but it could just as easily have been from nerves as from the unseasonable April heat.

Kate sat silently. Silence was an important part of her work, though not something that came naturally. But she had learned that at times stillness and space were all that were needed.

Not today apparently. Brian pulled his eyes guiltily away from hers and looked around the office. Instead of the usual museum reproductions, all of the wall space not covered by bookshelves displayed pictures done by children – some of them very disturbing. Kate watched, waiting to see if Brian's attention focused on one. Like Rorschach's ink blot test, artistic expression often helped to open doors. She withheld a sigh. She was trying to wait Brian out but was conscious of their time ticking away and for his sake she needed immediate results. Brian was obviously in crisis. His teacher said he was showing signs of obsessive-compulsive disorder or even schizophrenia and was disrupting the class. And disruption simply wasn't allowed at Andrew Country Day School. A private school in a smart neighborhood in Manhattan, it accepted only the best and the brightest – of students and staff. Every amenity was provided, from an indoor swimming pool to a state-of-the-art computer center, to language lessons that included Japanese and French for six-year-olds. That's why there was a school psychologist. Kate had only gotten the plum job recently, and Brian, like other kids who showed the slightest 'difficult' behavior, seemed to be immediately remanded to her office. Nothing was to disrupt the smooth daily ingestion of information by the children of the elite.

'Do you know why you've come here, Brian?' she asked, her voice gentle. Brian shook his head. Kate rose from her desk, moved around it and sat down in one of the small chairs beside her eight-year-old 'client'. 'Can you guess?' He shook his head. 'Well, do you think it's for eating gummy elephants in school?'

He looked at her for a moment then shook his head again. 'There's no such thing as gummy elephants.'

'Gummy rhinos?' Kate asked. Brian shook his head again. 'Eating peanut butter and raccoon sandwiches at your desk?'

'It wasn't for *eating* anything,' he said. Then he lowered his voice to barely a whisper. 'It was for talking. Talking in class.'

Kate nodded, the pencil fell out of her bun and her hair cascaded down over her face while the pencil clattered to the floor. Brian smiled and actually let a giggle escape before he covered his mouth. Good, Kate thought. She leaned closer to her little patient. 'You're not just here for talking in class, Brian. If you were just talking in class, then you'd be sent to the principal's office, right?'

Brian's adorable face gazed up at Kate with terrified eyes. 'Are you *worse* than the principal?' he whispered.

Kate felt such empathy for the boy at that moment that she was tempted to take his hand in hers, but he was so very anxious that he might shy away. This kind of work was so delicate – like dealing with Venetian spun glass where the slightest jolt could shatter it – and she often felt so clumsy.

'Nobody is worse than the principal,' Kate said. Then she smiled and winked at Brian. None of the kids at Andrew Country Day liked Mr McKay and – as so often – their instincts were good. 'Do I look as bad as Mr McKay?' Kate asked, feigning shock.

Brian shook his head vigorously.

'Well. Thank goodness. Anyway I do something different. You aren't here to be punished because you didn't do anything wrong. But everybody hears you talking – even though you're not talking to anybody.' She watched as Brian's eyes filled with tears.

'I'll be quieter,' he promised. Kate wanted to scoop him up onto her lap and let him cry as long as he needed to. After all, his mother had just died of cancer and he was still so very young. Kate's own mother had passed away when she was eleven, and that had been almost unbearable.

She dared to take one of the boy's hands in hers and said, 'I don't want you to be quiet, Brian. You do what you need to. But I'd like to know what you're saying.'

Brian shook his head again. His eyes changed from tearful to frightened. 'I can't tell,' he whispered. Then he averted his face. He mumbled something else and Kate only managed to hear one word but it was enough.

Go slow, she told herself. Go very, very slowly and casually. 'You're doing magic?' she asked. Brian, face still turned away, nodded his head, but didn't speak. Kate was already afraid she had gone too far. She held her breath. Then, after a long moment, she lowered her own voice to a whisper and asked, 'Why can't you tell?'

'Because . . .' Brian started, then it burst out of him '. . . because it's magic and you can't tell magic or your wish won't come true. Like birthday candles. Everybody knows that!' He got up and walked to the corner of the room.

Kate actually felt relieved. The boy wasn't schizophrenic. He was caught in a typical childhood trap: total power-lessness combined with hopeless longing and guilt. A toxic cocktail. Kate gave Brian a moment. She didn't want him to feel trapped. Yet he shouldn't be alone with this pain. She approached him slowly, the way you might move toward a strange puppy. She put her hand on the little boy's shoulder. 'Your wish is about your mother, isn't it?' she asked, her voice as neutral as she could manage to keep it. Brian didn't need any of her emotions – he needed space for his own. 'Isn't that right?'

Brian looked up at her and nodded. His face registered a cautious relief. The dreadful burdens of childhood secrets always touched Kate. Though she was a long-lapsed Catholic, she still remembered the power and release of the confessional. She had to serve this child well. 'What are you wishing for?' she asked, her voice as gentle as she could make it.

Brian began to cry. His face, usually so pale, flushed deep rose. Speaking through his tears, he said, 'I thought if I just said "Mommy, come back" a million times that she would be back.' He sobbed and put his face against Kate's skirt. 'But it isn't working. I think I've said it two million times.'

Kate's own eyes filled with tears. She took a deep breath.

She could feel the heat of Brian's face through the thin fabric of her skirt. The hell with professional detachment. She scooped Brian into her arms and over to one of the chairs. He was as small and light as a crushed sparrow. The boy nestled against her. After a time he stopped crying, but his silent neediness was even sadder. They sat for a few moments, but Kate knew their session was nearly over and she had to speak. 'Oh, Brian, I am so sorry,' she told him. 'But magic doesn't work. I wish it did. The doctors did everything they could to help your mommy. They couldn't fix her and magic can't fix that. It's not your fault that the doctors couldn't save her.' She paused. 'And it's not your fault your mommy can't come back.' Kate sighed. Breaking children's hearts, even to help them, had not been in her job description. 'But she can't and your magic can't work.'

Brian suddenly pushed against her, wriggling his way out of her embrace. He stood up and looked angrily at her. 'Why not?' he demanded. 'Why can't my magic work?' He glared at Kate for another moment then pushed her hard and barreled out of the room, nearly knocking over the dollhouse. The office door crashed and rebounded open. From down the hall, she heard a voice – Elliot Winston's – try to stop Brian. 'Shut up, you stinky dick!' Brian shouted. Kate winced and listened to the little boy's footsteps recede.

A moment later, Elliot stuck his head around Kate's door. 'Another satisfied customer?' he asked, his eyebrows raised nearly to his receding hairline. 'Perhaps you should have stuck with French.'

Kate had majored in French as an undergraduate. For a while she had even considered continuing her language studies in graduate school. She had never regretted not doing so, because her work with the children was so satisfying, but, occasionally, particularly at moments like this one, Elliot – one of the math teachers, and her best friend – teased her about her choice.

'As I recall, the German for "stinky dick" would be *reichende Steine*. What would you say in French?'

'I would say you are very annoying,' Kate told him. 'That's good enough. And that Brian and I are making some progress. He expressed some of his true feelings today.'

'Brian also expressed his feelings about me and my genital odor. Congratulations on your progress.' Elliot stepped into the room and sat beside the dollhouse in an overstuffed chair – the only piece of adult-size furniture in Kate's office aside from her own desk and chair. Elliot was dark-haired, average in height, slightly over-average in weight and possessed a much, much higher than average IQ. As usual he was wearing wrinkled chinos, a baggy T-shirt and a clashing open-necked shirt on top. Putting his feet up on the toy box, he opened his lunch sack.

Kate sighed. She and Elliot usually had lunch together. But, today, Elliot had had the dreaded cafeteria duty and was just now, at nearly two thirty, getting a chance to eat. She delighted in his company but she was melancholy from her session with Brian. Elliot, fresh from the horror of the lunchroom, was blithely unaware of her mood as he pulled out several items and tore into a sandwich that smelled suspiciously like corned beef.

'Brian is in Sharon's class, isn't he?' Elliot asked too casually.

Kate nodded. 'Poor kid. His mother dies and his teacher is the Wicked Witch of the Upper West Side.' Kate had to smile. Neither she nor Elliot had much use for Sharon Jones, a truly lazy teacher and a deeply annoying woman.

'So aside from a recently deceased mom, what's bugging Brian?' Elliot asked.

Kate felt too brittle for their usual badinage. 'You have mustard on your chin,' she told him, but as Elliot reached up to wipe it, the glob fell onto his shirt.

'Oops,' he said and dabbed ineffectually at his shirtfront

with one of the hard paper towels from the school's bath-rooms. The yellow splotch looked particularly hideous on the green of his shirt. Watching Elliot eat, Kate often thought, was a spectator sport.

'He believes that magic can bring his mother back,' she sighed wistfully.

'See? See what I mean? They're all obsessed with witches and wizards. Damn that Harry Potter!' Elliot said, than took another huge bite of the sandwich. 'So what's your pre-scription?'

'I want him to give up the magic and get in touch with his anger and pain,' Kate answered.

'Oi vey!' Elliot said with the best Yiddish accent a gay man from Indiana could ever manage. 'When will you give up on this quest to get every little boy at Andrew Country Day in touch with his true feelings? And why discourage magic in his case? What else does the kid have?'

'Oh, come on, Elliot! Because magic won't work and he mustn't think it's his fault when it fails.' She shook her head. 'You of all people. A trained statistician. A man who could trade this job in, triple your salary and become chief actuary at any pension fund. *You're* telling me to encourage magic?'

Elliot shrugged. 'Haven't you ever had magical things happen?'

Kate refused the bait. Elliot, raised in the Midwest and stoic to the bone, had told her 'the unexamined life is the only one livable'. He often challenged her about the efficacy of psychology. Now, just to annoy her, he was going to take a perverse stand on magic. 'If you think you're going to start an argument today, Elliot,' she warned him, 'you're out of your mind.' Then, to annoy him – as well as for his own good – she added, 'I didn't think corned beef was good for your cholesterol.'

'Oh, what's a few hundred points one way or the other?' he asked cheerfully, swallowing another mouthful.

'You've got a death wish,' Kate said.

'Ooooh. Harsh words from a shrink.' Elliot winced mockingly as he opened a Snapple.

'Look, I'm leaving,' she told him, gathering some notes from her desk and putting them into her file cabinet. If she left now she'd be able to do a bit of shopping before meeting her friend Bina. She took a lipstick and mirror out of her purse, dabbed the color over her mouth and smiled wide to make sure she didn't have lipstick on her teeth. 'I'll see you for dinner.'

'Where are you going?'

'None of your bee's wax.'

'A secret? Come on. Tell! What if I threw a tantrum like Brian did?' Elliot reached into the toy box at his feet. Then he hurled a stuffed bear in Kate's direction. 'Would you tell me then?' The plush missile hit her squarely in the face. Elliot curled up in the chair, held his hands in front of his own face and started to beg rapidly. 'It was an accident. I'm sorry, I'm sorry, I'm sorry.'

'I'll show you sorry,' Kate warned as she threw the bear back at Elliot, but missed.

'You throw like a girl,' Elliot taunted. Then he picked up another animal and threw it at Kate. 'Duck!' he called as he reached for yet another toy to throw. It was indeed a duck, yellow and fluffy.

'Duck this, you math nerd,' Kate almost shouted as she grabbed a fuzzy rabbit and pummeled Elliot's head. It felt good to blow off some steam.

'Abuse! Abuse!' Elliot screamed in delight as he rolled off the chair to protect himself. 'Teacher abuse! Teacher abuse!'

'Shut up, you idiot!' Kate told him and rushed to close the office door. She turned from it just in time to get a stuffed elephant right in the face. Stunned for only a moment, Kate grabbed the pachyderm and lunged at Elliot. 'I'll show you abuse, you sniveling cholesterol warehouse,' she threatened as she fell on top of Elliot and beat him repeatedly with the toy.

Elliot fought back with both an inflatable flamingo *and* a stuffed dog. He might be gay, but he was no wussy. When he and Kate were both exhausted (and – sadly – the flamingo's leg was punctured), they sat panting and laughing together in the big chair, Kate on top. The door opened.

'Excuse me?' Mr McKay asked, but despite his words he wasn't the type to excuse anything. 'I thought I heard a ruckus in here.'

Mr McKay, the principal of Andrew Country Day lower school, was a hypocrite, a social climber, a control freak and a very bad dresser. He also had a knack of using words no one else had used for several decades.

'A ruckus?' Elliot asked.

'We were just testing out a new therapy,' Kate extemporized. 'Did it disturb you?' she asked innocently.

'Well, it was certainly loud,' George McKay complained.

'From the little I know of it, AAT – Airborne Animal Therapy – can frequently be noisy,' Elliot said, po-faced, 'although it's having significant measurable success in schools for the gifted where it's being pioneered. Of course,' he added, 'it might not be right for this setting.' He nodded at Kate. 'I'm not the expert,' he said as if he were deferring to Kate's professional judgment. She smothered a laugh with a cough.

'We'll put this off until after three o'clock, Mr McKay,' she promised.

'All right then,' he said primly. He left as suddenly as he had arrived, shutting the door with a firm but controlled click. Kate and Elliot looked at one another, waited for a count of ten, then burst into giggles that they had to stifle.

'AAT?' Kate gurgled.

'Hey, straight men love acronyms. Think of the army. He'll be on the internet in less than ten minutes searching for Airborne Animal Therapy,' Elliot predicted. He stood up and began collecting the stuffed animals. Kate got up to help him. The irony of the situation was that Elliot had helped Kate get hired and since then George McKay had told several teachers that he suspected them of having an affair. Ridiculous as that idea was, the sight of the two of them in the chair was not one to instill confidence in George McKay, who had frequently announced at teachers' meetings that he 'discouraged fraternizing among professional educational co-workers'.

When Kate and her 'professional educational co-worker' finished laughing she smoothed her skirt and put her hair back up, this time with a barrette she found in her drawer. Elliot was standing still, looking down at the chair. He heaved a dramatic sigh.

'Oh shit!' he told her. 'You crushed my banana.' He held up the mangled fruit from his lunch bag which had slipped under them during the battle.

Kate turned, struck the pose of a *femme fatale* and rasped, 'How times have changed. You used to like it when I did that.'

Elliot laughed. 'I'll leave all banana handling to you and Michael.'

Kate's new boyfriend, Dr Michael Atwood, was going with her to dinner at Elliot's place. Kate felt a little flurry in her stomach at the thought. She hoped they'd like each other.

'If I don't leave now, I'll be late tonight,' Kate told him.

'Okay, okay.'

She picked up her purse to prepare for leaving.

'So you like your work so far,' Elliot said. Kate nodded. She loved it. 'But even though I helped you get the job, you're still not going to let me know where you're going.'

Kate didn't bother to answer. Elliot was what people in Brooklyn called 'a noodge'.

2

In all the years Kate had known Elliot – over ten now – he'd always managed to cheer her up when she was sad and support her in her successes. Now, as they walked down the corridor to his classroom, she glanced at him affectionately. The stretched-out orange T-shirt, the ugly green over-shirt decorated with mustard, the slight love handles and the wrinkled chinos didn't make him look like much but he had a keen mind and was a loving and generous friend. She felt a swell of gratitude toward him. As always, he had cheered her up and helped her make the break from school. Kate was proud of the work she did with the kids. She had learned a lot from them, too. For one thing, the school catered to the children of the rich and successful but Kate saw that money, privilege, and education brought as much misery as had her own deprived childhood. She had lost her resentment of those with money and she was grateful for that. She had not picked her calling for the money it earned; in fact, she regarded her work as a kind of vocation. It was one thing she never made light of, and she often found it hard to leave it behind at the end of the day. But tonight she had to, to help Bina prepare for her big night, and then, later, to introduce Michael to Elliot and his partner Brice at dinner.

She waited just inside Elliot's classroom as he chucked the offending lunch sack in a bin and started messing about in his untidy desk.

'You know, it's very hard not to keep thinking about Brian. He's so adorable, and has had a really difficult time. And I think the disappointment when his magic doesn't work, which of course it won't, could cause real problems later.' Kate sighed. 'Boys are just so much more fragile than girls.'

'Tell me about it.' Elliot sighed deeply too. 'I'm still getting over the time Phyllis Bellusico told me I smelled.'

'Did you?' Kate asked, ready to be either his straight man or his audience. She was used to Elliot's shticks. Since college they had been amusing one another with dark humor from their childhoods.

'Well, yes,' Elliot admitted reluctantly, 'but I smelled *good*. I should have. I'd dumped an entire bottle of my mother's White Shoulders into my underpants.'

'Pee-yuw.' Kate imitated any one of her lower school 'clients'. 'Maybe Brian has a point. I'd have to agree with Phyllis,' she said. 'And this happened . . . ?'

'. . . In third grade, but with a little more therapy and Brice's love and support I expect to get over it in the next decade.'

Kate loved it when Elliot got going. She had to laugh.

Elliot had been tormented by kids in school. After a moment he said, 'I have to go to Dean & Deluca to get rice for our dinner tonight. Brice is making his world-famous risotto. You can tell Michael it's your recipe. The way to a man's heart . . .'

Kate looked up with a suspicious glance. 'Yeah, and please be on your best behavior. Elliot,' she began, 'can't you just . . .'

'No,' Elliot retorted, 'I can't just anything.' He walked over to her and gave her a quick hug. 'I don't want to discourage or criticize you. I just want to make sure you know what you're doing.'

'Oh, God, Elliot! Who knows what they're doing when they try to find a soul mate?'

'Well, you have a point there. But I don't want you to be hurt again, Kate.' He paused. Kate knew where he was going and she didn't want him to. Her last entanglement had ended so badly that she didn't know how she would have gotten through it without Elliot. She had invested a lot of time and emotion in Steven Kaplan, all of it worse than wasted. It had left her more suspicious and distrusting of men than she liked to admit. One of the good things about Michael was that she could trust him completely. He might not have Steven's banter and easy charm but he had substance and achievement and sincerity. At least she thought so.

'That's why you're meeting Michael.'

'Ever since Steven, I get to meet your *new* boyfriends. I'd like you to just find the right one and make him an *old* boyfriend.'

'He's thirty-four. Old enough?'

Elliot rolled his eyes. 'I worry about you.'

Kate looked directly at Elliot. 'This one is different. He's got his doctorate in anthropology and he's very promising.'

'Promising what? You always think they're different and you always think they're promising, until they bore you and then . . .'

'Oh, stop,' Kate interrupted. 'I know: I won't pick losers on account of my father and I won't pick winners on account of my father. Yadda, yadda, yadda.'

'Don't leave out your fear of commitment, yadda.'

'I'll have you committed if you bring that up one more time. How come for thirty-one years you're allowed to be a gay bachelor – in both respects of the phrase – and then one day you hook up with Brice. Bingo! But since then I'm neurotic for not doing the same.'

'Hey, I don't want you to hook up with Brice,' Elliot mock-protested. 'We're both strictly monogamous.'

'I can't tell you how relieved I am to hear that,' Kate retorted. 'But don't project your fears onto me. It isn't easy to find a kind-hearted, dependable, intelligent, sensual single man in Manhattan.'

'Tell me about it!' Elliot exclaimed. 'I had to try almost every guy on the island before I met Brice.'

'Try not to be bitter, Elliot. I try so hard not to be.' She reached up and wiped off a remaining bit of banana from his mouth with her thumb, then gave him a little peck on the lips. 'Do you really have to be gay?' It wasn't the first time she had asked him that. Ever since their college years – when the two of them became instant friends during a calculus class that bored him and that Kate had barely managed to pass – Kate had depended on Elliot to be her friend, sometimes her brother, more often her sister, and occasionally even her father. Elliot was family. Still, like family, he could be a pain in the ass. Then she smiled. Elliot was everything to her, except her lover. And sometimes she thought that's what made her love him the most. Elliot was safe. Unlike the other men in her life, Elliot would always be there.

'What makes you think I'm gay?' Elliot asked with wide-eyed innocence. 'Is that your professional opinion, Doctor, or just a guess? Is it my spectator pumps?'

In fact, Elliot was not a flamboyant homosexual. He didn't look or act like what Kate's old Brooklyn crowd might have called 'a fag' and, like most of the young gay men in New York, he didn't go in for the high-maintenance *GQ* look. Elliot looked and acted like a grade school math teacher – no, what he looked like, she thought affectionately, was a classic nerd: the only thing missing was the broken glasses held together with a paper clip.

'How did a little queer kid from Indiana get to be so well adjusted?' Kate asked him, also not for the first time.

Elliot reached over, took one of Kate's hands and held it in both of his. 'Listen closely,' he told her, 'because I am

14

going to tell you something from Indiana about getting in touch with your true feelings.' He looked at her intently and asked, 'Are you listening, because I am *not* going to repeat this.' Kate nodded, and Elliot continued. 'I got in touch with my true feelings by learning how to mask them very early in life. When you realize that your true feelings are most likely going to get the shit kicked out of you, you learn how to hide them for as long as you have to. You wait for a safe place to express them.' He smiled and gave Kate's hand a gentle squeeze. 'Like I do with you and Brice. But I wouldn't tell a kid to try and find a best friend and a lover here at Andrew Country Day.'

'I hear you,' Kate agreed, and thought of poor Brian again.

'So, what *are* you doing before dinner? Feel like making the trip to Dean & Deluca with me first?'

Kate noticed the time – she'd have to hurry now – and gathered up her backpack and cotton sweater. 'No can do. I must run. I have a date.'

'You're meeting this early with Michael?' Elliot asked, surprised. 'You have a date with him *before* he's coming to dinner with us?'

'It's not with Michael.'

'You have another date with someone else before Michael? And I don't know about it?' Elliot's voice rose with shock and offense. 'How could that happen? On average we speak six point four times a day in person and two point nine times by phone. A date I don't know everything about is a statistical improbability.'

Kate rolled her eyes and decided to put him out of his misery. 'It's just a date with Bina. Barbie's told her Jack is finally popping the question tonight – they're going to Nobu because Jack wants to make it really special – and to help prepare her I'm taking her out for a manicure.' She wriggled her fingers in the air. 'They should look good for the ring,' she said in an accent similar to Bina's Brooklynese.

15

'You're kidding! And you didn't tell me?' Elliot asked.

She shrugged, slipped on her jacket, shouldered her bag and started toward the door. 'I guess not.'

Elliot followed her to the school door. 'The fabled Bina and the much-sought-after Jack. Together at last.'

'Yep, wedding bells have broken up that old gang of mine,' Kate said. 'Bye-bye Bitches of Bushwick. It's only Bunny and me left unmarried.' She looked down at her Swatch, refusing to engage with the depression this thought gave her. 'Gotta go.'

'Where are you and Bina getting together?' Elliot demanded.

'In SoHo,' Kate answered, as she pushed against the bar of the school safety door.

'Oh, good. I'm going that way. Just let me pick up my stuff.'

'Forget it,' Kate told him sternly.

'No. No. Wait for me!' he begged. 'We can take the subway together and I can finally meet Bina.'

Kate tried to keep her face still. Elliot had waged a year's-long campaign to meet her old Brooklyn gang. But Kate didn't need it. In fact, as she'd made clear more times than she could count, she loathed the idea. She'd tried in the dozen years since she'd left home to erase most of the dark memories of her troubled background and though she was still close friends with Bina Horowitz and occasionally saw her other pals, she didn't need Elliot's jaundiced eye appraising them.

Kate gave him a look. She disappeared out of the door, then called back, 'You need to meet Bina like I need another unemployed boyfriend.'

She thought she was safely away and down the steps of the school when she heard Elliot behind her. He had a madras hat on and was clutching his backpack with one hand while he ran in a crouch that was a cross between Groucho's walk and a begging position. 'Oh, come on,' he pleaded. 'It's not fair.'

'Tragic. Absolutely tragic. Just like so many things in life,'

16

Kate told him and kept on walking while he flapped at his other backpack strap.

'How come I never get to meet any of your Brooklyn friends? They sound so fascinating,' he demanded.

Kate stopped in the schoolyard and turned back to Elliot. 'Bina may be a lot of things, but fascinating is not one of them.' The girl had been her best friend since third grade and was still, in some ways, the most dependable. Kate had spent every holiday and most summer vacations at Bina's, partly because the Horowitz house was so clean and orderly and Bina's mom was so kind, but mostly because it allowed Kate to avoid the empty apartment that was her home or, worse, her father who was too often drunk.

If Kate had perhaps outgrown Bina, who'd dropped out of Brooklyn College and worked at her father's chiropractic office, it didn't stop her from loving her. It was just that they had different interests and none of Bina's would appeal to Elliot or any other of her Manhattan friends.

'Elliot,' Kate said sternly, as they made their way down the street. 'You know your interest in Bina is only idle curiosity.'

'Come on,' Elliot coaxed. 'Let me come. Anyway, it's a free country. The Constitution says so.'

Kate snorted. 'Like the US Constitution, I believe in the separation of church and state.'

'No,' retorted Elliot, 'you believe in the separation of gay and straight.'

'That's not fair. I let you have dinner with Rita and me only a week ago.' She wasn't going to let him manipulate her with his politically correct blackmail. 'You're not meeting Bina because even though she's my oldest friend, you have nothing, absolutely nothing, in common with her.'

'I like people I have nothing in common with,' Elliot argued. 'That's why I like you and live with Brice.'

'Don't be greedy, you're getting to meet Michael tonight,' said Kate. 'Isn't that enough for two yentas like you and Brice?'

'Yeah,' said Elliot, giving in. 'It will have to do.'

Kate laughed and said, 'Come on, I'm going to be late for my girly date. Let me give you some advice I gave Jennifer Whalen just a couple of hours ago. "Try to make your own friends dear."'

They were at the IRT subway entrance. She gave Elliot a big smile and then hugged him goodbye. He shrugged, admitting his defeat. As she descended into the shadow of the subway, Elliot shouted after her, 'Don't forget; dinner's at eight!'

'See ya there!' she yelled back and ran to get the train.

3

Kate and Bina walked down Lafayette Street, gazing in the windows of the fashion boutiques and art galleries that lined the SoHo strip. Kate looked and felt at home in SoHo. She would have liked to live in the neighborhood, but it was far too pricey for a school psychologist's salary. Her apartment was on the West Side, in Chelsea, but Kate could pass as a downtown hipster. Bina Horowitz, on the other hand, was still all Brooklyn: her dark hair too done, her clothes all 'matchy-matchy', as Barbie used to say back in high school. Short, a little dumpy, and wearing too much gold, the truth was that Bina stuck out like a sore thumb among the modelesque shoppers converging in one of the coolest sections of downtown Manhattan. That didn't stop Kate from loving her friend dearly but she was grateful for all she herself had learned about style from Brice, college, Manhattan boutiques and her current New York friends. She'd left her Brooklyn look far behind, thank goodness.

'My God, Katie, I don't know how you live here,' Bina said. 'These people in Manhattan are the reason girls all over the country go anorexic.' Kate just laughed, though Bina was far from wrong. Bina continued to crane her head around at every opportunity, slowing them down to look at a pedestrian painting of a nude at which she raised her brows, a dress shop window where the clothes were torn into strips, and to marvel at the boutique called Center for the Dull. Kate had to explain it was just a clothing store like Yellow Rat Bastard – a store that Kate didn't shop in though she did have a shopping bag of theirs.

'Why all the confusing names?' Bina asked. 'And isn't it hot?' she added, fanning herself frantically with a flyer for a failing off-off-Broadway show that some guy had just shoved into her hand as they walked by. He hadn't tried to palm one off on Kate, but then she didn't look like the kind of person who accepted garbage.

'Well, it *is* nearly summer,' Kate observed. She tried to quicken their pace – the salon was notorious for demanding promptness – but Bina was Bina and she simply couldn't be rushed or silenced. The Horowitz family had taken Kate in when she was eleven and Kate knew practically everything about Bina. Kate had once done the math and realized Mrs Horowitz had fed her more than five hundred meals (most of them made with chicken fat). Dr Horowitz had taught her to ride a two-wheeler bike when Kate's own father was too drunk or too lazy (or both) to bother to do it. Bina's brother Dave had taught the two of them to swim in the municipal pool, and Kate still swam laps three times a week. Kate was grateful and loved Bina, but she had to admit that Bina was the Mistress of the Obvious in most of her observations.

'It's really hot,' Bina said, as if Kate needed proof of her belief.

Back in Brooklyn, when Kate had had no other outlet and longed for more sophisticated friends – like Elliot and Brice and Rita – with whom she could banter or talk about books, Bina had sometimes annoyed her. But now that she had a circle of intellectual, cosmopolitan pals, she could give up the frustration over Bina's provincial interests and conversation and simply love her good heart.

'It's really hot,' Bina repeated – a habit she had when Kate didn't respond to her.

'Is it hotter in Manhattan than it is in Brooklyn?' Kate asked her, teasing.

'It's *always* hotter in Manhattan than it is in Brooklyn,' Bina confirmed, completely missing Kate's mild irony. Bina definitely had an irony deficiency. 'It's all these damned sidewalks and all this traffic.' Bina looked up and down Lafayette Street and shook her head in disgust. 'I couldn't live here,' she muttered, as if the choice was hers and million-dollar lofts were an option she and Jack could consider. 'I just couldn't do it.'

'And you don't,' Kate reminded her, 'so what's the problem?'

Bina stopped fanning herself abruptly, looked at Kate with wide-eyed appeal and meekly asked the question that she always asked midway through one of her anti-Manhattan tirades. 'Am I being horrible?'

Kate felt a rush of affection overcome her annoyance and, as always, remembered why she loved Bina. Then she gave her the answer that she always did: 'Same old Bina.'

'Same old Kate,' Bina responded, in the litany they'd used to make peace and settle differences for two decades.

Kate grinned. The two of them were right back on track. Kate could neither imagine introducing Bina to her Manhattan friends nor imagine life without Bina – although she sometimes tried. Bina absolutely refused to grow and that was both irritating and comforting to Kate – and sometimes downright embarrassing.

Just as they crossed Spring Street, Bina, as if reading Kate's thoughts, virtually shouted, 'God, look at him!'

Kate turned her head, expecting, at least, to see a mugging in progress. Instead, across the street a pierced and tattooed guy of about their own age was going about his business.

Not the slightest bit phased by the local wildlife, Kate didn't

21

even comment and merely looked down at her watch. 'We can't be late,' she warned Bina. 'I have something special reserved.' And, to change the subject – 'So have you picked out a manicure color?'

Bina dragged her eyes away from the local sideshow with obvious difficulty and focused instead on Kate. 'I was thinking of a French manicure,' she admitted.

Kate felt distinctly unenthusiastic and it must have shown. Bina had been having the tips of her nails painted white with the rest a natural pink since high school.

'What's wrong with a French manicure?' Bina asked defensively.

'Nothing, if you're French,' Kate retorted, having conveniently forgotten her teenage days when she, too, thought a French manicure the height of sophistication. Bina looked puzzled by Kate's remark. Kate had also forgotten Bina's irony deficiency. 'Hey. Why don't you go for something a little more up-to-date?'

Bina held out her hands and studied them. Kate noticed she was still wearing the Claddagh friendship ring Kate had given her for her sweet sixteen. 'Go for something . . . daring,' Kate suggested.

'Like what?' Bina asked defensively. 'A tattoo on my fingernails?'

'Oooh, sarcasm. The devil's weapon,' Kate said.

'Jack likes French manicures,' Bina whined, still looking at her left hand. 'Don't push me around like you always try to.' Then she dropped her hands to her sides. They were both silent for a moment. 'I'm sorry,' Bina said. 'I'm just a little nervous. You know, I've been waiting for Jack to propose for over . . .'

'. . . Six years?' Kate asked, forgiving her friend. She had to stop giving unwanted advice, which was difficult for a woman with her temperament in her profession. She smiled at Bina as they continued down the street. 'I think on your first date with Jack you started designing the monograms for your towels.'

Jack and Bina had been seeing each other for so many years. He had been her first and only real love. He'd made her wait while he finished college, got his degree and became a CPA.

Bina giggled. 'Well, I knew right away he was the one. Such a hottie.'

Kate reflected on the wide variation of people's tastes. To her Jack was so far from a hottie that he left her ice-cold. Of course she'd never, ever, in all the six years of their courtship revealed that to Bina. And Bina had thought Steven was sour and gaunt, while to Kate he'd been . . . Her thoughts were interrupted by Bina's continued chatter. 'I just can't believe now that he's leaving for Hong Kong for five months tomorrow, and tonight's the night . . .' Bina trailed off, her voice unsteady.

There were few secrets among Kate's old Brooklyn posse, so when Jack had consulted with Barbie's jeweler father to get 'a good deal' on an engagement ring, the news had traveled faster than e-mail among them. The day Bina had waited for for so long had finally arrived but when Kate glanced at her friend, Bina looked anything but happy. Surely she couldn't be having second thoughts. But Kate knew Bina well enough to see that something wasn't right.

Oh my God, thought Kate. Bina has changed her mind and she's afraid to tell anyone. Her parents – especially Mrs Horowitz – would be beside themselves if . . . 'You're starting to have doubts?' she asked, as gently as she could, stopping to look at her friend. 'You know, Bina, you don't *have* to marry Jack.'

'Are you crazy? Of course I do! I want to. I'm just nervous that . . . well, I'm just nervous. Normal, right? Hey, where is this place anyway?'

'Just to the left on Broome,' Kate said. And if Bina didn't want to talk about her nerves it was fine, she told herself. Give the girl a little space. 'This is the Police Building,' she said as a diversion while they passed the domed monument that Teddy Roosevelt had built when he was chief of police. 'It's condos now,' she went on, 'and they found a secret tunnel from here to the speakeasy across the street so . . .'

'. . . So the Irish cops wouldn't be caught getting drunk,' Bina said, then stopped in embarrassment. Kate just smiled. Her father, a retired Irish cop, had died three years ago from cirrhosis of the liver and she couldn't help but consider it a release for both of them. It was the Horowitzes who couldn't get over it.

'No harm, no foul,' Kate told her. 'We're almost there, and we're only four minutes late. You're going to like this place. They have great nail colors, but just in case I bought a few alternatives for you.' Kate scrabbled around in her Prada bag – the only purse she owned, and she carried it everywhere. It had cost her an entire paycheck but every time she opened it, it gave her pleasure. Now she pulled out a little bag. It contained three nail polishes, each one a wildly different seductive shade.

Bina took the bag and peeked into it. 'Ooooh! They look like the magic beans from *Jack and the Beanstalk*,' she said. Then she started to giggle. 'Get it? Jack and his Beanstalk?' she asked, suggestively raising her eyebrows.

Kate gave Bina her 'I'm-not-in-the-mood' look. Clearly her moment of nervousness had passed. 'Hey, spare me the details of Jack's beanstalk or any other part of his anatomy,' she begged. 'Consider that your bridesmaid's gift to me.' Kate took Bina's arm to get her around the guy selling used magazines on the sidewalk and across to their destination.

Just then, as they crossed the street, Bina stopped – as if the Manhattan traffic would wait for her – and pointed to the corner. 'Ohmigod! That's Bunny's ex.' Kate looked in the right direction as she simultaneously pulled Bina's arm down. She was about to tell her not to point when she caught sight

24

of one of the best-looking men she had ever seen. He was tall and slim, and his jeans and jacket had the perfect casual slouch. The sun reflected off his hair as if he had a halo around his head. He had stopped for the light, and before he began to cross the street he fished in his inside pocket.

'He went out with Bunny?' Kate asked. Of her posse, Bunny was probably the most garish and certainly the dimmest bulb.

Bina nodded. Kate could only see the movement in her peripheral vision because she couldn't tear her eyes off the man just twenty feet away.

'Are you sure that's him?'

Just then a taxi honked, the driver deciding he would warn them before he ran them over. With a shriek from Bina the two of them scampered across the street. By the time they had walked single file between parked cars and got to the sidewalk, the Adonis had put on sunglasses and strode away.

'What color do you think I should do for bridesmaids?' Bina asked.

Kate repressed a groan. Bev had them all in silver and Barbie had picked a pistachio green that not even a blonde could wear without looking sallow. 'How about basic black?' Kate asked, but she knew there wasn't a hope in hell. She sighed. She and Bunny would be the last of their high school crowd not to be married – at least there was still Bunny. Kate would try not to mind, but everyone else would. No one at Bina's wedding would leave the naked state of her left finger unnoted. 'Please, Bina! Don't make me walk down that aisle again. Why not just make me wear a sign that says "unmarriageable"?'

'Kate, you have to be my maid of honor. Barbie was always closer to Bunny and Bev . . . well, Bev never really liked me.'

'Bev has never liked anyone,' Kate informed Bina, not for

the first time, and took her arm. 'Hey, I'm really touched.'

The pair came up to the door of the salon. Kate held the door open for Bina, who nervously stepped inside.

4

Kate knew the spa was unlike any place Bina had ever seen in her life – a sort of post-industrial French boudoir with Moorish touches. That was exactly why she had chosen it. Not to show off, but to make it very special for her friend. 'This is,' she informed Bina in a dramatic stage whisper, '*the* most expensive spa in the city of New York.' She studied Bina's face to make sure what she was telling her was sinking in. 'And I mean the *entire* city,' Kate continued.

'Wow,' was all Bina could manage, looking around at the sheer curtains, the concrete floor and the Louis XVI bergère armchair.

Kate smiled and walked up to the counter. A chic young Asian woman smiled back and, without speaking, raised her perfectly shaped eyebrows. They did a good brow wax here. 'Kate Jameson,' Kate announced. 'There are the two of us here,' she added, because Bina had disappeared shyly behind Kate. 'For manicures, pedicures, and toe waxing.'

From behind, Bina whispered, 'Toe waxing?' but Kate ignored her. 'We have a reservation. I have the confirmation number.'

'It will be just a moment,' said the beautiful receptionist. 'Please, have a seat.'

Of course, that was difficult with just the one antique armchair, but Kate motioned for Bina to sit and she did, albeit gingerly.

Then she looked up at Kate and grabbed her hands. 'Oh, Kate. I'm nervous. What happens if I go through all this and it jinxes me. What if Jack doesn't . . .'

'Bina, don't be silly. You can't "jinx" things.' Kate sighed. 'I just spent an hour trying to convince an eight-year-old that magic won't work. Don't make me repeat myself.'

'Look, I know all about you. Little Miss Logic. But I'm superstitious, okay? No black cats, no hats on the bed, no shoes to friends.'

'Shoes to friends?'

'Yeah. You give shoes to a friend and she walks away from you,' Bina said. 'Don't you know that?'

'Bina, you are truly crazy,' Kate said. 'Anyway, this is your big day and I want to be a part of it. So relax and enjoy. Everything will be fine, and tonight with Jack will be wonderful.'

Bina still looked doubtful. She craned her neck and looked around again. 'It just must be so expensive,' she said. 'You know, I can have all of the same thing done in Brooklyn at Kim's Korean place for about one quarter the price. And I bet it's every bit as good, too.'

Kate smiled. 'Maybe – maybe not. But here you have ambience.'

'Well, my mother would say "ambience, schmambience, paint my nails".'

'You know I love your mother, but sometimes she's not up-to-date. And by the way, how do you spell schmambience?' Kate asked with a smile.

'You don't,' Bina told her. 'It's Yiddish. It's a spoken language.'

Kate laughed. This was typical of the verbal exchanges Kate and Bina had been having since Kate first entered the Horowitz household, and Mrs Horowitz pronounced that Kate's father knew 'bupkis' about raising a 'shana maidela'.

Kate, at the time, didn't know that 'bupkis' meant virtually nothing or that 'shana maidela' meant pretty little girl, but she figured it out from context. She learned what 'putz' and 'shnorrer' and 'goniff' meant, all words that sounded better, more accurate, than their English equivalent. And from that time on she had been asking Bina for Yiddish spellings and translations.

Kate had celebrated every holiday at Bina's house – even if they weren't Kate's holidays. And the cultural expansion wasn't just limited to Jewish events. When Christmas and Easter rolled around, Mrs Horowitz made sure Kate got a Christmas tree and an Easter basket, complete with a chocolate bunny, and just for extra, sweet noodle kugel (which had nothing to do with Easter but was a dish Kate loved). When the time came for Kate's first Holy Communion, Mrs Horowitz sewed up Kate's white dress and bought a headpiece. (When Bina wanted a white dress and headpiece too, she got one, though Mrs and Dr Horowitz drew the line at allowing Bina to get on line with the little Catholic girls for the ceremony.) And, though Kate didn't take the weekly ballet lessons Bina did, she did get a pink tutu just like Bina's. Not to mention a dozen Halloween outfits over the years. Kate sometimes thought of it as the Costume School of Child-rearing but she was always grateful.

Kate, told by a priest in her catechism class that trick or treating on Halloween was a mortal sin, felt tremendous disappointment. When she shared this with Bina's mother, the reassurance Kate got was, 'Sin – schmin! Do your best with that meshugana in a dress and go out to get your candy. Don't worry about it.'

'But I don't want to go to hell after I die,' Kate told her tearfully.

'Hell – schmell,' Mrs Horowitz had responded. 'Trust me,

there's no such place except here on Earth *before* you die.' She raised her voice. 'Norm, can you believe the chutzpah of these priests and what they say to children.' She drew Kate onto her lap and held her close. 'There's only heaven, honey,' she whispered. 'And that's where your mama is.'

Somehow, Mrs Horowitz's complete conviction sank in. A few months later, after catechism, when Vicky Brown told Kate and Bina that Bina's Jewish mother was going to hell after she died, Kate turned to Vicky and declared, 'Hell – schmell! What do you know?' Then she pushed Vicky into a pile of garbage cans and made a very satisfying mess of her. 'Yeah!' Bina had declared. 'And if you say that again, we'll turn you into a toad. And I mean it.' After that, Kate and Bina made a pact to stick up for one another.

Maybe it was from that day they became known as the 'Witches of Bushwick'. As teenagers, their posse grew, with Bev and Barbie and, later on, Bunny, but they stayed the same, though in the neighborhood their nickname changed to 'Bitches'.

Bina was still holding onto Kate's hand. 'Oh, Kate,' she said and squeezed it hard. 'I'm so excited! Tonight's the night I get proposed to by the man I love.'

'Don't forget to act surprised,' Kate warned her. 'You don't want Jack to know you already knew.'

'I wish Barbie hadn't told me that he bought the ring,' Bina sighed. 'I'm so nervous. Why couldn't she just let it be a surprise for me?'

'Oh, honey,' Kate laughed. 'You don't want surprises. You want to look your best.'

Just then another Asian woman, even more beautiful than the receptionist, walked into the waiting area. 'Kate Jameson?' she asked. Kate nodded. 'We have your room all ready. Follow me, please.'

'A room?' Bina repeated, sticking behind Kate as they followed the woman down the pristine hall.

'Highest luxury,' Kate told her and led her into their own private boudoir. Bina looked around her, clearly in a state of confusion.

'Take a seat,' Kate told her. 'And just relax.'

Kate sat down in one of two facing chairs. Each was throne-like, with a built-in foot Jacuzzi already filled with delightful-smelling bubbling water. The softly lit room, all in soothing sea blue, also had two glass tables on wheels prepared for hand pampering. Two young Asian women knelt on blue silk pillows on the floor beside the foot baths. They helped their clients out of their shoes and indicated that they should plunge their feet into the fragrant Jacuzzis, in preparation for the pedicure. Bina looked across at Kate in amazement. Kate merely smiled at her. Her plan was working. This would be something Bina never forgot.

The air smelled of freesias and Kate took a deep, appreciative breath. If she had to pay half her salary check for the 'ambience-schmambience', it was so worth it.

Bina, still a little dazed, turned to the shelf beside her left elbow and stared at the almost endless rack of nail polishes. The second beautiful Asian woman came back into their blue heaven and asked the pair, 'Would you like bottled water, coffee, tea, juice or champagne?'

'You're kidding!' Bina almost squealed.

'Champagne, I think.' Kate replied as if Bina hadn't reacted. Bina didn't usually drink but, 'This is a big celebration,' Kate told her.

The woman nodded, smiled, and walked out of the room.

'Kate, this is so nice of you,' Bina began. Kate was pleased to see she was beginning to relax. 'But how come a pedicure? Jack isn't going to put the ring on one of my toes.'

'No, Jack would never think of a toe ring,' Kate agreed. Jack was nothing if not conservative. 'I just thought it would be a nice treat.'

One of the two pedicurists began to massage Bina's feet.

She giggled, pulled them away, and giggled again.

'Oh, just relax, Bina,' Kate told her. 'Breathe.' For a moment the two were silent. Kate closed her eyes and let herself feel the strong hands work her heels and instep. It was delicious.

'This is great!' Bina leaned forward to whisper across the small room. 'It's better than when we both earned the Brownie badge for First Aid on the same day!' Kate looked at Bina in disbelief. 'Is this really where Sandra Bullock, Giselle and Gwen Stefanni get their manicures?' Bina continued.

'Yup,' Kate said. 'And it's where Kate Jameson and Bina Horowitz have their manicures, too.'

'Soon to be Bina Horowitz Weintraub,' Bina reminded her. She was silent for a moment, but Kate was nice enough not to shut her eyes. For, as she expected, in another moment, Bina spoke again.

'Kate, you know I love Jack so much. I'm just so . . . so happy today and so glad I'm spending part of it with you.'

Kate smiled at her friend, who was, at that moment, having her cuticles cut.

'I just want you to find your Jack and be as happy as I am.'

Kate laughed. 'As your mother would say, "From your lips to God's ears".' Before Bina could speak, the door opened and the woman entered with a tray holding two flutes of champagne. She offered one to Kate and one to Bina. 'Enjoy!' she said as she glided from the room.

Kate felt a slight change in her emotional landscape. There was a time when she thought she might be drinking champagne to celebrate something with Steven but she had been very wrong. She wondered if the time would come when she and Michael . . . She pulled her thoughts away and focused on the moment.

Bina looked at her glass. 'I don't think I should start drinking this early in the afternoon.'

Kate rolled her eyes. Bina never wanted to drink. 'Oh, come

on, Bina,' she said. 'Live a little.' She lifted her own flute. 'May your engagement be as happy as your dating and your marriage even happier than that.'

'Oh, Kate!' Bina was clearly touched. Tears softened her brown button eyes. Both girls took a sip of their champagne. Then Kate started looking through the polishes. She narrowed her selection to two but couldn't decide between them. 'Boy, I bet Bunny wishes she was in my chair,' Bina said, leaning back.

'How is Bunny?' Kate asked. Bunny was a dental hygienist with a poor record with men. Kate thought of the delicious-looking man they had seen outside. It was hard to imagine Bunny with him.

'You don't want to know,' replied Bina.

Bina was right. Kate *didn't* want to know. Bunny was really more Bina's friend. She'd entered Kate's life in junior high, taking the Bitches to five, and changing her name to begin with 'B' so she'd fit in with the gang. Kate had already drifted a little from the group by then, and though she still went to the movies, dances, and hangouts with all of her crew, she also spent more time studying and reading. While the others were worrying almost exclusively about hair, makeup and boys, Kate was worrying about SAT scores and college scholarships. And when graduation day came, the other Bitches set their sights on non-demanding jobs, good marriages and babies, while Kate declared that she was not just going to 'sleep away' college but also intended to graduate to become a doctor of psychology.

As Bev put it, 'She thinks she's who the fuck she is.' If it hadn't been for Bina, that would've been the end of Kate's association with the Bitches and everyone else in Brooklyn. When Kate left for Brown she truly believed she had left her loneliness, her father's alcoholism, and her grammar school friends behind. Of course she was wrong on all three counts. Bina made friends for life. At first Kate had resented what she had considered Bina's 'clinging'. Then she realized that there was no one who knew her the way that Bina did. And while some of Kate's other 'backlash' from Brooklyn were incidents and memories she'd prefer to drop, for Bina's undemanding friendship Kate was grateful.

She finished her glass of champagne and was immediately brought another. She realized she was feeling more than a little sentimental as she watched Bina slowly sipping her champagne and trying to repress a giggle every time the pedicurist touched her foot. She was still talking about Bunny.

'. . . So the guy drops her like a rock. You saw him. I mean Bunny should have known he wasn't for her, but she took it hard. And now she's on the rebound. She's going out with another guy – Arnie, or Barney, or something – and she's already telling Barbie they're getting serious.'

Big news flash. Bunny picked inappropriate man after inappropriate man, always thought they were 'serious', and was always wrong. Classic repetition compulsion, Kate thought, but what she said was, 'Denial ain't just a river in Egypt.'

'What?' Bina paused for a minute. 'Oh! I get it!' She paused again, then made her voice falsely casual. 'How are things going with this Michael?'

'All right,' Kate said noncommittally and shrugged. She liked to keep a low profile on her dating life with Bina and the others or else the Horowitz family would be sending out engraved announcements. 'He's very smart and seems promising. We're going over to Elliot and Brice's tonight for dinner.'

'Who's Brice?' Bina asked.

Kate sighed. When it came to Brooklyn, Bina remembered what day of the month each of her friends had their periods, but outside Brooklyn . . .

'Elliot's partner.'

'Elliot who?'

'You remember, Elliot Winston. My friend from Brown. The guy I teach with.'

'Oh yeah. So if he's a teacher, how does he have a partner?'

'His *life* partner, Bina,' Kate said, exasperated. Bina might live in a small world but she watched television and saw movies.

Bina paused then dropped her voice. 'Are those guys gay?'

Yeah, and so is your unmarried Uncle Kenny, Kate thought, but all she did was smile tolerantly. So what if Bina's gender politics were way behind the times. She'd change the subject. 'So what color are you going to go with? Remember, every shade goes with a diamond!'

'I don't know. What have *you* picked?'

Of course the question was completely irrelevant but Bina was like that. Before she selected anything from a menu she had to know what you were having. Kate shrugged, picked up her selection and tossed it over to Bina. 'Just for my toes, I think.'

'God, Kate,' Bina said as she looked down at the bottle of nail polish that had landed in her lap. 'That looks like black. You aren't going Goth, are you?'

Kate shook her head. 'It is not black, it's a very deep aubergine.'

'Is that what it's called?' asked Bina.

'No,' said Kate. 'Actually, it's called Chanel's Despair.'

'Well, no wonder,' replied Bina. 'If my toes were that color I'd despair, too.'

'There's no excuse for you,' Kate admitted aloud.

'That is so funny I forgot to laugh,' Bina responded. 'But not as funny as your face.'

'Okay, Bina,' Kate began. 'You're . . .'

'I'm rubber. You're glue. Whatever you say bounces off me and sticks to you,' Bina taunted.

Kate took a sip of her champagne. 'Why do I feel like I

35

am back in a session with a very troubled eight-year-old?' she asked.

Bina didn't say a thing. Kate looked at her and realized her face had changed. It looked . . . hurt or self-protective.

'I'm sorry,' Kate apologized. 'It's just I am around kids all day and . . . well, I didn't mean to hurt your feelings.'

'Oh, no. I'm not hurt,' Bina assured her. 'I'm just a little scared. And I can't think of any more old insults,' she admitted. 'Wasn't there something about a screen door on a submarine?'

'Same old Bina,' Kate said, smiling at her irrepressible friend.

'Same old Katie,' Bina slurred. The champagne was clearly starting to get to Bina, and, looking at her friend, ready to take such a big yet inevitable step, Kate shivered, though the salon air conditioning was just pleasantly cool rather than cold. Jack had never been her cup of tea – and he certainly was no glass of champagne – but he seemed loving to Bina, her family liked him and . . . well, looking across at Bina, sweet pedestrian Bina, Kate had to admit that Jack was probably a good match. Kate was torn between bursting into tears and laughing out loud. Bina smiled at her, slightly cross-eyed. 'I love you, Katie,' she said.

'I love you, too, Bina,' Kate assured her, and it was true. 'But no more drinks for you. You've got a big night ahead of you.'

Bina took a last sip of champagne. Then she leaned over, close to her friend. 'Kate,' she whispered. 'There's something I'm dying to ask you.'

Kate steeled herself. 'Yes?'

'What's a toe waxing?' Bina inquired.

Bina's tone made it sound obscene. Kate laughed. 'You know how sometimes there is a little bit of hair on the knuckle of your big toe?' she asked.

Bina pulled her foot out of the Jacuzzi and studied it. 'Wow,' she said. 'Look at it. Eeuuyew.' One of the Asian women turned to look at the other and both started to giggle. Bina's face turned a bright pink. 'It's kind of icky,' she admitted. 'Like Big Foot. God, Katie, you're making me feel like a freak. But I never noticed it before.'

'Well,' Kate continued, 'after it's waxed off, Jack won't either. You can let him kiss all your little piggies with pride.'

For a while they chatted about Bina's plans for the wedding, places to go on the honeymoon and a little bit about Michael. Then, after cuticle cutting, more foot massage, filing and the mysterious toe waxing, they were painted and prepared for their manicures. 'Get your ring finger ready,' Kate told Bina. 'So, what color have you decided on?'

Bina turned her attention to the gift bottles from Kate, and the others arranged beautifully along the wall shelf at her elbow. 'They don't have most of these colors in Brooklyn,' she admitted.

'Just one more reason why I live in Manhattan,' Kate declared. 'Step up to the plate. What's it going to be?'

Bina looked down at the Asian girl already working her left hand. 'Do you do French manicures?' she asked her.

5

Kate's Manhattan apartment was undeniably small, but a delightful haven. She had been lucky to find it: it was in a brownstone on West 19th Street, on a tree-lined block close to the seminary, a very desirable location. The apartment was on the first floor, above street level, and consisted of a large room that had once been a parlor, a small bathroom and smaller kitchen behind it, and then a cozy bedroom.

Because it was on the first floor of the brownstone, Kate had all the advantages of beautiful moldings, mahogany pocket doors, a parquet floor and a marble fireplace which, though it had been bricked up years ago, still looked lovely even if it no longer served any functional purpose. Kate, with her neighbor Max's help and Brice's input, had painted the room a color that could almost be called yellow, but was just a little bit lighter than that. Benjamin Moore had called it 'sunlight' and the name on the paint chip may have affected her selection as much as the color itself. But it was a happy choice, and even on overcast days like today, the room had a cheery brightness.

The main room faced the back garden – which, unfortunately, belonged to the apartment below – so she had quiet and a green view in summer and a chance to watch the snow in winter. She hadn't had much money to spend on furniture, but she had splurged on a blue-and-white Chinese rug. Elliot, always alert for bargains, had helped her find and carry home the sofa – a small one with down cushions that she had slip-covered in a blue-and-white awning stripe. Someday she would buy an armchair but in the meantime an old wicker rocker which she had bought in a thrift store and sprayed blue made a comfortable, if slightly rickety, seat. And the yellow cushion on it made a cheerful spot of color.

Max, who lived upstairs, had also helped her put up book-shelves that filled in the recesses on either side of the fireplace. Max was a friend of Bina's brother and, it turned out, a cousin of Jack's from Brooklyn and worked on Wall Street. When Kate had heard about the apartment through him they hadn't known each other well. Kate had rushed over on the day the old tenants moved out and had signed a lease the next afternoon. Max, to whom she would forever be grateful, had been interested in her, but Kate wasn't *that* grateful. He was nice and good-looking but they had nothing to talk about, although Max didn't seem to mind that. And though her father had given her precious little advice about life, he had expressed his philosophy to 'never crap where you eat'. Kate had interpreted that to mean it was best not to sleep with anyone you worked with, but to paraphrase and extend her father's concept, she also knew it was best not to crap where you slept, either. While Max was attractive, he didn't attract her, and she couldn't be less interested in his Wall Street work. She had managed to handle it all diplomatically, though, and they were good friends as well as good neighbors. Though Max would never need to stop by to borrow a cup of sugar, he might well ask for a cup of coffee, a shot of vodka or, less frequently, a fix-up with some girl Kate knew.

Kate opened the curtains. It looked like rain. She threw her purse down on the sofa and hurried across to her bedroom. The beauty treatment with Bina had taken more time than she expected and she only had a half-hour before Michael came over. Although she had been cavalier about it with Elliot earlier in the day, Kate was actually a little nervous about bringing Michael over. Introducing a boyfriend to Elliot was like taking him home to meet her family, and she wanted everything to go smoothly.

Kate's bedroom was really just a part of the larger room that had been partitioned off. Its biggest disadvantage was the smallness of its closet. Each spring and fall Kate had to pack up the previous season's clothes and store them in boxes under the bed to make room for the next.

Kate decided she didn't have the time to shower, so she selected the Madonna blue sleeveless dress she'd just bought and ran into the bathroom. She had enough time to wash her face, take her hair down, brush the cascades of wavy red that fell below her shoulders and pull out her makeup bag for a quick fix.

She never wore much makeup. Her skin was pale and she'd finally outgrown the tiny freckles, no bigger than pinpoints, that used to dance across her cheeks and the bridge of her nose – a sort of Irish trail. Now, her face was simply creamy, and most of the time she only bothered with lipstick so that her hair didn't overpower her oval countenance.

Admittedly, as a kid, she had hated her freckles and the shape of her head – when her hair was pulled into pigtails, the kids called her egg-head – but with maturity her cheekbones showed, setting off her eyes, and the frame of her hair around her face pleased her. Because she was seeing Michael, she took out her mascara. She couldn't wear black because it made her blue eyes stand out like marbles in a plate of milk, so she applied the brown wand carefully to her upper and lower lashes. She blinked in the mirror to make sure she wouldn't smudge and, because it was a special night, she added a little lip gloss.

She now had only ten minutes before Michael was supposed

to arrive, though he was often a little late. That, she'd come to understand, wasn't because he was disrespectful – Kate hated lateness as a pattern and thought it was a narcissistic trait – but Michael was often so wrapped up in his work and thoughts of his research that he occasionally forgot to get off the subway or overshot the bus stop.

She smiled at the thought of him. He had a good mind, good hands, and a strong jaw. She liked his silver-rimmed glasses, his earnest peering through them and his dedication to his work.

She had only just recently slept with him: she wasn't usually so prim but her affair with Steven had left her more cautious than she had been before. They had met at her friend Tina's; Tina and Michael worked at the same university. Tina hadn't 'fixed them up' because she hadn't thought that Michael was Kate's type, but since Steven Kate wasn't sure what her 'type' ought to be. Michael's courtship had been slow but steady and when they had finally taken the plunge, she'd been delighted to find he was caring and generous in bed. It seemed as if he was just as taken with her. But this was the point of the relationship where things could go on for a long time without actually moving forward. Kate had spent two years with Steven, a writer, before they'd broken up eight months ago. She'd been shocked and hurt when she realized that he would never want to marry her or possibly anyone else. She had gone slowly with Michael because she didn't want to spend another year only to let that happen again.

She sat down on her bed and looked down at her painted toes. For a moment she could even imagine herself envious of Bina, who had her life settled. But she reminded herself that Bina had put in her time with Jack. Kate couldn't imagine waiting six years for anyone. She knew she wanted children, and would marry just for that. Her life was focused on kids and making their lives better. The work she did with Brian, Clara, Jennifer and the others at Andrew Country Day was satisfying, but, growing up, she'd been denied a normal family of her own and she wanted one. At thirty-one, she wasn't so old that she had to be frightened of the biological clock, but she had made the decision that she couldn't afford any more two-year dalliances that merely left her feeling bereft, disappointed and foolish.

Michael seemed solid. They had not yet discussed exclusivity, but as he called her almost every night and since they saw each other regularly, Kate thought the talk would only be a formality. She wasn't in a rush and wouldn't make ultimatums. Still, deep down, she wanted to know her goals were shared.

Kate slipped into the silk dress and scrambled under the bed for her high-heeled sandals. Black and strappy, they would show off her newly painted toenails. They were killers to walk in, but she didn't have to walk far to Elliot's.

When there was a knock at the door a couple of moments later, Kate was ready. She clicked across the floor and opened the door. But it wasn't Michael. Max was there holding a bouquet of snapdragons and statice. 'Hey,' he said. 'You look great.'

Max's smile was adorable, as one of his incisors showed because it had moved up on the tooth next to it. Max was a bit like his incisor: he often tried to push in where he didn't belong. There was no harm in him, though.

'Thanks.' Kate smiled briefly, trying to show she didn't have the time to chat. Max held the flowers without moving.

'Are those for me?' Kate asked.

'You betcha,' Max said. 'The Green Market was open when I walked by. The snapdragons reminded me of your hair. You can't say no.'

Kate didn't and took the bouquet. But sometimes she worried that Max still had a crush on her. She didn't want to encourage him, nor did she want to be rude. She tapped across the living-room floor to the tiny excuse for a kitchen and fumbled for a vase. Max followed her and stood in the doorway. Kate filled the vase and couldn't help but smile when she saw the red snaps with the orange centers. 'I wish I could wear two of these as earrings,' she joked.

'You don't need any earrings,' Max said. 'You look perfect. And as cool as a cucumber.'

Kate took the flowers and set them on her small dining table. They did make a pretty spot of color. 'Thanks, Max,' she said and kissed him on the cheek, leaving a small imprint of lip gloss.

Before she could tell him, he asked, 'Where you off to?'

'Oh, just dinner at Elliot's.' Max, an accountant and actuary, occasionally enjoyed talking higher math with Elliot. She hadn't yet told Max about Michael.

'Well, that dress is wasted on him,' Max said and, to Kate's dismay, he sat down. It wasn't that she had any reason to feel guilty, but she didn't want Michael to arrive and find another man in her apartment, and to have to introduce them to one another. Michael didn't seem overly possessive. On the contrary, he seemed a little nervous. But Kate wanted him to feel secure so she also wanted Max to get up and go, although she didn't want to have to ask him. Michael was already five minutes late but he was sure to be there soon.

Max shifted position on the striped sofa and pulled some envelopes and a rolled-up magazine from his back pocket.

'Oh, here. I picked up your mail.'

Kate sighed. There were no separate mailboxes for the four tenants of their brownstone and mail was left on a radiator in the vestibule. She had been in such a hurry she had forgotten to check for hers, and punishment for this tiny sin was a *New Yorker Magazine* completely ruined and the requirement to show fake gratitude to Max. 'Thanks again,' Kate said. 'Are you being so nice to me because you wanted to borrow a bottle of Absolut?'

43

'No, I try not to rustle booze until it's Absolut necessary.'

Kate gave him an obligatory smile. 'Well, hey, I've got to go. Elliot and Brice won't wait.' Max shrugged, got up and ambled over to the door. Perhaps he had only been fishing for an invite to join them. Brice's cooking was legendary. Whatever. At last she saw his back and closed the door. She took the mail he had brought over to the wastepaper basket beside her desk. She tried to smooth out the *New Yorker*, picked up a catalogue from Sak's, tore it in half and threw it into the basket before it could tempt her, filed a bill from Con Ed next to her checkbook and threw away junk mail that informed her that Ket Jemson had just won One Million Dollars! More junk mail into the basket. Then, at the bottom of the small pile, she found an almost square envelope addressed to her in gold calligraphy. Oh my God, she thought, has Bina jumped the gun and sent out wedding invitations before the proposal?

She turned the ominous communiqué over and saw Mr and Mrs Tromboli's address written across the back. Kate's hands began to tremble. She tore open the envelope and accidentally tore off the corner of the enclosed pasteboard. She pulled out the inevitable: an invitation to the wedding of Patricia (Bunny) Marie Tromboli to Arnold S. Beckmen. For a moment, Kate felt dizzy. How could this have happened? What had Bina been saying earlier about that Brooklyn bartender who had broken Bunny's heart? Now Kate felt her own heart quiver. With Bina engaged and Bunny about to get married, she would be the very last of her old friends to be single. When they started having children, she would really be alone. And Bev was already pregnant. Inevitably, young mothers got involved with playground, preschools, play-dates, and pregnancies – the four 'P's. Four peas in a pod, the 'B's would be busy reproducing and Kate would finally be completely closed out of the circle.

Kate put the invitation down, feeling a little dizzy. Then

the buzzer rang. She and Michael had no time for a drink now and she had no desire for one either. She hit the intercom as hard as the wedding invitation had hit her and when he said 'hello', instead of inviting him upstairs she told him she'd be down in a minute. Stuffing the stiff square of card into her purse, she told herself she wouldn't think about the Bunny situation, but on her way down the stairs, careful not to trip in the sandals, the idea of Bunny reproducing like a rabbit came to her. As much as she loved the children at school, and as dedicated as she was to them, Kate felt mournful. She knew she always would do if she didn't have a child of her own to raise and love.

Michael was standing in the vestibule. He was wearing pressed chinos, a white Oxford shirt and a tweed sports coat. It was a little heavy for the season, but Kate had noticed that he was always careful to dress conservatively and just a little 'scholarly'. He was both a good-looking and nice-looking man, just slightly taller than Kate was in her heels, and she liked his abundant curly brown hair.

'Hi,' she greeted him, trying to put away her concerns the way she had stuffed Bunny's wedding invitation into her bag. They kissed, just a peck on the lips. 'You've had a haircut,' she said.

'Nope, just had my ears lowered,' he replied. Kate wished he hadn't cut his hair, especially just before meeting Elliot and Brice. It made him the tiniest bit geeky-looking, but she put that thought out of her mind as well. Michael looked fine and was a fine person. He had put himself through undergrad and graduate school on scholarships and his own work. He'd already published papers in important journals and was poised for a brilliant career in academia. He was well read, well informed, and well intentioned, as far as she could tell. The fact that he'd been married – but only for one year, when he was too young to know any better – made him even more attractive in her eyes. He knew how to commit, even if it had been to the wrong woman.

45

Now Michael looked at Kate and his deep brown eyes sparkled behind his glasses. 'You are breathtaking,' he said and Kate smiled. The cost of the dress was well worth it.

'We better go,' she said. 'Brice hates late guests when he's cooking.' Despite her words, Michael gently pushed her against the doorway and kissed her. He was a good kisser and Kate let her tongue and mind wander. Then Max, clothed for the gym, came bounding down the stairs. They pulled apart, but Max, of course, had seen them. He raised his eyebrows as he walked past them, Kate's lip gloss still on his cheek.

'Dinner at Elliot's?' he asked as he walked by and down the stoop. Kate felt a twinge of guilt. Of course, she *was* going to dinner at Elliot's, but by withholding the information that she was going with an escort she now looked like a liar. Michael, unaware, took her hand and they walked outside and down the steps.

Kate couldn't help but think of her two years in Catholic school. Sins of omission and sins of commission: she thought she remembered they were equal. She promised herself she would find some way to apologize to Max later.

Now she took Michael's arm as they walked down the shady street. Chelsea was very pretty west of Eighth Avenue. 'Let's walk through the seminary garden,' Michael suggested. Kate smiled her agreement. At this time of day the block-sized park enclosed by the church and seminary buildings was at its most lovely. They walked arm in arm. The tulips made swathes of color against the deep green grass and the gray weathered stone rising from it.

'Kate, stop for a minute,' Michael said. 'I have something for you.'

Kate stood beside him. He fumbled around with his briefcase straps for a moment. He had given Kate a gift before – an out-of-print English psychology book by Winnecott. It had been very thoughtful, and just now she expected another book. But instead he took out a small, oblong box wrapped in

46

silver paper. Unmistakably a jewelry box. 'Do you know today is our three-month anniversary?' he asked. Kate actually hadn't and she was really moved that he had. 'I saw this and thought of you,' he said. He handed Kate the box, which she unwrapped. Once she opened it, a thin silver bracelet with a tiny 'K' hanging from it was revealed. She looked from it to the expectant expression on Michael's face. It wasn't anything she would have chosen for herself, but it was very sweet nonetheless.

'Oh, Michael. Thank you.' They kissed again and this time there was no interruption.

'Do you like it?' he asked.

For a moment, Kate thought of sins of omission again, but even Sister Vincent couldn't believe they would extend to this. 'Yes. It's lovely. Would you fasten it for me?'

Michael leaned forward and fiddled with the tiny clasp. It took a moment, but at last he had it around her wrist. She stretched out her arm. 'It looks nice,' she said.

'It looks great!' Michael said and tucked her arm in his.

Kate felt better than she had all day.

6

Brice and Elliot had met three years ago, and had only moved in together in September. Brice's stylish retro furniture in orange and lime green had taken precedence over Elliot's collection of thrift shop purchases and off-the-street finds. Their two-bedroom apartment in a Chelsea brownstone near Kate's had large windows in the living room overlooking a tiny backyard. An old refectory table was set before the windows and, despite their protests, Michael and Kate were given the chairs that faced the garden view.

'The tulips are just over and the roses haven't started so it's not at its best,' Brice apologized as he seated them, then excused himself to bring dinner in from the kitchen. Kate noticed they were using Brice's good glassware and Havilland china and she was really touched. Elliot brought in a wine cooler and set it on the oak credenza. 'A coaster! A coaster,' Brice exclaimed, and slipped one under the crystal cooler. Kate repressed a smile.

In a few moments dishes were being passed around. Elliot, standing, began to pour wine in the waiting goblets. Michael picked up his glass and almost ostentatiously set it upside down.

'None for me,' he said.

48

Kate winced. She should have seen this one coming. Michael didn't drink at all. He just said he didn't like it. Given her father's bad habits, it seemed a good trait to Kate but she knew it wouldn't go down well with Elliot. He prided himself on his wine cellar – even though it was actually in the linen closet – and must have taken pains selecting this Pinot Grigio. Elliot raised his eyebrows.

'Don't you drink?' Brice asked, his voice, rather than his eyebrows, slightly raised. Kate could imagine the talk afterward – 'Is he an alcoholic, is he in AA? No? Then he's a control freak or a born-again Christian.' Oh, it would be endless.

'I prefer to keep a clear head,' Michael answered.

'Yeah. You never know when someone might need to see through it,' Elliot muttered beside Kate's ear as he filled her glass.

Once they all had their plates and the drinking crisis was past, they began on Brice's famous appetizer: a beautiful, multicolored vegetable terrine. There was some cursory conversation but the tension seemed thick in the air, especially between Elliot and Michael. Of course Elliot was always very protective of Kate. And he had already made his dislike of this accomplished and nice-looking new boyfriend clear. The fact that Michael was a bit priggish and overly fastidious wasn't lost on Kate, but he did have other, compensatory traits. He was clever, he was generous in bed, and he seemed very, very stable.

'There's a good chance I'm going to get that Sagerman grant,' Michael said to Kate as they finished the first course. 'I saw Professor Hopkins and Charles told me that the committee discussions seemed to be very, well, promising.' Kate saw Elliot and Brice exchange a look. It was rude of Michael to ignore them, even briefly, but he was a single-minded academic.

Kate held back a sigh. Even when she and Michael were alone it was sometimes difficult to remember all the cards in his academic deck. Now, to make the conversation general, it would be necessary to explain to the others about the Sagerman Foundation, Michael's interest in a post-doctorate appointment, and his complicated relationship with his mentor Charles Hopkins. It was the kind of thing that made a difference to a couple, but didn't make for good dinner talk.

'Great,' Kate said. No one else spoke. Elliot refilled their glasses and Brice passed around the second course. Kate looked at it and knew that her friends had spared no expense to impress Michael. This was Brice's risotto with truffles and she knew what the price of truffles was. They all took a bite of the steaming rice. As the awkward silence stretched out, Kate turned to Brice in an attempt at light conversation. 'Brice. This risotto is really delicious.'

'Very good,' Michael agreed.

Brice beamed at the compliments. He was proud of his cooking, his design sense, and his extensive collection of pristine Beanie Babies. Those were arranged meticulously on a series of long floating shelves over the credenza. Kate had watched Michael notice them and avert his eyes. He was not, she had to admit, very playful in his attitude to décor or dining chat.

'So, what happened at the salon this afternoon?' Elliot inquired of Kate. She smiled. She knew him so well: he was taking pity on her and trying to make the dinner less painful. And because he figured she'd spill her guts more readily just to keep the conversation going. Nice try, she thought, but it wouldn't work.

'Oh, I just had my nails painted,' she said. She showed ten gleaming fingertips and still managed to hold the fork. 'Do you think Mr McKay will feel they're subversive?' The previous semester the principal had declared toe rings subversive and all the kids had to remove their socks and shoes to have contraband foot jewelry confiscated.

'That and cock rings,' Elliot said.

50

'Elliot, please!' Brice reprimanded. 'Not in front of the Havilland.' He flashed a smile at Kate and Michael. Their conversation continued in fits and starts but Kate knew Michael was not a hit. Of course Elliot had really liked Steven and that hadn't worked out, so . . . perhaps Elliot's first impression was not as important as she had thought it was.

'Salad or cheese and fruit before dessert? I have lovely Bosc pears,' Brice asked.

'No thanks, Brice,' said Kate.

'None for me,' Michael agreed. Across the table, Elliot stood up and began to clear away the dishes. 'It was very good,' Michael added.

Even to Kate it seemed a bland thank you. 'Wasn't the terrine terrific?' Kate prompted. She looked at Michael who in turn looked at the empty serving plates with an expression of confusion.

'Which was the terrine?' he asked.

Kate's face flushed pink. She knew how much effort Brice had put into the dish. 'The vegetable pâté,' she explained to Michael.

Elliot, still picking up plates, circled around behind Michael. 'With your head so clear you probably just call that "thick dip", huh?' he asked.

Kate winced. From behind Michael's back, Elliot held his nose and gave Kate a thumbs-down sign, almost dumping the plates he had gathered.

'Watch out for the Havilland!' Brice warned again.

'Elliot, you don't have to do that,' Kate said, referring both to his comment and the clearing.

'Oh, but I do, I do,' Elliot replied, his double entendre obvious.

She gave him a look. Clearly they needed some private time in the kitchen. 'I'll help you clear,' she offered, noticing Michael didn't even attempt to help.

Brice began to protest and rise as well, but Elliot shook his

51

head and looked pointedly at Michael. Brice gave him a pleading look, but Elliot leaned close and whispered, 'Somebody has to talk to him.'

Brice gave Michael a weak smile. 'So, what's new in anthropology?' he asked Michael in a bright voice. 'Is the Sugerman grant a sure thing?'

'Sagerman,' Michael corrected. 'From the Sagerman Foundation for the Studies of Primitive Peoples.'

Kate sighed, picked up some glasses and followed Elliot into the kitchen. It was small but efficient, with black and white floor tiles, red walls and cabinets, and the latest stainless steel appliances. Kate tried to steel herself. Elliot was silent as he put the dishes in the sink. Then, as she knew he would, he turned to face Kate, his hands on his hips like an accusatory nun. 'Where did you dig him up?' he demanded. 'This guy's the worst of the lot.'

'Oh, Elliot! He is not,' Kate protested. 'And keep your voice down.'

'Come on, Kate. Wake up and smell the primitive peoples. He's dull, he's pompous, he lacks humor and, aside from his haircut, I don't see anything superior about him,' Elliot said.

Elliot *would* like that haircut, Kate thought. She whispered, 'Oh, come on, Elliot. You never like any of my boyfriends.'

'Neither do you,' Elliot retorted. 'Not since Steven. And this one is not only boring, but also self-involved, pompous *and* a homophobe.'

'Oh, Elliot! He is not!' Kate exclaimed. 'You blame everything on that.'

'Kate, the guy didn't address a single word to either of us through the whole meal.'

'That doesn't make him a homophobe. Maybe he's just shy. Or doesn't like you personally,' she added. 'It could happen.' She put the wine goblets – one of them clean, on the counter.

'Doubtful. And he's probably an alcoholic. That's why he doesn't drink. Anyway, coming here to dinner is like meeting your family,' Elliot explained as he rinsed a plate. 'He should at least pretend to like us, since we're *in loco parentis*.'

'Well, loco, anyway,' Kate agreed. Elliot made a face. She opened the dishwasher and started to put in the china.

'Oh, no,' Elliot sighed. 'Not the Havilland. It's a hand-wash job. Brice wants gold leaf Brice washes it.' He rinsed his hands. 'We better get back in there. The coffee ought to wake up Brice. Would you fill the creamer?' Kate nodded. Elliot popped the chocolate sauce for the profiteroles into the microwave to heat.

Kate opened the refrigerator and stuck her head in. 'Hey, Elliot, I've told you before. It isn't easy to find a good, interesting, educated stable man who doesn't want to date a supermodel.'

'You may be right, Kate,' Elliot agreed. 'I certainly don't think you'll find him in the Sub-Zero. But you could take out the profiteroles.'

'Very funny.' Kate pulled a quart of milk and a pint of half-and-half out of the fridge and placed them on the counter. 'I admit you didn't see him at his best. Trust me. Michael is much better one on one.'

'I bet.' Elliot smirked.

Kate ignored his innuendo. 'No. Honestly. Evidence. He can be funny. And he's really smart. He got his doctorate at twenty-one, was teaching at Barnard when he was twenty-four and is considering his post-doc. I think he's going to get tenure at Columbia.'

'I didn't ask for his curriculum vitae,' Elliot snapped. 'He's just dull. Your father was an alcoholic and you never knew what to expect when he came home. Your mother died before you hit puberty. I know you want a responsible male, someone you can depend on. But this guy isn't just stable, he's inert. Where's the magic between you? And he's not nearly good enough for you. Don't let your snobbishness over academic achievement blind you.'

'I don't,' she assured him, but a nagging voice in the back of her consciousness wondered about that. Despite all her professional training and the analysis she herself had been required to undergo, she still sometimes felt that much of what she did was a reaction to the desperate childhood she'd had.

Elliot shrugged, turned around quickly in order to pick up the tray of coffee cups, and knocked over Kate's purse which had been sitting on the counter.

'There goes my cell phone,' Kate said.

'Is it the Havilland?' Brice called.

'No. It's the Melmac,' Elliot yelled. 'He's obsessed with the damn stuff,' he told her. 'Be right in, sweetheart.'

Then he knelt down to pick up Kate's handbag and all the objects that had scattered over the floor. 'I'm so sorry. I think I broke your makeup mirror.'

'Uh oh. It was a magnifying one. So do I have fourteen years of bad luck, or just seven years of more intense bad luck?'

'Stop it, Kate. I'm a statistician, a mathematician, not a superstitious bumpkin.'

'But you talk about magic . . .'

'Not Harry Potter magic. Not superstitious nonsense. I'm talking about magic between two people.'

'Need any help?' Brice called. 'We're waiting out here.'

'No, dear,' Elliot responded. He handed Kate her purse. Kate, kneeling beside him, picked up the remainder of the detritus and threw it in.

'Hey, what's this?' Elliot asked. Kate looked up. He was waving an envelope in the air.

'It's an invite to Bunny's wedding.' Kate sighed.

'Bunny of the Bitches of Bushwick is getting married?' Elliot asked. 'When did this happen? You never tell me anything.'

'Hey, I got it today. And you're on a need-to-know basis.' Kate stood up. 'Can you believe it? She was just dumped by a guy a month ago. I don't know where this came from.'

54

'Brooklyn. And on the rebound,' Elliot said. 'Can I go? Please, can I go?'

'No,' Kate replied. 'See, this is another valid reason why I shouldn't break up with Michael. With Bina getting engaged and now this, I have to go with someone viable.'

'But Michael is so . . .' Elliot didn't get a chance to finish his critique because, suddenly, a loud and frantic pounding came from the front door of the apartment. 'What in the world?'

The two of them hurried into the living room where Brice was standing at the door. He looked at Elliot and Elliot shrugged. Brice opened the door. A woman, her hair wild, her face covered by her hands, threw herself into the room, sobbing uncontrollably. Everyone stood in silent amazement and Brice actually took two steps back. It was only after a moment or two that Kate saw the woman's fingernails and realized, with a horrible shudder, that she had a French manicure.

'Bina!' Kate gasped. 'Oh, Bina! What's happened to you?'

7

Bina looked around her wildly. 'Katie! Ohmigod. Oh, Katie!'
Then she threw herself onto the sofa and heaved with sobs.
Kate, paralyzed for a moment, stepped forward and put her
hand gently on Bina's shoulder. Could she have been raped?
Had someone mugged her? Her clothes were such a mess
and her hair so disheveled that, at first, Kate only thought
of physical tragedies.

Elliot stood looking down at the weeping woman on his
couch. 'It's Bina?' he whispered. 'This is the famous Bina?'

Kate ignored him. 'Bina? Bina dear, what's happened?'

Bina shook her head violently. Kate actually felt one of
Bina's tears hit her own cheek and put her arms around her
sobbing friend. 'Shhh,' she crooned and stroked Bina's hair.
Somehow all the times Kate had witnessed Bina's hysterical
outbursts over the years, at sleepovers and parties, flashed
in a visceral way through her consciousness. Kneeling, with
her arms around Bina, was familiar. Then she looked up and
remembered the audience of three men surrounding this
drama. And that the drama was happening in Manhattan
on a borrowed sofa. She hoped the whole thing wasn't as
bad as it seemed. Then a new thought occurred to her. 'Bina,
how did you find me here?'

'Max,' Bina said, struggling with her tears. 'He heard me crying in the hall and told me where you were.' She took a gulping breath and burst into tears again. Elliot and Brice drew closer to the couch, like rubberneckers, while Michael had withdrawn to a spot behind the dining table. Kate couldn't help but think that she was watching the epitomes of men: the straight ones retreating in the face of emotional turmoil and the gay ones jumping right in.

She looked back down at her friend. 'Bina, what's happened?' Kate asked again.

'Choked,' Bina wailed as fresh tears poured from her eyes.

'Are you choking?' Kate asked, confused.

'I can do the Heimlich. Does she need the Heimlich?' Brice asked, a bit too hopefully.

Bina, still sobbing, violently shook her head no.

'I *never* get to do the Heimlich,' Brice sighed. 'Do you?' he asked, turning to Michael, who was now folding and unfolding a napkin, obviously completely unnerved by the situation.

It was unnerving to anyone who didn't know Bina, but Kate had witnessed many a hysterical outburst like this before, once over the dress Bina's mother had selected for the prom. Now Kate took Bina's hands in her own and spoke to her firmly but gently. 'Who choked? Who's choking, Bina?' She turned to Elliot. 'Would you please get her a glass of water?'

Elliot, turning to Brice, repeated the request. 'Brice, get her a glass of water. This is better than *One Life to Live*.'

Brice didn't budge. '*One Life to Live*? This is better than *The Young and the Restless*.' He turned to Michael, still in the corner behind the table. 'Put down the linen,' Brice told him. 'You get the water.'

Michael seemed all too happy to leave the scene and disappeared into the kitchen. Bina gave another wail.

'Bina, you have to calm down,' Kate said, turning her attention back to her. 'You have to. And you have to tell us what's wrong.' Bina took some trembling breaths and got the sobbing under control. It occurred to Kate that Bina might have had an accident or be sick. 'Does something hurt?' she asked.

Bina nodded her head.

'Do you need a doctor?' Kate continued.

Bina nodded more vigorously. 'Yes. Jewish and unmarried. The kind who likes my type and who's looking for serious commitment.' She broke out into sobs again.

Elliot and Brice moved even closer to the circle. 'Uh oh,' Elliot said. 'Kate, check out her hand.' He and Brice exchanged meaningful looks.

Kate, not quite understanding, thought of their manicure that afternoon. Had Bina had some allergic reaction? 'Bina, have you hurt your hands?' She looked down at Bina's hands but didn't see anything more alarming than the French manicure.

'Not her right hand, Kate,' said Brice. 'Her *left* hand. Second finger from the pinkie.'

Kate finally understood. She wrapped her arms around Bina and said, 'Oh, my God. Jack . . .'

'. . . Jack choked,' Bina told her. 'He had the ring in his breast pocket. I could see the bulge the box made.' She began to cry again. 'Oh, Katie! Instead of asking me to marry him, he asked if we could spend this time apart . . . exploring our singleness.'

'That son-of-a-bitch!' Kate, who thought that she understood enough about people and their motivations to no longer be surprised, was shocked. While Jack had finished school and entered corporate life, Bina had waited, worked and collected every issue of *Bride*. She watched as all her other friends became engaged, she'd relentlessly thrown shower after bridal shower, a virtual pre-connubial fountain. And now, when at last it was her turn, Jack had choked? Bina didn't deserve this. 'That goddamn son-of-a-bitch!' Kate was ready to spit.

She looked up to see that Michael had returned from the

kitchen just in time to hear her undeleted expletives and recoil at the outburst. Lucky that she hadn't called Jack a motherfucker, she thought, as she watched him approach the sofa and gingerly hold out the glass of water to Bina. Bina ignored the gift.

'I can't believe it!' Bina said, wiping ineffectually at her face and only making the raccoon eyes worse. 'He got the ring from Barbie's father. Mr Leventhal gave him a break. It was princess cut, Barbie said – just under a karat and a half.' She paused for breath while Michael gaped and Elliot and Brice shook their heads in sympathy – and almost in unison.

'Everyone will know,' Bina said, and began sobbing again. 'I can't believe he'd do this to me. Just drop me. And shame me in front of everyone.'

Kate took the napkin from Michael's hand, dipped it into the water and held it up to her friend's face. 'Bina, honey,' she said with all the assurance she could muster. 'You've been going out with Jack for six years. He loves you.' She wiped mascara from under Bina's eyes. 'Blow your nose,' she said, and Bina did. 'Look, this is just a temporary thing. Sometimes it happens. Picking a life mate is a serious decision. It isn't that Jack doesn't want to marry you. It's a lot more probable that he just got frightened. I'm sure he'll call you tomorrow.'

'Tomorrow he'll be in Hong Kong. With my ring! I'll be dumped in Bensonhurst and he'll be the Christopher Columbus of singleness,' cried Bina, who had a penchant for wildly inappropriate metaphor when under pressure.

'Maybe you should drink the water,' Michael said awkwardly, and pressed the glass into her hand.

Bina looked down at the glass. 'Is there strychnine in it?' she asked without lifting her eyes.

'Uh . . . no,' Michael replied.

In a single smooth motion Bina dumped the water out over her shoulder and down the back of the sofa. 'Then what good is it to me?' she said to no one in particular. She fell back onto the sofa and burst into a fresh batch of tears.

'That was a gesture,' Elliot said, grabbing a napkin.

'On Fortuny fabric,' Brice added. 'This is *so* Brooklyn.'

'I knew I'd love Brooklyn,' Elliot said.

Kate looked up over Bina's head at the two of them and gave them a warning squint, her blue eyes narrowed to lizard slits. She wondered if she could get the girl home to her own apartment and calm her and put her to bed there, but either getting a cab or walking back with Michael seemed impossible. Better to deal with it here and then go home. But first she needed to free the frightened Michael and stare off the spectating twosome, though, to be fair, it was their own home. 'I'm sorry, guys,' Kate started, looking up at the three men. 'It looks like we might have to put off dessert.'

'Don't be ridiculous,' Brice said. 'In times of pain nothing works better than drowning your problems in profiteroles.'

Elliot nodded, but Michael began backing toward the door. 'I think you're right, Kate,' he agreed, relief shining from every pore. 'I'll just see myself out,' he added, picking up his briefcase and heading out of the door into the foyer. 'Have a nice evening,' he said as he closed the door behind him.

Kate jumped up. 'Just a minute, Bina,' she said, giving another narrow-eyed glance at the guys as a deterrent, and ran to the hallway. She was just in time to see Michael step into the elevator. 'Hold it!' she called, got to the button and pressed it. Michael stood in the fake mahogany cab like an insect suspended in amber. 'You're leaving like that?' she demanded.

'Like what?' he asked, looking down at himself as if it was an unzipped fly she was commenting on.

'My friend just had her life shattered and you go out the door saying, "Have a nice evening"?' Kate had learned not to expect too much of a date in the early stages of their mating dance, but Michael was *way* out of tempo. 'Have a nice evening?' she repeated, mirroring him.

'Kate,' Michael began. 'Bina is your friend, not mine. I don't really think it's my place . . .'

'. . . To be what? Nice, kind , caring? Can't you just pretend to be sensitive?' Kate realized she was holding him hostage and took her finger off the button. The door closed slowly across his miserable face. Kate turned away, hoping he would press the door-open button and return, at least to give her a kiss and a moment of sympathy, but the elevator door remained as smoothly closed as Michael's emotions had been. She shook her head to clear it. She had to return to Bina.

She entered the apartment and found to her surprise that Bina had stopped crying. She was sitting up on the sofa beside Elliot, who was holding her hand and sharing his own heartbreaks. '. . . And then he said, "I'm going back to my place to get my things and move in." I was thrilled, just thrilled, so I said, "Can I come and help" and he kissed me and said, "No, sweetie. It won't take but a few hours," and I never saw or heard from him again.'

Bina shook her head in mute sympathy.

'Just as well,' Brice said. 'Street trash. It's all worked out for the best.' He kissed the top of Elliot's head. Kate saw Bina blink.

'Well, let me bring out the profiteroles and actually nuke the chocolate sauce,' Brice said and headed for the kitchen.

'Meanwhile I'll get a blanket,' Elliot offered and disappeared into the bedroom. Bina nodded gratefully to Kate.

Kate, with nothing else left to do, sat beside her. 'I'm sorry,' Kate said, comforting her friend now they were alone. 'You must be devastated.'

'Oh, Katie, how could he do this? Who does he think he is? The Magellan of certified public accountants?' Bina asked. 'How could he?'

Kate looked into her imploring eyes. But she had no easy answers. 'Even if he leaves for Hong Kong he'll have that long flight alone, he'll miss you, he'll remember the good times and how much he loves you . . .' Kate paused, hoping that all she conjectured was true. She wanted to comfort Bina but not lie to her. If an eight-year-old like Brian had to face the reality of the death of his mother, Kate believed it would be best for Bina to face the death of her relationship with Jack, if that was what it was. But she was sure it couldn't have suffered a mortal wound. Bina was lovable and Jack, slow-moving as he was, had always seemed to adore her. 'I'm sure he'll call. Even if he leaves for Hong Kong I bet he sends you a ticket to join him and proposes there,' Kate ventured hopefully.

'Men are just funny . . .'

'Not homosexual ones,' Elliot said as he walked back into the room carrying a knitted afghan throw. 'We're fucking hysterical.' He knelt down beside Bina and wrapped her up in it. Brice came out of the kitchen carrying a full tray which he put down gracefully on the coffee table. Arrayed before them were four dessert plates, the plate of profiteroles, a silver server of piping-hot dark chocolate sauce, lace-trimmed napkins, a crystal shot glass and a frosted bottle of Finlandia. 'All for you,' Brice said.

Bina looked at the tray. 'I'd love some dessert but I don't drink,' she told him.

'You do tonight, honey,' Brice said and poured her a shot. 'Chocolate and alcohol together beat shit out of Prozac.'

Bina looked at him, at the brimming shot glass, and, to Kate's utter surprise, took it from him and knocked it back.

'Good girl!' Elliot said.

'And here's your chaser,' Brice added and handed Bina the pastries. 'You know what they say: just a spoonful of sugar . . .'

Bina picked up the plate to dig in.

'Wait just a minute,' Brice said. 'The doctor is in.' He picked up the silver pitcher, raised it theatrically and poured out the bitter chocolate over the ice cream pastry.

Kate looked at the three of them entranced, not sure if she

was experiencing pleasure or discomfort. Her two worlds had merged here on the Fortuny-upholstered sofa and all one could have said was that it seemed quiet on the western front. Then Brice filled the shot glass again and handed it to Bina who, docile as a kosher lamb, drank it down. That broke Kate's trance. 'Guys, this is more serious than something a drink and an overdose of carbohydrates will cure,' she told them.

'Honey, there's nothing that will cure this. But alcohol and sugar will temporarily dull the pain,' Brice replied. 'Trust me. I know.'

Bina, back at her dessert, looked up from her plate with a dazed expression on her face. Elliot wiped the chocolate from around her mouth with the lace napkin.

'Who are these guys, Katie?' Bina asked, looking at Elliot and Brice with some confusion. 'Are they therapists, too? They're very good.'

'No, dear. This is my friend Elliot, who works with me at school, and his partner Brice,' Kate told her. Bina smiled, but it was obvious that Kate's words were merely washing over her. She suddenly realized just how drunk Bina was.

'Why am I here?' Bina asked. 'And why are they room-mates?' She slurred her words, and only God knew how slurred her mind was. Again Kate wished that she hadn't mixed Brooklyn with Manhattan. They were parallel universes, and, like parallel lines, should never ever touch.

Despite her concern, Kate was just slightly amused watching surprise mixed with curiosity and a *soupçon* of horror cross Bina's face as she looked from Elliot to Brice and back. Her amusement dissolved, however, as Bina opened her mouth. 'Oh, so you're the . . .' she started, and Kate winced, afraid of what word she might hear next.

'. . . the mathematical one,' Elliot finished for her.

'And I'm the emotional one,' Brice said with an exaggerated sigh. 'Somebody's got to do it.'

Kate had to get Bina home and onto her own couch before

it became necessary to carry her. She knew once Bina was forced to stay here, Brice and Elliot would dig themselves in deeper. They were kind, but they couldn't help Bina now and Kate knew she had a big job to do. 'I know the floor show traditionally precedes dinner, but I did the best I could without hiring tap dancers,' she said.

'Ooooh, I love tap dancers,' Brice crooned and Elliot gave him a look. It didn't stop Brice from pouring out the next drink for Bina.

'Put that down,' Kate said, her voice as stern as the one she had to use in the Andrew Country Day School cafeteria. Here, just like there, it worked. 'I'm taking Bina home,' Kate said.

'Nooooo. I can't go home. I can never go home again,' Bina said. 'Not until I'm engaged anyway.'

'You're coming to my apartment,' Kate said. 'It isn't far and you could use the fresh air.'

'She's welcome to stay here,' Elliot offered, and Kate knew his kindness was mixed with an equal part of curiosity.

'Show's over,' Kate said. 'Say good night, Gracie.' She pulled the dazed Bina up from the couch and began to walk her to the door.

'Good night, Gracie,' Elliot and Brice chorused.

8

Later, Kate could not remember much about the nightmare
of getting Bina back to her place that night. It was called
'selective memory' in her textbooks – some things were just
too gruesome to keep in your consciousness. In the four long
blocks from Elliot's to Kate's own apartment, Bina alternately
wept, sang, tripped, wailed, and sat down at one point on the
sidewalk, refusing to move. Kate didn't think Bina had tried to
throw herself in front of a bus or wet herself but she couldn't
be absolutely sure of either. It was lucky that Max had been
home and heard her trying to get Bina up the stairs. Asking
no questions, he took over. Kate didn't remember if he carried
Bina up the stairs in his arms or over his shoulder. She did
remember holding Bina's head as she vomited violently, and
washing her up. Max had left her to that thankless task. Kate
made an executive decision not to put Bina in her bedroom
but instead to tuck her up on the sofa. Made in haste, it was
a decision that Kate would not regret.

The next morning Kate was up early brewing coffee, laying
out the Tylenol, and waiting to call in sick to work. One look at
the bedraggled, unconscious Bina gave Kate a pretty good idea
of how she was going to spend her next twenty-four hours.
She took down her favorite coffee mug. It was the only gift

she could remember her father giving her. A molded, ceramic one, the handle was shaped like Cinderella bending over the top of the mug and looking into whatever liquid would be put there, as if it were a wishing well. Then she added another, plain cup to wait until Bina woke. She thought of calling Mrs Horowitz or even trying Jack before he left, then thought better of it. Kate didn't mind being involved, but she didn't want to become the puppeteer pulling strings. Bina – despite her many childlike qualities – would have to decide on her own what actions to take and Kate would support her as best she could. She retied her cotton bathrobe tighter around her waist. The radio alarm, when it went off in her bedroom, hadn't made a ripple on the dark pool of Bina's unconsciousness, but it had informed Kate that the day was going to be a scorcher for April.

When the phone rang Kate glanced at the caller ID, picked up the receiver and without preamble said, 'Yes, she's still sleeping. No, I'm not going into school today and no, you can't come over.'

'Good morning to you, too,' Elliot's voice said briskly. 'Can I at least drop off a couple of bagels on my way up to Andrew?'

'Forget it. I don't think Bina is going to want to eat anything, and if she does I have plenty of Saltines.' Kate poured the hot coffee into her Cinderella mug. She was careful, as always, to avoid the little blond head peeking over the rim.

'God, Brice and I feel so bad for her.'

'At least you're not feeling as bad as her . . . I mean, she is. Bina doesn't have the genetics to handle a hangover,' Kate told him. 'You shouldn't have let Brice pour all that booze down her throat.'

'Well, he's not apologizing for getting her drunk and I think it was the best thing for her . . .' Elliot began.

'Well, it wasn't the best thing for me,' Kate interrupted,

peeking at Bina. It wasn't a pretty picture. 'I've had quite a mess – literally and figuratively – to clean up.'

'Oh, the poor girl,' Elliot said, his sympathy real. 'How can I help?'

'Short of teaching Michael to deal with human feelings and finding Jack and slapping some sense into him, I don't think there's much you can do,' Kate said.

'Yeah, I told you Michael was a dud. What went on between you two in the hall? I'll bet he got a pounding.'

Kate thought of Michael's face before the elevator door closed and chose to change the subject. She spilled some coffee as she moved her mug to the counter beside the refrigerator. 'I don't think there's much anyone can do, but I'm taking a sick day.'

'Maybe you should call it a mental health day,' Elliot said. 'Except this one isn't about your mental health.'

'Don't worry, it will be mine soon enough,' Kate predicted and poured some milk into her coffee. She preferred half-and-half, but she hated skim so she had compromised on regular milk. The coffee took on the exact shade that Bina's skin used to tan to back on the beach when they were kids. Kate had always envied that beautiful color, but now her friend's complexion had a distinct green tinge. Kate just hoped she didn't wake up and throw up again. She liked her rug. 'I've got to go,' she told Elliot.

'Do you want me to take the day off, too? The kids have standardized testing most of the day. I can keep you company and help with Bina.'

'Forget it,' Kate told him. 'I know you're just afraid you're going to get my cafeteria duty,' she joked. 'Anyway, you had your first and last dose of the Bitches of Bushwick. It ought to be enough Brooklyn to last a lifetime.' Before he could protest, she added, 'I have to go. She's waking up.'

'I'll call you later,' she heard him say as she put the phone down.

67

She quickly poured a glass of club soda – her favorite remedy for the dehydration of a hangover – and walked from her kitchenette into the living room with her mug in one hand and the glass in the other. Bina groaned, put a hand to her forehead and then opened her eyes, which she closed again quickly. 'Ohmigod,' she said and Kate wasn't sure if it was a reaction to the light or a remembrance of things past. She groaned again.

'It's okay, Bina, drink this.' Kate held the glass in front of her friend and Bina squinted at it.

'What is it?' she croaked.

'Well, it's not vodka,' Kate told her. 'Come on, sit up and take your medicine.'

Bina did as she was told, took the glass, drank three or four big gulps and then began to choke. She put the glass down on Kate's coffee table and Kate moved it onto a coaster before she went to Bina's side.

'Ohmigod,' Bina repeated. And Kate knew that this time she had remembered Jack and the night before. Bina looked up at her. 'Oh, Kate. What am I going to do?'

Kate sat down in the wicker chair and reached out and took her friend's hand in her own. 'Bina,' she said, 'what happened last night?'

'You were right about the French manicure,' Bina said. She shook her head and Kate could see the physical pain register on her face.

Kate went back to the kitchen and brought her three Tylenol and a couple of vitamin Cs. 'Here,' she said, thrusting them into Bina's hand. 'Take these. You'll feel better.' She left Bina again and returned to the kitchen where she took out her emergency stash of Saltines. Bina had just downed the last pill when Kate returned. She didn't want them all to lie there in an empty stomach so she handed Bina a Saltine. 'Eat it,' she said.

'Oh, please,' Bina responded in a world-weary voice.

'Eat it,' Kate commanded, 'and now tell me what happened last night.' She watched as Bina made an entire meal of the Saltine taking many tiny bites and washing them down with the club soda. The moment she was finished, Kate handed her another Saltine and refilled her glass. 'Good girl,' she said. 'So what happened?'

Bina lay back among the cushions and put a hand across her forehead. This time the tears were silent ones. Kate rose, went to her bedroom, and came back with a box of tissues. Wordlessly, she handed one to Bina who mopped at her eyes and began to talk in an unsteady voice. 'You know that I was meeting him at Nobu and I was excited because it's one of the kinds of places you go to.' Kate almost smiled. Nobu was one of the most expensive, stylish, Asian restaurants in the city and Kate couldn't afford to eat there even on her birthday. Sometimes Kate wondered about Bina's vision of Kate's reality, but she didn't have the time to do that now. 'Anyway, the place was beautiful and when I walked past the bar I could see that all the women looked better than I did. I don't know why, because their clothes weren't as good as mine – at least they didn't look as good, but somehow they looked better, if you know what I mean.' Kate just nodded. 'Anyway, when I got to the dining room the hostess wasn't there. I looked around, kind of self-conscious, then I thought I saw her. She had her back to me and was talking to some guy at a table and she was holding his hand up and laughing. When he laughed back, I realized it was Jack. I nearly plotzed.'

Kate had a vision of Bina going into hysterics and throwing a scene in the middle of the Zen of Nobu. God, she thought, that would end a romantic evening quickly. Bina did tend to overreact. 'So did you . . .'

'For a minute I didn't do anything,' Bina said. 'I couldn't believe it. Then I walked over to the table and . . .'

The phone rang and Kate looked at the caller ID. 'It's your mom,' Kate said.

'Don't pick up,' Bina nearly screeched.

Kate let the phone ring until the answering machine kicked in. Mrs Horowitz's concerned voice came on and Kate turned the volume down. 'You will have to tell her what happened. After you tell me, of course,' Kate said. 'And she must be concerned. Where does she think you are? Did she know about your plans last night?'

Bina covered her eyes again. 'I can't talk to her now,' she said. 'And I didn't tell her anything because she would have nudged me to death. But I'm sure she knew about the ring and she knows Jack is leaving . . .' Bina stopped for a moment and began to wail. It was a high-pitched keen of misery. 'He's leaving tonight. Ohmigod, he's leaving tonight.'

Kate crouched at the edge of the sofa and took Bina in her arms. She felt Bina tremble against her, shaking with every sobbing breath. 'Bina, you have to calm down and tell me what happened. We probably can fix this.'

Bina shook her head silently but lowered the volume of her crying. Just then the phone rang again. Reluctantly, Kate left Bina and went over to it. It was Michael. She had to pick it up, and wondered what people did in 'the olden days', as her kids would say, before there were things like caller ID. Kate looked over at Bina who had turned on her side and was quietly sobbing into a bunch of tissues. She picked up the receiver.

'Kate, you're home?' Michael asked.

'Yes.' She didn't need to tell him anything more. He knew that she was usually in her office by this time and as a post-doc he might have had the brains to figure out that based on what he had reluctantly witnessed the night before she might not show up at school.

'Hey, Kate, I . . . I just wanted to call to apologize.'

Kate softened. She sighed, but covered the mouthpiece to be sure that Michael didn't hear it. She had learned that there were two kinds of men: those who apologized and continued their behavior and those who apologized and stopped it. She hadn't known Michael long enough to know which type he was.

The way she looked at things at this point in her life, most relationships were compromises and all men had to be looked at as fixer-uppers. As a therapist, she knew people did not change unless they wanted to and worked very hard at it. As a woman, she knew she had to tolerate a certain amount of what her ten-year-old patient Susan called 'monkey clone behavior'. 'Okay,' she said to Michael in a voice as neutral as she could manage.

'I'm sure I looked like an unfeeling jerk last night. You know, it's just that . . . well, your friend was *very* dramatic.'

That pissed Kate off. 'I suppose a little drama is warranted when your entire life is ruined.' She purposely kept her voice low and looked over at Bina to make sure she went unheard. What good was an apology, she thought, if it was followed by a further injury?

'I've done it again, haven't I?' Michael asked. He might not be empathetic but he wasn't stupid, Kate reflected. 'Look, let me take you out to dinner one night this week,' he said. 'Let's talk about it. I know I can do better.'

Fair enough, Kate thought. But it couldn't be in a restaurant. There should be a lot of talking, a lot of negotiating, and maybe some reconciliatory sex. 'Why don't you come over for dinner?' she proposed. 'But not tonight.' She looked over at the sofa again. Bina was just raising her head. 'Gotta go,' she said. 'Let's talk later.'

'I'll call you this evening,' Michael promised and Kate hung up. She returned to Bina's side.

Bina, her eyes red, but not as red as her nose, looked up at her. 'How can we fix it?' she asked.

Kate sat down and the wicker creaked. 'Well, to know that, first I have to know what happened. Exactly what happened.'

71

'So I go over to the table, and Jack is laughing and the Chinese woman – who was smaller than a size two and taller than I am – looks at me like I'm the bus boy. But Jack, he jumps and pulls his hand away. "Hey, Sy Lin was just teaching me how to say hello in Mandarin. Nee-how-ma!" So I look at him and say, "Nee-how-ma, right back atcha." Then I turn to Sy Lin and say, "How do you say goodbye?" So she just gives me this smile, does one of those look-overs – you know the way Barbie does when someone is dressed really badly – and then looks at Jack and says, "Enjoy your dinner." Oh, and just to make it a really bad omen, she was wearing the color nail polish you picked out. I should always listen to you.'

'Bina, don't be silly. This isn't about manicures. So what happened next? Did you pitch a fit?'

Bina began to cry again. 'That's the worst part,' she gulped. 'I didn't do anything. It was Jack, Jack who . . .'

The phone rang again. Kate stepped over and looked at the handset and saw that it was Elliot's cell. 'Wait a minute,' she told Bina, who just ignored her anyway. Kate picked up the phone.

'Okay. Don't worry about a thing,' came Elliot's voice. 'We've got the situation under control. Brice and I will be there with bagels, cream cheese and lox. We also have two pints of hand-packed Häagen-Dazs,' he added. 'Rocky Road – Brice figured Bina was on one – and Concession Obsession. Maybe that was because this is all like a bad movie. And that's not all. I have a couple of ten-milligram Valium that Brice "borrowed" from his mother's medicine cabinet. We're the rescue squad. Don't try to get in our way.'

'Elliot, this is serious,' Kate admonished.

'That's why Brice and I took half a day off from work. Well, that and intense curiosity.'

'The two of you are gossipmongers,' Kate said.

'You betcha. Don't let Bina say another word until we get

72

there because even though I'm a social idiot, Brice knows how to fix up anything that's interpersonal. I hang the shelves.'

Kate found herself holding a dead phone and looking at her almost-dead friend. Maybe some food, ice cream, muscle relaxants and diversions were just what she needed. But first she had to find out the rest of the story.

'Was that Jack?' Bina asked.

'No,' Kate admitted. She sat down again. 'Tell me what happened next.' And then the door bell rang.

9

'It's Jack!' Bina shouted and virtually levitated off the sofa.
'Ohmigod! It's Jack and look what I look like!'

'It isn't Jack,' Kate told her and watched Bina struggle with
both relief and disappointment simultaneously. 'It's Elliot.
He's the only one who can get into the building without me
having to buzz. He has a key to the downstairs door.'

Kate went to the tiny foyer and looked through the safety
peephole. There, scary in the fish-eye lens, was Elliot, smiling
and gesturing to Brice, who was holding up the promised
goodie bag. Reluctantly, Kate turned the knob and opened
the door. If she didn't do it, the guys would come in anyway
– Elliot had a spare pair of keys for emergency purposes (like
the time Kate locked her purse in the office and got halfway
home before she noticed) and he wouldn't hesitate to use it.

Elliot and Brice almost tumbled in, the three of them
crowded into the tiny four-foot by four-foot entrance hall.
'Is she okay?' Elliot whispered.

'No,' Kate told him.

'Well, is she better?' Brice asked.

'No,' Kate repeated.

'Then it's a good thing we came,' Elliot said.

'I told you,' Brice responded and then all three of them

stepped into the living room, like all those clowns emerging from a tiny car at the circus. At least it felt like a circus to Kate.

'Oh, Bina! You poor girl,' Elliot said and flew across the living room to sit down beside her in Kate's good chair.

'Don't worry about a thing,' Brice said and began unpacking the shopping bag onto Kate's coffee table. 'What's the last thing you ate? And when was it?'

Bina, a bit dazed, tried to answer him. 'Well, I thought I was going to eat last night with Jack but then I never finished the meal. I was too upset. Then I couldn't find Kate. I remember having some vodka . . .'

'Well, you need one of these,' Elliot said and took out a waxed paper parcel and handed it to her.

She opened it up. Kate winced at the poppy seeds that went rolling off the bagel and onto the sofa, the floor, the rug, and places that she would vacuum for months to come. 'Oh, I can't eat,' Bina said.

'You have to keep up your strength,' Elliot told her.

Kate nodded. 'It would be good for you to have some breakfast,' she coaxed. 'Just take a bite.'

Brice nodded, moved to the foot of the sofa, sat down and rearranged Bina's feet so they were on his lap and covered with the quilt. 'Now, just tell Uncle Brice all about it,' he said, his voice a combination of mockery and sincerity.

'I can't believe yesterday was supposed to be your big night and nothing happened,' Elliot said. 'You must be distraught.' At that point Kate realized she was fairly distraught herself, and taking a throw pillow from the sofa, sank down to the floor on it beside the coffee table.

'Tell me about it! I thought Jack was nervous. Like he was making sure the ring was still safe. Jack Weintraub was finally going to propose to me and he was nervous. You know, he's such a perfectionist – Barbie said he insisted on a perfect stone: Flawless D color.'

'Flawless D!' Brice said approvingly.

'Right. See? I love him for a reason. He knows things. He wants things right. And I thought he wanted me to be happy. So I was happy and I decided to forget about Tokyo Rose.'

'Yes, forget the hostess,' Kate pressed. 'Unless he asked *her* to marry him. You didn't fight over her, did you?'

'We didn't fight at all,' Bina protested. 'I was a little upset about the dragon lady – it just isn't like Jack to flirt with strange women – but I couldn't have loved him more. Anyway, he raised his glass of champagne and I think he was about to make a toast when he realized I didn't have a glass. So he tried to get a waiter or a waitress and they were nowhere to be seen. So Jack says he has to go to the men's room and on the way he'll order me a drink. But I think he might have been looking for the hostess . . .'

'Her and many like her, the man-whore,' said a heated Brice. 'I just hate it when a man . . .'

'Hey. Don't make this personal,' Elliot said, cutting Brice and God only knew what story off.

'Focus, darling,' Kate said, touching Bina's face gently. Kate was quickly losing hope that a simple phone call before Jack got on the plane might put things right.

'Okay. So he excused himself and headed for the men's room. I watched him walk away from the table. I couldn't help thinking he was so handsome.'

'I know. Men are so cute from behind,' said Brice.

Bina nodded her agreement. 'I mean, people are like "Jack is just ordinary", but that's what I like about him,' she continued, paying no heed to the sexual orientation of Brice's comment nor being the slightest bit shocked. It seemed to Kate as though Bina was bonding with Brice the way she did with her girlfriends. 'Jack reminds me of the Goldilocks story,' Bina went on. 'He's not too tall or too short, he isn't too skinny or too fat, he isn't too handsome or too ugly. He's just right,' she said. 'At least just right for me.' Then she realized anew where she was and what had happened. 'He *was* just right, but I wasn't just right for him. Maybe it's me that's ordinary.'

'Oh, Bina,' Kate said and put her arm around the girl, squeezing tightly. 'You're not ordinary.' That might not have been totally true, but that she was Jack's equal was a sure thing. Kate had never met anyone more ordinary than Jack. 'What happened then?'

'Jack was gone for a little while. So finally that stupid hostess came back and asked me if I wanted a drink. I told her that my boyfriend was getting me something, and she said, "Your boyfriend? He said this was a business meeting. Otherwise I would have given him a more private table."'

'The bitch!' Elliot and Brice said simultaneously.

'Yeah. The beautiful, thin, exotic bitch,' Bina agreed bitterly.

'This is not productive,' Kate said. No matter what the story was, Kate was going to be sure they didn't criticize Jack too much, because when he and Bina patched things up – and they would – Bina would forever remember Kate's criticism. Kate had learned that lesson the hard way with Bev, before she married Johnnie.

'Bina, you are so beautiful. Any guy in the world would be lucky to share the same air as you,' Kate told her friend and meant it. Every bit of Bina's soul was generous and giving. Her heart was loyal and loving. And she had an adorable, round little face, and a curvy figure. Kate stroked Bina's dark shiny hair. What the hell was wrong with Jack? It must have been a panic attack. Commitment was a very frightening prospect. 'Didn't you tell me just last week that Jack said he found you beautiful in so many ways?'

'Honey,' Brice said with a tilt of his head, 'greeting cards can tell you that.'

'No, he said I was too beautiful and too good for him,' Bina corrected.

'Uh oh,' Brice and Elliot said, again in unison, and exchanged a look.

Kate gestured to them behind Bina's head, then focused on Bina again. 'Well anyway, Bina, you *are* beautiful and I am sure Jack still feels the same way.'

'Yeah? You haven't heard the end of the story,' Bina said.

'We're trying to,' Kate told her, attempting not to snap.

'Go on. Get it all out,' Elliot advised.

'Well, of course I was hating this . . . woman.' Bina paused and Kate was pleased that she didn't stoop to any slur. 'So I told her to go away. Jack finally came back with my drink and said – and you won't believe this –' Bina mimicked Jack's deep Brooklyn baritone voice. '"I looked at you from across the room. You looked good from over there." Was that a compliment or a diss?'

Kate pursed her lips but refrained from speaking. It seemed clear that her theory was right – Jack needed distance in both senses to see Bina. But up close and intimate his anxiety paralyzed him. If only he could have stayed at the bar and proposed by cell phone, Kate thought ruefully. He could have sent the waitress over with the ring and everyone would be happy. Instead, here Kate was, stuck with an immovable object on her sofa, trying to stave off an irresistible force. And uptown at Andrew Country Day there were children who wouldn't get to see her while she practiced adult psychology in her cramped living room.

'What did you do?' Kate asked.

'I just gave him a look,' Bina said.

'And what did he do?'

'Well, I think Jack saw my reaction. He asked if something was wrong. He sounded so sincere, so concerned, that I felt bad and figured I had to let up on the poor guy. I thought he was a nervous wreck about proposing. Also, to tell the truth, Jack has never been . . . well, let's just say he's careful with his money.'

'Oh hell,' Brice said. 'Let's say he's cheap.' Bina opened her eyes wide, and for a moment Kate thought her friend was going to giggle.

'Go on,' Kate said.

'Well, I just shook my head and suggested that we make a toast. And all he said was "To us". I waited for more, you know like "and to our future as Mr and Mrs Jack Weintraub, the perfect married couple", but there was nothing more.' A tear slid down her cheek and Brice took her hand.

'So?' Kate prompted. She wondered what time Jack's plane was actually taking off, whether Jack planned to be on it, whether he had called the Horowitz household, whether he had called his cousin Max across the hall.

'Then he said he really wished he didn't have to take this trip, but said some of that stuff about markets misbehaving. So I suggested that in the future maybe we'll make the trips together.'

'What did he say to that?' Kate asked.

'Well, of course, then the waitress shows up before he can answer. Just my luck. And you know it takes Jack a long time to order. And then he has to make sure none of the things on his plate are going to touch any of the others.'

Kate had forgotten about that phobia. She nodded to Bina.

'So we had our drink and it seemed that the dinner was going fine until I told him how much I was going to miss him. I mean that's okay to say, right? The guy is going away for months and it's halfway around the world. Jack and I haven't been separated by more than ten miles since we first started dating.'

'Really?' Brice asked. 'That's so romantic!'

'It's true, right, Kate? She was there the night Max, you know, Kate's neighbor from across the hall, had the party where I met Jack.' Kate rolled her eyes. Bina had the habit of playing what her friends called 'Jewish geography'. Kate had gotten her apartment because Bina's brother knew Max from summer camp and he had told Kate about it. Kate got the place and Max invited her to one of his parties to which Bina had also come – on one of her few sallies across the East River – and Max's cousin Jack had . . . well, it could go on endlessly, between Hebrew schools, summer camps, bar mitzvahs, weddings, cousins, and on and on and on. Kate didn't know the Yiddish word for six but there seemed to be fewer degrees of separation between the Jewish communities than the six in the John Guare play and film. Thankfully Bina didn't overindulge. 'The weird thing is we had both grown up in Brooklyn just six blocks from each other but we were introduced for the first time that night, and we haven't been apart since. I mean, he took me out for a drink after the party and asked me out for the next night. And that weekend he came over for dinner with my parents and brother and . . . well, there we were, saying goodbye to each other for a very long time. So I thought it was appropriate to say I would miss him. And I thought it would be good to kind of, you know, get him started. I mean, we were finished with our appetizers and entrées. Did I have to wait until he popped the question?'

'Men spook easily,' Brice offered. 'I remember the time when Ethan Housholder told me . . .'

'Not now, Brice,' Kate interjected.

'Right, sorry. Continue, honey.' Kate had to admit that Bina couldn't have had two more sympathetic listeners than Brice and Elliot. And sometimes simply talking was the best therapy. But then, just when Kate thought they had safely gotten out of the water, Bina began to cry again. Elliot's soft pats and Brice's coos of sympathy only made it worse.

'Well, it was like all the color drained out of his face. And then he said, "Bina, you know I have to be in Hong Kong for almost five months and that's not going to be easy." He kept touching his breast pocket and the tension was almost overwhelming. I couldn't help but think "here it comes". Then he just sat there. I wanted to scream, "*Why*

80

don't you just take the damn thing out of there and ask me to marry you?" But, nothing. The man just sat there and then looked down and finished eating his fucking Chicken Rangoon.'

10

'What did you do?' Elliot asked.

Kate was afraid that she would hear that Bina had become hysterical, attacked Jack physically, made a huge scene, or something even more dramatic. But Bina surprised her.

'I went to the ladies' room, of course.'

'Of course,' Brice agreed. 'I can't tell you how many times I wished I could go there myself.'

'So, anyway . . .' Bina continued. She opened her eyes wide and they glazed over as if she could see the scene replaying itself.

Kate, Elliot and Brice all held their breath, as if at last they were to find out what had actually happened. Then the phone rang. 'Shit!' Kate said and grabbed for the receiver, peering at the number. 'It's your mother again,' Kate said. 'I think you better talk to her.'

'Kill me first!' Bina pleaded. Kate froze for a moment. She couldn't bear to explain the situation to Myra Horowitz and she didn't have the heart to give the phone to Bina. But she couldn't refuse the call again . . .

'I'll take it,' Elliot said.

'Don't be ridiculous,' Kate told him, realizing he was getting deeper and deeper into her Brooklyn life. She pressed the 'answer' button.

'Katie! Thank God! Listen, do you know where Bina is?'

'She's fine. She's right here with me,' Kate told Mrs Horowitz, only telling one lie, not two.

'Well, put her on.'

Bina was wildly shaking her head, her hands in front of her face as if to ward off a blow.

Kate was grateful for every moment she had spent at the Horowitz house because even with her training it took more than therapeutic skills to talk Mrs Horowitz down. Kate said soothing words, then distracted her with questions, then reassured her, then sent her love to Dr Horowitz. All the while Elliot circled his hand, telling her to move it along, while Brice pulled his index finger across his throat, giving her the sign to cut it short. As if she wanted to be the middleman! She finally hung up.

'At last,' said Brice.

'So you were in the ladies' room,' Elliot prompted.

'Yeah. You know, I just wanted to be by myself for a minute; just long enough to get it all together again,' Bina said. 'So I fixed my makeup – and I still had to give the woman there a dollar, even though I hadn't used the toilet – but I just looked at myself in the mirror and said, "Bina Horowitz, this is the night that's going to change your life. Be nice and be happy."'

'Good for you,' Kate said, though in the face of obvious tragedy to come.

'So I get back to the table and Jack stands up. He always does it when we're in a fancy restaurant. So he leans over to help me into my chair and . . .' She gulped. 'The ring box slipped out of his pocket. It was like a car accident in one of those movies. I saw it all happening in slow motion. The ring box fell over and over and over. The moment the box hits the floor, Jack lets go of my chair. The ring flies out of the box and he scrambles to retrieve it. I'm as frozen as a Swanson TV dinner, and I see the ring skid across the floor and that stupid bitch hostess bends *all* the way over and picks it up.'

'Wow,' was all Kate could say.

'Wow, indeed,' Brice added.

'What did you do?' asked Elliot.

'I just sat there, like the turkey dinner that I am, and I realize that Jack, on the floor, can see up the woman's skirt – well, it was *so* short and she bent right over. And not from the knees like you're supposed to but from the waist. And she isn't wearing any underwear.'

'What?' all three said in collective amazement.

'None. And Jack is on the floor, looking straight up her – well, up her . . .'

'We get the visual,' Kate said.

'So did Jack. Everyone was looking. I think that was when he lost his mind. It must have been then. So Jack manages to get off the floor and tear his eyes off that woman's naked crotch and she turns around and hands him the ring. He stands up and puts it in his right pocket. Then he scoops up the box and puts it in his left one.' Bina stopped for a moment and shook her head. 'He walked back to the table.' She turned to Kate. 'I couldn't stay happy anymore, Katie. I told Jack that if he was trying to make it a memorable evening, he was succeeding. I mean I could have smacked him, I was so mad. And you know what the asshole said?'

'What now?' Kate asked.

Bina, using her Jack voice again, said, '"This isn't how I want to remember you, Bina."'

'Uh oh. Here it comes,' Brice said.

'Wait for it,' Elliot warned him.

'Please, you two – it's like Tweedledee and Tweedle Very Dumb,' Kate admonished. 'Let the woman finish her story, which, I pray, is almost over.'

'Almost,' Bina said. 'So, I was wondering which pocket my ring was in now. It made me think of that game, Kate, that my father would play with us when we were little girls. You know, when he would have surprises for us and we would have to guess which pocket they were in.'

Kate nodded, almost smiling in remembrance. Dr Horowitz had been so kind to her. He used to give his daughter her allowance every Sunday morning and since Kate's father was usually sleeping one off on Sunday and rarely gave her money, Dr Horowitz always gave Kate the same allowance as well. A big Sunday event was going to the candy store and agonizing over Junior Mints or Bit O Honey. Not to mention the *Betty* and *Veronica* comics. Bina and her family were good people, and she hated hearing how she'd been subjected to this hurtful slapstick. But maybe the situation could be salvaged. After all, Bina and Jack had years of history and were made for each other. 'So then what?' she asked.

'Well,' Bina continued, 'Jack then looked me in the eyes and said, "Bina, I have something I want to say to you." And I'm thinking at least someday we'll tell our grandchildren about all this and laugh! But then Jack says, "I have to be honest; Hong Kong is far away from here. Very far away." Like I didn't take geography, right? So I think maybe he's going to want to elope. It would break my mother's heart, and I want the dress and all, but I was like dying by now. I kept waiting for Jack to reach for the ring, but his hands are staying folded together on top of the table. He takes a deep breath, looks up to the ceiling, and says, "I think it would be unfair of me to leave and ask you to just wait for me." I told him I agreed and I looked down at my hand to get my finger ready. But then he said, "I think this time apart might be a good chance for us to – well, for us to – I think this might be a good chance for us to explore our singleness."'

'I could kill him, Bina,' Kate said.

'Oh, me first,' Brice added.

There was silence in the room. Kate, Elliot and Brice sat there with their mouths open wide, until Bina started sobbing

85

again. All three snapped back into action. Kate moved closer on the sofa and held Bina. 'Oh, honey,' she said. Brice got up, took a cushion and put it under her feet as if she had internal bleeding. Elliot got up, went into the bathroom and returned with a wet towel, a glass of water and a blue pill. Ever neat – except in his clothes – he looked for a coaster. Before Kate could hand him one, he found a piece of cardboard.

'Take this and drink all the water,' he told her. Bina did as she was told without question.

'What was that?' Kate asked.

'Oh, I just felt she needed a visit from cousin Valerie,' Elliot told her. It was his code word for Valium, and Kate knew a blue one was ten milligrams.

'She'll sleep for a week,' Kate said.

'What a good time for that,' Elliot told her.

'Okay, Bina. Tell us what happened next.'

'I just ran out,' she said. 'Well, ran as best I could in my heels. I went straight to your apartment, Katie, and when I couldn't find you Max helped me. You can't believe how hysterical I was.' Kate silently disagreed with her on that. Bina blew her nose and continued. 'Max was home. And he told me he thought you were out to dinner and where Elliot lived and I went straight there in the pouring rain and . . . Ohmigod!'

'What! What is it, Bina?' Kate asked. Had Bina had a bad reaction to the pill? 'What is it?'

Bina reached over to the coffee table and picked up the coaster for the water. It was Bunny's wedding invitation. 'Bunny? Bunny is getting married?' she asked.

'Is that a bad thing?' Elliot wanted to know.

Bina ignored him. 'Why didn't you tell me, Katie?'

'I just found out,' Kate told Bina. 'I got the invitation yesterday.'

'Oh, this is it! It proves I'm a complete loser,' Bina wailed. 'Bunny is going to be a bride and Jack is off to become the Marco Polo of singleness. Why don't I just open my veins?'

'Well, it's very messy, for one thing,' Brice told her. 'And it's almost impossible to get blood out of clothes. Very cold water and hydrogen peroxide . . .'

Bina put her head under the pillow and sobbed into it. It wasn't that she was competitive with Bunny, Kate knew. It was just that Bunny had been last to join their group, hadn't had a date to the prom, had never been pinned. Bunny didn't do well with men, picking a string of bad boys and scoundrels. One she had lived with had stolen everything – even her sofa and kitchen table – when she went away for the weekend. 'How can Bunny be getting married? She just got dumped by that guy we saw in SoHo. She's only just met Barney or whatever.' Bina squinted at the card. 'And how did they get invitations so quickly? They must be Xeroxed.'

How had Bunny met someone? Kate wondered why it was so much more complicated for her than for Barbie and Bev and Bunny. When Kate found a warm man, he was often devoted to her but just a little . . . dull. Or second-rate. And when she found a man with a first-rate mind and an engrossing life work, a man like Michael, he was lacking in emotional heat. Of course, she reflected, Bina's father, a successful chiropractor, had doted on her. So, in spite of her current troubles, it seemed only natural that she would eventually find a successful accountant who doted on her. Kate sighed. It didn't bode well for her. 'Bina, everything is going to be okay,' she promised.

'Fine for you to say. You've got that doctor Michael to go with. What am I going to do? Go with my brother?'

'Oh, I don't think Katie will want to bring Michael all the way across the Brooklyn Bridge,' Elliot began. He turned to Kate and gave her a little smirk. 'Unless you want to prepare him for his journey to Austin, you know, a little bit at a time.'

Kate grimaced at him. Elliot turned back to Bina. 'Anyway, if my calculations are correct – and they always are – we have here two women who need dates and two men with an insatiable curiosity for the customs and rituals of deepest, darkest Brooklyn.'

'Really?' asked Bina.

'Not only that, but I have fabulous formal wear. I'll definitely be better-dressed than the bride,' Brice said.

'In a dress?' Bina asked, her voice about to rise into hysteria again.

'No. A great tux. Versace. And I'll do your makeup. You'll look absofuckinglutely great and all your friends will want to know who the great-looking guy you're with is. You can tell them whatever you like. I once passed as the Prince of Norway.' Brice turned to Elliot, gave him a loving but exasperated look and then stared at Kate. 'I know what he looks like in a rented tux,' Brice told her. 'You're on your own.'

'Thanks,' Elliot said. 'No offense meant, I'm sure, and none taken. So it's set. Brice and I will take you two girls, and we will all have a wonderful time.'

'Maybe that's a good idea,' Bina said. 'But right now I think I have to take a little nap.'

Kate watched as Bina's eyes fluttered shut. 'You guys must be joking,' she said.

'No way.'

11

Two weeks later, Kate and Bina, both carrying presents, were waiting for Elliot and Brice three blocks south of St Veronica's Roman Catholic Church, the place where Kate had made her first Communion in the dress Mrs Horowitz had sewed for her. Kate, all grown up now, was unaware that in the simple, calf-length, navy-blue dress that set off her fiery hair she looked stunning. She didn't think of her Communion dress; she was just grateful that she didn't have to wear one of the loopy bridesmaids' gowns she was usually stuck in. They were always ugly and the polyester in them was always hot.

Bina, at Kate's side, was already hot and actually holding Kate's hand. She felt really damp, looked totally Brooklyn and smelled like fear. She wore a pink dress that poofed at the skirt. Her dark-brown hair was done up in lacquered swirls of French twist curls as if she were going to their senior prom. Sal, the hairdresser who had 'done' both of them for the prom, had probably done Bina this time, too.

'Is it going to be a High Mass?' Kate asked, remembering her boredom at the standing, the kneeling, the standing again in the interminable services of her youth.

'Mass-shmass,' Bina said, dismissively. She craned her neck, looking for the guys. 'I'm safe during the ceremony. It's afterward that I'm dead meat.'

'Bina, this isn't a firing squad. These women are your friends,' Kate tried to reassure her. 'You've known them since we were little girls. They're not going to judge you.'

Bina turned back to stare at Kate. 'Are you kidding?' she asked in amazement. 'That's exactly what they're going to do. That's what friends are for.'

'Hey, look: we got a great strategy,' Kate reminded her. 'Everyone may assume that Elliot is Michael, it will take a while to straighten that out and I'll distract them with it. If Bev opens her big mouth and calls him Michael I can do half an hour of material to make it look like I'm embarrassed. And everyone knows Jack left. So showing up with Brice will just daze and confuse them, or maybe even blow them away; I mean, he *is* gorgeous.'

'Yeah,' Bina agreed dispiritedly, 'but he's no Jack.' Jack had gone to Hong Kong without calling, and Bina had heard nothing from him since. Now, she looked up and down the street again. 'Where are they?' she demanded.

'They'll be here,' Kate reassured her, looking down the all-too-familiar Woodbine Avenue. She felt slightly dizzy and she wasn't sure if it was the heat or the location. Returning to Brooklyn and the old neighborhood gave her a kind of vertigo.

'But, Kate, what if they don't show up? I'll have to go in alone. I can hide in the back during the ceremony, but if at the reception I have to go Jackless and ringless they'll all want to know the reason he broke up with me and . . .' She was working herself up into what Kate was starting to think of as Bina-less-Jack frenzy.

'Bina, calm down,' Kate said, with more than a bit of concern in her voice. For the past two weeks, Bina had been spending every day and almost every night alternating between Max's and Kate's. After a few days Kate had remonstrated, but Bina refused to cross the bridge. 'I can't go home. Everything reminds me of him' was Bina's first excuse. Kate had been happy, initially, to provide Bina with a safe haven but after four days she'd insisted that Bina call her father and mother herself and break the news. Dr Horowitz had threatened to fly to Hong Kong right there and then to 'knock that pisher's block off' but Bina had implored her father to stay in Brooklyn and had thereby kept Jack's block safe. Mrs Horowitz, in the face of all the evidence to the contrary, remained convinced that her daughter was engaged. Denial was a great temporary convenience at the time.

'I can't take this,' Bina said. 'I'm melting from nervous perspiration. I'll never wear this dress again.' Kate thought that was probably a good thing. Just then, a black Lincoln town car pulled up and Elliot and Brice emerged.

'You're late,' Kate said in place of a greeting, but she was happy to see the two of them.

'Well, hello to you, too.' Elliot smiled, his usual cheerfulness intact. 'Who's late?' He looked at his watch. 'You said the ceremony was three o'clock. It's two fifty-seven.'

Kate sighed. 'Being on time is late in a situation like this.'

'Haven't they heard of fashionably late?' Brice asked.

'This is Brooklyn,' Kate reminded him. But as she looked both men over she couldn't be angry.

'Wow,' Bina said. 'I love your outfits.'

Kate smiled. 'You two do clean up well.'

'Of course,' Brice said. 'We're gay.' With that he grabbed Bina's arm. 'But not for this afternoon.' He lowered his voice to a baritone. 'This afternoon I'm devoted to you. Can't keep my hands off you.' Bina actually smiled.

'Shall we, honey?' Brice asked. Bina nodded. 'Hmm. Who did your hair?' Kate heard him ask Bina, that 'anything-she-can-do-I-can-do-better' tone in his voice.

'Sal Anthony. He has a little shop at the corner of Court and . . .'

'Burn it down,' Brice ordered. 'And we'll see if we can't soften it up a bit.'

'He's so bossy,' Kate said softly to Elliot.

'Yeah. Isn't it great?' Elliot asked. They got to St Veronica's and walked up the formidable steps to the entrance of the church. Once inside, Kate indicated the way to the ladies' room downstairs.

'Follow me, princess,' Brice told Bina and led her off to the basement.

Coming in at the very last minute wasn't a bad strategy, Kate thought. There was no time to meet and greet – and to be interrogated. Kate and Elliot left the foyer and took a place in the next-to-last pew. Soon Brice and Bina joined them. They tried to be unobtrusive, but by now everyone was waiting for the ceremony to begin and, with their entrance, heads turned. Then, to Kate's relief, in only a moment the organ began to play the wedding march.

Bunny, a meringue of tulle and taffeta, made her way down the aisle on her father's arm. There was the usual 'oooh' from the guests. Oddly, Kate felt tears well up in her eyes. She'd never been very close to Bunny – she couldn't honestly say she even liked her. But the tears were there nevertheless. She wondered if she was simply being empathetic for Bina, who must be finding this almost unbearable, but it felt far deeper than that.

Kate blinked away the moistness, then took a chance and looked around at the other guests. She wondered if they had as many doubts and fears as she did about picking a mate for life. Certainly, Bina and her other friends had talked of little else for many of the years they were in school together. Boys, and then young men, who was going steady, who was breaking up, marriages and honeymoons were the fodder of many – maybe most – conversations. Yet, despite all the talking and all the romantic notions, hopes and dreams, Kate didn't see intelligent or realistic choices being made, and she also didn't see any marriages or relationships she envied.

She wondered sometimes if her view was darkened by her early home life or her professional training. But the truth was that she remembered very little of her parents' marriage and didn't believe that it was bad or violent. Her father's serious drinking had started after her mother's death. So why was she so frightened? Was everyone frightened and they just hid it better? Specializing in child psychology, she knew when the seeds of relationship problems to come were planted but her training with and for children certainly hadn't focused on dysfunctional marriages – or how to avoid them.

So what was Bunny doing now? She'd just met this guy. Was she simply on the rebound from whoever had dumped her? Or was she smitten, deep in that sex haze of infatuation that never seemed to last longer than several months? How could she be taking these steps so quickly down the aisle beside her father? Though her Catholicism had lapsed, Kate was still idealistic enough to believe marriage should be forever.

Here, standing in St Veronica's watching Bunny meet the groom at the altar, she felt an uncomfortable combination of jealousy and fear: jealousy because she doubted she could give herself to Michael or any man without hesitation, and fear because she wanted to and might lose her opportunity to do it. Though she had made up with Michael, his lack of compassion for Bina had made her look at him in a new way. Would he always dwell on his own issues and concerns and be insensitive to others? He had seemed sincere in his apology, but Kate felt it was important to watch him. Above all, she needed a partner with empathy for others.

Kate sighed. Elliot, beside her, gave her a smile, then craned to see ahead. Maybe it was Manhattan. Here in Brooklyn love seemed so much easier, Kate reflected. Young women met young men. They dated for a while and either broke up or made a commitment to make a commitment. Women

pressed for marriage and the men, albeit sometimes reluctantly, seemed eventually to fall into line. It was expected.
And families, ever present in the background, pushed for it.

There were, of course, the exceptions like Jack, but despite
this glitch, Kate felt almost certain that he could get over the
hump, have some fun in Hong Kong and return to Bina, the
woman he loved. But for how long, if they married, would
they love each other? Looking at the older couples in the
pews beside and ahead of her, Kate saw bored, middle-aged
men and stoic or overly sentimental women. Many held
handkerchiefs or tissues to their eyes. When Kate saw an older
woman cry at a wedding – and she'd been to a lot of weddings
– she often thought they cried because unconsciously they
remembered their own hopes and the subsequent disappointment that marriage had brought them.

Kate stood there, between her two best friends, and between
two worlds, and realized that she was not only envious but
also very, very sad. Even if Michael wound up being the right
man for her, and it was possible, she simply couldn't imagine
wearing the gown, she certainly wouldn't be in a church,
her father couldn't walk her down any aisle, and it seemed
impossible she'd feel the joy that she'd glimpsed on Bunny's
veiled face. Worst of all, she'd probably want Elliot as her
matron of honor, which would cause all kinds of difficulties
and hurt feelings among her old crowd.

Kate had to smile at the thought. Of course, Elliot would
love it. She looked over in his direction and saw that, behind
Bina, on the cushion of the pew, Elliot and Brice were
discreetly holding hands. It was so sweet that Kate, without
a Kleenex, again felt tears rise to her eyes and film them over.
She was so happy for Elliot, who had searched and searched
for a wonderful partner. But it sometimes made her feel more
lonely than she had felt in years.

'Having fun?' Elliot asked in a whisper as he nudged her
out of her reverie.

'Just thinking,' Kate murmured.

'Bad idea at any time,' Elliot advised. '*Particularly* bad during rituals.' He flashed Kate another quick smile. 'And did I tell you, you look extremely fetching in that dress?'

Kate smiled but put a finger over her curved lips. Religion was serious in Brooklyn. The ceremony was beginning. And so was the trouble.

Even though she was not Catholic, and was standing yards and yards from the altar, the moment the priest began to speak Bina began to sob. At first they were silent, shoulder-shaking sobs. For a few moments Kate didn't notice them. But by the time Bunny and her groom had knelt and stood up and knelt again, Bina was audible halfway up the nave. Kate and Elliot eyed one another, then leaned forward and gave Brice a look. He already had one arm around Bina's shoulder and shrugged in the traditional what-else-can-I-do gesture.

Kate looked toward the altar, desperate to think of options. A little crying at a wedding was acceptable, even mandatory, but this was getting out of hand. For no reason, her eyes focused on the incense-filled censer, hanging from the hands of an altar boy. Really handy-looking. For a moment Kate wished she could get a hold of it and give a swing at Bina's head. Not, of course, to knock her out, but merely to knock some sense into it. It was going to be hard enough to get through the reception without Bina blowing her cover now by making a spectacle of herself.

Already a few heads had turned toward them. Kate smiled and nodded, wiping at her own eye, as if she was acknowledging everyone's tears of joy. 'So beautiful,' she mouthed to someone's mother. Brice, in a moment of brilliance, turned Bina to him and planted a kiss on her lips. For a few seconds Bina's total surprise silenced her. Elliot, putting his arm around her neck from the other side, discreetly covered her mouth with his hand. Bina took the warning and they all watched as the couple stood up, knelt yet again, then stood up and faced one another.

'Is this a wedding or an aerobics class?' Elliot asked. Kate would almost have laughed out loud but when the couple got to 'love, honor and cherish', Bina cut loose, crying louder than the baby somewhere up front.

Before everything got completely out of control, Brice reached over, turned back Elliot's cuff and removed a straight pin. Then, without a moment of hesitation, he stuck it into Bina's upper arm.

Kate, shocked, was not as shocked as Bina, who yipped, shut up and looked from Elliot on one side to Brice on the other. Brice just leaned forward, whispered in her ear and, magically, the crying stopped.

At last the service was over, the bride and groom kissed, and Brice and Elliot had to let go of each other's entwined hands to hold Bina's down so she didn't cover her face and begin to sob again. 'Hey, look,' Kate said, taking Bina by the shoulders because she felt that Bina needed some more tough love or she wouldn't be able to get through the next phase of the event. 'Pull yourself together. This isn't the worst part,' she told Bina. 'The worst part is about to begin.'

'Oh, boy!' Elliot said. 'Will there be a family feud?'

'With guns,' Brice added hopefully.

Kate ignored the two of them despite her gratitude. 'We have to get Bina out of here before the rest of the rabble,' Kate told the two men.

'You aren't kidding. Just look at her.' Elliot tilted his head toward Bina.

Kate had to agree. Bina's makeup was mostly smeared off her face, and mascara had run down her cheeks. Kate gestured and Elliot tapped Brice on the leg.

'Time to go now,' Elliot told Brice.

'No fucking kidding,' Brice responded. 'The last thing Bina

needs right now is to have rice land on her face. It would stick.'

Elliot scrunched up his face in disgust at that thought. 'Then let's strike the set,' Brice suggested. Elliot and Kate nodded enthusiastically and they crept as quietly as they could out of the pew, out of the foyer, and out of the church.

They were lucky to snag a passing cab – not so easy in a borough dependent on car services. They piled out at Carl's of Carroll Gardens, where everyone in Brooklyn, it seemed, had their wedding reception.

'Well, here we go,' Kate said as they stood before the entrance. Kate gave Elliot a nervous smile and they linked their arms and went through the revolving doors, followed by Brice and Bina. Thankfully, the reception area was empty except for a few bustling waiters who had seen a lot worse than Bina's ruined face.

'Where's the bathroom?' Brice whispered in Kate's ear. 'I'm going to take Little Miss Three Mile Island in for a makeup makeover. She's had a serious meltdown.'

'It's down the hall, to the left,' said Kate. She had been to this banquet hall many times in the past. Maybe a dozen people she knew had got married here, but it would be a quiet day at Andrew Country Day School before *she* ever would. Assembly line wedding, with the same music, the same guests, the same MC, the same cake. 'Take her away,' Kate said. 'And Brice, darling, please be gentle.'

'I'll do my best,' Brice said and started to push Bina from behind. 'Come on, honey. Time for some surgery from Dr Brice.'

Kate heard Bina's nasal protesting voice trail off as she and Brice disappeared down the hall.

'Well,' said Kate, turning her attention to Elliot. 'Are you ready for your first Brooklyn reception?'

'Oh, Katie! This is going to be so much fun,' Elliot said with a smirk.

'Cut the Katie before you get your tongue cut out,' Kate warned him. 'I've got a mission. Let's see where we are supposed to sit, change it if we can and then avoid everyone until we've regrouped.'

'Sure. I'm happy just to gape.' Elliot craned his neck almost the way Linda Blair had in *The Exorcist*. 'Where do they get these smoked mirrors? Are they left over from the sixties or can you still buy them?' he asked, his voice low. It was kind of like Halloween in Greenwich Village. Then he looked down at his watch. 'Kate, I'm starting to worry about what Brice is doing to Bina. Let me go and find them. I'll be right back. You wait here for the resurrection.' Elliot darted off in the direction of the bathroom.

Once alone, Kate walked over to the gift table and placed her box from Tiffany's right in the center. She knew it wouldn't be the only one there wrapped in distinctive robin's-egg blue, but she was fairly certain the beautiful cut-glass bowl would be the only gift that actually came from Tiffany's. Those blue boxes were often more highly prized than the contents they carried and were passed around over and over, filled with gifts from Bed, Bath, and Beyond, or Pottery Barn.

The reception area was beginning to fill up. But where the hell was Elliot with Brice and Bina? Kate could hear the cars pulling up outside. It wasn't only Bina who would be tortured at this event. Kate was definitely not in the mood to deal with all these people – well-meaning or not – asking her about her 'love life' and whether wedding bells were in her future, too. People from the old neighborhood neither thought deeply personal questions were off limits nor took notice of how she had managed to add a 'Dr' before her name. All everyone here would talk about was when there would be a 'Mrs' in front.

Kate put this all out of her mind because she had a goal to achieve. She had to get over to the table where the seating plans were and make sure her party of four was at the same table. Then she had to get into the closed banquet hall and move the place cards on that table around so that Bina would be tightly cordoned off from attacking hyenas, the type that tried to take down a straggler or the weakest member in the herd.

She approached the assignment table with complete authority. If she didn't she might get stopped by one of the staff. They were used to unmarried women putting themselves beside bachelors, bitter aunts removing themselves from tables with their relatives, even parents who moved their kids to other tables so they could eat dinner in peace. Kate quickly spotted the two important cards. *Miss Katie Jameson and guest.* Table nine. She shook her head. Not only had the 'Dr' been omitted but she didn't even get her full name. She hated being called 'Katie', but Bunny and her mother wouldn't care about such subtleties.

Two cards above her own was *Miss Bina Horowitz and Mr Jack Weintraub*. That was something Kate knew she couldn't afford to let Bina see. Bunny's mother obviously hadn't remembered about Jack's trip. Kate picked the card up, turned it over and, using a black marker she had put in her purse for this very situation, she wrote *Miss Bina Horowitz and guest* on the back of the card and replaced it. She hoped that Bina wouldn't turn the card over and that Elliot and Brice were smart enough to pocket them. They'd probably want them as scrapbook souvenirs anyway.

So far, so good, Kate thought. Next, and last, was getting to the actual table to manipulate the place cards. If Bina was seated next to Bev or Barbie she wouldn't last five minutes. Of course, they might be seated in the traditional boy-girl-boy-boring arrangement. Kate sighed, thinking of one more dinner beside Bobbie, Barbie's excessively dull husband. She walked to the closed entrance of the banquet hall and, as luck would have it, a hassled-looking waiter came out. She grabbed at the door closing behind him as he departed with an armful of linens and stepped into the room.

A sign said 'Tromboli–Beckmen Wedding Saturday'. Under it was 'Eisenberg Bar Mitzvah Sunday'. Kate surveyed the room. The interior of the hall was Bunny Tromboli's dream come true, amazingly close to Kate's nightmare. The decorations, the centerpieces, the candles – everything was a middle-class version of photographs Bunny had been clipping and saving from society pages since she was ten. All of the Bitches, except Kate, had done the same. Kate sighed deeply. If she had ever allowed herself to imagine the elements of a dream wedding, the major emphasis had been on the groom, not the flatware.

Yet despite the inconceivably garish tablecloths and place settings – hot pink and orange, a combination Kate saw no use for in either clothes or furnishings, along with black dinnerware and centerpieces that looked like patent leather with flourishes of net – there was something lovely, calm and even . . . magical about a vacant room prepared for but empty of revelers. She allowed herself to pause for a moment to take it all in. Then her mission moved her forward. She found table nine, looked it over and saw that she was right on the money not only in checking it out but also 'editing' it. She moved the cards so that the line-up on their side of the table was Elliot, then Kate, then Bina and, lastly, Brice. She had to juggle Bobbie and Johnnie, Barbie and Bev's husbands, to get it to work out, but in a few moments it was done. She pulled out the four chairs for her party and leaned the backs against the table – a very déclassé way to show the seats were taken and to ensure that nobody re-edited her editing.

The noise of new arrivals outside the banquet hall had gotten much louder and then, without warning, the doors swung open. The guests began to pour in. Kate, not wanting to be found alone in the room, a target worse than a lonely duck before the hunter's blind, decided to make her way out to the terrace that ran along the east wall of the room. She would wait outside, get a breath of air and a bit of privacy before the onslaught. Once her crew came back there would be enough people and enough noise to allow her just to slip back inside the French doors, find the 'Trouble Trio' and begin the minimum required mingling. She'd mingled at dozens of weddings before, and she could do it again, she told herself.

Out on the terrace Kate had a moment to reflect. She was overwhelmingly glad that she had not invited Michael to the affair. She would have been self-conscious and, although she shouldn't be, rather ashamed. The clothes, the accents, the loudness, the . . . well, the vulgarity of it all, made her wince. She was used to it, and loved many of these people, but did not want to have to translate them for Michael or anyone else. At the same time, she wasn't enjoying how much Elliot and Brice were enjoying their Brooklyn visit. It was too much like a visit to Great Adventure Safari Park. They were observing the wildlife with the detachment of another species.

Kate peeked into the room. It wouldn't take long for it to fill. And then Elliot and Brice would get to talk to the creatures they had been observing at the church. Somehow, while it was all right that Kate thought of these people as strange, outré, or louche, she didn't like the idea of outsiders observing them in that way, not even Elliot and Brice. Yes, she reflected again, it was the right thing to do to leave Michael out; and how on earth would she have managed Bina without the help of the guys? Kate couldn't even imagine Michael's reaction to Bina's overreaction. Despite the breeze, she actually felt herself breaking into a light sweat. She wasn't sure if it was the humidity or her discomfort.

Kate, on the terrace, continued to watch as people entered, rearranged their own place cards, hugged or kissed one another, and went for the drinks. Even through the windows, she could hear them speculating about the estimated per-plate cost of the upcoming meal, where the bride had got the dress, whether there was a bun in the oven and . . . then Kate saw Elliot, Brice and Bina enter the room. She had to admit it: Bina did look a thousand times more sophisticated with the terrific makeup and more gentle upswept hair style Brice's lengthy ministrations had created. Kate reached for the handle of the French door to let herself in, only to find that the door had locked itself behind her. She tried the second one, then the third. All locked.

Stranded. She knocked on the glass and tried desperately to get someone's attention, but the hall was abuzz with noise. She could make out older female guests loudly declaring the ceremony to be the most beautiful wedding they'd ever seen, while the men called across the room to each other, inquiring about the outlook for the Mets.

In moments, the room had changed from tranquil to chaotic, from empty to full, and myriad poof skirts and treacherously dangerous high hair-dos blocked her line of vision. She had lost sight of her friends. Kate thought she caught a glimpse of Brice and someone who might be Bina, now on the side of the room opposite their table, but she couldn't be sure. She ran back down to the remaining doors of the terrace to try to get in but they were all locked. Well, she would just have to wait until someone . . .

Just then, a tall blond man stepped out of the door at the other end of the terrace. What a relief!

'Wait!' Kate yelled. 'Wait! Hold the . . .' but before she could finish her sentence or make a move he had turned away and the door slammed behind him.

12

'Damn it,' Kate muttered under her breath. She walked over to the slammed door and tried the handle, but it was locked. Meanwhile, behind her, the guy had moved to the ivy-covered wall and was looking around casually. He was, she couldn't help but notice, one of the best-looking men she'd ever seen. His blond hair must have had a dozen shades in it – the kind of hair women paid hundreds of dollars to salons for but never achieved. He was probably only a little over six foot tall, but his wide shoulders and the way his jacket tapered from them, along with legs that didn't quit, made him incredibly well proportioned. Kate wondered whether his upper arms were muscled and cut in the way she found so attractive. She could barely see his profile but even from here she could see that he didn't have the usual pale coloring of a blond. There was a golden tone to his skin that . . . well, he was altogether a golden guy, the type who is all looks and no substance.

Then he saw Kate and turned to face her. From a full frontal he was – if it was possible – even more alluring. To her dismay Kate felt a blush rise from her chest to her neck and cursed her involuntary muscles.

He didn't seem to notice, he just asked, 'At the risk of cliché, what's a pretty girl like you doing alone in a place like this?' He took a few steps toward her. 'And you look distressed. Um, in the damsel, not the furniture sense.' He smiled.

The smile was the coup de grâce. It was marvelous the way his teeth lightened his face, parenthetical dimples formed around his mouth and his eyes, unlike most people's when they smiled, stayed wide open. He was what might be called *un canon*, a living embodiment of male beauty. Kate took a step back. She was suspicious of men this good-looking and with charm as well but she couldn't help staring. Something about him looked familiar, but she would never have forgotten him if they had met. Perhaps he was a newscaster, or someone she had seen on television. She forced herself to take her eyes away from his.

Kate tried to keep her embarrassment from showing. 'You could have helped by holding the door open. Now we may have to wait until someone from the Eisenberg bar mitzvah lets us in tomorrow afternoon.' The words had come out more sharply than she meant them to. He cocked his head and observed her. She felt a trifle self-conscious at the way he looked at her. Not that it was an up and down examination. Merely because it was so intent – as if he were memorizing every detail of her, from her exposed collarbone to her Jimmy Choo shoes. She turned and looked in at the party through the long window.

'Is that such a bad thing?' he asked.

At the far side of the room Kate could see Bina, flanked by Brice and Elliot, looking around, presumably for Kate. Oh no, she couldn't let Bina sit down among their old crowd without her protection! There would be a feeding frenzy. She rattled the door handle. No luck. '*Merde!*' she said.

'*Ah. Parlez-vous français?*' he asked, almost too quickly.

She turned away from the party to look at him, face to face. This guy wasn't just an average hottie. He had the smile of a man who knew he was more than handsome and very acceptable to women. It was a well-practiced smile that bathed Kate in warmth. She felt as if she were the first woman in the entire world to ever see such an expression of welcome. The guy was absolutely gorgeous, what French slang would describe as *un block*.

'*Oui.*' Kate blushed, and cursed the paleness of her skin. She might as well have her feelings written in neon on her forehead. '*Je parle un petit peu, mais avec un accent très mauvais,*' she told him.

'*Mais non. Pas mal. Vraiment.*'

Handsome as the guy was – and his accent was perfect – Kate was in no mood to test her skills in a foreign tongue right now, though the thought of his tongue was a momentary distraction from her desperation. She turned and tried once again to open the doors, but they were clearly catchlocks, only openable from the inside. 'We're stuck out here,' she said.

'What an unexpected bonus at an affair like this. Maybe it's an omen,' Mr Gorgeous continued. Perfect damn teeth. 'Maybe we're not meant to participate in the Bunny Tromboli and Arnie Beckmen nuptials.' He leaned back on the terrace railing, crossed one foot in front of the other, and gave Kate another appreciative once-over. 'Personally, I would take that as a gift.'

Kate was too uptight to flirt or respond to compliments, especially from a guy as practiced at them as he was.

'You don't look like you're from around these parts,' he said, doing a passable Gary Cooper accent. He looked a little like the late actor, too, and probably knew it.

Kate had always preferred slightly nerdy boyfriends, no matter what Elliot said. They were more real, more sincere. Ever since a really handsome Oxford exchange student had asked her on their first date, 'How can I possibly keep from falling in love with you?' and subsequently dated her room-mate a week later, she'd been wary of charm. '*Et vous?*' she asked, just as a test.

105

'*Oui, je suis un fils de Brooklyn*,' he answered with a mischievous smile.

'Your accent is perfect,' Kate observed admiringly.

'My French accent or the Brooklyn one?' he asked and smiled again. Looks like his should be against the law, she thought. They could turn the most pedestrian package into someone who seemed special. Despite that thought, Kate couldn't help taking a glance at his hand, checking for a wedding band. There was none. Not that it mattered to her, she told herself. Kate didn't know what this guy was about – the answer was probably *rien* – and she didn't have the time to find out.

Turning around, she peered through the glass. She could see that Elliot had found the table where she knew the place card that said *Katie Jameson* was, now directly next to one that said *Elliot Winston*. She couldn't see his face, but she could see Bev Clemenza and her husband Johnnie headed directly toward him. Predictably, Barbie and Bobbie Cohen were right behind them. 'I have to get in there,' Kate said in a panic. She grabbed the knob and shook the door frantically.

'Are you a friend of the groom or the bride?' the hottie asked her.

She knocked again on the window. 'Bride,' she answered tersely. But then realized how rude it sounded. 'Bunny is one of my oldest friends,' she added. Through the glass she watched in a paralysis of horror as Elliot shook Bobbie's hand then Johnnie's.

'A much older friend, right?' the charmer asked and moved beside her.

Kate was not in the mood. 'Bunny and I have been friends since grade school,' she told him, waving wildly through the glass, hoping someone would notice the movement. 'And yes, in fact, Bunny *is* older by – almost a month. But we didn't let that come between us.'

'So what's the problem if you miss some of the earlier festivities?'

'I have to be there to support a friend from my posse.'

'Your posse?' he asked and smiled. 'Anyone I know?'

'Bev Clemenza, Bina Horowitz, Barbie Cohen.'

'You're kidding!' he began and he stepped away to get a better look at Kate. She turned to him, just for a moment.

'*C'est incroyable, mais vraiment.*' What was it, she wondered, with the friggin' French? She looked back in at the party. God! The DJ was starting to play! 'You must be one of the infamous Bitches of B-Bushwick,' he said. 'I've heard about *you* girls.'

'Excuse me?' Kate asked, turning to him in surprise.

'How come I've never met you?' he asked, oblivious to her hostility. Typical narcissist, Kate thought. He looked over Kate's head into the room and pointed. 'I already know Bev, Barbie and, of course, Bunny. All the busy Bs. Who are you? Betty?'

'My name is Katherine Jameson,' Kate told him.

'I'm Billy Nolan. Why haven't I met you before?'

'I left Brooklyn to go to college.'

'I left Brooklyn to go to France. What did you do in college? And where have you gone since?'

'I got my doctorate. I live in Manhattan now where I work as a psychologist.' She paused. 'Look, Billy, I have to get in there.'

'So I see. I'm willing to cover my hand with my jacket and bust through the glass, but it . . .'

'It might be a bit much,' Kate finished for him.

'They'll open the doors once it gets too hot in there,' he said, sitting down on the balustrade. 'Have you noticed how no one from Brooklyn ever outgrows having their name end with an "ie"? Barbie. Bunny. Johnnie. Eddie. Arnie.' He chuckled as he ran through the roster of juvenile nicknames. 'Here in Brooklyn I'm never William or even Bill. I'm Billy.' He held out his hand and Kate couldn't resist shaking it.

She tried to appear casual, despite the thrill that had run up her back, causing hairs on her neck to rise. 'Do you prefer Billy to Bill?' Kate asked.

'Hey. We're in Brooklyn,' he answered. 'Go with the flow. Here I'm Billy Nolan. And should I call you Doctor Katherine? Kate? Kathy or Katie?'

'Oh, please, Kate not Katie. I hate it,' Kate confessed. 'Oh, look, they must be playing their song.'

To her complete surprise Billy stood up, grabbed her hand and started to dance. Before she could make a move he stopped abruptly. '"Doo Wah Diddy" is their song?' He made a face, looking puzzled in a really exaggerated way, his head cocked to the side.

Kate laughed. 'Well, maybe not.'

'I hope not. If it is, I give the marriage three weeks. You have to at least *start* with some romance.'

She bet he did. And that for him romance wore off fast. Kate looked him over. The sun glinted on his golden hair. He was one of those very few lucky Irish with the kind of skin that tanned and made their blue eyes bluer. 'So you don't think you can keep romance going?' Kate asked him.

'If I thought that I'd be married.' Billy Nolan laughed. My God, he is handsome, Kate thought. Perhaps because of the brief exchange in French the phrase *un coup de foudre*, a lightning bolt, entered her mind and she felt almost as if she'd been jolted by one. He was something – and he knew it, she reminded herself.

'Ah. The tyranny of commitment,' Kate said, nodding.

Billy reacted with widened eyes. Then he clutched at his chest. 'Now they're doing the "Hokey Pokey"!' he said, as if that upset him.

'So unusual for a Brooklyn wedding,' Kate agreed, a bit sarcastically. They always played the 'Hokey Pokey' or the 'Alley Cat' or both. She looked in the window, where dozens of old ladies were dancing, their backs to them. 'We definitely won't be able to get their attention now.'

'Uh oh. I think I'm in trouble,' Billy said and began to shake. Kate wondered if he was still reacting to the word commitment. 'Good thing you're a doctor,' he said.

Kate looked at him suspiciously. 'Why is that?'

'I may need treatment right now. I have a terrible phobia of the "Hokey Pokey".'

'Really?' Kate said. He'd been putting her on. There was something irresistible about Billy Nolan, but she didn't need this kind of banter now. She just wanted to get into the reception. Well, as long as they were stuck outside . . . 'As I say in my practice "Why do you feel that way?"'

'It seems obvious,' Billy told her. 'Did you ever think about it?'

'About what?'

'About the song? I mean, "You put your left foot in, you put your left foot out." Yadda, yadda. "You do the Hokey Pokey and you turn yourself around. And that's what it's all about."' He shivered exaggeratedly.

'So?'

'Well, what if that *is* what it's all about? What if life is just putting one foot in front of the other and that's it? Doesn't the thought terrify you?'

Before Kate could decide how tongue-in-cheek he was being and come up with an answer, the doors at the other end of the terrace at last flew open and a big guy in a wrinkled blue suit stuck his head out. 'Hey, Nolan!' he shouted. 'Get your ass in here. Arnie wants to talk to you about the toast.'

Before he vanished again, Billy shouted: 'Larry! Hold that thought and that door!' He gracefully ran the length of the terrace, catching the handle just in time. Then he turned back to Kate, held the door ajar and said, 'After you, *chère mademoiselle*.'

Kate felt her cheeks color again, but wasted no time stepping through the doors and into the crowded room. She was about to thank Billy when she heard Bev Clemenza's high-pitched voice cut through the ambient noise like a knife through an angel food wedding cake, 'Katie! Katie! Over here,' and didn't dare look back.

13

As Kate crossed the room toward her posse she almost felt a gravitational pull at her back caused by Billy Nolan. She was deeply embarrassed by the strength of her attraction and decided to put it out of her mind. He was just a superficial Brooklyn flirt. And she had an important job to do now.

'Katie!' Bev called again. Kate didn't want to see how terrified Bina was going to be. Though it wasn't her choice, she bitterly regretted that she hadn't been beside Bina during the first few critical minutes. As she moved through the crowd – now twisting again as they did last summer, or at the last wedding – she silently cursed Billy Nolan and the time on the terrace, diverting as it had been.

At last she managed to get across the dance floor and could clearly see table nine. Luckily, Bina was still somewhere in the crowd and Elliot had apparently abandoned the table for greater intrigues. There was Bev, her frosted hair slicked back and her now visibly pregnant belly stretching her unsuitable Lycra dress. Barbie, with her big hair hanging halfway down her back, was already seated too. Barbie's dad, in the jewelry trade, had been more successful than the other friends' fathers had been. She'd always had more clothes, trips to Florida, weekends in the Poconos and things that seemed enviable

111

at the time. But now she was a Brooklyn wife, a buyer for a women's clothing store on Nostrand Avenue. Her husband, Bobbie, was an accountant. Kate could look at her now and feel no envy at all.

Barbie sat beside Bobbie, her plunging neckline revealing the half of her breasts not covered by her push-up bra. Kate averted her eyes, but the husbands were, in their own way, more difficult to look at. If each of them hadn't been wearing a bow tie and cummerbund that matched his wife's dress, Kate wouldn't have been able to tell them apart. They were nice-looking Brooklyn boys, but neither of them was the kind of handsome that Billy – or Bill – or William – Nolan was. And behind their eyes was none of the genuine intellect that Michael possessed. The thought of Michael trying to communicate at table nine raised goosebumps on her arms.

'Hey,' Bev yelled. 'Look who's here.'

For a moment Kate thought she was being greeted, but Bev was staring past her. Kate turned to see Billy Nolan join the wedding party at the head table. Bunny looked down from the dais and gave Kate a quick wave and a big, proud smile while taking Arnie's arm. Kate waved back but her eyes strayed to Billy, talking earnestly to the groom, then laughing with him. Well, there would be no laughs at table nine, Kate reminded herself. She forced herself to turn back to her own companions.

'Wow, Kate, you look great!' Bev said. 'Of course, you're a Scorpio and your ruling planet has come out this month, so no wonder.'

'Yeah, there's that. And the sale at agnès b,' Kate said with a smile. Kate's simple dress, sleeveless and high-collared, with a placket that covered the buttons, was the antithesis of all the overdone outfits of her old friends. If she but knew it, she was easily the most elegant woman in the room. It was always curious to Kate that while her Brooklyn crew never missed an issue of *Vogue*, *Allure* or *Cosmopolitan*, they never

112

seemed to dress any differently than they ever had. Or, if there had been a change, it seemed merely to be that blouses had gotten tighter and patterns had gotten louder. Bev, despite her belly, was wearing a black and lemon tiger-striped Lycra thing. Barbie wore a tight, strapless dress in a Hawaiian floral print, all banana leaves and toucans wreathing (and writhing) around her torso. Kate could never quite decide if their taste was unbelievably bad, or whether hers had been permanently repressed by the nuns at Catholic grade school, when she'd worn a uniform.

'You could use some accessorizing,' Barbie opined by way of a hello. 'A scarf, or maybe a pendant.' Barbie herself was wearing an emerald – no doubt real – that was suspended just above her cleavage.

'I have to wait until I get the chest and the gem for it,' Kate said smoothly.

'You are so cynical,' Bev snorted. 'Such a Scorpio.' Since she had become pregnant, Bev, always a horoscope reader, had *really* gotten into astrology. Hormones, or something, Kate thought. Or perhaps the feeling of being out of control and the comforting compensation of a system to predict the universe. Kate turned to face the wedding hall again to try to spot Bina and the guys. She was getting nervous about them. At last she saw Elliot making his way across the room. He arrived carrying three drinks.

'For you, and you, and you,' he said and gave each of the women a Cosmopolitan.

'Ooh. Thanks,' Bev said, 'but I can't.'

'What a gentleman,' Barbie said appreciatively, then dug Bobbie in the ribs.

'This is my friend Elliot.' Kate took Elliot's arm.

'We've already met,' Elliot said. Kate raised her eyebrows. 'Out in the reception area. Your friends are as unique as you are, Katie.'

'Oh, we're very unique,' Bev said.

'Where's Bina?' Kate asked Elliot out of the corner of her mouth. She scanned the room and saw Brice and Bina making their way toward the table.

Bev tugged on Kate's elbow. 'Hey, that guy with Bina, is he her date or what?'

Barbie raised her highly waxed eyebrows. 'I love the tuxedo,' she cooed. 'Armani.'

Kate had to smile. If Judaism was a religion to Bina, fashion had always been Barbie's creed. And Kate remembered that Brice had predicted the impression he would make.

'But do you think Jack would approve?' Barbie asked. 'I mean he's gone only a week or so and she's . . . Does he know?'

Kate shrugged. Let 'em guess. Keep 'em busy and distracted.

'His name is Brite, or something,' Bev said, rubbing her belly.

'Brice,' Kate corrected.

'So, what's this guy Brice's sign anyway?' Bev asked.

'I think he's a Sagittarius; you'll have to ask him,' Elliot said, holding out a chair for Kate, who was grateful to sit down. It was going to be a bumpy ride.

'Oh, Katie, a Sagittarius! Not for Bina!' Bev complained. 'Dangerous while her fiancé is gone.'

'Oh, he's a dangerous man,' Elliot agreed.

'Is he on the cusp?' Bev added, hopeful.

Kate didn't need or want to explain that Brice was way over the cusp as a mate for Bina. 'I think they're just friends,' she said.

'That's not what it looks to me,' Barbie said as she sat down next to Kate, 'and he's *gorgeous*. Like a *GQ* model. He'd be perfect for my cousin Judy. What does he do?'

'He's an attorney,' Kate told Barbie.

'In a big firm or a sole practitioner?' Barbie asked.

'You'll have to ask him,' Kate sighed. Same old Barbie.

Putting everyone in boxes, then fixing them up with one another. She turned to watch Brice and Bina, who were caught in the Electric Slide on the dance floor. She couldn't help but smile a little at Brice's artful steps as he sidestepped between the slides, dragging Bina behind.

'What happened to Michael?' Bev asked. 'Is that all over?' Except Bev pronounced it 'uvah'. They all dropped final 'Rs' and added inappropriate ones at the ends of words that didn't have them.

Kate didn't have time to consider diction because Bina and Brice arrived at the table at that moment. Bina said, 'Hi there, everyone,' limply and sat down immediately without making eye contact. In fact the only contact she seemed interested in was grabbing what would have been Jack's waiting glass of wine with her right hand and pinning down Kate's hand with her left. To Kate's astonishment, she knocked back the entire glass.

'Hello,' Barbie said, but not to Bina. She leaned over the table and extended her hand to Brice while exposing more breast than most foldouts did and a lot more than Brice needed or wanted to see. Well, maybe she was trying to scoop him for her cousin, Kate thought charitably.

Meanwhile Bina picked up Kate's wine glass and drank off half of that. Before Kate could say something to slow her down, eagle-eyed Bev noticed. 'Since when do you drink? Cancers don't drink!' she cried.

'*Plus ça change, plus c'est la même chose*,' Kate said, perhaps because of her encounter on the terrace.

'What?' Barbie and Bev asked in unison. Kate just smiled and shrugged. No time for French class now.

'Bobbie, Johnnie, this is my friend Elliot and this is Bina's friend Brice,' Kate said to the men, interrupting a deep conversation about the pros and cons of moving some football team to Dallas. 'Elliot, Brice, meet Bobbie and Johnnie.' The husbands nodded a greeting in unison.

'What do you boys think of them moving the Rangers to Dallas?' Bobbie asked.

'I'm not really into spectator sports,' Elliot said.

'Oh, I love football. Tight ends, wide receivers. *You* know,' Brice said, smiling at them.

For a moment the two husbands looked confused. 'You a Jets or a Giants fan?' Johnnie asked, a little suspicion in his voice.

'Definitely a Giant. Love a Giant . . .'

'Brice!' Elliot said, trying to interrupt.

'. . . a Giant game,' Brice finished, and Kate let her breath out.

Bev and Barbie, now also totally confused, stared across the table and looked the two men over more carefully. But, as Kate hoped, they were at least temporarily distracted by their looks.

'What's your sign?' Bev asked Brice.

'Do Not Enter,' Brice replied, raising his eyebrows and smiling innocently.

Elliot, always ready with a peacemaking lie, smiled at Bev. 'Oh, he's a bull,' Elliot told her and gave Kate a nudge under the table, as if she didn't get the joke without it. On the other side, Bina was still clutching Kate's right hand with her ringless own.

'Hmm. A Taurus,' Bev reappraised, Elliot's innuendo sailing right over her over-gelled hair.

Meanwhile, Bina reached out and picked up the Cosmopolitan Bev had refused. In another moment she'd gulped it down.

'Bina!' Barbie exclaimed. 'What are you doing?'

'Yeah, you have to pace yourself,' Bobbie advised.

Brice nudged his chair closer to Bina and took away her empty glass. They had created a Bina sandwich, insulating her from her friends. Bina reached out for Brice's glass of wine. He paused for a moment, then shrugged and handed

116

it over to her. She downed it in a few breathless gulps. Bev and Barbie stared at Bina. Kate could see Barbie reevaluating Brice as a candidate for Judy.

There was a moment of complete silence. Then Barbie asked the dreaded question. 'Bina, you have to tell us about Jack's proposal. Let's see the ring.' Kate clenched Bina's hand and tried to change the subject.

'Look at the bracelet Michael gave to me,' she said hurriedly, holding her wrist up for them to see the sad little silver chain and the thin charm that hung from it. Despite the contempt they'd feel for it, she'd do anything to distract them from Bina's sorry state.

They barely glanced at Kate's wrist. With her usual amount of discretion, Bev opened her mouth. 'Yeah, what happened to Michael the doctor?' she wanted to know. 'Bina told me about him.'

'Why isn't he here? Is he gone already?' Barbie asked.

Kate shook her head. 'He's away at a conference. Elliot is a nice change.' Elliot and Kate exchanged looks of love. Barbie raised her eyebrows.

'What is Michael's sign, anyway?' Bev continued questioning.

'Well, I'm not sure, but I think it might be . . .' but that was as far as Kate got when Barbie interrupted her.

'Wait a minute. What's going on here?' Barbie said. Kate watched suspicion bloom on her face. 'Bina, the ring!' she exclaimed. Then suddenly, without a moment's notice, Barbie reached across the table and grabbed Bina's wrist, yanking her hand from Kate's grip. There was a moment of total silence at table nine. Bina's naked hand, still French manicured, lay like a dying whitefish on the hot pink tablecloth.

14

'Where the hell is it?' Barbie asked accusatorially. 'My father sold you a perfect stone.' She looked down at the ringless finger and then back up at Bina, whose face was scrunched up as she tried to hold back tears. 'Wait a minute!' Barbie said as the light began to dawn with some approaching horror. To her credit, there was true concern in her high-pitched voice. 'Bina, is everything okay with Jack?'

Two waiters arrived and began distributing plates of chicken and vegetables. Kate hoped it would give Bina a distraction but she paid no attention to the bland food in front of her.

'Yes . . . in a way,' Bina managed. Bev and Barbie exchanged looks, then frowned.

'Okay. How is it okay?' Barbie asked.

'Well, after his trip we'll get . . . we'll probably get engaged then, after . . .'

'I knew it!' Bev exclaimed. 'Mercury is in retrograde!'

'Very true,' Brice said. 'It's affected my whole law practice.'

But the distraction didn't work. 'You lost him, Bina!' Barbie said. 'After six years on the hook, you still couldn't reel him in?'

'Barbie!' Kate remonstrated. Elliot put his arm protectively around Bina's little shoulder.

'Oh, God! Are you holding up okay?' Bev asked with genuine sympathy.

'Yes . . . and no,' Bina said, and then began to cry outright.

'Well, is it yes or no?' Barbie asked.

'Looks like no to me,' Johnnie said. 'Uh, we'll get some drinks,' he offered and he and Bobbie abandoned the table.

'Honey, is there anything we can do to help?' Barbie asked.

'Well, I've been staying with Kate, and Elliot, Max and Brice have been a major support,' Bina told her friends through her tears. 'Look, I'm fine,' she began. 'I cried for a little while but now I have found' – she looked fuzzily at Brice – 'a new focus.'

'Right!' Barbie chimed in. 'Focus on the possibilities.' She smiled at Brice. 'You miss one bus there's always another. A door closes and a window opens. You lose one house and you find one next door.'

'Wrong street,' Elliot muttered, sotto voce, to Kate who shushed him.

'Yeah, look at Bunny,' Bev said, waving her hand with its unbelievably long nails toward the bridal table. 'Less than three months ago she got dumped. Then she met her Arnie . . . and everything turned around.'

'I don't want everything to turn around,' Bina sniffed. Kate was actually grateful for the wine Bina had consumed, because without it there would have been floods of tears. 'I want Jack . . .'

Just then the waiters returned and removed the dishes, replacing them with a limp salad. A waltz began and, after the earlier nonsense music, the seductive swell of Strauss drew their heads to look out on the dance floor. Kate was, at first, glad of any diversion, but then realized the only dancers were Billy and Bunny whom he was expertly twirling around the floor. Kate had a momentary flash from the wonderful dance scene in *The King and I*, but Billy Nolan outdid Yul Brynner. Kate, along with every other woman in the room, admired his moves, his mastery and all the rest of him. His grace made Bunny look good. Spontaneous applause broke out and then other couples started to join them on the dance floor. Kate was about to casually ask about him when Bobbie and Johnnie returned to the table carrying a tray full of drinks. Kate was thankful for hers, but had trouble swallowing at the sight of Bina guzzling down a Jack Daniel's and Coke.

'Oh, look at Bunny! Thank God she lost those last five pounds,' Barbie said. 'I told her not to buy a size six when you're an eight. It wasn't like she had eight months to lose the weight. She'd been on the Häagen-Dazs diet after she got dumped the last time. Then bim bam boom and she's getting married.'

'It was in the stars,' Bev said. Kate figured it was on the rebound but said nothing.

'She bought the dress three weeks ago,' Barbie told them. 'And they only got this date at all because another couple eloped. It's too bad. If she had done some Pilates she could have worn a bias cut. They're big now.'

'Stop!' Kate interjected. 'She looks beautiful because she's happy.'

Brice looked out at the couples on the dance floor. 'I'm not sure I like her dress but I like her taste in grooms,' he said, snapping a Polaroid of Bunny and Billy as they passed by. There was greater interest and enthusiasm in Brice's voice than Kate would've preferred, but it didn't seem as if anyone else noticed.

'Oh, that is *not* her husband!' Barbie sneered. 'That's Billy.' Apparently a raw spot had been touched. 'He's the guy who dumped her, but introduced her to Arnie.'

Then, as clear as a movie flashback, Kate remembered the glimpse she had gotten of the man in SoHo, the one Bina had pointed out. Of course. She *had* seen him before.

'See, Bina? It could happen to you,' Bev said, her voice warm with encouragement. 'I'll do your chart and see what's up. It could be a Taurus,' she added archly to Brice.

'And what a lucky Taurus he would be,' Brice said gallantly. He sat back in his chair and picked the developed picture of Billy off the table. 'Ooh, pretty,' he said to himself and slipped the photo into his pocket.

'Sure,' Bina slurred.

'One day dumped and the next engaged,' Barbie told her.

'I have not been dumped!' Bina exclaimed.

'Can you believe Billy's actually the best man?' Barbie asked the table at large, apparently still stuck on the subject.

'Didn't you date him right before you met me?' Johnnie asked his wife. Bev blushed as she nodded that indeed she had dated the man in question. 'I went out with him for a few weeks, right before we met, but it didn't work out.' She leaned over and kissed her husband. 'Anyway, he's an Aries,' she offered by way of explanation.

'He's an asshole,' Barbie clarified. 'He's the asshole who dumped Bunny.'

For once Kate was forced to agree with Barbie. Her assessment of the guy had been right: too good-looking, too facile, too smooth.

'Good old Billy,' Bina said, clearly close to drunk. 'Let's drink to "Dumping Billy".'

'"Dumping Billy"?' Elliot asked with interest. 'Why do you call him that?'

'Because he's turned dumping women into a major lifestyle,' Barbie told him.

'He's not really a bad guy,' Bev said in Billy's favour. 'It's hard for an Aries to commit.'

'I can't believe you actually dated him,' Johnnie said, which indicated to Kate just how quickly his mind was moving.

'Yes,' she answered. 'But I wasn't the only one,' she added defensively, 'was I, Barbie?'

'No,' Barbie said bravely. 'Billy was the last guy I dated

121

before I got married to Bobbie. But he didn't mean a thing to me. When I broke up with him . . .'

'Excuse me?' Bev asked. 'Reality check. He broke up with you.'

'Whatever. He's not really so terrible. He's fun and he's got a great sense of style. It's just that the word "commitment" isn't in his vocabulary.'

Brice leaned across the table to whisper to Kate. 'I was so right. This is much better than *The Young and the Restless*. But a lot less realistic.'

'That's because soap operas are art and this is not real life,' Kate told him. She didn't even want to imagine the feedback she'd get from these two after this nightmare was over.

Kate looked over at Elliot who had taken out a pencil and paper. 'Let me see if I have all the facts right . . .' he said to himself. She wondered what in the world he could be up to but didn't get a chance to ask.

Because, just then, Bina stood up unsteadily and decided that this was the moment to announce to the assembly just how unhappy she was. 'Ladies and gentlemen,' she said. 'You are looking at Bina Horowitz, loser and future spinsper.'

'Spinster,' Brice corrected.

'Whatever,' Bina said and tried to climb up on her chair. Elliot caught her before she fell but he couldn't stop her from raising her voice. 'Single women can have children, you know. Not just Rosie O'Donnell. Michael Jackson did it and he wasn't even a woman. I'm a woman, goddamnit!'

Despite the incredible din in the room, people were beginning to stare. Luckily, at that moment, the sound system crackled and Billy Nolan's voice covered Bina's.

'*Excusez-moi*,' Billy tried once, and then tapped the microphone and said more loudly, this time in English, 'Excuse me. Everyone?' The chattering continued until finally he tapped the microphone so firmly that the high-pitched squeal of feedback quieted the crowd. 'Stop talking!' Billy nearly shouted at them all.

It was a perfect opportunity to get Bina calmed down. Kate and Brice tried to take her by the hand as Bina resisted. Meanwhile, over the speakers Billy Nolan seemed to be having trouble of his own. 'Jeez, I know it's imp-possible for B-Brooklyn women to b-be quiet, b-but if you could just g-give a guy a b-break here.'

Kate cringed as Billy struggled to regain control of his stammer. She looked down at the bracelet Michael had given her and sighed. Then she turned to see what Elliot thought of Billy, but he didn't seem to be paying attention. In fact, he looked as if he was trying to solve a math problem. As the best man started to lift his glass in a toast, Elliot was frantically scribbling on his napkin with a pen.

'I raise my glass to Arnie and Bunny,' Billy began. '*Toujours l'amour.*'

'Oh, Jesus,' Barbie spat, rolling her eyes, 'he's pretending to be French again.'

'Who in the hell does that guy think he is?' Bobbie wanted to know. 'Speak English!' he shouted from the table.

'Sorry.' Billy blushed. 'English it is.' He took a deep breath and continued. 'I, uh – I introduced Arnie to B-Bunny,' he said quickly. 'I've known Arnie for years and B-Bunny . . . well, I've known her, too!' There was a general eruption of salacious hoots and catcalls that caused Bunny to blush, Arnie to hang his head in shame, and Billy to make his toast brief. 'Congratulations to Arnie and Bunny!' he said. 'They're good people. And marriage is a beautiful thing . . . to witness from afar. To Arnie and Bunny.' He lifted his glass to signal that he was finished.

The crowd cheered and clinked their glasses with their silverware and Arnie and Bunny obligingly kissed. When the cheering and jeering had abated to a dull roar, Kate turned to the others at the table and asked, 'Did you two really date him?' Bev and Barbie nodded ruefully and shrugged their shoulders.

Dancing resumed. This should have been all right, since it would make slipping out unnoticed easier. It was a reception to dip into and out of, not swim in. Except Elliot stood up and excused himself from the table. 'Where do you think you are going?' Kate asked. 'We ought to get Bina out of here.'

'I'll be right back,' he said and hurried into the crowd.

Kate kept hold of Bina and watched as couples did the Twist and slow-danced to 'Every Breath You Take'. Finally, Elliot returned. He had a self-congratulatory look on his face.

'Where have you been?' Kate demanded. 'We must take Bina home. She's ready to start doing the hora all by herself.'

'I was just doing a little probability research,' Elliot replied.

'Great!' Kate snapped. 'Why? Going to set up a whole new group of word problems for third-grade math in a wedding hall? If X serves four cocktail wieners to three guests and Y serves two stuffed . . .'

'Look, statistics are involved,' Elliot said, 'but no word problems will be solved. Merely a romantic one. You'll see.' He turned to Brice. 'Get her left arm,' he said, pointing at Bina. 'And I'll get her right.' Without a word the two men surrounded Bina and coolly and unobtrusively led her away from the table, across the room and to the exit. Kate followed, forbidding herself to turn and take one last look at Billy.

15

Some days later, Kate walked down the wide, quiet hall of Andrew Country Day. She hadn't seen Michael for over a week: he'd been off on a seminar and she'd been held hostage by Bina since the wedding. Tonight he was coming round to dinner and she expected he'd sleep over. She was looking forward to it.

She'd had a rough afternoon. Stevie Grossman, a fifth grader, was showing disturbing signs of schizophrenia – very unusual in a child his age, and heart-breaking. Kate knew he needed to see a psychiatrist – she had a friend at Ackerman Institute for the Family who might help – however, not only his parents but also Mr McKay were trying to minimize the boy's troubles in the face of her professional advice.

As she passed Elliot's third-grade classroom she caught a glimpse of him teetering on a chair, sticking transparencies on the windows. 'MATH IS FUN!' they said. He was hanging them so they showed their faces to the outside world and read backwards to the class.

'Well, that ought to convince them,' she teased. She needed her dose of Elliot to cheer her up. 'Good for the dyslexics, at least.'

Elliot whirled, startled by her voice, and nearly fell off the chair. He grabbed at the window to steady himself, then looked down at her and smiled. 'Nice to see you, too,' he sighed. 'Andrew Country Day. Home of learning for learning's sake.' Quite apart from Wall Street, Elliot could have made a lot more money as an academic or working in a New York City public school, but he loved teaching mathematics, hated disciplining kids and wanted to work with the best and the brightest. The trouble with Andrew was that every child was expected to be the best and the brightest by their type A parents, and a single B on a report card was testament to failure. Kate thought again of poor Stevie's frightened face.

Kate walked in and took a seat in Elliot's chair, putting her feet up on his desk. Maybe he could suggest something she could do for Stevie. But he beat her to the punch. 'How's Bina doing?' he asked, swiping at her feet to get them off the desk.

'As well as can be expected,' Kate said, shrugging her shoulders. After the wedding Bina had agreed to go home to face the music and begin her 'exploration of singleness'. Somehow that translated into coming over to Kate's constantly for sympathy, and getting gossip about Jack from Max.

'Poor Bina,' Elliot said. 'I really like her.'

'So do I,' Kate agreed. 'She's like a sister to me.'

'I liked Bev and Barbie, too,' Elliot said. 'What a hoot.'

'Well, I wasn't as close to them,' Kate reminded Elliot. 'But I'm glad you and Brice had fun.'

'Fun? Brice hasn't talked about anything else since. He's dying for the next installment.'

'There is no next installment. It's not a soap opera. It's life, sort of. Bina is back managing her father's office. Maybe she'll meet some guy who needs a spinal adjustment.'

'I'd like to see Bina,' Elliot said.

'Look, Brooklyn isn't a spectator sport.' Kate stood up. She didn't want to hold her friends up to derision and criticism, even if she derided them and criticized them herself. 'Bina is

126

very low. She had a lot invested in Jack.' She sighed. 'I've gotta go. I have a date with Michael tonight.'

'Sit down another minute,' Elliot requested, for once without saying a word against Michael. Kate was surprised enough to do it, but only at the edge of the seat, ready for a quick exit if he got started. 'Look,' he said. 'I think I have a way to help Bina.'

'Oh, Elliot. Please . . .' Kate began, rolling her eyes. 'Unless you have a written proposal from Jack in your pocket there's nothing you can . . .'

'Just listen,' he told her. 'This might be as good as a written proposal.'

Kate looked at him with false expectation, as if he were about to reveal the secrets of the mummy's tomb.

'Remember how at the wedding Barbie said she got dumped by that gorgeous guy?'

'What gorgeous guy?' Kate asked as if she didn't know. She had had a dream and though she couldn't remember it clearly when she'd awoken, she thought Billy Nolan was in it. She'd put it out of her mind until this moment and it irritated her that Elliot had brought it up.

'The best man. Billy,' Elliot reminded her. 'Remember? The one who looked like a much more handsome Matt Damon.'

'Oh, yeah. The toaster. What about him?' Kate said, her irritation showing. She tried to look bored.

'Well, Barbie dated him.'

'Barbie dated everyone,' Kate said. 'She'd just about run out of Brooklyn and had to start on Staten Island.'

'Try and hold your focus,' Elliot said. 'As you may or may not remember, Bunny also dated and got dumped by Billy. Right before she married Arnie.'

'Bunny had really bad luck with men,' Kate said. 'So?'

'Well, she had good luck, as you call it, after Billy . . . if you consider Arnie good luck.'

Kate shrugged and tried to remember if she had picked up

her white blouse from the dry cleaner's or not. She wanted to wear it tonight. 'And your point would be?'

'Well, Bev had dated Billy, been dumped, then got married too. When I noted this odd probability my brilliant mathematical mind went into high gear and I started to do some digging.'

'And?' said Kate.

'And so . . .' Elliot continued, sounding a little annoyed. 'And so, I went on a little fact-finding mission and found out six women at the wedding dated Billy and got dumped by him.'

'So he's a slut,' Kate said. She thought of the way Billy had charmed her and was surprised there weren't thirty women there he'd disappointed. 'Wow, Elliot. You're a regular Sherlock Holmes.'

'You're not getting the picture here. You remember how I had to help you with statistics?'

'How could I forget? You remind me at every possible opportunity.'

'Well, I'm a genius,' Elliot told her. 'Geniuses are always disrespected.' He spoke primly, holding his nose a little higher. 'Stay with me here, Kate. You'll see. All six of these women, after getting dumped by Billy, *married* the very next man they dated.'

Kate shrugged. 'Anyone would look good after that guy. He's just a player.'

'Kate. Kate! Don't you get it!' Elliot almost shouted, clearly exasperated. 'It's not about him. It's about what happens *after* him. Do you know the statistical likelihood of that phenomenon?'

'Obviously not,' replied Kate, who herself was getting pretty annoyed. She stood up. She wouldn't have time to stop at the cleaner's and if her white shirt wasn't at home she'd wear the green silk one. She picked up her purse. 'Gotta go.'

'Kate, I've worked it out and the probability ranges from

one in six million three hundred and forty-seven to one in eighty-two million six hundred and forty-three. And that's *with* standard deviation.'

'Talk about deviation,' Kate said, blowing off Elliot's ridiculous mathematical discovery, 'when do you have time to shampoo your hair?' She got to the door. Then she stopped for a moment. 'Anyway, how does that help Bina?'

'Don't you get it?' Elliot yelled, actually pulling at his very clean hair. 'We *use* it in Bina's favor.'

'Use it?'

At that moment Mr McKay showed up in front of Kate like a migraine on a sunny day. 'Is there an altercation going on in here?' he asked.

'Certainly not,' Elliot assured him. 'We were testing the acoustics of this room. For some reason the students in that corner near the door don't hear all of the class discussion. Kate thought it might be the cork boards.'

Kate nodded. 'Proust and all,' she said.

Mr McKay blinked. Kate almost laughed out loud. He was so easily impressed by literary allusion. 'Oh, I see. Well, that will suffice for now,' he said, and was gone as quickly as he had appeared.

'He thinks we're having a lovers' quarrel,' Elliot said.

'That, or he's going off to bake some madeleines.' Mr McKay brought his own baked goods to the cake sale. 'So just tell me what the point of all that was before I run for the subway.'

'The point,' Elliot told her, 'is that Bina is supposed to explore her singleness, right? So we get her to date Billy, get her dumped, get her to see Jack, and wham, bam, thank you ma'am, he'll ask her to marry him.'

Kate could hardly believe what she'd just heard. 'And I thought Stevie Grossman needed therapy,' she said. 'Elliot, you're certifiable. Next you'll tell me to adopt Bev's black magic and that Bina needs to be a Pisces so she can swim to happiness.'

'Kate,' Elliot said, his voice deeper, as it got when he became serious. 'We're talking statistics and probability here, not astrology. I'm not Bev. I calculated it out, and it's as close to a sure thing as possible.'

'Oh, come on, Elliot!' Kate exclaimed. 'You've lost it. I don't even begin to have the time to tell you how flawed your plan is.'

'Try,' Elliot challenged her.

'Number one: Bina doesn't want to date anybody else. Number two: Billy is an asshole who has slept with every truly attractive girl in Brooklyn – and possibly lower Manhattan. Number three: Bina, as much as I love her, couldn't pick up a guy if he had a handle on him, much less get a date with Billy Nolan. Will that suffice for now?' Kate said, pleased with herself.

'Okay,' Elliot conceded. 'But give me one more good reason it won't work.'

'You're insane.' She began to walk down the hall.

'You won't be saying that when I am Bina's maid of honor,' Elliot called after her.

Jesus, Kate thought, McKay would be on them in a private school minute. Kate turned around to where Elliot stood complacent and so annoying in his doorway. 'No, Elliot. Just no.'

Elliot examined her face. 'Kate, who tutored you so you passed your GMATs?'

'You did,' Kate sighed. She knew the litany.

'And who graduated top of his class from Columbia?' he asked her.

'You did, but . . .'

'And who was invited to accept an adjunct professorship and a grant at Princeton?'

'You, but that doesn't . . .'

Elliot interrupted her. '. . . But that doesn't mean that you can still doubt my abilities?' He shook his head. 'In the land

130

of the blind . . . Kate, this is an absolutely fascinating finding, and a tremendous opportunity to exploit and you are calling it hooey?'

'I don't think I ever actually used the word "hooey",' she said. 'That sounds more like something McKay might say.'

'But you know I'm *never* wrong when it comes to numbers,' Elliot told her.

Kate looked down at her watch and then again turned to leave. Let him screech down the hallway if he wanted to. 'Elliot,' she said as she began to walk. 'I don't believe in magic, I don't believe in superstition, or horoscopes, or coincidences that predict the future. Now I've got to go. I've got a date with Michael and I haven't shaved my legs in a week.'

'Ah, yes, Michael,' Elliot said, walking past the lockers. 'I thought . . .'

'I would rather not go into your thoughts right now.' She got to the entrance. 'Bye-bye.'

Elliot put his hand on her shoulder. 'Look, Kate, this doesn't just involve you, it involves Bina and *her* future. At least let me present the facts to her. It ought to be her decision.'

Kate looked back at her friend, shook her head and shrugged her shoulders. Then she hurried down the steps on the way to her date.

16

Kate strolled along Eighth Avenue with the pleasant anticipation of the weekend before her. She decided that after the
Bina siege, Bunny's wedding and Elliot's insane reaction she
wouldn't allow herself to think about any of it. She wouldn't
even think about her little clients at school. She had done
a bit of what she thought of as 'luxury' grocery shopping:
stopping at some of the superb food specialty stores in her
neighborhood and buying prepared curry chicken salad, a
bunch of perfect red grapes and poached sole with lemon
zest garnish.

Friday afternoon was a special pleasure to Kate. She had
finally reached the point in her adulthood where she had
hired a cleaning lady. Teresa only came for half a day each
Friday but the forty dollars was well worth it because, at the
end of a hard week, Kate could look forward to walking into
a vacuumed, dust-free living room, and a bed freshly made up
with clean sheets. When Kate remembered her teenage years,
she thought of the reluctance she had felt in going home to
the four dirty rooms that she shared with her father, and the
misery of shopping for the cheapest basics – sardines, canned
soup and cereal. She would open the door fearfully, never
knowing what she would find inside. All this had given her

an enormous appreciation now for the security of knowing what to expect when she opened her own door, as well as a pride in order and cleanliness.

She passed by a Korean market and her eye was attracted to roses of an unusual apricot color. It would be nice if Michael brought her flowers, but if he didn't it would be lovely to have some of these roses in a bowl in the living room and a vase beside her bed. She stopped, and when the old merchant offered her 'special discount two bunches for ten dollars only for pretty lady', she smiled at him, took out a ten-dollar bill and walked away with the paper-wrapped roses tucked under her arm.

Kate turned the corner and walked along her block. Many of the windows were open and as she passed the brownstones she could see people in basement kitchens preparing dinner, others in living rooms with a book or a glass of wine and even a few children playing on the stoops and tiny yards in front of the buildings. When she got to her stoop she strode up the steps quickly, had her key ready, entered the vestibule and managed to pick up her mail and get up the flight of stairs to her apartment without dropping the delicacies, her purse, the flowers or the mail.

She entered her small but orderly space and sighed, kicking off her shoes and leaving them at the door. It was past five and she needed enough time to put away the food, arrange the flowers, take a shower and change her clothes. She would have to rush a little bit, but it was a pleasant domestic kind of rush and the afternoon sunlight slanting in across the living-room floor and over her bed made both rooms particularly enjoyable. She was just putting the last rose into the vase for her bedroom when the phone rang. She checked her caller ID. She simply didn't have time for another call from Bina. Cruel as it might be, they were starting to annoy her. She picked it up while she carried the flowers to her bedside table.

133

'Look, I don't want you to be angry,' Elliot's voice said.

'I'm not angry, I'm just in a rush.'

'Of course you're not angry yet,' Elliot said. 'I don't want you to be angry after I tell you what I'm going to tell you.'

'Is it that I look fat in this skirt?' she asked. 'It's too late for me to take it back now. You told me it looked good.' She put the flowers down and stood back to get the full effect. The room looked charming.

'I know you're just joking, but I'm serious. Don't be mad. I'm inviting Bina and your friends to brunch on Sunday.'

Kate, who was slipping out of the new skirt while she cradled the receiver between her shoulder and her neck, nearly dropped the phone. 'What would you do that for?' she asked. 'What in the world would you do that for?'

'I knew you would be mad,' Elliot said. 'But, Kate, I've done a little more sleuthing and . . .'

'Who are you? Nancy fucking Drew?' Kate asked. 'No one does sleuthing, no one drives a roadster and no one is inviting my Brooklyn girlfriends to their Chelsea apartment for brunch except me – and I'm not even sure I'll do it.' She hung up her skirt and was delighted to see that she *had* brought home her white sleeveless blouse from the cleaner's. She would wear it with the top two buttons undone and the gray pants from Banana Republic. But first she'd get rid of Elliot and stop this stupid plan.

'Kate, it isn't just Barbie and Bunny. There are six women that have dated Billy and right afterwards – right after he dumped them – they got married to other men.'

'Are you still on that?'

'The statistical probability is almost unheard of. Kate, you owe it to Bina to . . .'

Kate, truly annoyed, put her clothes down on the bed and held the phone so that she was speaking right into the mouthpiece. 'Elliot, I don't know why you've gotten this bee in your bonnet, but kill it right now. You only want to have

134

the Bitches over so that you and Brice can watch them up close and personal and then make fun of them later.'

'That is so unfair! This is just a way to help Bina.'

Kate looked at the alarm clock on her dresser. 'Michael is coming over. I have to go. Bye.' As she replaced the phone she could hear Elliot whining.

'But Kate . . .'

She rushed into the bathroom, showered, but kept her hair dry, got dressed and primped for a few minutes in front of the steamy bathroom mirror. Then she picked up her hairbrush, went into the kitchen and began brushing out her hair while she poured herself some peach ice tea.

Then she walked over to the window of her living room, and looked out into the frieze of maple leaves. Since their reconciliation after the night of Jack's failed proposal, she and Michael were slipping into that comfortable stage where both of them assumed that they would spend most of the weekend together and called one another just about every day.

Kate sat at the open window, sipping the tea and waiting for Michael's arrival. She had only to toss a few greens and take out her purchases and they would be ready for a pleasant dinner. Michael, as usual, was just a little bit late, but Kate didn't mind. It gave her more time to enjoy the peace of her apartment and the pleasant view of brownstones.

Last winter, after she had broken up with Steven, when the trees were bare, the view had seemed gray and empty, just as her life had done. Elliot had nursed her through, and time . . . well, time had passed and done what it does.

She smiled for a moment, grateful that she had put those days behind her. It was funny; someone should write a book about the new, twenty-first-century stages of commitment and separation in relationships. Perhaps she would suggest it to Michael. Each action represented either a step in growth or a diminishment in love and trust. First a couple only had each

135

other's home numbers. Then they exchanged phone numbers at work. Then there was the important moment when you program both numbers into your home and cell phones. Followed by the ceremonial leaving of the toothbrush, followed quickly by the leaving of the personal hygiene products – deodorant, moisturizer, a razor. Then, most symbolically, the critical exchange of keys. Eventually, of course, each of these actions was reversed. Kate didn't know when Steven had wiped her name from his cell phone but she remembered clearly the day she had deleted him.

While she and Michael had not yet exchanged keys, Kate felt that they were moving nicely from the dating phase into what she would call 'a relationship' if the word didn't make her wince. And that was a relief. In her twenties, it seemed that dates had either been more casual or guys had played games, and when they parted after a time together Kate never knew if they would call her the next day or the next week or even at all. Maybe it was because she was in school and there was a big pool of people to date so that it was easy to meet someone to replace the someone of the previous month. Now, however, since Steven, she felt some kind of shift. Dates always seemed to be an assessment on her part of the chance for a long-term hook-up and if she didn't feel a strong level of interest from a man she found herself losing interest in him.

As she looked down at the street, thinking of him, Michael appeared round the corner. From her vantage point she could observe him and remain unobserved. There was something about his walk that, seen from above, looked a bit prissy, but Kate put the unworthy thought out of her mind.

'Yo, Michael!'

Down below, he stopped, looked up to the trees for a moment and then caught her waving from the window. 'Hey,' he yelled up. 'Sorry I'm late.'

She hadn't meant to make him feel guilty. She just shrugged, smiled and gestured for him to come up. She left the window-sill and buzzed to unlock the downstairs door, then opened the door to her apartment and waited for him.

She heard his steps on the stairs before she saw him, ignored his second apology and kissed him instead. He held her for a moment and it felt so good that she was disappointed when he stopped. But dinner was pleasant and Michael was appropriately delighted and grateful. She talked about the progress she was making with Brian Conroy, the motherless little boy, and about trouble they were having with two brothers – twins – who kept trading places and confusing not only the staff but also their classmates. Michael told her about his week. All of his news lately had been about the mutual courtship between him and the Sagerman Foundation. Michael was still hoping for an offer to chair a department at the University of Texas. Kate wasn't sure whether or not she was included in his Austin plans. He didn't speak about it and she didn't ask. Did he plan for her to go? Or would he bring it up at some point in time? Maybe he only wanted to be offered it and then wouldn't accept. Austin. Kate tried to put it out of her mind. Texas was not for her. He was young to head up a department, and while it would be a coup and almost irresistible she didn't want to think about it. Michael, today doubting the likelihood of the offer, helped her clear and produced a white paper box containing a poppy seed pound cake for dessert. 'I have some vanilla ice cream that might go well on top of that,' she told him.

'I can think of something that might go well on top of something else before dessert,' Michael said. He took her hand. 'Did I tell you how pretty you look?'

She shook her head. 'Are you telling me now?' she asked, hoping for more.

Instead he looked down at her. 'You have a problem with the buttons on your blouse.' From his height he could see her modest cleavage. She smiled up at him. 'You've made

137

a mistake.' He put his hands on the next button. At first, she thought he was about to button her up, but then she realized what he was doing. 'You silly girl. You've neglected to leave them all open,' Michael said. And in a moment, he had undone them.

In a few moments more, they were on her bed and she was – in the Victorian sense – being completely undone.

After Steven, with whom she'd shared such an intensely passionate relationship, Kate had been afraid that anyone she slept with would be second best, but if Michael lacked a little in humor or banter he more than made up for it in bed. Kate was so engrossed in her own thoughts that when she felt his hands move deftly over her body she had to rouse herself to put her arms around him and do more than simply lie back and enjoy it. Usually, she liked to turn him on, to hear his breathing change. Together, they kissed, fondled, and held one another. When Michael pressed his hands against her shoulders and rolled onto her she was more than ready.

17

When Kate awoke on Saturday morning, she was smiling. She stretched out, arching her back in the delicious relaxation of post-sexual doziness and in anticipation of the weekend of leisure ahead of her. She wanted to snuggle up and whisper a thank you to Michael, perhaps even entice him into an encore, but when she turned on her side, she realized he was gone. It took her a moment to remember that he always ran for an hour between six and seven. 'No matter what', he'd told her when they'd first met and she'd admired his self-discipline. Now she was just disappointed. He'd come back wide awake, he'd shower, he'd want coffee and she'd have to do all that too if she wanted to spend the time with him.

Kate sighed, lifted herself up, saw that it was a quarter to seven and lay down again. She considered her options: she could either get up, shower, and begin to make breakfast, or go back to sleep and wait for his return. Despite wanting some snuggle time, she knew if she waited for Michael, he would go straight to the shower, thoughtfully leaving her alone to sleep. He'd probably read the *Times* quietly until she got out of bed. Kate decided to replay last night's sex in her mind's eye and was just closing her eyes when the phone rang. No one would be calling her this early on a weekend morning except . . .

'Hello, Elliot,' she said. 'Do you know that it is ten minutes to seven on a Saturday morning?'

'Am I interrupting something?' Elliot asked archly. 'I can call right back. Or does he take longer than a few minutes?'

'Elliot! You are interrupting my sleep,' Kate said. 'What's the emergency?'

'Look, Kate, I don't want you to be mad.'

'Mad? What have you done?'

'Look, I know how you are. And I didn't mean for it to be more than Bina, but she told Barbie, and you know how *she* is . . .'

Yes, Kate reflected, she did know how Barbie was but she didn't need to hear about it, and certainly not from Elliot before seven a.m. on a weekend. Anyway, Bina had gone back to Brooklyn, the wedding was over, and her old friends no longer needed to be a source of entertainment to her newer ones.

'I had to do it. The mathematics and the potential for happiness here were just too big to be ignored.'

'Elliot, what are you going on about?' She wondered where Michael was.

'About the brunch. I had already told Bina about the findings and she wanted to hear more, and Brice suggested a brunch but then I was going to cancel after I spoke to you. Now, though, she's invited Bev and Barbie. And Bunny is back from her honeymoon, so Bev told her and now . . .'

'Oh, God,' Kate interrupted. 'Don't tell me you bothered Bina with this geeky idea of yours. Stop it, Elliot! And what does it have to do with the others? Or a brunch?' Kate had hoped for a Bina-free weekend, a time to relax with Michael and refuel. She tried to focus on what Elliot was saying but she wanted to be unfocused, soft and fuzzy and feminine and infantile. 'Elliot, don't get Bina crazy with your nonsense.'

'You don't understand the clarity and magnitude of the numbers, Kate,' Elliot told her. 'Since Bina talked to the girls, they found two other cases where women married *immediately* after Billy broke up with them.'

'So what?' Kate heard the door to her apartment squeak open. Maybe, if she got up right now, she could negotiate a little more time in bed. She liked Michael sweaty, but he was too fastidious to comply with her wishes. Still, there was a chance . . .

'I have to go,' she told Elliot.

'I understand,' Elliot said meaningfully. 'Have fun. Just close your eyes and think of England. And be here tomorrow at eleven thirty.'

'I hate you,' Kate said.

'But doesn't it feel good, in a strange and exciting way?' Elliot asked. 'Eleven thirty tomorrow. Be there or be . . . talked about.'

On Sunday morning, Kate knocked on Elliot's door at a quarter to eleven. She wanted to arrive before the Bitches, lay some ground rules, vent a little anger and limit the way Elliot and Brice would toy with them.

'Kate!' Brice shouted in false surprise when he opened the door. 'You're early! Whatever could be the reason?'

'I thought perhaps I could help you get ready by putting some ground glass in the chicken salad,' she said with an insecure smile.

'My, my. Little Miss Hospitality,' Brice said.

She stepped past him and walked into the apartment. She had a bone – well, more like a whole skeleton – to pick with Elliot.

Her quarry was standing at the sofa, barely visible behind an armload of charts and graphs. When he saw her he dropped everything onto the coffee table. Brice, never dumb, disappeared into the kitchen, from which delicious smells were emanating. 'What's all this?' Kate asked Elliot, who had begun to sort out the charts, placing them on an easel.

'This is the evidence,' Elliot replied. 'I thought putting the facts right in front of Bina's eyes would convince her.'

'Elliot, I absolutely forbid this. You are not allowed to interfere in people's lives in this way.'

Elliot gave an exaggerated blink, lowered his chin and looked over his glasses at her. 'This from a woman who is attempting to reshape two dozen kids at Andrew Country Day.'

Kate bristled. She thought of Brian, who seemed to have begun mourning his mother, Elizabeth – whose parents made promises they never kept – and the twins she was working with who didn't seem to relate to anyone but each other. 'Elliot, my work is very different. I'm professionally trained to assess and assist children, some of them in crisis, while they are developing their personalities. I am trying to prevent future problems. You're dealing with adults, you have no training and you're going to *create* future problems.'

'I beg your pardon, Dr Jameson,' Elliot said, 'but you forget that I am a professional in my field and this data is astonishing.' He touched the charts for emphasis. 'And I'm dealing with adults who have free will. Bina doesn't have to listen to me. She is not a captive audience.'

Kate did not like the implication; her kids were not captive, but maybe she was being a little unfair to Elliot. Maybe he was only trying to be helpful, even if it would end in tears.

'Just take a look, Kate,' Elliot coaxed.

Kate picked up the first chart. She had no idea if what she saw there was true or not, but, if it was accurate, it was fascinating. She looked at the other carefully constructed models. She sighed. Kate was impressed by the work Elliot had put in, but was not going to budge from her veto. Elliot was smart. He knew Bina and the others would be gaping and amazed by the brightly colored charts and graphs, just the way the tourists in Times Square were stunned by the lights and ads. But the tourists didn't change their lives based on a huge Pepsi ad, did they?

'Kate, it really can't hurt. At the very least, it's a distraction for Bina and that's what she needs right now. She can't keep herself in her father's office and wait for something to change.'

Kate sighed. She thought of the three or four long messages from Bina that were on her answering machine each night when she got home.

'Okay,' Kate said, 'but I want you to play this down, not up. It may be Fun With Math for you, but it's Bina's life. Anyway, even if all of this crazy nonsense were true, a troublemaker like Billy Nolan would never be interested in dating someone as ordinary as Bina Horowitz. So don't get her hopes up.'

Elliot vehemently nodded his agreement. 'No hopes up,' he said.

Brice came back out of the kitchen carrying two bottles of white wine. He put one down and popped the cork on the other. 'Bottoms up,' he said, pouring a glass and handing it to Kate. 'How does the buffet look? Kate, those Brooklyn friends of yours are fabulous! Well, not Versace fabulous, but more like *Absolutely Fabulous*. But younger and with Brooklyn accents.'

'Brice, my friends are not toys,' Kate told him.

'Of course not. Even if one is named for a doll and another a stuffed animal.'

Kate had to smile. Still, she didn't want her two worlds to collide. Elliot and Brice were getting too involved with all this. Just then the buzzer rang. 'I'll get it,' Brice sang as he strode over to the door and opened it. 'Hello, ladies!' he greeted the group.

And there they were, in all their splendor, the Bitches of Bushwick. Barbie came first, wearing a bright-pink halter-top with a leather jacket over it. She was followed by a nervous but hopeful-looking Bina. Next came Bev and her belly, and

143

then in walked Bunny, who had just come back from her honeymoon and had the tan to prove it.

'You're Bunny, the bride,' Brice said. 'I'm Brice and that stud muffin over there is Elliot.' The girls giggled, except for Bunny, who actually blushed. Without the 'breaking in' that had happened at table nine, Kate could see that the adventure wasn't comfortable for her. She had grown up in a very strict Italian Catholic home where, Kate was sure, homosexuality was synonymous with sin, perversion, and the molestation of little boys. Brice, sensing her hesitancy but never one for subtleties, threw his arm around Bunny's shoulders. 'We didn't have a chance to talk at your wedding. But it was beautiful. Absolutely beautiful!'

He couldn't have said anything better. 'Wait until you see the video!' Bunny exclaimed, suddenly ready to bond.

Kate winced. The ordeal of watching that video might be worse than the trauma of going to the event itself but Brice was enthusiasm itself. 'Oh, you *have* to show us. And what a dress!'

'Size six,' Bunny said proudly. 'Priscilla of Boston.'

'I knew it!'

'She got lucky,' Barbie told him. 'It was a special order but the bride was pregnant and didn't tell. By the time the dress arrived, well, you can imagine.'

'I got it at cost,' Bunny told Brice.

The attention seemed to ease her. Soon they were all standing around the buffet, filling their plates and – with the exception of Bev – drinking wine. Kate covertly looked around at them. Bev's belly looked as if it had expanded since the wedding. Kate tried to avoid staring at it with horror, although she couldn't escape the twinge of jealousy as she felt her own flat but empty stomach.

Elliot, too, was caught by Bev's very apparent expansion. 'Wow,' he said to her. 'Are you going to go into labor right here, or are you carrying twins?'

144

'I know, I'm huge and I've got months to go.' Bev looked down at her belly and shrugged.

'Remember after graduation you dieted all summer and were a size four by September?' Bunny asked. She was the group's weight historian, and could tell any one of them what they had weighed at any event or moment since they met.

'I'm trying to cut back on eating so much,' Bev explained to Elliot. 'I think I've gained about forty pounds.' Despite her confession, Kate watched as Bev piled her plate with nova, cream cheese, a poppy *and* a sesame bagel, finally adding some herring in cream sauce with a guilty final flourish. 'Unless I give birth to a thirty-five-pound baby, I'm gonna be in big trouble,' she laughed.

'Do you know if it's a girl or a boy yet?' Elliot asked her.

'Nah,' Bev said, waddling to the sofa from the buffet, Bina and Bunny right behind her. 'Johnnie says he wants to be surprised.'

'He's got a real surprise coming when he sees your ass after the baby is born,' Barbie snickered.

Kate never stopped being astonished by the way the women merely passed over cruel taunts without a ruffled hair. She watched as they sat down and checked out the apartment around them as if they'd just stepped into a den of unimaginable iniquity. It was a big adventure for the four girls from Bushwick to finally see the inside of a homosexual couple's apartment – even Bina hadn't really had a chance to look around the last time she was there. Kate could only imagine what they thought they were going to find. And she wasn't going to point out that Bina's Uncle Kenny and Barbie's youngest brother were most certainly gay but hadn't come out. Anyway, it must have been reassuring to see that there was nothing terrifying or exotic about Elliot's home – thanks to Brice, it was all done in stylish taste (though the Beanie Babies were a little camp). The situation made Kate smile.

She knew how frightening good taste could be to someone from Bushwick.

They all sat down on various perches like colorful birds with big mouths. Toucans, maybe, Kate thought. Despite their provincialism (and some morbid curiosity) it was really moving to see that all the girls had shown up for Bina. Kate loved them for that.

Barbie was more brazen – of course. She looked around as if she was assessing everything – and she probably was. 'How much does a place like this cost in Manhattan?' Barbie needed to know.

'It's a steal,' Brice willingly obliged. 'It's stabilized. We're still only paying eighteen a month.'

'Eighteen dollars a month for rent?' Bina asked in utter amazement. 'My grandmother's apartment on Ocean Parkway is rent-controlled but she pays sixty-six bucks a month.'

The better-informed Bunny was not as confused. 'Jeez,' she spat in disgust, 'for eighteen hundred dollars a month, you'd get three bedrooms and a balcony in Brooklyn.'

But why would you want them? Kate thought, then felt wildly guilty.

'Honey,' Brice replied, 'call me crazy but I'd rather have a closet in Manhattan than a palazzo in Prospect Park.'

'I thought you guys were all out of the closet,' Barbie said, obviously pleased with her heavy-handed witticism.

'Sweetie, some of us were never in it,' Brice said. There was silence for a moment.

Kate felt obliged to break it. 'Well, isn't this nice?' she chirped, turning to Elliot, as if to say 'I told you so'. 'Finally, all of my girlfriends together in one room.'

Bina let out a rather nervous little giggle in response to Kate's observation, but Bev just agreed. 'You have a lot of girlfriends, Kate. But then you're a Scorpio. Scorpio women always have lots of girlfriends.'

'And lots of boyfriends,' Elliot added sotto voce.

'So you have some plan to kill Jack, the scumbag?' Barbie asked.

'Not exactly!' Elliot told her.

'Well, why don't we get started?' Brice suggested as he began collecting dirty dishes. 'Bina, I can't wait for you to hear all about Elliot's plan.'

'Okay,' Bev began, 'so, Elliot, what's this huge discovery of yours?'

Elliot put his fork down, stood up and self-consciously stepped up to the easel. He looked first to Bina and then to Kate. He laid one hand on the first chart, turned it over so they could all see it and said, 'Bina, I made an incredible mathematical discovery while we were at Bunny's wedding.'

'And I thought we'd paid for all the extras,' Bunny said.

'The almonds in the net bag were lovely,' Brice assured her. 'But this is something no one could pay for.'

'Like what?' asked Bev.

'Genius,' Brice told them all proudly.

'Probability,' Elliot said. 'Some events can be predicted because of constancy and reliability of past data.'

'Huh!' Bina said. Kate suppressed a giggle. Poor Elliot.

'This helps us take down Jack the scumbag?' Barbie asked.

'Hey, what good would that do anyone?' Elliot asked. 'What if I told you that instead of revenge I've found a sure-fire way to get Jack to propose to Bina?' he asked the room. 'And marry her.'

There was a buzz of noise, part verbal, part flatware. Bina dropped her coffee spoon, Bev choked on her last mouthful of bagel, Barbie turned to Bunny and they began to murmur appreciatively.

Only Kate let out a snort of derision. 'Elliot!' she warned. Then she turned to Bina. 'Remember, this is just a theory, a suggestion, Bina. It may not be correct. You don't have to pay any attention to it. Personally, I think it is a lot of hocus-pocus.'

147

Elliot looked down at her from his full height. 'Kate,' he said. 'I think we all know your views on magic. So it's a good thing this has nothing to do with it,' he added. 'This is mathematical theory put into practice.'

'What's wrong with you, Katie?' Bev asked. 'Such a spoilsport. I think it sounds interesting.'

'What are you actually talking about?' Barbie asked.

Elliot nodded. 'It *is* interesting, more than interesting.' He pointed to the chart and said, 'Bina, these statistics are . . . well, they are just incredible. But they are absolutely accurate. I've done a bit of research and worked out the probability and you'll see that even with a differential for the . . .'

'Is he a college teacher or something?' Bina whispered.

'He's an obsessive neurotic gone compulsive,' Kate snorted.

'I know. Isn't he wonderful?' said Brice, placing his hand emphatically on his heart.

Elliot was in his teaching mode and ignored them both. 'Remember how Bev and Barbie both said that they had once dated that Billy guy who had just dumped Bunny?' He turned to her. 'No offense.'

'None taken,' Bunny said. 'When I dated him I was a size four – and weighed one hundred and sixteen pounds. My personal best.'

'Well, we both got dumped by him, too,' Bev added.

'Which was just fine with me,' Barbie assured everyone. 'The guy's a jerk.'

'That's right,' Elliot said, nodding to Barbie, 'and right after that you met Bobbie and got married.'

'Well, it wasn't right after. It was at least three weeks.' Barbie paused, then added, 'And Bev got married to Johnnie, right after she got dumped.'

'My Johnnie and I had our moons in Venus. It was fated,' Bev observed. No one paid any attention to her.

'So at the wedding, Elliot . . . well, began to snoop,' Brice explained.

'I collected data,' Elliot corrected Brice with dignity.

'Did I tell you about Gina Morelli and Nancy Limbacher, Elliot?' Bev asked, already eager to be part of the plan. 'Billy dated and dumped them, too.'

'I found that out on my own. Both of them married right after Billy Nolan. They were at Bunny's wedding.'

'Sure. I worked with Gina, and Nancy is best friends with my cousin Marie,' Bunny said.

'Marie Genetti?' Elliot asked. 'Billy dated her, too.'

'He dated Marie? You're kidding. She never told me!' Bunny exclaimed.

'So now we know that Billy Nolan has dated and dumped every woman from here to Albany. Who cares?' Kate spat out angrily. She thought of him charming her on the terrace. And to think that she'd been attracted to an idiot like him. 'Who cares?' she repeated.

'Bina should, and as her friend, so should you,' Elliot told her. 'I did some digging, and I made some calls. Everyone this guy drops gets married.'

'How did you find that out?' Barbie asked. Kate smiled. As the professional gossip of the group, she must be feeling a bit defensive.

'He pretended he was doing an article for *Jane* magazine,' Brice told her proudly.

'You're a regular Columbo,' Bev said admiringly. 'What sign are you again?'

Elliot laughed, didn't bother to answer but acknowledged Bev's compliment with a slight bow. Then he turned back to his first chart. 'Look at this,' he said, pointing to it. 'All five of these women dated William Nolan.' On the chart were the names of each woman and the date, time, and place of their first encounter with Billy Nolan. 'Now here,' Elliot said, flying to the next chart, 'is a timeline that follows the period of each relationship. Please note that where Billy drops out there is a segment of between three point two weeks and four point seven months before each woman marries.' The room was silent. Even Kate was momentarily impressed.

'Was the bastard going out with Gina Morelli the same time he was dating me?' Bunny asked.

'From the data I've collected, he only goes out with one woman at a time. Anyway, that doesn't matter,' Elliot said to silence her. 'The point is,' and he indicated the first chart, 'soon after each woman got dumped by Mr Nolan, each met or returned to another man – and sometimes, as in Bunny's case, she was introduced to that man by Billy himself. In all cases, that very next man was the man that they married.' Elliot stopped and looked at Kate and the Bitches with a broad smile as if his message was perfectly clear.

'Wow, congratulations, Elliot – it's quite an achievement,' Bev said, more serious than necessary.

'Right. Now you qualify as the biggest gossip in all five boroughs,' Kate said coldly.

'Yeah. What's the big deal?' Bunny asked. 'We all know that Billy Nolan is the biggest player that has ever lived.'

'But you didn't know this,' Elliot said, and flipped over a third chart. There was a list of fourteen names with a column listing the time they dated Billy and another column with wedding dates beside each name – except two. 'It isn't most of the women Billy Nolan dates. It's *all* of the women Billy Nolan dates.'

The friends examined the list.

'Don't you get it?' Elliot asked. 'Do you know the statistical likelihood of this phenomenon?' He flipped to his next chart. 'I've worked it out with and without the standard deviation, the probability ranges from one in six million three hundred and forty-seven to one in eighty-two million six hundred and forty-three.'

Kate wondered about the two out of the fourteen but figured she'd get her chance to debunk all this later.

'I don't get it,' Bunny admitted. 'I don't think even Billy

Nolan could date and dump eighty-two million women. It's just not humanly possible. Are there even that many women in New York?'

'He doesn't have to date eighty-two million women,' Barbie told Bunny dismissively. 'He just has to date Bina. Right, Elliot?'

'Really? Really, Elliot?' Bina asked, her voice filled with more hope and animation than it had been since the afternoon of the manicure.

'Oh, Jesus H. Christ,' Kate said, no longer able to control her disgust. She stood up and started to pace around the room. 'Elliot, you know I don't approve of this whole scheme. It is just ridiculous.'

'Be quiet, Kate,' Bev said. 'I'm trying to understand this.' She narrowed her eyes and looked at Elliot. 'You're saying that anyone who dates Billy gets married right afterwards?' she asked.

'Everyone?' Bina asked.

Kate felt she couldn't let this go on. Instead of spending the morning in bed with Michael, then reading the *Times* together and having a nice meal before they parted, she was stuck with this burgeoning bunch of maniacs with a berserk plan. She never thought any of them would buy it. 'It's a pile of superstitious crap,' Kate told Bina and the rest of them.

'This isn't about superstition,' Elliot insisted, his voice showing his hurt. 'These are the facts.'

Bunny kept staring at the charts, and now tried to sound smart. She used to do it in sixth grade to about the same effect. 'Are you saying that the odds against Bina ever getting married are about eighty-two million to one unless she dates Billy Nolan?' she asked Elliot.

'Well,' Elliot said, pretending to give the ridiculous question some thought, 'that's not *exactly* what I'm saying. I can't compute the odds of Bina getting married. I don't have

151

enough data. But the odds are eighty-two million to one in her *favor* if she does date Billy.'

Kate saw Bina pale and felt her own face grow warm with anger and agitation. This was all madness. She'd just stop it, send them all back to Brooklyn and never talk to Elliot again – or at least not for a week. She was about to speak when Barbie stood up and brushed off her skirt.

'Then it's settled,' Barbie said. 'Bina has to go out with Dumping Billy. That's all there is to it. After all, what has she got to lose?'

Bina stood up too, but she hesitated before she spoke. 'Elliot, I appreciate all the time you must have put into this, but I'm not interested in dating anyone except Jack.' Kate watched as tears rose in her eyes. 'I just want Jack back.'

'This is a way to *get* Jack, Bina,' Elliot said. 'You date Billy, then get dumped, then see Jack and . . . *voilà*!'

Kate turned to Bina. 'This is all ridiculous. I didn't know it was quite as insane as it is, but I promised him I'd let him show you . . .'

'Why is it insane?' Bev asked.

'Well, it's a long shot that we could get Billy to go out with Bina in her current state . . .' Barbie said and then narrowed her eyes speculatively. 'But if we did some work on her . . .'

'Just look at the numbers, sweetheart. The numbers don't lie,' Brice said to Bina. He took her hand in his, but was watching Elliot with the look of a proud mother on his face.

Kate was sure that Bina, monogamous for so long, wouldn't consider this nonsense.

'They *all* got married?' Bina asked Elliot in disbelief.

'Yes. Well, to be totally accurate, one joined a convent and one came out as a lesbian,' Elliot confessed, 'but both are hooked up, one to God and one to her girlfriend. So that makes fourteen for fourteen.'

'Isn't he wonderful?' Brice asked no one in particular.

'He's absolutely nuts,' Kate snapped. 'Bina, don't even consider it.'

'We'd have to time it so that Jack was back at the strategic moment – just after the break-up,' Bev said.

'And to be safe, we have to make sure he drops her,' Elliot cautioned. 'I have no indication of what happens to his partner if she dumps him.'

Bev and Barbie laughed. 'No one dumps him,' Barbie said.

'Of course he's gorgeous,' Bev said (it sounded like 'ov cous he's gowjus'). 'But that doesn't explain it. That only explains why he gets women.'

'And probably why he dumps them,' Elliot said.

'No,' Bunny told him. 'To be fair, he is always nice and he seems . . . well, I don't know.' She thought for a minute. 'Like really disappointed when things don't work out.'

Elliot took a deep breath. 'I don't really care about his psychology,' he told them. 'The key question is why women marry right after he leaves them.'

Kate wondered too.

But Bina wasn't listening. She was staring at the charts before her. Kate knew how desperate she was. Elliot, seeing that he had Bina hooked, asked, 'Do you want a detailed cross section?'

Kate could see Bina's love for Jack and the longing for him written all over her face. 'I don't need one, I'll do it!' Bina exclaimed.

'Bina!' Kate was shocked at her friend's declaration.

'Then it's all settled,' Bunny said and stood up. 'I've gotta go back to Arnie.'

'Well, we're not exactly finished,' Barbie said in the tone that had driven fear into many pre-teen girls in their junior high days. 'He doesn't just go out with anyone. He looks for a certain . . . style.' She preened for a moment. 'Do you think Billy would go out with *Bina*?'

'Barbie!' Despite the usual cruelty of the girls to one another, that went too far.

'The boy is certainly hot,' Brice said to himself, pulling out the Polaroid from the wedding. He put it down on the table.

'Very hot,' Bev said, also looking at the photo while pretending to fan herself.

'Good point,' Bunny agreed. 'Maybe Bina would be out of her league.'

Before Kate could jump to Bina's defence, her friend took control. 'I'm still in the room!' Bina suddenly exploded. 'Why are you talking about me like I'm not here?'

Kate couldn't help but feel bad for Bina. Here she was, alone and reduced to believing in ridiculous statistics. Kate knew her friend and knew that all she really wanted was to be with Jack. 'We're sorry, Bina,' she apologized for the group. She tried to be diplomatic while she sided with the Bitches so this whole idea could be plugged up.

'We didn't mean to hurt your feelings, honey,' Bev said and put her arms around her friend as far as she could manage.

'Look, no one said you couldn't become Billy's type,' Barbie said by way of an apology.

'Right. We only wanted to help, not to hurt,' Elliot added.

'And to make it up to you . . .' Brice began to a mimed drum roll. 'A makeover!!'

Once the magic word had been spoken, Kate knew there was no going back.

18

Kate sat in her office and tried to put Bina, Jack, Billy and –
what for a moment she was thinking of as – 'the rest of that
nonsense' out of her mind. Bina's makeover, the problem of
getting Billy to date her and the idiocy of the same was not as
important as the problem in front of her. Jennifer Whalen, a
pretty and neatly dressed nine-year-old, was sitting in front
of her doing what she seemed to do best. 'So my father opens
the door to the limousine and Britney Spears steps out. And
she came into our building and right up to our apartment.
She even had dinner with us. We had meatloaf. And if you
don't believe me, she gave me this bracelet.' Jennifer pulled
the elastic of the bead bracelet she had around her wrist. 'See?
I have proof.'

Kate withheld a sigh. She knew there was no point in
discussing this particular lie or any of the other whoppers
that Jennifer had told not only her classmates but also her
teachers. The question was why Jennifer needed to lie. Did she
crave attention? She was a middle child, with an older sister at
Andrew Country Day and a year-old brother at home. Had the
baby usurped her position in the family constellation?

Or was it feelings of inferiority? Kate knew that both
Jennifer and her sister were receiving financial aid because

their family, though well-off by Kate's childhood standards, were only middle-class and could not afford full tuition for both girls. Maybe Jennifer felt inferior to her friends simply because their homes were bigger, their school vacations were often spent in Aspen, the Hamptons, or even Europe, and Jennifer couldn't compete.

The worst-case scenario, of course, was that Jennifer was showing early signs of bipolar disorder. However, as Kate looked at her, she felt that she was studying a healthy, outgoing little girl who doubtless knew the difference between fantasy and reality.

Kate didn't want Jennifer's lies to continue, nor to argue with her. She had listened quietly without showing much reaction. She could, of course, recommend a therapist for Jennifer, but Kate felt that she and Jennifer had a good rapport. This business was always tricky, but Kate thought of a quote from A.S. Neal: 'Sometimes you simply have to trust your instinct with children. Analysis with them is an art, not a science', and decided to take a chance.

'Want to know a secret?' she asked. Jennifer nodded her head. 'I'm going to get married. And I'm going to have a really big wedding. It's going to be in a castle and Justin Timberlake is coming.' Jennifer's eyes opened wide. 'He's going to bring the Backstreet Boys but my sister is really angry because *she* invited the boys from 'Nsync and you can just imagine what would happen if they came, too.' Jennifer's eyes were popping and she nodded her head.

'I bet they hate each other,' she said.

'They do. And they all hate my husband-to-be. Do you know who I'm marrying?'

Jennifer shook her head back and forth, her mouth slightly open.

'Mr McKay,' Kate said.

Jennifer's face froze. Then Kate watched as doubt, then disbelief, then relief and even – perhaps – understanding

156

bloomed on it like one of those flowers opening in time-lapse photography. 'No way!' Jennifer said.

'Way,' Kate insisted and nodded. 'Know what else? We're both going to ride white horses down the aisle of the church.'

'No way!' Jennifer repeated more vehemently. Then she started to giggle. 'Mr McKay on a horse!'

Kate laughed too. Then she paused. 'I really like you, Jennifer. You know why?' Jennifer shook her head. 'Because you are smart, and cute, and funny. And you have a great imagination. You have a gift for fiction.'

Jennifer's brows went down. 'What does that mean?'

'It means that I think you could write really good stories. Or maybe books. Or maybe movies.'

'I could write down a movie?'

'Sure.' Kate nodded. 'Movies all start from someone writing down a story.' She didn't want to set off another round of lying. 'Not every story is good enough to be a movie, but once you write one down you never know what could happen.' She paused, letting the compliments and the idea settle in. 'Of course, it isn't easy. Do you think you would like to have some special time with Mrs Reese?' Joyce Reese was the creative writing teacher for the sixth grade, and a friend of Kate's.

'I'm only in fourth,' Jennifer said, but that, of course, added to her enthusiasm.

'That's true,' Kate agreed, 'but I would say that you could probably write sixth-grade stories. Maybe even eighth-grade stories. If one was in the school magazine everyone would read it.'

Jennifer stared at her. The two of them sat like that for a few moments in silence. Kate could virtually see the child's mind working behind her gray eyes. 'Britney Spears didn't come to my house,' Jennifer said.

'But it was a good story,' Kate told her, keeping her tone neutral. 'If you tell it like a story or write it down like one,

157

people would want to hear the next part. They'll think you're special because you can make up really good stories.'

'But then they get mad,' Jennifer said. 'They get mad when it isn't true.'

'Did you feel angry at me when I told you about my wedding?'

Jennifer sat for a moment, looking down at her nails. 'First I liked it. I thought it was a secret. But then when I knew you were . . . lying . . . I got a little mad,' she admitted.

Kate nodded. 'That happens when you fool people. They get mad.'

Out in the hall, the bell rang. In a moment, they could hear the sound of doors being thrown open and the noise of classes getting out.

'Why don't you come in and visit with me next week? And in the meantime I'll talk to Mrs Reese.'

Jennifer nodded her head.

'But now, I'm sorry, you'll have to go or you'll be late for the bus.'

Reluctantly Jennifer stood up. 'You told a lie,' she said.

'Don't tell anyone,' Kate whispered. 'And especially don't tell Mr McKay.'

Jennifer laughed. '*Nobody* would want to marry him,' she said and marched out of Kate's office.

Kate had just gotten home, thrown her purse onto the sofa and kicked off her shoes. She hadn't even had a chance to sit down before there was a knock at the door. God, she wasn't in the mood for a visitor! She turned around and opened it. Max stood there, still dressed in his suit and tie, clearly just back from work, though he was not usually home until after dark. He was leaning against her doorway, one arm raised, his head resting on his inner elbow. He must have been away during the last weekend because he had a bit of a tan. It made his blue eyes bluer. 'Hi,' she said.

'Hi,' he returned. 'Is Bina here?' he asked, his voice lowered.

Kate felt a stab of irritation. Since Jack had flown the coop, she felt like Bina Central. 'No,' she answered, not as hospitable as she might be. 'You can call her at home,' she added shortly and began to close the door.

'No, that's a good thing,' Max told her in a normal tone. 'See, I want to show you something and, well, I don't know if she should see it or not.' Kate rolled her eyes, but she let Max take her hand to lead her up the stairs.

His apartment door was open. Inside was the usual requisite bachelor setup: the black leather couch, workout equipment, an expensive stereo and the pile of newspapers that seemed a requirement for all male apartments. Max also, of course, had the latest titanium laptop, and it was that to which he brought her over.

'I want you to look at this and tell me what to do,' he said. He loosened his tie before he punched in a few keystrokes. For one crazy moment, Kate thought he might be asking her opinion about some stock melt-down, but Kate had never had a share of anything in her life except a dorm room. But instead of charts, graphs, or analysis, Kate watched as the screen filled with a photo. It was Jack, bare-chested, standing on a balcony with a view of a beautiful harbor behind him and an equally beautiful woman next to him.

'Oh my God,' Kate said. 'Where did you get this?'

'He e-mailed it to me today,' Max said. 'Do you think I should show it to Bina?'

'Do you think I should set fire to your hair gel?' Kate asked. The thought of Bina seeing this grinning ass literally made Kate sick to her stomach. When she'd found out Steven had been cheating on her she'd been so distraught that she couldn't get out of bed for three days. Bina would just collapse.

Unconsciously Max smoothed down his wavy hair. 'I didn't

159

think so either,' he said. 'But, you know, I feel responsible for this. I introduced them and all . . .' Kate felt her irritation melt away, replaced with growing respect for Max Cepek. She had always thought of him as a stereotype; a kind of Wall Street/jock/yuppie clone. When he'd had girlfriends for any length of time he didn't seem particularly committed or passionate. In fact, if pushed to describe him, Kate would have used adjectives like 'shallow' and 'self-absorbed'.

Now, his concern seemed genuine and moving. Kate began to feel a new warmth toward Max and a little guilt over how she might have misjudged him.

'I know Jack and he is a one-woman guy.' He shook his head. 'I saw Bina. I know what this has done to her and I told her that he was just talk. I mean, who would think Jack . . .' Max stared at the picture displayed on the screen. Kate could feel him getting lost in it for a moment. 'She is very pretty,' Max said, and Kate took back any good judgment she thought Max had.

'Well, I hope they're very happy together,' Kate said tartly. 'I'm sure they share common goals and interests.'

'Hey, he isn't married!' Max protested. 'Even Jack isn't that stupid.'

'How do you know?' Kate asked.

'Read the e-mail,' Max said and displayed the message from Jack.

What a place! The views are incredible, electronics are cheap, and the women are incredible and cheap. You gotta come! Money is king here and the dollar rules.

Kate didn't bother to read any more of it. 'He is disgusting,' she said. She turned away and started to walk out of the apartment.

'So you don't think I should show this to Bina? Right?'

'Right, Einstein,' Kate said and ran down the stairs to her

own place. As she walked in her door the phone began to ring. Kate grabbed it and saw Elliot's number on the caller ID. 'Shoot me in the head,' she said into the receiver.

'And a happy Memorial Day to you, too,' Elliot said. 'I didn't catch you before you left school, but Brice and I are getting together with Bina on Saturday morning for the big renovation. Are you in?'

Kate hesitated for a moment, torn between the news from upstairs and her disapproval of the whole scheme. Wasn't a makeover a kind of lie not much different from little Jennifer's stories? It was a visual way of saying you were someone different. But Jack's e-mail had shocked her. 'I'm in,' she said.

It was only after she hung up that she realized her commitment would mean canceling Michael. They spent every Friday night together, and each Saturday. After Steven's unreliability, Kate appreciated the fact that Michael saw her every Wednesday, Friday and Saturday night. During the week they usually went to a movie and stayed at her house afterward. They alternated places on the weekends. Perhaps Michael was a little too routinized, because he always seemed upset when she had to change their schedule, and apologetic when he – though it was rare – had to do the same. Well, Kate would regret the pleasant, leisurely Saturday they would lose, but perhaps she could persuade him to work while she was off with her friends instead of on his usual Sunday night. She picked up the phone again and, a trifle uneasy, dialed Michael's number.

19

Two days later, the Bitches accompanied by Brice and Elliot were walking down Fifth Avenue. They had all insisted on being a part of Bina's makeover.

'All I can say is it's about time,' Barbie said. 'You're starting to look like an orthodox Jew.'

'It's the hair,' Brice agreed. 'It looks like a bad wig.'

'Brice!' Elliot warned, before Kate could.

'The truth hurts,' Bev said, patting Bina's arm and then her own tummy.

'I think I need to, uh, go to the bathroom,' Bina said. 'I'm so nervous. Jack liked my hair.'

'Not enough,' Barbie said.

'Don't worry. They have a ladies' room at Louis Lacari's,' Brice told her, and took her into a marble lobby. Kate shook her head. She had made it clear that she totally disapproved of this ridiculous idea but that hadn't seemed to ever slow the rest of them down for a moment. She hated to admit it to herself, but that had shocked her. After all, the plan was crazy; she, not Barbie, Bev or Bunny, was Bina's best friend; none of them knew Elliot or Brice; Elliot, her other best friend, knew she disapproved, yet the whole crew seemed to be disregarding her completely, except Brice, who now turned to her and said,

'You know, while we're here Pierre can cut your hair, too.' She'd given up a day with Michael – would she have to live with his testiness because of this?

'I don't think so,' Kate snapped. She loved her hair long. So had Steven and so did Michael. It was sexy, and easy to put up if she had to. Now, completely offended, she joined the party as they got onto the elevator to go up to the fourteenth-floor salon, overlooking St Patrick's Cathedral.

'Wow!' Bina said as she stared out at the skyline. 'It looks almost as good as Epcot.' Kate rolled her eyes. Leave it to Bina – she'd compare the fake Disney version to the real and prefer the ersatz.

Brice didn't bother with the view. 'Pierre, please,' he told the woman at the desk. 'Tell him it's Brice and we have a cut with him and consultation with Louis.' Bev, Barbie and Bunny looked at one another, obviously impressed. All those years of reading *Allure* magazine had familiarized them with Louis Lacari, the god of hair color. And Brice had just called him by his first name. 'Now c'mon. I think we can do everything your head needs here,' he instructed Bina as he clutched her hand and escorted her to the stylist chair.

'Except get it examined,' Kate muttered. She looked over to Elliot but he just shrugged. Barbie, Bunny and Bev were right behind them. Kate was delighted that Bina was getting so much help and attention. It was just what she needed at a time like this. But oddly, she also felt a bit of envy. She had never asked for help when her crises with Steven had taken place, not that the Bitches would have been much help.

'Do you really think this whole thing is a good idea?' Kate asked Elliot. 'You know it won't change things between her and Jack. And it's just getting her hopes up for nothing. I can't imagine that the narcissist prince will go out with Bina anyway.'

'Oh, come on, Kate. She's got nothing to lose,' he said as he held the door for her. 'And at least she's off your couch. And

163

anyway, according to my statistics, the plan can't fail. Figures don't lie.'

'But liars figure,' she said and gave him her darkest look. As she watched Bina being led off to her appointment, Kate thought of Jennifer and her lies. Wasn't changing yourself nothing more than an elaborate lie? What was the difference between a nine-year-old's self-aggrandizing stories and Bina's upcoming makeover? The big difference was, in this case, her friends were encouraging her and reinforcing her feelings of inferiority. Kate shrugged. Yet a small doubt persisted. If she herself had been beautiful – truly drop-dead, gob-stopping stunning – would Steven have left her? Would Michael be more attentive? She put the thoughts from her mind, though she certainly had plenty of time to think about whatever she wanted.

Bina spent four hours at the salon. While they were there, Barbie got a good cut, Bev had a facial, and Bunny got a massage – as a belated wedding present from Brice and Elliot. Kate merely had a manicure, and didn't even care for the color she had selected.

But it was Bina who was transformed. Her hair moved. It had been lightened a bit around her face, and then streaks of ash blond made the dark brown of her natural color glow. Kate was stunned by the subtlety and artistry of it. And the cut, a chin-length, undercut masterpiece, made it seem as if Bina had a head of moving light, a kind of nimbus of hair. Even Kate had to admit the transformation was remarkable.

'Holy haircut, Batman,' was all Elliot said, as he looked up from the papers he was marking. Bina giggled and shook her head from side to side. The nimbus moved like a saintly glow in a chapel. The receptionist and two cashiers 'Ooohed' and 'Aaahed' as they were paid to do. Barbie, Bev and Bunny kept cooing like demented pigeons. For an insane moment, Kate wondered if she should get her own head shorn. Maybe a haircut, a few highlights and a makeup makeover would . . . Kate took a deep breath. Then she got a grip.

'Okay,' Brice said. 'We did the drapes. Now on to the upholstery.' He looked at Bina's outfit, an old Gap blouse and a charity skirt. 'First stop, Prada!' Brice called and the entire group got into two taxis.

Before Bina even had a chance to take note of the ambience or the price tags she was standing in front of a three-way mirror while a saleslady pinned up the hemline on a skirt that – in Kate's opinion – was already far too short and far too tight. It draped to one side, exposing a thigh. 'Do you really think this is *me*?' Bina asked the admiring group.

'We left *you* back in your closet,' Bunny told her.

'Oh,' Brice said. 'Doesn't being in the closet seem a bit harsh?'

'How would you know?' Elliot asked.

Barbie backed away from Bina and gave her an approving once-over. Kate remembered squirming under those looks back in tenth grade. Barbie liked what she saw. 'Isn't it nice to wear something red? It's the new beige, you know,' she confided.

Kate didn't have a clue as to what that meant, but she thought that Bina looked ridiculous. But that didn't stop them from buying the skirt and moving on to Victoria's Secret. Brice picked up a Wonderbra and then handed it to Bina. 'Here you go, honey,' he said. 'Every girl needs a little support.'

'Don't forget this.' Bunny handed her a lacy black thong.

Bina looked down at the bra and dental floss in her hand. 'I'm not wearing these.' She lifted up the thong and held it two ways. 'I . . . I don't even know how to wear this,' she admitted. 'Besides,' she added, 'I'm not sleeping with him. My underwear isn't relevant.' She looked at Elliot; the only man in the store who seemed neither embarrassed nor interested. 'The charts didn't say I had to have sex with him, did they?

165

Because I'm not doing that.' Kate felt relief. They might all be crazy but at least Bina wasn't self-destructive as well.

'Honey, it's not about having sex, it's about feeling sexy,' Brice said. 'And if you feel sexy, you'll look sexy to others. Right, Elliot?'

'I plead the Fifth,' Elliot responded.

'Bina, you're a Capricorn,' said Bev, 'and, trust me, they need all the help they can get when it comes to attracting men. See what it does for you.' Bina disappeared into the dressing room and came out with her eyes bulging as much as her breasts were. She'd put her blouse on to step out of the dressing room but she hadn't buttoned the top two buttons.

Barbie leaned forward and unbuttoned the third. 'Now, that's a nice rack,' she said.

Bina stared at herself in the mirror. Then she turned to Kate. 'I wish Jack could see me now,' she said. Kate's breast, unexposed, felt a stab of sympathy for her friend. Little cheerful Bina, a cupcake of a girl, now looked more like a pop tart and still thought of only Jack. She was doing all of this because of him, and Kate honestly couldn't decide if it was an act of self-mutilation or love. Kate doubted that any of this would make a man like Billy Nolan want Bina. After all, she was still Bina-the-good-girl-from-Ocean-Avenue. At least, she decided, it gave Bina something else to concentrate on and who knew? Looking like a hot tamale, she might meet someone else. One thing that Kate did know was that while she could go on without Michael and even without marriage to anyone, Bina always had only one goal: marriage and children, preferably to and by Jack.

'Hey. Turn around,' Bev said. 'Let's see if there's a panty line.'

'How can there be?' Bina asked. 'There is hardly any panty.' She turned as directed. 'This is so uncomfortable,' she said.

'Beauty has to hurt,' Bunny told her.

*   *   *

At Tootsie Plouhound Bina once again followed Barbie's directives and bought her first pair of serious 'fuck me' sandals.

'You need a low-cut top,' Bev said, taking inventory of their progress to date. 'I mean you've got 'em, and you've lifted them, might as well show them. And you've always had a small waist so we should find something tight.' She looked down at her own stomach. The Lycra she was wearing couldn't be any tighter without crushing the fetus, Kate thought.

'Yes, that would complete the outfit,' Brice agreed.

'Bina, wait a minute,' Kate said. 'How do you really feel about all of this so far?'

'I feel like that thong could perform a colonoscopy,' Bina answered. 'I don't know if it will make me think I'm sexy but I'll be thinking about my crotch every moment I wear it.'

'And so will every man you meet,' said Brice.

'But it seems so uncomfortable,' Bina said.

Bev, overhearing them, laughed. 'Try it when you're pregnant.'

'You're kidding,' Bina gasped, 'you don't – do you?'

'Sure. Barbie and I call them crotch-eaters.'

'If only my Bobbie would get the message,' Barbie said.

'More information than I require,' Elliot said.

As the seven of them walked down the busy West Broadway sidewalk, Kate had to marvel at how seamlessly Elliot and Brice seemed to join in with her Brooklyn friends. She'd avoided this for years and never introduced Bina and the others to Rita, her friend from graduate school, or Maggie, a choreographer she'd met in her exercise class. Somehow she didn't think a mix like that would work as smoothly and she suspected it was because Brice and Elliot were observing all this as they participated.

Kate felt distinctly uncomfortable. She had worked diligently for as long as she could remember to change her style, her look, her vocabulary . . . well, almost everything that she had believed didn't reflect who she was or wanted to be. She

167

thought she had succeeded in creating a unique persona. Hers, she felt was valid. Now watching Bina's overnight instant transformation she wondered if it wasn't valid as well, even if it had been overseen by others. After all, Kate had made all of the changes to herself based, in part, on what others – even if they were people in magazines or strangers she'd observed in Manhattan – had shown her.

As Elliot led the way to hail yet another pair of cabs, Barbie took stock. 'Let's see,' she muttered. 'Bra, thong, skirt, top, shoes, hair, nails.' Barbie stopped and turned to Bina. 'Okay, now the electrolysis!' Bina froze in terror. 'Just kidding, Binie,' Barbie warbled. Then Brice grabbed Bina by the hand and pulled her into one of the waiting cabs.

'Give me half an hour in Make Up Forever and I'll have you looking like a queen,' Brice promised.

A look of horror came over Bina's face. 'Not *that* kind of queen, Bina,' Brice assured her.

'I'm not changing my makeup,' Bina protested as the cab pulled out into the traffic.

'You have to *wear* makeup if you want to *change* makeup,' Bunny said sharply. She reached into her purse and pulled out a lipstick tube. 'Just try a little of this.'

'Oh, leave her alone!' Kate begged. She wondered what all the criticism and change was doing to Bina's self-esteem. But Bina took the tube and applied it. It was awful – it made her look like Mrs Horowitz at a funeral.

'I don't think red is her color,' Kate objected, and then realized she had now added to the critique.

'I agree with you there,' Brice said from the front seat beside the driver. He handed Bina a tissue. 'I see you more in a sizzling salmon.' He appraised her face as best he could through the small aperture in the plastic shield that kept the passengers safe from the driver. 'We'll have to stop at Make Up Forever on the way home.'

By the time the afternoon was over, Bina had charged more

on her credit cards in one day than she had in all of the last three months. Kate was exhausted but happy to see that Bina finally seemed to be enjoying herself, even if it was over silly things and a hare-brained scheme. It was the first day Bina had paid more attention to herself than Jack since he left. Elliot helped Bev waddle up the steps of Kate's building.

'A fashion show!' demanded Brice once inside. Barbie, Bunny and Bev joined the demand, and so did Kate, a little reluctantly. All of them in her living room felt not just crowded but claustrophobic. It was a clash of cultures and sexual orientation in the tiny space that was, in a way, sacred to her, but only Kate seemed disoriented. Bev had her feet up, her hands over her belly, Barbie sat primly in the rocker. Bunny stood in front of the fireplace glancing every so often at her honeymoon tan in the mirror that hung over the mantel, and Brice was busy going through the bags, while Elliot just sat back on the sofa smiling to himself.

Bina took the shopping bags into Kate's bedroom and, a few minutes later, returned completely transformed. There was a moment of silence. Kate was shocked. In a single afternoon Bina had changed literally from head to toe and Kate could barely recognize the hot little number turning around and around in front of them. She thought of Billy Nolan and the look he had given her out on the terrace. Would a man who had approved of her style and looks want a woman arrayed the way Bina was?

'Wow! You look great!' Bev said, breaking the silence.

Then Elliot gave an excellent wolf whistle (Kate wondered what, if anything, he had used that for) and Barbie, Brice and Bunny began to applaud. Kate joined in.

'Okay, so now all we have to do is bring you over to Billy and serve you up on a platter,' Elliot said.

'How?' Bina asked, as if playing the trussed fowl on a plate came naturally.

'We go to his place of business,' Elliot said. 'A bar in Williamsburg . . .'

'Is that where he works?' Kate interrupted. Elliot ignored her and laid out the time, the rendezvous spots, the assault on the watering hole, and all the rest as if he were the Iron Duke planning an invasion.

'Now, not that you can't do it, but let me come over and do a touch-up to your hair and makeup before Saturday,' Brice said. 'And I'll have a surprise for you.'

'I'll hafta be surprised later,' Bev said. 'I need to get home for my Johnnie. And I can't walk another block. Hey, Barbie, I know Libras have an overdeveloped sense of ownership, but maybe you want to share a cab back to Brooklyn?' she asked.

'Sure, Bev,' Barbie said, ignoring the comment. 'Bunny, are you in?'

'If you're sure, then all right, Barbie,' Bunny said hesitantly, apparently taking the fact that Barbie was a Libra to heart. No one but Bunny had ever paid any attention to Bev and her astrological nonsense. Kate looked at Bunny, and wondered if she had put the weight back on during her honeymoon. Kate thought the idea of a honeymoon in days when most couples live together before marriage was ridiculous and sometimes not healthy. Travel often put a lot of stress on people, and time completely alone for days and days when a couple wasn't used to it created pressures that caused 'Honeymoon Remorse', a sort of minor depression that descended after the excitement and hoopla over the wedding had ended and the focus changed abruptly.

Kate wondered if she'd like to go on a 'honeymoon' with Michael. They had spent one weekend at the Jersey shore, which had been pleasant. Two weeks, though . . .

Kate brought her focus back to the party that was breaking up. Barbie, Bunny, and Bev got up to leave. 'We'll see you all later,' Barbie told them. 'Oh, Bina, I'm so excited for you. Good clothes open all doors.'

Kate tried not to laugh or cry. How had Barbie's mother known in advance how to name her so accurately?

There were many kisses and hugs. They all hugged Bina hard and the three women disappeared out the front door.

Bina was left with Brice and Elliot, who were walking her to the subway. At last Kate was left alone. She wondered, as she took off her clothes, ran a tub, combed her hair and brushed her teeth, what Dr and Mrs Horowitz would say when Bina walked in the door. Mrs Horowitz had a mild heart condition, some minor mitral valve problem, and Kate wondered, for a moment, if their daughter's makeover might cause an infarction.

It wasn't until she was in bed, just at the edge of sleep, that she wondered again what she would look like after a makeover. Then she closed her eyes and slept – poorly – for the rest of the night.

20

The following Friday, Kate sat in her office across from two identical twin boys wearing identical green corduroys and white T-shirts, each with the same picture of a Tyrannosaurus Rex clawing across their chests. Each had a name tag stuck to his shirt – one reading 'James' and the other, 'Joseph'. Kate was perched on the front of her desk purposely to appear to tower over the two small third-graders. The three of them had been talking for a while already and Kate thought she'd cleared up the situation.

'Now, I am going to take you back to Mrs Gupta's class, James,' she said, pointing at one of the boys – the one who was wearing the 'Joseph' name tag. 'And you, Joseph, are to go back to Mrs Johnson's . . .' she said sternly to the other boy. 'Where each of you belong,' she added.

The Reilly twins were good boys, well behaved and intelligent. But they had been assigned separate classes this year with the consent of their parents and, since the separation, they had developed a bad habit of fooling not only their classmates but their teachers and even Mr McKay about their identities. They switched at will, but when Kate suggested to their parents that the third-graders might be better off if they dressed individually instead of in matching clothing they had

172

insisted that it was up to the boys and they still wanted to dress alike.

Lately, the mischief had escalated, but Kate felt her talk about trust and fooling people had penetrated into the strange and interesting world of twinship. 'So we're agreed?' she asked.

Just then the phone rang. Kate turned her back to the twins and reached for the receiver. 'Dr Jameson,' she answered.

'Dr Jameson? This is Dr Bina Horowitz. I'll be at your office ready for our conference tomorrow at six. I've been told we have to consult with Dr Brice first,' Bina said.

'No one is listening in, Bina,' she told her friend. Years of eavesdropping by her mother on the extension had made Bina paranoid. 'Come on over for Operation Ridiculous. I'll be there at five. Gotta go. I'm working.'

Kate hung up and turned back to the twins. 'I want the two of you to exchange your name tags now,' she said. They nodded, peeled off the sticky-backed strips and handed them to one another contritely. Her phone rang again. She sighed and turned her back on the twins who quickly re-traded name tags and seats.

'A Dr Michael Atwood is here to see you,' Louise, the secretary from the front office, informed Kate in her nasal voice.

'Thanks, I'll be right out,' she said, and laid down the receiver. This was unexpected. Kate wondered what had prompted such a spontaneous visit. An emergency? Michael was nothing if not a man of routine. She'd seen him go, step by unchanging step, through his morning ritual: plugging in the coffee maker he had prepared the night before, turning on the shower, brushing his teeth while he waited for the hot water to hit the shower head, and so on. In a way she admired it, since he, unlike her, never forgot his cell phone, misplaced his glasses, left his bed unmade or his coffee mug unwashed in the sink. She also knew, of course, that too much of that

173

behavior became obsessive-compulsive and it always masked deeper fears of reality and the uncontrollable nature of life. But she thought, in Michael's case at least, it was more a demonstration of his good service and organizational skills. He was stable, rather than a madman about to spin out of control if he forgot to straighten a sheet or wake up exactly at seven thirty.

Kate's mind was so preoccupied with these thoughts that she didn't notice the twins' subterfuge. 'Remember,' she said to them absently, 'it isn't just a trick to switch places. It's unkind to fool people. And after you fool them, they won't trust you when you want them to. Understand?' Normally, Kate wouldn't have repeated herself to Joseph and James, but she was a little thrown by this surprise and was anxious to hear what Michael had to say.

The twins nodded innocently. She jumped down from her desk and took each boy by the hand. She led them out the door and down the hall, at the end of which Michael was standing. He gave her a big, if somewhat sheepish, smile. Kate didn't acknowledge it and instead stopped in front of a classroom door and nodded for 'James' to go in. 'Joseph' let go her other hand, gave her a triumphant smile, and raced to another door on the opposite side of the hall.

Only then did Kate smile back and walk up to Michael. 'Nice surprise,' she said, reinforcing his spontaneous behavior. 'What are you doing here?'

'I thought I'd see you in action. Very stern.' He smiled. 'You're such a natural with kids.'

'Thanks,' Kate replied. She wondered – just for a moment – if he ever thought of her as a mother of his children but stopped herself. It was too early for that.

'You almost ready to go?' he asked. 'Do you mind that I dropped by?'

'Not at all,' Kate said. 'I like it.' And she did.

'I have something else I wanted to show you before tonight,'

174

Michael said, reaching into his briefcase. He pulled out an academic journal with a bit of a flourish.

'Oh, Michael! Your article!' He had been working on this piece for months. He had even gone into the field for research. It meant a lot to him, and to his career. Kate was delighted for him.

'Hot off the press from the University of Michigan's *Journal of Applied Sciences*,' he said proudly.

Kate gave him a big hug. 'I'm so pleased for you,' she said. 'What a great surprise!' She took the journal and opened it at the article. He had already marked the page with a bright red sticker. She smiled at that. There were things about him that were . . . surprisingly childlike. It was endearing rather than immature.

They walked back to her office. 'That's the very first copy,' he told her. 'I thought as soon as you were done here we could go out for a drink and then maybe dinner.' She smiled at him and nodded. 'I'm looking forward to our weekend,' he said, put his arm around her and nuzzled her neck. She felt his stubble tickle her and giggled, just as Mr McKay appeared at the door.

'Excuse me,' he said.

Michael pulled away and Kate did her best not to look like a guilty schoolgirl. In fact, she found herself having to suppress a smile since Mr McKay's face clearly showed his confusion as well as his disapproval. She could imagine him trying to decide if she was two-timing Elliot or had moved on, slut-like, to a new man. Since it wasn't his business, she smiled at him. 'Yes, Mr McKay?'

'There seems to be a problem with the Reilly twins,' Mr McKay told her. Kate could see him forcing himself to keep his eyes off Michael.

'I know,' she told him. 'I had them in my office and we had a talk about it. Mr McKay, I would like to introduce Dr Michael Atwood.'

175

Mr McKay nodded curtly in Michael's general direction, but turned back to Kate. 'I know you saw them,' Mr McKay told her. 'But apparently they pulled a switcheroo again.'

'Oops,' Kate said. 'I guess I will have to do some more in-depth work with them.'

'I guess you will,' Mr McKay rapped out, then turned and disappeared.

Michael looked at Kate. 'Oops?' he asked. 'Is that a Freudian or a Jungian term?'

Kate had to laugh, though she felt some embarrassment and concern. Well, she would deal with it on Monday. Now she had to deal with her changed plans for the weekend.

As they walked out of the school and passed the playground, Kate took Michael's hand. 'I'm so glad you came to the school,' Kate said. 'It gives us some extra time together.' Michael nodded and smiled. So much for the setup, Kate thought. 'The thing is, Michael, I have to go out tomorrow night.'

'Tomorrow night? But it's Saturday.'

'I know. But it's Bina . . .'

'Oh. Bina.'

'It will just be for a few hours,' Kate told him.

'A few hours on Saturday night,' Michael said, and Kate could hear the reproach in his voice. They always spent the weekend together and on Sunday, after the ritual reading of the *New York Times*, parted at about two o'clock. Kate had learned not to extend the stay at his apartment, nor try to keep him at hers. Michael's Sunday afternoons and evenings were reserved for work, but she knew his Saturday nights were reserved for her.

'I'm sorry,' she said. 'It's not going to be fun. I just have to.' As she voiced the words, she felt annoyed with herself and him. She didn't have to apologize. Why did she feel so guilty? It was a small change and it wouldn't hurt him to learn to be a little more flexible.

Michael nodded, then looked down at his shoes for a

moment. Kate watched him adjust and then he put his hand in his pocket. He held it out to her and opened his fist. There, nestled on the pink palm of his hand were two shiny keys on a new key ring. 'Well,' he said, 'I'm glad I got these for you. It'll make Saturday more convenient. You can let yourself in to my place.'

Kate took the keys as if they were a piece of jewelry. Indeed, exchanging keys was the equivalent of getting pinned decades ago. It was a sign of trust, and commitment. 'Oh, Michael,' Kate said, taking the keys. She kissed him, and then realized that she would now have to give her keys to him. She also realized that she didn't really like the idea.

The next evening, a guilty Kate and a now hot, trendy Bina met Elliot and Brice at Kate's apartment to begin their trek into Brooklyn. Kate looked down at her own simple blue knit dress – short but with a turtle neck – and felt distinctly under-dressed, though she knew it was flattering. Steven had liked it. Then she reminded herself this was about Bina, not her. Billy meant nothing to her.

'This is even better than that trip to Nevis last fall,' Brice said. 'The cultures of indigenous people always fascinated me.'

Kate cleared her throat to catch Brice's attention and gave Bina a sideways glance. Bina, however, was too absorbed in trying to learn to walk in the 'fuck me' sandals to notice Brice's comment. Brice, taking pity on Bina's poor soul, not to mention poor soles, cocked his head and said, 'Think up, dear. Lift! Lift!'

Kate, just for a moment, tried to imagine how a corporate lawyer knew all the drag tricks of the trade, which Brice did, but put that thought out of her mind.

Meanwhile, Bina jerked her shoulders up higher and in just a moment the look of total concentration on her face passed into a smile. She took a few tentative steps, then walked around Kate's small living room almost confidently. 'Hey!

177

Wow!' she exclaimed. 'Thanks, Brice. That really works.'

Kate couldn't resist. 'Brice?' she asked. 'Where did you learn about walking in stilettos?'

'Let us draw a veil across those things unnecessary to expose,' Brice said with Victorian hauteur.

'Oh, tell them. He used to be the lead singer of Destiny's Child before Beyoncé pushed him out,' Elliot told her. Bina opened her eyes wide, but Kate tipped her off with a headshake.

'Enough. We're going to be late meeting the girls,' Elliot said.

'I thought we *were* the girls.' Brice pretended to pout.

'Hey, is there a party going on?' The voice, muffled by the door, but clearly Max's, stopped the conversation. Elliot, closest to the entrance, reached out and turned the knob. Max, stopped in the hallway with his dry cleaning hooked over his shoulder and a bag of take-out in his other hand, now stared across Kate's living room at Bina. His eyes moved up and down and Kate watched as both his hands opened in surprise, and both the take-out and the slippery plastic-wrapped dry cleaning fell to the floor. For a moment, despite the spills, Max couldn't pull his eyes away. 'Bina?' he asked. 'Is that you?' Then, as if waking from a spell, he looked down, flushing with embarrassment. He crouched down to pick up the hangers while Elliot went for the plastic containers of what looked like Chinese food which had scattered but, thankfully, not opened.

'Hi, Max,' Bina said. Kate had to turn away from the wreckage in the hallway because she could hardly believe it was Bina who had managed to pack so much flirtatiousness into the two syllables simply with her tone. In all the years she had known her, Kate had never heard a coy sentiment escape Bina's lips. But there was definitely something new, some come-hither timbre packed into her words which made Kate believe that perhaps Bina could just manage to nail a date with Billy Nolan.

'Here's your dinner,' Elliot said cheerfully to Max, handing the bag back to him. 'Gotta go.'

Right. No more distractions. Kate grabbed her purse and ushered Bina out the door behind Brice's broad back. Unfortunately, she had to stop to lock the door and in the moment it took her to do so, Max, still immobilized, asked Bina, 'What happened to you?'

Bina opened her mouth but before she could put her sandaled foot in it Brice intervened. 'Only I and her hairdresser know for sure. Toodles.' He took Bina's hand and led her to the stairs.

As Kate followed them she turned and saw Max, still frozen, above her. 'Don't worry. It isn't Bina,' she told him. 'It's Bina's evil twin.'

Once in Brooklyn, for some reason known only to himself, Elliot told the cab to stop on an inauspicious corner in Williamsburg. There wasn't a bodega, much less a bar anywhere to be seen. It was an industrial neighborhood of converted warehouse factories, and a few dilapidated private homes that had become the hot place for twenty-somethings who had been priced out of Manhattan. On her forays to clubs and galleries there, Kate had actually found herself feeling old and out of place. She also couldn't figure out the geography, or even which way was north or south, east or west. 'Do you know where this place is?' she asked now in bewilderment.

'Sure,' Elliot said. 'It's just a block or two. And I need some time to coach Bina.' Turning to her, he said, 'Now remember, if you want this to work you have to remember LAID.'

Kate spun around in horror. 'Is that part of your research, too?' she asked. 'If that's a requirement we may as well go home now. Bina already made it clear that she's not going to sleep with that man.'

'I thought I didn't have to go to bed for this to work,' Bina whined. 'I love Jack and don't . . .'

179

'Although I can't be certain, evidence leads me to believe that neither the repressed lesbian nor the nun-to-be had intercourse with Billy Nolan,' Elliot informed them.

'I can't believe you!' Kate exclaimed. 'How do you . . .'

'Oh, calm down both of you,' Elliot interrupted. 'Not laid, LAID. L-A-I-D,' he spelled. 'God, I hate acronyms. They're so military and butch. Lick, Arouse, Ignore and Disturb.'

'What am I supposed to lick, Elliot?' Bina asked him, her voice very tentative.

'Your lips,' Elliot answered.

'And that's all you lick, Missy,' Kate added, like a disapproving mother.

'And that will arouse him?' Bina asked.

'I can't guarantee it would work on me,' Elliot said, 'but, yes, it appears that most straight men are aroused when their dates lick their lips.'

'I know *I* am,' Brice offered.

'And what do I ignore?' Bina wondered, missing the joke.

'Him!' Elliot answered, as if to say 'Uh, duh!'

'And why?' Kate demanded, not liking this acronym at all. She was only afraid that Billy would ignore Bina and the entire plan would fall apart, Bina along with it. 'Why should Bina ignore him?'

'Because he obviously has intimacy issues,' Elliot explained, turning to Kate with exasperation. 'God! You're the shrink, not me.'

'I don't get it,' Bina admitted.

'If you ignore him, he won't be afraid of you,' Elliot said, turning back to her and speaking very gently, as if to a child. 'And if he's not afraid, he'll ask you out – and maybe even again after that. We just have to get past the two point seven month requirement.'

'Fine,' Bina said good-naturedly, 'I've licked, I've aroused, and I've ignored. What was next?'

'Disturb,' Elliot answered.

'That should be easy,' Kate told them. 'Just tell him why we're doing this. I think Billy Nolan would find this whole idea very disturbing.'

'But not *too* disturbing,' Elliot told Bina, pointedly ignoring Kate's comment. 'Try to be just disturbing enough to be a challenge, but not challenging enough to be a turn-off. You get it?' he asked.

'I think so,' Bina stammered, obviously trying to sort out all of the advice, keep the acronym in order, walk on the broken sidewalk and keep a smile on her face.

'Well, come on, kids,' Brice said as he flagged down another cab. 'The Bitches and Billy are waiting!' He looked them over and started to laugh. 'This is a little like the Osbournes visiting Sesame Street.'

The cab pulled up to the subway stop at Bedford Street, where they had all agreed to meet. Bev and Barbie were already there. Bev was looking *very*, *very* pregnant while Barbie appeared to have raided the closet of a fifteen-year-old girl without regard for the difference in size.

'I haven't had a night out with the girls in I don't know how long,' Bev squealed.

'Me, either. Biological girls at least,' Elliot said, looking lovingly over at Brice, who had immediately gotten into a 'deep' conversation with Barbie about hemlines.

'We're going to meet Bunny at the bar,' Bev told them.

'Isn't she newly married?' Kate asked in disbelief. 'They're barely back from their honeymoon. Doesn't she want to spend her weekend with Arnie?' Once the words were out of her mouth she realized how her new culture was colliding with her old.

'Hey, she just got married to him and finished their honeymoon. How much do you expect?' Bev asked. In the darkness Kate had to smile. The gang had a very split but pragmatic view of marriage: that it was necessary to have but easy to

181

ignore. The girls hung with the girls and the guys hung with the guys.

Kate, looking at her motley crew, was having serious doubts about the whole expedition. Even if the outfit and hair were great, Bina looked very uncomfortable. Kate quietly pulled her away from the rest of the group. 'Bina, you don't have to do this,' she said in a near whisper. 'I know you really love Jack and I really believe he loves you. This is just a momentary aberration.'

'Is that Manhattan for "fucking around"?' Bina asked bitterly. Apparently the new look also put a slight new edge on Bina's personality.

They continued to walk down Bedford, which looked more and more disreputable.

'He probably regrets what he said,' Kate said, trying to talk her out of the whole thing. 'He'll call.'

'Kate,' Bina began. 'After I've dedicated six years to him he wants to explore his singleness. Who does he think he is? Ponce de León?' She looked over at Bev. And more specifically, Bev's swelling belly. 'Neither of us has found the fountain of youth. Don't you worry about your biological clock?'

Elliot, having heard the entire conversation, chose this moment to interject. 'Like every modern girl,' he said, putting his arm around Kate, 'Kate has had her eggs frozen for future reference.'

'You have?' Bina said in awe.

'Really?' Barbie joined in.

'Don't listen to him. He's crazy,' Kate told them as if his nonsense didn't embarrass her although a telltale blush had pinked her cheeks. 'Anyway, where the hell is this place?' she asked, diverting the attention away from her frozen eggs and on to the task at hand.

Bev looked down at the piece of paper in her hand. She had to squint because of the near darkness. 'I think we turn

182

down at the next corner.' She indicated a side street. Kate was very grateful for the company of Brice and Elliot now. 'Bunny gave me these directions. I know it's here somewhere,' Bev said. They turned the corner. 'There should be a barber's pole . . .'

'A barber's pole?' Kate asked, raising her eyebrows.

'Yeah, it's a converted barber shop!' Barbie informed her.

'There it is!' Brice pointed down the block to a barely visible red, blue and white striped pole.

'How did you ever notice that? It must be because you're a Taurus. They are very talented at acquiring sight,' Bev said.

'Oh, honey. It's not the stars,' Brice said with a smirk. 'If there is a pole, I can find it!'

21

'Since I'm supposed to meet Billy here, I'm buying.' Bina's voice cut through Kate's thoughts. 'What's everybody drinking? Beers?'

'Not for me, beer gives me gas,' Bev said, 'and no alcohol for the baby. You know, sometimes, alcohol that the mother drinks can affect the baby,' she said, patting her swell.

'Really? I would have never thought,' Elliot said, not bothering to conceal his sarcasm. 'Beer for everyone and a Shirley Temple for the mother-to-be,' he told Bina.

'Okay,' she said, 'so now what do I do?'

'I'll help,' Kate offered. 'The rest of you see if you can find us a table. And if we're not back in ten minutes, send a search party.'

Kate led Bina through the crowd to the bar. 'Try to get Billy's attention,' Kate said. Kate could see Billy Nolan down at the end of the bar. His white shirt emphasized both his wide shoulders and his tan. Kate wondered, briefly, if he was so vain that he went to a tanning parlor, but there wasn't time for much reflection. 'Call him,' Kate told Bina.

'Call him what?' Bina asked.

Unfortunately, at that moment an older man, balding and with a beer belly, came at them from the other end of the bar.

'What will it be, ladies?'

'Ohmigod!' Bina whispered to Kate. 'That's not him.'

'Great pick-up line,' Kate told Bina. Then, turning to the bartender, she said, 'Thanks anyway, we're just looking.'

'Okay, Red. But if you're looking for a guy to buy you a drink, look no further.'

Kate hated it when anyone called her 'Red' or 'Carrot Top' or 'Freckles' or any of the names she'd lived with in her childhood. Anyway, her freckles had faded and her hair had darkened into what she liked to think of as auburn. But what dumb bartender would offer a drink to 'Auburn'?

'Don't worry,' she told Bina, 'we'll get to him.'

Kate did a quick scan of the crowd at the bar. It was clear that it was far busier at Billy's end, and that a gaggle of girls had monopolized the stools, while she could barely see Billy. She grabbed Bina and pulled her through the crowd to the other end of the room, and then, mostly by pushing and a couple of shoulder moves, got the two of them right up to the bar again, this time at the right place.

As she waited to be served, Kate had time to look around. They were almost crushed at the packed bar. She sighed. She felt way too old for the bar scene. Did that mean she was getting old at thirty-one? At least this place was a little more imaginative than most, she had to admit that. The old barber chairs, obviously restored, were still screwed into the black-and-white marble floor, and the bar, a dark mahogany, was backed by what must have been the original mirror and shelves of the barber shop. Among the vodkas and malt Scotches lined up, there were also antique shaving cups and old bottles of hair tonic, aftershave and the like. The place had obviously been expanded from the original shop. Aside from the bar and the row of chairs where people were clustered, there were banquettes along the far wall, and tables and booths in the back.

Above the noise she heard a middle-aged bartender holler,

'Hey, Laurie! Long time no see. What you been up to?'

'I found a real man, Pete,' the Laurie person's voice told him. 'Meet Ralphie.'

Kate had to smile. She, like Ralph, would have an 'ie' added to her name. It must happen when you crossed Court Street, because it wasn't the case in Brooklyn Heights.

'You owe me a drink at least,' Laurie said.

'How about champagne?' the bartender offered. 'You used to like it when I popped your cork.'

'Well, this time you can pop it up your ass,' Laurie told him.

'Ah, the wit of the boroughs,' Elliot murmured in Kate's ear, making her jump. 'See. I knew this would be fun,' he said.

Kate couldn't help herself. She had to see what kind of people could be so vulgar in a public place, even if it was a bar. But when she turned her head to look, she was surprised to see that Laurie and Ralph didn't look a whole lot different from her and Michael. She thanked God that she had chosen not to bring him, despite his hurt feelings.

'You must have picked up those moves in Manhattan,' Elliot commented on her push through to the bar.

'There are a lot of things I've picked up in Manhattan,' Kate replied.

'Now, get to work,' Elliot whispered urgently, and hurried away back to the others.

Bina looked behind Kate. 'Ohmigod! It's really him.'

Kate kept her back to the bar, facing away from Billy and toward Bina. 'Yep. Elvis has not left the building. Get on my left and get his attention,' she commanded and hoped it would work.

'What comes first?' Bina whispered desperately. 'Was it the lick or the annoy?'

'Just call his name and order our beer,' Kate demanded, turning toward the bar to help her. Billy, his teeth as white as his luminous shirt, his hair more golden than

Kate remembered, finished pouring a drink for another customer. 'Say something,' Kate whispered and gave Bina a hard elbow.

'Billy! Here,' Bina gasped. Perhaps he heard her urgency because he came right over to Bina.

'What'll it be, ladies?' he asked, flashing his perfect Crest commercial smile. Kate turned away but it was too late. Billy looked straight into her face and she didn't think it was her imagination that she saw his eyes change in recognition. She elbowed Bina again.

'Two pitchers of Shirley Temples and a beer,' Bina sputtered, and then flushed bright red.

'Better line, but not effective,' Kate said softly to Bina, who had apparently frozen with an exaggerated smile, her eyes bulging.

Billy narrowed his eyes for a moment and searched Kate's face but Kate was careful to keep hers perfectly blank and slightly behind Bina's, hoping he wouldn't remember her. 'Is this for a whole table of designated drivers and one drunk?' Billy smirked. He ignored Bina's embarrassed giggle and looked directly at Kate.

'It's two pitchers of beer and one Shirley Temple,' Kate replied, not as amused.

Billy wouldn't take his eyes off Kate. 'At the risk of sounding like a cliché,' he began, which sounded like a cliché in itself to Kate, 'have we met before?'

'I think you met my friend, Bina. At Bunny and Arnie's wedding,' Kate said. 'Bina, this is Billy.' Kate noticed how Billy did not even look at Bina, but rather kept his gaze on her. Her face felt hot under his stare.

'Nice to meet you,' Billy said to Bina without so much as a nod in her direction. 'But you and I,' he said, still looking intently at Kate, 'we met . . .'

'Bina lives here in Brooklyn, too,' Kate interrupted, pulling her eyes away from him and focusing on her friend.

'Oh, yeah? Nearby?' Billy asked, glancing over at Bina for the first time.

'Well, kind of. In Bensonhurst,' Bina replied, much too anxious.

Billy began to pour the two pitchers of beer. 'Hey, there's a big difference between Bensonhurst and Williamsburg, Reina.'

'Bina, her name is Bina,' Kate said. Who did this guy think he was anyway?

Billy shrugged and handed over the tray with the drinks on it. Kate took the tray and hustled Bina to the table where the rest of the group was sitting.

'That was him!' Bina exclaimed.

'Who?' Elliot said slyly.

'HIM!' Bina squealed.

'Mel Gibson?' Bev asked, playing along.

'Bill Clinton?' Barbie joined in.

'If so, honey, tell him if he comes back to be our president he can have all the interns he wants,' Brice said. Brice didn't exactly feel positive about what he called 'the Bush league' and was verbal about it.

'It was Billy,' Kate said aside to Elliot, 'but he didn't have the ightest-slay interest-ay.' Elliot grimaced at Kate's ridiculous Pig Latin message. Bina was going to need all the help she could get. 'Well, here are your pitchers, ladies,' Kate said, handing over the tray. 'I'm going to run to the bathroom.'

Kate made her way through the crowd to the tiny one-stall bathroom. It was surprisingly clean. Kate had just entered when she heard two voices outside.

'Hey, did you see the way that redhead looked at me?' one voice said. It was that bartender, the middle-aged guy named Pete. 'Man, she's hot! Did you see the eyes on that girl? And she had two other beautiful things.' Evidently, he was talking about Kate.

'What redhead?' Kate recognized Billy's voice immediately.

'The one who carried off those two pitchers of beer,' Pete said.

'She wasn't looking at you,' Billy said, thinly veiling his contempt of Pete's illusions.

'You know,' Pete grunted, 'you do all right for yourself but sometimes you miss the subtleties. She wants me.'

Kate heard Billy groan and the two were quiet for a moment. Then Billy's voice broke the silence. 'Susie was in earlier.'

'Shit!' she heard the other man curse. 'And I missed her. She was so fucking hot. Why did you dump her?'

'I dunno,' Billy answered. 'Anyway, she comes in and tells me that . . .'

'Don't tell me,' the other guy interrupted, 'she's engaged, right?'

'How did you know?' Billy asked.

'Billy – buddy, look. I don't know what it is that you do to these women, but once you date them they become like marriage roach motels. Other guys check in but they don't check out.'

Kate was finished, and she really didn't want to hear any more of what they had to say, but even as she flushed, washed her hands, and hit the dryer button, she could still hear the men talking.

'Usually it wouldn't bother me,' Billy said, 'but I was at Arnie's wedding a few weeks ago and I realized that I'm like the last single guy out of all my friends.'

'You're a bartender,' the other guy said. 'Bartenders are supposed to be single. You're not the marrying type. Besides, what's happening with Tina?'

Kate didn't need to hear any more. She was just glad that Elliot wasn't there to listen. She opened the door quickly, hoping to get back to the table before Billy and his friend were finished with their break, but she was moving too late. Just as she stepped into the passage beyond the restroom door, she found herself face to face with Billy Nolan.

189

'Whoa! Slow down, Red,' he said as Kate tried to continue on her way without speaking. She ignored him. Then he actually reached out and touched her arm. 'We met at the wedding, didn't we, Doctor?' The hallway was narrow and a guy pushed past them and nudged her up against Billy. He steadied her with a hand on each shoulder and looked at the passing customer. 'Hey, watch it,' he shouted. He looked again at Kate. '*Je pense . . .*' He stopped. '*Je n'oublie pas,*' he said, slipping back into French.

What was it with this guy and French? Kate wondered. 'I haven't forgotten you either,' she admitted, but as a throwaway line.

'Right. We discussed existential issues. I always like to combine Sartre and weddings,' he added, and Kate couldn't resist smiling though she tried. This guy was impossibly self-assured. How could she entice him to date Bina? 'So what are you doing on this side of the river?' Billy asked.

'Having a drink with my friends in that corner,' Kate said, pointing to their table. Just then the big-bellied bartender tapped Billy on the shoulder from behind.

'Yo, Bill,' he said. 'Forget the conquest. I can't carry the bar by myself.'

Kate blushed against her will, angry at the thought of being considered 'a conquest'. As if. 'See ya,' she said. And forced herself to give him an enticing smile.

Kate returned to their table and hoped the hook had worked. Sure enough, just moments after their glasses were empty and Barbie had refreshed Bina's lip gloss, Billy appeared at their table, a pitcher of beer in each hand. 'Welcome,' he said and put the pitchers down. He smiled at Kate. 'So, you weren't lying about your posse at the wedding.'

All eyes at the table focused on Kate. She hadn't mentioned their little *pas de deux* on the terrace to anyone. Now, she regretted that. Across the table, Kate saw Bev dig an elbow into Bina's side.

190

'Hey, Billy,' Bunny said, 'business looks real good.'

'You gotta pretty full crowd,' Bev said approvingly. 'And dancing.'

'Yeah,' Billy said and then looked back at Kate. 'We do a little "Hokey Pokey".'

'Don't you get a night off?' Bev asked.

'Usually Saturdays. But one of my guys called in sick. Lucky I was here and got to see all you beauties,' Billy said.

Above the general noise, the middle-aged bartender bellowed, 'Yo, Billy! This ain't a one-man band. Where's Joey?'

Billy didn't turn around. Bunny, clearly desperate, grabbed his hand. 'This is my friend Bina,' she said. 'You two ought to get together.'

Billy looked at Bina blankly for a moment. 'Yeah. Nice to meet you.' He turned back to Kate who felt desperate herself.

'How about bowling with Bina and me next Wednesday?' she asked.

He blinked, then smiled. 'I wouldn't have guessed you for the bowling type,' he said.

Barbie, always prepared, pushed Bina's phone number scribbled on a piece of paper into Billy's hand. 'Here,' she said. 'Give Bina a call to set it up.' There was another yell from the bar and this time Billy turned.

'Coming,' he said and gave the group another dazzling smile before he disappeared into the crowd.

'My God,' Brice said. 'He's gorgeous. Can I come too?'

Elliot gave Brice a look, then turned back to Kate and gave her a more searching one. Before he could say anything Bev began to high-five everyone at the table. Next, Kate thought, they'd do The Wave. 'Nice work,' Barbie said, slapping Kate's palm.

'Good save,' Bunny agreed.

'I think he believes he's going out with you, Kate,' Brice said.

'Well,' she told the table, 'he'll find out differently when he meets Michael. Anyway, he has Bina's number.'

'Thanks, Katie,' Bina said, and looked totally exhausted. Kate smiled at her but wondered how she would talk Michael into a Wednesday night of bowling.

22

Kate felt guilty as she pressed the buzzer before she remembered she had Michael's keys. She silently cursed herself. She checked her watch and was even more concerned when she realized it was already a quarter to one. She was sure he was sleeping, and equally sure she had more beer on her breath than she would like him to smell. Somehow it was all right to go out with friends because of obligation but not to have a good time.

When Michael came to the door, still dressed but obviously rubbing the sleep out of his eyes, she greeted him with a quick hug and passed him in the narrow foyer.

'You shouldn't have waited up,' she said. What she meant was she should have gone home to her own apartment or, better yet, not gone to Brooklyn at all.

But Michael just yawned and stretched. 'Time to go to bed,' he said. Kate agreed with a nod but headed to the bathroom.

'I have to pee,' she said.

Once she had the door closed, she washed her face, brushed her teeth, gargled and then brushed her teeth again. She caught a glimpse of herself in the mirror as she reached for the face towel and stopped. She looked so . . . furtive. For a moment Kate saw – in her jaw, the set of her eyes, and her hairline – a frightening similarity to her father. It sent a shiver through her. Then she realized that rather than physical resemblance it was the guilty, skulking body language and expression that had conjured up his long-dormant image. She stood immobile under the light of the bare bulb in Michael's bachelor bathroom and looked herself in the eye. *You have nothing to be guilty about,* she told herself. *If Michael is rigid with his schedule there is no reason for you to feel guilty. Having drinks with your girlfriends is nothing to feel guilty about.*

But Kate knew it wasn't just that. Her thoughts of Billy Nolan were unsettling. She didn't want those thoughts; she didn't want the feeling she had had as she flirted with him. And even if she had done it for Bina, and even if she was only tricking Billy, the fact was she had acted as if she were making a date with another man and the other man believed it. Wasn't that kind of cheating on Michael? She thought about Jennifer and her lies to members of her fifth-grade class. Raised as a Catholic while her mother was alive, Kate had never quite gotten over the concept of sins of commission as well as sins of omission. Was she guilty of the latter? But how could she possibly discuss this with Michael?

Now she was returning to sleep with her lover and she felt uncomfortably like a slut. It wasn't the beer on her breath or the smell of cigarette smoke on her clothes that embarrassed her. It was her own feelings that she felt ashamed of.

Kate washed quickly and emerged from the bathroom in her panties and bra. As she walked into Michael's bedroom she was dismayed to see that he was completely undressed under the sheet and had lit the candle on his nightstand. Michael usually slept in pajama bottoms and a T-shirt. The lack of them and the lighted candle was almost always a sign of desire.

'May I borrow a shirt?' Kate asked meekly.

Michael nodded and gestured to the bureau. She took out

a plain white Fruit of the Loom and slipped into it, then slid into bed beside him.

'Was it fun?' Michael asked, putting his arm around her.

'Not really,' Kate said. 'And I'm so exhausted.' She paused. Michael was good with this kind of sexual nuance. She waited a minute. 'Can we just spoon?' she asked and turned her back to him, feeling his chest against her shoulder blades.

'Sure,' Michael said and Kate was relieved not to hear disappointment in his voice. He shifted for a moment, blew out the candle and pressed his body up to hers. Kate sighed, and either out of shame, exhaustion or too much beer, she closed her eyes and was asleep in moments.

Kate woke up slightly hung over on Sunday morning and took two aspirins, washing them down with club soda. She and Michael then fell into their comforting and usual ritual; he had gotten the *New York Times* and bagels, and they spent two hours reading bits of paper to one another and nibbling on cream cheese and pumpernickel. Kate opened the Styles section to read a continuation of a story about beauty parlors in Afghanistan and accidentally ran into the Weddings/ Celebration page. It was something she tried to avoid, something unsettling like stepping around a dead pigeon on the sidewalk. A picture caught her eye. Two men, their heads cocked toward each other, had celebrated a commitment ceremony in Woodstock, Vermont. Kate thought of Elliot and Brice. Since the *Times* had begun running gay couples on their wedding page, the two of them read them, usually laughing hysterically. This one, she had to agree was pretty silly. 'Listen to this, Michael,' she said. *'We met through a personal ad.* Can you believe it? *He wrote "NICE JEWISH BOY 22. The kind your mother would love." And we had coffee and then dinner and went out the next night and we've been together ever since.'*

'That's nice,' Michael said, absently.

'I think it's dreadful,' Kate said. 'Publicly admitting that

195

you met through a personal is bad enough, but bragging about it . . . pathetic.' As if in punishment for her judgmental comments she then went on to read the rest of the section, as she always had to when she forgot to avoid it. It was a bad mistake. Column after column describing happy unions, listing the groom's parents, the bride's family, with quotes from their siblings and descriptions of the celebrations always left her feeling depressed and different from everybody else. If she married Michael, what would the *Times* possibly run about her wedding? 'The bride, close to her 32nd birthday and an orphan, had elected to have a small wedding. "I couldn't really afford a big party, and I don't have enough family and friends to attend one," Katherine Jameson-Atwood said. "In fact, I'm not sure I'm doing the right thing, but then, who is?"' She covertly looked over the top of the paper at Michael and wondered how he would look in one of the grainy gray photos, his head leaned toward hers. She closed the paper and put it aside.

Restless, she got up and went to the window. Michael's building, a large white brick post-war complex, consisted of several hundred boring apartments, but the views from the upper floors were spectacular. She looked out the window down at Turtle Bay. She could even see a glimmer of the East River. 'It looks like it's clouding over,' she said.

Michael came up behind her and wrapped one arm around her chest and shoulder, like a high collar on a coat. 'Well,' he said, 'we could either go out and competitively skateboard or we could lie down in the bedroom. The choice is yours.'

Kate laughed and let him take her hand, leading her to the bed, though she wasn't certain she was in the mood. But when they were lying down and he had undressed her, Kate relaxed into his kisses. When he bit her, gently, on the back of her neck it sent a pleasant shiver down her spine. She began to forget herself in the trance of sexual pleasure that began to rise slowly like a tide at full moon. She felt his hands slide over her, deft and knowing, if a little predictable. When he rolled from his side on top of her she wanted him. Swept away by the rhythm of his movements and her hungry response, Kate felt good for the first time that weekend. She closed her eyes and had the delightful feeling of an irresistible orgasm about to take place. At the edge she whispered, 'Yes.' She squeezed her eyes shut and then Billy Nolan's face flashed before her, as clear as it had been the night before. She caught her breath and groaned, but it was not with pleasure.

When Michael came, Kate realized – to her dismay – that she was relieved.

As they lay there together Kate thought about the bowling plan. She couldn't imagine Michael running down the lane, but she had to go with him or Billy would continue to believe that she was his date. She couldn't take Elliot, because any man could tell there were no vibes between them – at least not the sexual kind. And her guilt compelled her to end the charade as quickly as possible. 'Michael,' she whispered. 'Are you asleep?'

'Not quite,' he murmured.

'I want to ask you something.'

He turned to her with that deer-in-the-headlights look men got when they thought you were going to talk about 'the relationship'.

'How do you feel about bowling?' Kate asked.

23

'Pee-yeuw!' Bina said as she, Kate and Michael struggled to get their rented bowling shoes on.

'STRIKE!'

'You lucky sonofabitch!' Behind them some blue-collar bowlers were either in a fierce bowling or a drinking competition – or perhaps both.

They were at Bowl-a-Rama. The noise was thunderous as pins fell and madmen screamed. 'The thrill of victory, the agony of defeat!' Kate chirped, echoing a television sports show intro line.

'The agony of de feet is only starting,' Michael quipped. Kate knew how fastidious he was, and the idea of putting her own foot into these skeevey bowling shoes gave Kate the willies. It seemed that Bina had qualms too, but they were more fashion-related.

'Do you think this red goes with my outfit?' she asked Kate nervously.

'Sure,' Kate told her, though the shoes were hideous, as was Bina's new outfit. Kate could see that Barbie had 'helped' in dressing Bina for the big occasion.

Thinking of that, Kate scanned the crowd, looking for Billy Nolan. All was chaos. In the lanes next to them, a league was

198

just finishing up and the clash of orange and brown shirts was almost nauseating to look at. Kate herself was wearing a simple white shirt and jeans while Michael was wearing a sports coat, perhaps the only sports coat in a ten-block radius.

Bina stood up. Kate reassessed her outfit and realized that the short black miniskirt would reveal all when Bina bent over to release the ball. Her green clingy top was set off by a fuchsia scarf, Barbie's trademark color. Unfortunately for Bina, the scarf reflected onto her face, giving it a mauve cast that clashed with the blouse. Oh, well, Kate thought, nothing would make this double date from hell work anyway.

They were assigned an alley and as they slipped into the molded plastic seats Michael, ever the gentleman, asked if they would like something to drink. Bina asked for a cola and, before she thought about it, Kate ordered a beer. She imagined that Michael raised his brows before he went off to get them.

The moment he was gone, Bina turned to her. 'Where is he, Katie?' she asked, eyeing the entrance. 'He said he'd be here on time. Maybe he's going to stand me up. Oh, I'm so nervous.'

'Calm down, honey,' Kate said. 'He'll be here.' In truth, Kate was nervous herself. She knew she had deceived Billy, though Bina hadn't a clue. And if she couldn't make the transition gracefully and make it look as if any confusion was a natural mistake on Billy's part she was afraid of the fallout. Billy Nolan wasn't going to be thrilled when he realized that he'd been tricked into an evening with Bina.

'God, I'm sweating through my blouse,' Bina said. 'I'm going to run to the ladies' room and check my makeup one more time.' She stood up and wound her way through the bobbing heads and fat bellies in the crowd that milled around the lanes and the bar. Kate noticed that many heads turned, but probably not the heads most women would strive to turn.

199

Michael returned with the beverages and Kate saw he had also bought some snacks.

'Bina's looking, um, different since the last time I saw her,' Michael stammered.

'Well, I think you only saw her when she was having a case of the hysterical fantods,' Kate reminded him.

'No, that's not what I mean,' Michael said. 'She looks . . . jazzier.'

'Please! She looks like she belongs in the cast of *42nd Street*,' Kate told him. She realized she sounded as tense as she felt. She put her arm out and took Michael's hand. 'It was sweet of you to come,' she said. 'Launching Bina in her new life is really important after what she's been through.'

'Well, it didn't seem to take her long to recover,' Michael said. He sat down and picked up a paper cup of soda. For a moment Kate felt irritation. Because of her background she had always looked for a man who was sober, but perhaps never drinking at all was a bad thing. It occurred to her for the first time that Michael might be terribly afraid of losing control.

He squeezed her hand. 'It was sweet to see you at work,' he told her. 'I suppose that you could do that anywhere. Or even have a private practice.'

It seemed to Kate, wondering if his comment was significant, that in the midst of the apocalyptic surroundings a discussion of career moves might be difficult. 'I like working in the school setting,' she said. 'You get more feedback about behavior and change.'

As he didn't say anything, she craned her neck looking first to the ladies' room and then to the door, hoping that this mad scheme with Billy would work out. At that moment, Billy walked into the bowling alley. He spotted Kate before she could even raise her hand and walked over to their lane. Damn Bina, Kate thought. It was going to be difficult enough to subtly show him who his date was; now it would be virtually impossible. What the hell was Bina doing in the ladies' room for so long, taking a shower?

Kate introduced Billy to Michael. They shook hands. Kate couldn't help but notice how incredibly attractive Billy looked. He was wearing very old black jeans and a slightly clingy T-shirt of the same color that revealed the body of a natural athlete. She could see his arms, and figured the guy didn't have two percent body fat. Typical narcissist, she thought. He must be a gym rat to have that kind of biceps definition. And she was amused to see that he had his own equipment. She hadn't known anybody who owned their own bowling ball in fifteen years.

Billy dropped his bowling bag on the seat next to Kate. 'Let's rock and bowl!' he said, looking down at her a little too intensely.

Kate stood up quickly, scanning the bowling alley. 'Bina will be back in a moment,' she told him.

'Fine,' Billy said, clearly not at all interested in Bina's whereabouts. To her alarm he put his arm around Kate's shoulder. 'Hey, you look great,' he said, his voice way too personal.

Kate quickly stepped out of his embrace and moved closer to Michael, who was still seated. She put her hand on Michael's shoulder. Billy paused for a moment, then sat down and began to put on his own shoes. Kate, feeling both guilty and awkward, sat down beside Michael. Michael, as if in response to Billy's overly warm greeting, put his arm across the back of the seats and rested it on her shoulder. Kate prayed for Bina's arrival.

Billy looked up from his laces and eyed the two of them. 'You two just meet?' he asked. 'Or are you related?'

'No. We've been going out for a while now,' Michael replied innocently. Kate thought she saw Billy's face color up but he looked down again at his shoes.

Just then, to Kate's enormous relief, Bina returned to the

201

lane. She looked as if the entire research staff of Max Factor had worked her face over. A great look for bowling. But when she smiled, her natural warmth showed. 'Well, hey,' she said to Billy, crossed the tile of the bowling pit and sat down beside him.

Billy looked from Kate to Bina. And he looked back across at Kate, along with Michael's proprietorial arm. 'I was afraid you weren't going to make it,' Bina told him. Kate tried to avert her eyes, but not soon enough. From the look on Billy's face, Kate knew that he now understood what was going on and he was clearly unhappy with the territory as it was now staked. She decided to hope for the best.

'Okay,' Kate said, sliding into the double seat behind the scorekeeping board. She quickly entered their information into the keypad and the names lit up on the overhead screens – hers with Michael's and Bina's with Billy's. 'Now we can get started.'

'Yeah,' Billy said, looking at the screen, 'but what are we starting?'

Kate thought she heard some anger or maybe bitterness in his voice but felt it was best to just ignore it.

'We can't start,' Bina whined. 'I haven't found a ball.' She looked at Billy and did everything except bat her eyelashes. 'Would you help me?' she asked. Then she licked her lips.

Kate wondered if she had confused Elliot's ridiculous instructions and was trying to annoy instead of arouse.

Billy shot Kate a look, and it said everything. Then he grabbed Bina's hand and, without ever taking his eyes off Kate, stood up. 'Sure,' he said. 'I'm no expert with balls, except my own, but I'll try. Though it often seems to me that other people have a lot of balls.'

Kate blushed. She knew this type of behavior; she had seen it with her child patients. He was going to act out and make sure she paid for her little deception by being as horrible as possible. Billy and Bina left the pit and Michael waited until they were out of earshot.

'Charming,' Michael said. 'Will he discuss other parts of his anatomy as the night progresses?' He sat beside Kate in the spring seat. 'How long have you known him?' he asked, echoing Billy, consciously or not.

Kate was surprised to feel a slight surge of pleasure at his possessiveness. 'Oh, he picked up Bina at that wedding I went to,' Kate replied.

'A friendly guy. And well-equipped,' was all Michael deigned to say.

Then Bina and Billy returned from the rack. Bina was carrying a hideous-looking bowling ball, blue with patches of fuchsia. 'We finally found a ball that matches my scarf!' Bina said, with what seemed to Kate overdone enthusiasm. 'Billy helped me.' Kate restrained herself from shaking her head. Bina was acting as if the selection of a piece of sporting equipment was akin to slaying a dragon. She held up the hideous ball then nearly dropped it. Kate remembered, all at once, just how klutzy Bina was. 'Klutzy-shmutzy', Mrs Horowitz used to say. 'As long as you get good grades.' Bina then attempted to stick her plump fingers into the tiny holes.

Billy, meanwhile, unzipped his bag and took out a much larger black ball. 'And look,' Billy exclaimed, laying on the sarcasm. 'I found a ball that matches my outfit too!'

Kate, concerned about him hurting Bina's feelings, decided to comment. 'Well, you're wearing all black and you brought your own ball.'

Billy served Kate an insincere smile. 'That did make it less of a challenge.' He looked over at Michael. 'Hey, Mike, how big is your ball?'

'Ten pounds,' Michael answered. 'And I prefer to be called Michael,' he added flatly. Kate saw him narrow his eyes. It was clear that he wasn't enjoying himself. But it seemed as

203

if he also sensed that something was going on between her and Billy.

Bina reached over for her cola. 'I haven't been bowling since Annie Jackson's sixth-grade birthday party. Remember, Katie?'

'How could I forget?' Kate said, smiling at the memory. 'I threw up Pop Rocks all over myself.'

'Oh, yeah!' Bina squealed. 'Gross.' She looked over at Billy and licked her lips again.

Billy joined the two of them at the scoreboard. 'Oh, I don't know,' he said and put his foot down right beside Kate's and on her shoelace. Kate moved her foot away, pulling out the bow. 'I think some women look cute in their own vomit.' Kate, totally nonplussed, pulled her foot up to the seat and quickly retied her shoe.

'Well, I'm sure you've had plenty of opportunity to see it,' Kate said. She turned to Michael. 'Billy works in a bar.'

'Lots of chances at drunken women,' Billy said. 'Right, Mike?'

'Michael,' Michael corrected. 'Not in my experience.'

'Well, owning my own bar, I'm sure I have more experience,' Billy said coolly.

Kate was surprised to hear that Billy owned the Barber Bar if that was, in fact, the truth.

Billy stared her down for a moment and then wrapped his arm around Bina. 'I'm sure I have a lot more experience in quite a few things,' Billy said.

24

'Ouch!' Bina yelled. 'Ow. Ow.' She shook her hand like a limp fish at the end of a pole, then put her index finger into her mouth. Kate hadn't been looking, but as Bina tried to retrieve her ball from the ball return her finger had been crunched by another ball spewed from the maw of the machine.

Billy bent over her hand, taking it in his. 'Are you okay?' he asked. Kate looked away from the two of them engrossed in examining Bina's nail and turned to Michael who was sitting beside her. When she had put together this ridiculous scheme she had thought of Billy and how he might be angry and difficult. She had thought of Bina, and how she might be disappointed. But she hadn't thought of Michael and the effect that a night of Brooklyn bowling might have on him. She put her arm around him. He was morose; a lot quieter than usual and obviously disturbed by his poor performance. While he was not a jock, Michael was fit and played squash regularly, where, she knew, he was a tough competitor. He didn't like to lose.

Kate looked down at the board, then put her head on Michael's shoulder. 'The score doesn't matter,' she cooed, and realized once she had said it that her tone was the one she used when she was talking to her young patients. 'Are you having fun?'

Michael ignored the question, as he so obviously was not. 'I can't believe I'm coming in third,' he said and shook his head. Kate wondered if she should try to do poorly, just so Michael would have a shot at second place, but she knew that her score and Bina's didn't matter. Michael was pissed because Billy was beating him, and doing it by so wide a margin.

Just then, Billy approached them. He picked up his drink from the holder, then shook his head as he observed the scoreboard. 'Well, we're all having a pretty dismal night,' he commented, but Kate thought she saw him smirk as he went up to help Bina prepare for what would almost certainly be yet another gutter ball.

Kate ignored them and turned to Michael. She felt responsible for this and didn't like to see him upset. If she was completely truthful with herself, she'd have to admit she also didn't like to see him bested by Billy. It was foolish, she told herself, to feel that way or to allow Michael to have that view. It was some vestige of the Homo sapiens fight for Alpha male position. 'People often confuse athletic scores with personal identity,' Kate said.

'Sure. When the Cubs lose I feel my world falls apart,' Michael almost sneered.

Michael was from Chicago and the fact was that he did root for the pathetic Cubs each year but they never performed. He didn't mind, he said, because it was just a tradition in his family. Kate felt now was not the time to point out that this wasn't the Cubs pitted against another, superior baseball team. It seemed to be Michael pitted against Billy Nolan. And Michael, in a word from her youth, was getting schmeisted. Despite that, his concern was ridiculous.

'This isn't that hard. I can't believe I haven't rolled a strike.'

'Oh, it's just for fun,' she tried to remind him. 'Bowling was never your game. It's for the working classes. Anyway,' she said, waving toward Bina, who was still at the line dithering. 'No one does worse than Bina.'

Billy, sipping his soft drink, overheard her, grinned and laughed. 'Eye on the head pin, Bina,' he encouraged. Then he put down his cup. 'Hey, wait!' he called. He left the pit and stepped behind her, put his arms around her and changed her stance. Kate, watching them, felt a twinge of what she wouldn't admit was jealousy. Then Bina, guided by Billy, released the ball down the lane – this time with her eyes closed. The group watched as the ball rolled directly down the middle of the lane and almost miraculously knocked over all the pins. Kate's mouth dropped, but not as much as Michael's pride did.

'OHMIGOD! OHMIGOD! I hit them. I hit them all!' Bina shouted.

She did a victory dance which included her reaching both arms up to the ceiling and, incidentally, exposing a significant part of the fuchsia underpants beneath her tiny skirt. Kate watched as bowlers from other lanes smiled, pointed, and gave her a thumbs-up sign. It was at that moment that Kate spotted the Bitches! That was all she needed, for them to come over and congratulate Bina on the bowling and the boyfriend. 'Touchdown!' Bina yelled. Then she gave Billy a big hug. Kate thought she saw him use the opportunity to clutch Bina's butt, though she couldn't be sure because Bina immediately let go of Billy and ran over to Kate. 'I can't believe it! I can't believe it,' Bina said, her arms under Kate's own while she jumped back and forth. 'I knocked them over!' Just then Bina's celebratory embrace knocked the beer out of Kate's hand and all over the front of Michael's shirt.

'Bina, you are on a roll at knocking things over,' Kate said, as Michael jumped up. Kate rose to survey the damage and checked to make sure the Bitches weren't coming over. But Barbie was at the ball return and Bunny seemed to be playing, though Bev sat it out, her hands on her bowling-ball belly. Phew, all was safe, except for Michael.

'I'm so sorry,' Bina said to Michael, flushing bright red. She

207

grabbed for the already damp Bowl-a-Rama cocktail napkin that was lying on the scoreboard top. Michael was holding his shirt out from his body, his elbows extended like a man impersonating a rooster. Kate could see it wasn't only his shirt but also his lap that was wet. Bina began to ineffectually dab at his chest and crotch. Michael took a step backwards. 'No. Let me help. I can get it right out. Club soda on the shirt. Club soda and salt on your pants.' Kate almost smiled in spite of Michael's discomfort. The Horowitz family were experts in removing every stain from every possible material: wine on linen, ballpoint on silk, tar on leather. The list was endless, and often discussed. Kate took Michael's arm. He looked helplessly at her.

'Hurry up,' Bina insisted, taking his other arm. 'We have to do it before the stain sets. Trust me, I know.'

'She does,' Kate said, nodding at him.

'Maybe it's all right,' Michael volunteered, but then looked down at himself. It was anything but.

'Go with her,' Kate said.

'Yeah. Let's get you cleaned up,' Bina told him as she led Michael away from the lane.

Kate watched him go and felt deeply sorry for inviting him. He disappeared into the crowd, like a damaged ship being pulled by a little tug boat. Bina would take care of this. It was her forte. Kate sighed.

'Not Mike's day.' Kate turned around to face Billy, who was leaning on the side of their banquette, his legs crossed and his eyebrows raised. 'Not much of a player.'

'Just because he's in third place . . .' Kate began.

'Last,' Billy interrupted.

'Excuse me?' Kate asked. Billy pointed at the electronic scoreboard. He took a step closer to her. She felt his arm against her shoulder. She also felt heat rise up from her chest to her neck and hoped it wouldn't show as a blush on her face.

'Last,' he said again, and leaned forward to tap the score.

'Since Bina's strike he's in last place.' Kate felt a little lightheaded. Billy Nolan was so very close to her she could smell his soap and the heat of his healthy body. For an insane moment she had an impulse to simply close her eyes and fall into his arms. Instead she took a step away and picked up a bowling ball.

'You're just jealous,' she said, almost panicked and not exactly sure of what she meant.

He turned to face her instead of the score. 'You're right, I am,' he said in a steady voice.

'You are?' Kate asked, but couldn't match his steadiness. She was surprised at this admission.

'Yeah,' Billy said. And then continued, a lot less casually. He lowered his voice but it rose in intensity. 'I thought I was going on this date with you. And you knew that. I can't believe I fell for the old bait and switch, or that you played me that way.'

Kate dropped the ball back into the ball return. Despite the truth of what he said, she felt indignant. She'd done it for the best of reasons, and who was he to claim a higher moral ground? 'You're on a date with my best friend,' she said defensively.

'Really?' Billy asked, his voice heavy with sarcasm. 'Is that what you thought?'

'Yes,' Kate lied. 'And then you insult my boyfriend and come on to me. What is wrong with you?'

'Well, for one thing I like to pick my own women,' Billy said. And he looked her over from head to toe. He paused, took a couple of steps away from her and sat down on the banquette, crossing an ankle over his knee. 'For another, I certainly wouldn't pick Bina,' he said bluntly.

Kate felt a surge of anger on behalf of her friend. She had feared something like this would happen and now her main concern was that Billy wouldn't humiliate Bina. She silently cursed Elliot, Barbie and the whole bunch of them. Playing

209

with people's lives was always dangerous and right now she was the one about to face retribution for their stupidity. 'That is just plain rude,' Kate told him.

'Rude to be angry when I'm tricked? I'm just calling it as I see it,' Billy said and he reclined back on the seat.

'I guess that's why everyone calls you like they see you,' Kate accused, almost ready to launch into a sermon about his predatory reputation.

'What's that supposed to mean?' Billy said, sitting upright and putting both feet on the ground.

Kate controlled herself, but with difficulty. She just didn't want to see Bina hurt and she had to try to get out of this somehow. She turned away from him. 'It means every woman in Brooklyn, perhaps with the exception of Brooklyn Heights, knows your reputation,' Kate said and went to pick up her purse.

'What reputation?' Billy asked. He stood up and followed her. When she didn't answer him or turn around, he put a hand on her shoulder and turned her to him. 'What reputation?' he asked again.

'Oh, come on. Don't you know everyone calls you "Dumping Billy"?' Kate was exasperated.

'"Dumping Billy"? Why?' Kate looked up at him. He was tall, at least seven or eight inches taller than she was, but she could see his eyes cloud. He seemed to have been completely unaware of his nickname. 'Why the hell would they call me that?' he asked.

'Because you dump every woman you date.' Kate looked toward the bar and the restrooms beyond. When would Michael and Bina return? She was tired of this conversation, and only wanted to salvage the rest of the evening.

'I don't dump women,' Billy said. For the first time he seemed defensive. 'I mean I've broken up relationships, but I don't dump people.'

'Oh, come on,' Kate said. 'My friends know a dozen women

you've dumped. I didn't make up the nickname. Anyway, your behavior is pathological.'

'What?' Billy demanded. He'd clearly gone from defensive to angry.

Kate knew she'd gone too far and spoiled what was left of the evening but couldn't resist taking a deep, annoyed breath. 'Path-o-log-i-cal,' she said slowly, as if for a child. 'It means . . .'

'. . . Any abnormal variation from a sound condition,' Billy finished for her. Kate blinked. She was taken aback that he could spit out the accurate definition so quickly. Billy pushed past her, grabbed his bag and turned back. 'It also means I'm out of here. The bad news is, I did just dump Bina but I wish I could've dumped you. The good news is that now your friend Michael has a chance of coming in third.'

He was gone in a minute and Kate stood beside their almost deserted lane wondering what she could possibly say when Bina and Michael returned.

25

The next morning, Kate sat in her office face to face with a
young girl. Tina, a high spirited third-grader, was sitting in
one of the tiny chairs with a big bandage on her arm. Tina
had injured herself over and over, but Kate didn't think it
was caused by clumsiness or by a need for self-mutilation.
She thought that Tina probably had a repetition compulsion:
for some reason she had to keep acting out the trauma of being
challenged and frightened and forced to respond. While many
professionals in her field dismissed the idea, Kate had always
found the concept of repetition compulsion very valid.

Kate had been talking with the child for over an hour now
and she felt that progress had been made. 'So you won't do
that again?' Kate asked Tina.

Tina looked up at her and smiled. 'No,' she said, then added,
'Not unless Jason dares me.'

'If he dares you to jump off the roof . . .' Kate stopped
herself. Where had that come from? It was the kind of line
her father might have used. Instead, Kate smiled, almost
closed her eyes and leaned forward toward Tina, the girl
who couldn't refuse a dare. 'I dare you not to,' Kate said.
'I bet that you have to do anything Jason dares you to.'

'Do not,' Tina said.

'Dare you not to,' Kate said.

She wasn't sure if the counter dare would work or if Tina really might jump off the roof. Just then the bell rang and interrupted her thoughts. 'We'll talk about your friendship with Jason next time, okay, Tina,' Kate said.

Tina nodded again, slid off the chair and bounded from the room.

'I told you, it just won't work.' Kate said each word slowly and distinctly so Elliot might possibly get it through his mathematical head. 'Zero, null set, no way. *Impossible*. Finished. *Kaput*.'

'But are you sure?' Elliot asked.

She gave him a look. They were going to their gym, Crunch. A place that ran cool ads on television and that had as its motto: 'No judgments'. But Kate was ready to make a few judgments now. Even for him, Elliot looked awful. They were walking up Eighth Avenue and he was wearing baggy shorts, a torn T-shirt and a madras fishing hat that must have come from some thrift shop, while his feet displayed two mismatched socks. 'You know,' Kate said, trying to change the subject, 'you look like a recently released mental patient.'

'Thank you,' Elliot said. 'It was the look I was going for. Brice helped me.'

Against her will, Kate smiled. How a guy as fashion-impaired as Elliot could couple up with stylish Brice was unimaginable to her. But they were a solid and happy couple with enough things in common to make their lives congenial and enough respect for their differences to make life interesting. It was hard to imagine how Brice would have let Elliot out of the house dressed so embarrassingly badly, but she knew that he, always immaculately clad, just shrugged, laughed, and hugged Elliot. Then the image of Michael and his sports jacket the night before came unbidden to her mind. Just because Michael dressed inappropriately was no reason for her to judge him, but somehow she was.

'I want to find out exactly what happened, sentence by sentence, word by word, act by act.' They turned west on Eighteenth Street and Kate looked at Elliot with hostile amazement.

'How does it feel to want?' Kate asked. 'If you think I'm going to go through last night all over again, you can think again.' They reached the door to the gym. 'And you can warm up by yourself.'

They had both gotten memberships at Crunch so that they could work out together and force one another to go. It usually worked pretty well but Kate was in no mood to dissect the previous evening. The fact was she was a little bit ashamed, both of her ruse and her behavior. But that didn't mean she had to tell Elliot that. At the door to the women's locker room she turned to him and said, 'Spot yourself. I'm going to find a straight guy to work out with.'

After she had changed into her workout pants and loose top, twisted her hair into a scrunchie and stuck it on top of her head with hair pins, then stowed her stuff in the locker, she came out, only to find Elliot standing there, just where she left him.

'Oh, come on,' Elliot pleaded, as if she hadn't just been gone for ten minutes. 'You never tell me anything anymore.'

'Oh, for heaven's sake,' Kate laughed, exasperated. But she couldn't refuse him. She went into detail about the whole awful night – how Barbie dressed Bina up like a Las Vegas showgirl, how Billy showed up thinking he was her date and not at all happy to find out he was Bina's, and how they finally got into an argument at the end of the evening.

'I give up,' she laughed. They walked to the mats and Kate grabbed a big blue plastic ball to begin their warm-up. She leaned backward over it to stretch the front of her body. The stretch felt good and Kate took a deep soothing breath. Stretching was the only part of working out that she actually enjoyed and she needed it after last night and today.

While Brian Conroy had improved and was able to cry over the loss of his mother, a new child, Lisa Allen, had been sent to her because she seemed 'withdrawn'. From the girl's body language and some indefinable intuition, Kate suspected abuse. That was the most troubling of all the problems she ran into. As if that wasn't enough, Tina Foster had been sent to her for the second time because she had taken a ridiculous dare and jumped off the top of the playground wall simply because Jason Franklin had said she couldn't do it. Kate sighed. Releasing some of her tension felt good. She would even relish a good session on the treadmill because after a mentally exhausting day at work, Kate thought the best way to ensure a sound night's sleep was to physically exhaust her body.

Kate and Elliot now clasped hands and bent away from each other in order to stretch out their backs. They had been coming to the gym together for eight months now and had their routine down pat. They continued to pull one another, first arms, then legs around and across the big blue ball. 'Well, you know,' Elliot said, 'I got a partial report from Bev last night.'

'Bev called you?'

'Oh, yeah. She and I are bonding. I want to be the godfather to the baby.'

'God forbid,' Kate said. She really felt annoyed that Elliot was so . . . integrated with her Brooklyn friends and really pissed off that Bev would rat her out. 'Look, I didn't think Billy Nolan would like Bina. It turns out that he resented the way I manipulated him and – shock, shock – he doesn't want to go out with Bina despite Barbie's outfits, Brice's haircut and your plan. Not only that, *I* don't like him. He isn't a nice person.'

'*You* don't have to like him,' Elliot began. 'I don't have to like him. Bina doesn't even have to like him. She only has to date him for two point seven months. That's roughly ten and a half weeks or seventy-three days – give or take.'

'But he has to like Bina,' Kate pointed out. 'And he doesn't. Case closed.'

'Technically we don't know that,' Elliot gurgled with his head tilted backwards. He was arching himself in a back bend.

'What do you mean?' Kate asked, standing upright again.

'I mean, from your re-telling it sounds like he had the argument with you,' Elliot said.

'Yes. So?' Kate was not entirely sure what Elliot was getting at but something in his manner made her nervous.

'So his problem is with you NOT Bina.' Elliot looked at her sternly.

'Elliot, trust me. There was no chemistry between them.'

'Kate, from what you told me and what Bev reported, I think last night was an opener. The fact is, you did trick the guy and he was angry at you and he doesn't like you but he might, given the chance, like Bina – at least long enough to date her for seventy-three days.'

'Oh, Elliot, don't be ridiculous,' Kate snapped. She let go of his hands and he went sprawling, his butt hitting the mat with a splat. 'Are you trying to tell me the fiasco was my fault?'

Elliot rose slowly from the mat, his hands rubbing his ass. 'That's exactly what I'm telling you. That and the fact that you owe him an apology.'

Kate stared at him in amazement. 'That is the most out-rageous thing I ever heard,' she told him. 'I would never apologize to the insufferable, arrogant . . .' She turned and began to walk away.

'You like him, don't you?' Elliot asked. And Kate stopped where she was, swung around and looked at him.

'I do not!' she said.

Elliot shrugged his shoulders. 'Just asking,' he told her. 'It's just that I've never seen you this excited about Michael.' He threw his towel over his neck and sauntered toward the treadmills.

'Leave Michael out of this,' Kate snapped. She took a deep breath. Elliot, who probably knew her better than anyone, was pressing all of her buttons. But Kate wouldn't let him. As she watched him set the program on his treadmill, his back turned to her, she made herself slowly and carefully go over the facts and the feelings from the previous night. Maybe she *had* been both a catalyst and a stumbling block. Maybe if she hadn't been in the way Billy would be interested in Bina. He seemed to have dated every other woman east of Court Street. However, even if she had gone about it badly, she knew her intentions had been good. She got onto the treadmill beside Elliot and punched in her own stats and program.

As she started walking, she said, 'If you believe in this and Bina believes in this, I'll do what I can to make it work. But I can't make him date her. And not for two point seven months. I don't believe he could rise to the challenge.' She stopped walking as the thought hit her, and almost flew off the back of the treadmill. She just grabbed the handlebars at the last moment. She thought of Tina Foster, and the jump from the wall. She'd bet that Billy had about the same mentality as Tina.

'Have you thought of something or are you just being klutzy?' Elliot asked as she regained her position and matched her stride to his.

'Maybe I have,' Kate admitted. 'But I hate the idea of apologizing to him. Do I have to?' she said, using her best Baby Wheedle voice.

'Kate,' Elliot said, ignoring her tone. 'I don't see you have much of a choice. It doesn't matter that you don't believe in the "silly" plan. Bina does, you are her best friend, and you alienated Billy. You have to apologize.'

God, Kate thought. I hate how Elliot is always right.

217

26

The following Tuesday morning, Kate stood in her bedroom before a full-length mirror holding a hip but dignified blouse up to herself. Deciding against it, she threw it onto the pile of rejected clothes that had already formed on her bed. 'What am I going to wear?' she asked her reflection. She turned away and paused for a moment. Why did she even care? Billy meant nothing to her, despite his obvious attractions. She went to her tiny closet and began to look for the green crew neck top that looked so good on her. As she pulled it off the hanger she stopped dead. Billy Nolan was taking up more space in her mind than he ought to. And he had seen her before. It wasn't like she was going to make a different impression on him this time.

She took a deep breath and looked back steadily at herself. 'Hello,' she said as if talking to someone else. 'Billy, I wanted to apologize for my behavior the other day.' Kate gritted her teeth. Apologies – especially to those you didn't like – were galling. But she tried to barrel ahead.

It was more difficult than she had imagined. She thought of all the children that she had asked to do role play: children who were supposed to talk to the fathers who had left the family, children who were tired of being scolded, children who had to practice asking for what they wanted. Now, when she had to try – and she was doing it without a witness – she had a new compassion for her little clients.

The phone rang and she was relieved at the distraction, until she saw the phone number. Somehow, she didn't feel like speaking to Michael right now and it was odd for him to be calling her on a school morning. Reluctantly, she picked up the phone.

'Hi,' he said cheerfully. 'Did I wake you up?' Kate assured him that he hadn't. 'Look, I just thought that we might get together tonight.' For a moment, Kate was confused. They never got together on Tuesdays. It was always Wednesdays.

'Is something wrong?' Kate asked.

'Yeah. I miss you,' Michael said, and Kate was surprised to feel mildly irritated.

'I miss you, too,' she lied. She paused for a minute, surprised by her own fib. She wondered whether the space that she should reserve for missing Michael might now be taken up by Billy. It was absolutely absurd and she would put a stop to it. Meanwhile, there was a growing silence between her and Michael. 'I'm sorry,' she told him, 'but I have errands I have to run tonight.'

'Oh. Okay. No problem. See you tomorrow, I guess.'

'Yes,' Kate said. 'I'll see you tomorrow.' She hung up the phone, sighed, and went back to the task at hand.

Later that day, after school had finished, she arrived at the Barber Bar, her hair perfectly coiffed, looking as if she was about to take over a Fortune 500 company. She'd taken the subway from school to the stop she thought was closest to Billy Nolan's place of business. All was quiet in the area, and the bar itself looked very closed but she knocked on the door anyway.

'We ain't open until . . .' a woman's voice called out. Suddenly the door opened and a tall, skinny blonde in her late thirties in old jeans and a cut-off top stood before her. She was polishing a glass with the apron she had on and looked at Kate suspiciously. 'Hey, listen. If you're lost, I'm dyslexic so I don't give directions. And unless you're a customer you don't get to use this toilet,' she said. She was about to slam the door when Kate put up her hand and held it open. Then the woman paused. 'The Redhead,' she said as if she already knew everything about her.

'Excuse me?' Kate asked. Had her reputation preceded her? 'Actually I am looking for someone who works here . . . Billy Nolan.' Kate blushed. She thought of all the women he had dumped and realized that this barmaid had probably seen dozens of them. How many women must have turned up on this door step and said the very same thing?

'Of course you are,' the woman said tiredly, confirming Kate's fear. 'But he ain't on tonight until six.'

Kate looked at her watch. She had almost two hours to wait. She sighed, more aggravated than ever. 'Well, thank you anyway,' she said, and turned to leave. She'd find somewhere in this ruin of a neighborhood to have a cup of coffee. She doubted there would be a Starbucks for miles.

But before she'd taken more than three steps the barmaid must have taken pity on her. 'Hey!' she called after her. 'You the one who told him his nickname?'

Kate turned around and nodded. 'Dumping Billy,' she said. 'Isn't that what everyone calls him?'

'Yeah. He just didn't know it.' She laughed. 'Put him in quite a spin.' She looked Kate over again.

'Well, I'll come back later,' Kate said. At least she'd had some impact on the arrogant bastard. That might help her on this errand she had reluctantly taken on.

'Look, if you gotta see him now, he just lives above the bar.' She pointed to a buzzer on the other side of the doorway.

'That's okay. I'll come back another . . .' Before Kate could get the words out, the woman rang the buzzer and shouted up.

'Hey, Billy! You got company and – surprise, surprise – it's a woman,' she shouted into the intercom.

'Thanks, Mary,' Billy's voice said through the speaker. 'I'll buzz.'

Kate gave Mary a small half-smile. 'Thanks,' she said, but she wasn't sure she meant it.

'Don't mention it, Red,' the barmaid replied.

'I'm Kate,' Kate told her, just to prevent 'Red' from ever escaping the woman's thin lips again.

A smile spread across Mary's face. 'Oh. Kate . . .' she said knowingly, and she turned back into the bar. Meanwhile the door buzzed open. Kate smoothed her hair once, and put her hand on the doorknob. She ascended the steps to the landing of the first floor where a door stood open. She peered in at the room before her. It was not at all what she would have predicted. Instead of being a 'bachelor pad' filled with empty pizza boxes and furniture that looked as if it had fallen from a truck, the room had a polished wooden floor, a shabby but attractive Persian rug, a big worn brown leather Chesterfield sofa and two walls of bookshelves filled to the ceiling with hundreds of books. A window seat was built into one bookshelf wall and the window was open. Through it there was the view of a tree in new leaf and a bit of the sky, though the billowing white curtains kept obscuring the small vista. Altogether it was charming, and far more homey and sophisticated than Kate would ever have given Billy Nolan credit for.

Billy sat with his back to her at a mahogany desk, trans-fixed by the laptop screen in front of him. Kate entered the room and looked around. Her surprise continued to grow. Almost half the books on the shelves were in French, and she now could see two nicely framed Daumier prints. A woman must have furnished this place, she thought. 'Hello,' she said.

Billy did not move his eyes from the monitor. 'Hold on. Hold on. I'm just catching up on my e-mail,' was all he offered as a greeting.

'This won't take long,' Kate began. Billy pulled his hands off the keyboard and spun around. There was an awkward silence.

'I d-d-didn't realize it was you,' Billy stammered. 'I thought I had to interview a n-n-new barmaid.'

'I don't think I'm qualified for the job,' Kate said and was then ready to bite her tongue. She sounded snotty, and she really hadn't meant to.

Billy stood up. 'So did you just come over here to turn down a job offer or is there more to this unexpected visit?' he asked.

The two of them stood across the room from one another, the sofa and plenty of tension between them. Kate tried to decide whether it would be best to just blurt out her apology and throw out her dare or try to first bridge the gap between them. Everything she had practiced seemed inappropriate, as if she were about to deliver a lecture to a Sunday school. 'I wanted to . . .' she began.

'Yes?' Billy raised his eyebrows. It was annoying to her to see how attractive he was, even when he was in deshabille; his hair in disarray, his shirt untucked and open to the third button. She tore her eyes away from him.

'I wanted to apologize for . . .' but it all came out wrong. 'I wanted to apologize for not telling you the truth the other night.'

Billy laughed. 'That doesn't sound like much of an apology to me,' he told her.

'I realize after what happened I may not be your favorite person, but that's not what counts,' she explained. She put her purse down on the desk.

'It isn't?' Billy asked.

'No. What counts is that Bina really likes you,' Kate said. This was going badly. She was being either too direct or too indirect, and was annoyed at her inability to really express herself to this guy. 'And I think you might like her.'

'Oh, really?' Billy smirked. 'And what would give you insight to my feelings?'

'Look, it's none of my business but . . .'

'Well, you finally got something right,' he said, and sat down on the Chesterfield. 'What is your business anyway?'

'I'm a psychologist,' she said.

He shook his head. 'I should have known,' he muttered. 'Nothing worse than a psychologist except a psychiatrist.'

'How would you know?' she asked. 'Have you dated both?'

'No. I consulted both. A long time ago. And they were ineffectual intellectuals.'

She wondered what a mook like him had gone into therapy for but knew better than to ask. She just walked over to the little window seat and tried again.

'I don't like this "Dumping Billy" stuff,' he said.

'I'm sorry. I shouldn't have said anything, but I'm not responsible for the name. Apparently, everybody uses it.'

'Apparently,' he said dryly. 'As if my personal life is anyone else's business.'

Here was her chance to put in one more plug for Bina. It was only because she had promised Elliot that she pushed forward. 'Well, that's why I dropped by. Of course, it's none of my business but I think you two would be very . . . you know . . . good for one another . . . which would be quite . . . something . . . so what I am saying is basically what I have already said . . . you know?' What the hell did she just say? she thought. She'd never been less articulate in her whole life.

'Actually, no,' Billy said, gently smiling at her obvious unease.

'Oh, I just knew you would make this difficult!' Kate stood up and walked to the door in frustration. It was never so hard to speak with children. Or to Elliot. Or Bina, the girls or even

Michael. Why was she having such a hard time talking to Billy Nolan?

'Why should I go out with Bina? I pick my own women. And she looks like a husband-hunter anyway,' Billy said. 'Not my type.'

Kate could take his slight mocking of her, but how dare he insult her friend! 'That is totally out of line! You're a loser!' she almost shouted at him.

'Me!?' Billy asked. He got up from the couch and faced her. 'Hey, I own this place. I built it up from nothing. I've got bigger plans, too! I'll be opening a restaurant next year.'

'Yes. But can you manage one decent relationship?' she asked.

'And I can date anyone I want!'

'NOT ANYONE. YOU CAN'T DATE ME!' Kate flared. 'You are still just a Mick who never even got out of Brooklyn. The trick with you is you are slightly better-looking on the outside than you are on the inside and they're in constant conflict. That is why you don't know you're a loser.' Kate was out of breath and her face was hot. This was not going well. She looked at Billy, who was surprisingly cool.

'Are you speaking as a doctor, or as a bitch?' he asked with a coldness that cut right through her.

Kate turned to leave, then checked herself, remembering her mission. She crossed to the desk, picked up her purse and muttered almost under her breath. But she made sure it was loud enough for Billy to hear. 'You couldn't do it anyway.'

'Do what?' he demanded.

Kate turned around to face him, her eyes blazing. The heat was really on. They stared each other down as they had in the bowling alley the other night. 'Nothing,' she spat. 'Absolutely nothing.'

'Tell me,' he said through clenched teeth, leaning across the back of the sofa toward her.

224

Kate almost smiled because she knew that she'd be victorious. He was no more difficult than Tina Foster. 'It's just that when I came here I knew you couldn't date Bina for more than a week or two,' she said, self-assured, almost as snotty as possible. 'You obviously have a repetition compulsion.'

'A what?' Billy asked, indignant.

'A repetition compulsion,' Kate replied impatiently.

'What's that? Some jargon from the DSM 4?'

Kate was surprised he knew about the DSM – the bible of mental dysfunctions that was compiled regularly for mental health professionals. Still, she didn't show her surprise. 'It's not a DSM 4 construct. It's an older Freudian theoretical position.'

'I thought Freud was unpopular these days? Oedipus complex, penis envy. Isn't that all pretty much out of date? After all, he was a guy who didn't know what women wanted.'

Once again, Kate was surprised by his casual familiarity with things she figured he had never heard of. 'I think it's still valid,' she said. 'Especially in your case. It roughly defines a compulsive neurotic behavior where a person repeats an altered version of traumatic events from their past. Once it starts, the compulsion requires the person to keep doing the maladaptive behavior.'

'Oh, really?' Billy asked, and, as she hoped, he was definitely becoming belligerent. 'And what maladaptive behavior would I be repeating?'

'An attempt at intimacy that has to be followed by abandonment. And each time you pick an inappropriate partner to ensure the eventual split.'

'And how do you know all of this about me?' he asked.

'Well, I am a doctor,' she said, 'and I do know several of the inappropriate women you've played the pattern out with. I just thought Bina might be a real person, someone you could actually bond with. She isn't one of your typical Brooklyn big-haired Bitches. And she's quite sad at the moment, with

225

Jack away. Anyway, it didn't work, and it doesn't matter to me or to Bina. I'm just sorry I gave you an easy excuse not to conquer it.'

'You didn't give me anything but a headache,' he shot back.

'Well, we're not really talking about me, are we? We're talking about you. And you find it impossible to date a nice girl with any kind of commitment.'

'That isn't true,' he told her.

'I guess that isn't why you have the nickname, then,' she said.

'I'd have no problem dating Bina. She's a nice enough girl and she knows how to have a good time. Unlike some uptight, word-dropping psychologists I've met. And I don't have a petition . . . whatever.'

'Sure you don't,' she said.

'I don't,' he insisted.

'Great. Then prove it,' she said. 'Date her for a couple of months without dumping her and I will be proven totally and utterly wrong. Well, if you can manage a real relationship you might also lose the nickname. But I don't think you can do it.'

'Done,' he declared. 'And only because I want to. And because she's a nice girl. Not my type, but nice. And I'll see her as long as I want to. I don't need a shrink to manage it, or to psychoanalyze me later.'

'I wouldn't dream of it.' Kate smiled, and picked up her purse and headed to the door. She put her hand on the knob, but before she turned it, she looked back at Billy.

'I can give you Bina's number,' she said.

'Thanks, but I already have it. Bina Horowitz, 378–143. 1742 Ocean Parkway.' He looked at her with a glint of triumph in his eye. 'I had thought of looking her up myself. She gave me her number, you know.' And Kate, for some reason she didn't quite understand, was annoyed.

226

Well, her feelings didn't matter in this ridiculous escapade. She'd accomplished what she'd promised to do. So she simply opened the door, exited and slammed it behind her.

27

Kate was almost a quarter of an hour early at LaMarca on Wednesday evening because she didn't want to be late. The restaurant, a pleasant if undistinguished bistro in Chelsea, was not the kind of snotty place where you had to 'wait at the bar until your party has joined you'. Kate was seated at a windowed table and had a chance to freshen her lipstick and twist her hair up into a knot. Then she waited, trying hard not to think. Nestled next to her lipstick in the makeup bag she carried in her purse were a pair of new keys on a silver Tiffany key ring. The ring was actually more like a 'U' than a circle, with sterling silver balls at each end that unscrewed so that keys could be added and subtracted easily. It also had a small silver dog tag on it. The number engraved on the sterling was registered at Tiffany's and, if the keys were lost and dropped in a mailbox, Tiffany's would return them. Kate felt that perhaps she had gone overboard, and she was afraid that she might be compensating with the gift for a diminution in her passion for Michael.

She'd tried, over and over, to analyze why she had cooled. Certainly their sex was fulfilling and their relationship sound and based on shared interests, though she had never felt truly passionate about Michael as she once had about Steven. That, however, she had considered a good thing. After Steven, Kate had promised herself she would never allow an obsession with a man to take over her life. And until now she had been more than happy with her union with Michael. Despite Elliot's prejudice against him, Michael was a grown-up – perhaps the first male grown-up in her life – and he respected and liked her. Michael, unlike a lot of guys, wasn't intimidated by her work, her looks or her independence. And he was not the kind of man to run from intimacy. So why, she wondered, did she find herself resisting? Was she afraid of the next step in their relationship? She didn't think so. But, as Anna Freud had pointed out, resistance was an unconscious thing.

'Would you like something to drink while you're waiting?' the waiter asked, startling her.

'A glass of Chardonnay, please,' she said, and then felt a bit guilty, which in turn made her feel annoyed.

As she was taking her first sip of the wine, Michael strode in, an unusually wide smile on his face. He was, she reminded herself, very nice-looking. Not dramatically gorgeous like that idiot in Brooklyn, but handsome in an understated way. His hair was thick, and a little silver was prematurely mixed with the brown. The steel-rimmed glasses he wore went well with his hair, and Kate had sometimes wondered if he knew that. If his shoulders were slightly narrow, he made up for it with his height. Now, he bent over her, took her chin in his hand and turned her head so he could kiss her on the mouth. She smiled at him and he slipped into the banquette opposite her.

'Very nice choice,' he said, looking around. They alternated in choosing restaurants, Michael most often referring to Zagat's on-line while Kate depended on Elliot – her own personal restaurant rating service.

'You seem in a good mood,' she said.

'Better than good!' Michael told her. 'I've gotten the offer from Austin.' He beamed. 'It's almost too good to be true.'

'It's official?' Kate asked. She felt her stomach lurch.

229

'Well, as good as. I got a call from Brill at the Sagerman Foundation and he told me, in complete confidence of course, that they had selected me and that I'd hear from Austin soon.'

'Wow. So you'll chair a department?' Kate was impressed and delighted for Michael, but her feelings were mixed with a tightening of her chest, as if her bra had suddenly become two sizes too small. Austin, Texas was supposed to be a lovely place, with a great university and very pretty countryside. And to get the chairmanship of a department was almost unheard of for someone as young as Michael. But Kate didn't want to think of the ramifications: if Michael chose to go would he ask her to go as well? And if he did, what would she say? She loved her job and her friends and . . .

The waiter approached again. 'Something to drink, sir?' he asked, and Michael nodded.

'A bottle of champagne, please.' Kate was startled but merely smiled. He was very excited, but perhaps he was more pleased that he had been selected than willing to go.

When the champagne came, Kate toasted him. 'To the smartest, most deserving man I know,' she said, and she thought Michael blushed. The moment seemed appropriate so she reached into her purse and took out the little blue Tiffany box. 'I'm not sure these would be useful in Austin,' Kate said and placed the box between them on the table. 'I would have picked something else, if I had known.'

Then Michael did flush, either with pleasure or embarrassment – some men were awkward with gifts – and Kate felt that he would surely be disappointed. But he opened the box, held up the key chain and grinned. 'How nice,' he said. 'How very nice.'

They ordered dinner and Michael actually took a sip or two of champagne. He spent most of the time chatting about the Sagerman Foundation and the University of Texas and Kate tried not to feel left out or frightened. She was surprised to discover how unprepared she was for this eventuality. Texas! She couldn't think of any place less attractive to her, why, she'd rather move back to Brooklyn. And was he simply giving her this news in what seemed an impersonal way or was he talking about their plans without saying so in so many words? She felt confused and ill prepared for something that a part of her had been expecting for months. But what did it mean? Kate hadn't the slightest clue.

After dinner they walked to her apartment. It was a balmy night and Michael, swinging his briefcase with one hand, held hers with the other. When they got to her door he reached into his pocket and took out the keys. 'Allow me,' he said and opened the door for her. As they walked up the steps, Kate reached in to her own bag. For some reason she wanted to open her own apartment door, and she managed to beat him to it.

When they entered the living room, Michael threw his briefcase down on the sofa and immediately pulled off his tie. Kate thought he might be a little bit high from the bit of champagne that he had drunk, but she was sober as a judge. In fact, she felt like a judge, busy weighing the pros and cons of the situation before her. When Michael took her hand and led her to her bedroom, she simply followed.

He began unbuttoning his shirt, sitting on the side of her bed. He took his shoes off, unsheathed his feet from their socks and carefully tucked them into his shoes. When he stood up and undid his belt buckle, his chest bare, he looked over at her and smiled. 'Do I have to undress you?' he asked.

Kate smiled back, and hoped the smile didn't show her uneasiness. She wasn't sure if she was uneasy because she was afraid Michael would leave her or because she was afraid he might ask her to come with him. His great good humor was certainly inappropriate if he was planning to go without her, and Michael was not an insensitive man.

Yet, like most men, he didn't feel her mood as he began

231

to make love to her. She felt his hands on her waist, then lower and he slipped her panties off. Then he moved his hands upward to cover her breasts. He kissed her, long and deeply, but Kate felt unmoved. When he began to touch her she realized that there was no way she could possibly have an orgasm. Ashamed to reveal herself, she simply climbed onto him and worked to make sure he achieved pleasure, but when they were finished Kate cradled him in her arms and, looking over his head at the dresser and the statue of the Virgin on it, she wondered what was wrong with her.

28

It had been a few days since Kate had heard from Bina. When she did call she didn't even leave a moment's opening for Kate's news but chattered on. Apparently, she had been kept pretty busy by Billy. Kate supposed it was a good thing, since Kate needed time to figure out her own emotional landscape.

Still, after a few moments, Kate found herself feeling oddly resentful of Bina's harmless chatter. She went on and on about Billy: how funny he was, what a good time they'd had over dinner, how sophisticated he seemed to be and, lastly, 'What a gentleman he is.' This, Kate knew, was Bina talk for him not jumping her bones when he said goodnight. 'I can see why he gets all the girls,' Bina said. 'He just seems to really listen when you talk. You know how guys are so busy talking or else how they kind of glaze over when you start talking?' Kate, thinking of Michael, reluctantly had to admit she knew. 'Well, he doesn't do that.'

'How refreshing,' Kate said dryly. 'So all is going well.' Not that she was coming around to believe in Elliot's ridiculous plan, but this distraction, Kate had to admit, must be a welcome break from the recent drama of Bina's life.

'Oh, we had the best time,' Bina was saying. 'He's just

so much fun. When we went to this club that he knew
he . . .'

Kate found it hard to listen. Besides, she had her own
tribulations to deal with. She hated to admit it, but she was
beginning to believe that Elliot's assessment of Michael had
been right. Michael, although sweet and caring in some ways,
was self-involved and lately she had found him . . . dull. In
the past week, he had called her daily, giving her updates
on what Kate was beginning to think of as the Sagerman
Situation. Since their dinner, he had spent most of their time
together talking about nothing else.

'So then he goes, "I would if I was crazy" and I go, "You
are crazy".'

Kate had had a half-day at Andrew Country Day today as
the school year was winding down, and she had another one
tomorrow. She felt like having some company but Michael
was going to a lecture and Kate, mercifully, didn't have
to accompany him. Suddenly it came to her that tonight
would be the perfect evening to take a break from her own
relationship and catch up with Bina's. Once she thought of
it, the idea burgeoned. She was, she had to admit, morbidly
fascinated with the progress of Bina and Billy's dating. If she
was interested in anything else she certainly wasn't going to
admit it. And, as a psychologist, she felt an additional interest
in seeing if Billy could manage to keep dating Bina for more
than fifteen minutes. So far, all seemed well, but she would
find out this evening – if Bina had the time and inclination
to see her.

'Hey,' she said, breaking into Bina's monologue, 'you wanna
walk the bridge?'

Since they were teenagers, Kate and Bina had found
pleasure in walking from one side of the Brooklyn Bridge
to the other. Now, since Kate had moved across it, they
occasionally met in the middle and then walked to one side
or the other.

'You're kidding?' Bina said. 'God, we haven't done that in ages.'

'Why not?' Kate asked. 'I'll buy you dinner in Brooklyn Heights. At Isobel's.' They both loved the restaurant, and Kate knew it would be great bait.

'Same old Kate,' Bina said. 'I'll go Dutch.'

'Same old Bina,' Kate laughed and they agreed to meet in the middle of the bridge.

The walk was good for Kate. It felt as if it blew some of the cotton out of her clogged head. She thought about some of the children, and how they might get through the summer, she thought about Michael and his new offer, but mostly she thought about herself. She had to be prepared for either Michael's decision to go to Texas without asking her to come or, alternatively, what she would do if he did ask her. She felt as if she should be happy. After all, wasn't this possibility what she had been hoping for? Even if it was, though, there was something that nagged her about the way Michael was going about it. It wasn't that he was cold exactly; it was more like self-centered – but then weren't all men? If she was brutally honest with herself she also had to admit that she didn't like the arrogance of his assumption that she'd drop everything and go with him. Still, she had no one to blame but herself for that. And why shouldn't he assume (if he was assuming) that she would be willing to go to Texas with him? Unfortunately there were plenty of dysfunctional families and a need for child psychologists everywhere. She could set up her own practice. She would be the first member of her family not only to become a doctor but also to marry one. The Horowitzes would be so proud! And if there was something, well, something missing in her relationship with Michael, wasn't everything imperfect in some way or other? Relationships were built over time with both people willing to listen and try to understand one another. Michael would certainly listen.

235

Kate, her thoughts tumbling about in her head, walked faster than she expected to. When she hit the mid-point of the bridge she was alone and couldn't even see Bina in the distance. She stopped for a moment, turned north and looked up the East River. This afternoon the water looked almost blue, and the Williamsburg Bridge and the blue Triboro in the distance sandwiched Manhattan which rose on her left like a magical illusion. When she looked to the right, Brooklyn seemed flat and dull in comparison. The huge blocky buildings that housed the Jehovah Witness Complex and the warehouses along the harbor were prosaic. Kate felt something like a little tug on her heart. She looked back at Manhattan. There, small as it was, she had a place of her own, a place she had made and had lived in. Could she leave it? Why would she?

She was so deep in thought that she didn't hear Bina until her friend was beside her and put her hand on Kate's shoulder.

'A nickel for your thoughts,' Bina said.

'A nickel? I thought it was a penny.'

'Inflation. Plus your thoughts are better than other people's.'

Bina took her hand and led her away from Manhattan, just like they used to do.

'So how's it going?' Kate asked. 'Have you been proposed to?'

Bina laughed. With the wind catching her hair and the sunlight glancing off the blond streaks she looked almost as good as a shampoo ad.

'That guy is crazy,' she said. 'We went to this club where they know him. Well, they know him everywhere. So everyone was saying hello. We didn't even have to wait to get in.' Bina began to ramble on with details that Kate found tedious. She 'ummmed' and 'uh-huhed' for a while. '. . . And then they start playing "Flavor of the Week" . . . you know the song?' Bina asked Kate.

'Yeah. I know it,' Kate said.

'Well, it must be like his theme song.' Kate nodded, secretly amused. She was not really sure if Bina understood the lyrics entirely and how they pertained to Billy.

'Well, everyone in the bar starts shouting: "Billy! Billy!" And at first he's like brushing it off, you know what I mean?' Bina asked.

'Yeah. I know,' Kate replied. She was feeling odd, as if Bina's simple story was upsetting her on some high school level.

'Anyway, they won't stop. So he gets on the bar and starts singing at the top of his lungs. It was such a riot.' Bina laughed at the memory.

'Sounds like one,' Kate said, dryly.

'He's so not like Jack!' Bina said. 'Can you imagine Jack . . .' A look came over her face as if she had just heard her own words.

Kate knew her friend well enough to recognize conflict, though Bina was so rarely in a dilemma. Could Bina be falling for Billy? What a fiasco that would be.

'Thank God he's not,' Kate said, looking at Bina. 'Right?' Bina nodded, but she looked slightly dejected.

Max had dropped by several times to inform Kate of Jack's latest bulletins. It was hard to tell if he did it because he was trying to be helpful, if he was horrified, or just gossiping. Certainly he seemed outraged as he told her about Jack's bar-hopping and his delight in the beauty and apparent availability of Hong Kong women, both Asian and Caucasian. 'The guy is going nuts out there.' Kate was grateful he didn't share any more photos or specifics.

She wondered whether Bina had heard anything, but guessed that she still hadn't heard from Jack, who had been gone more than a month now. Kate didn't want to ask, because Bina seemed to be in good spirits and Kate was glad to finally see her smiling.

'Right.' Bina paused and took a deep breath. She shook her

237

head as if to shake the thought of Jack from the forefront of her mind. They came to the end of the bridge.

'Do you want to walk on the promenade before we eat?' Kate asked.

'Sure,' Bina said, and they made a right, crossed Cadman Plaza, passed Isobel's and walked up Cranberry Street. This was the charming part of Brooklyn which looked virtually unchanged since the late 1800s. Brownstones lined the blocks, complete with little gardens in the front, and the trees arched overhead, making a cool but shimmering shade. 'So how are things with the fruits and nuts?' Bina asked.

Kate raised her eyebrows, taking Bina's remark as a comment on Elliot as well as her little clients. Then she realized that Bina probably didn't know the connotation that 'fruit' had. 'They're not nuts,' she said. 'Although their parents sometimes are.'

'Sorry,' Bina said. 'Didn't mean to hurt your feelers.'

Kate had to smile. She and Bina had replaced the word 'feelings' with 'feelers' when they were ten years old and Bina still used the joke. Kate changed the subject. 'What have you bought Bev for the shower?' she asked.

'Ohmigod! Ohmigod!' Bina exclaimed, a new level of animation lighting up her face. 'I went with my mother to the Macy's on Flatbush. We got the most adorable outfit you've ever seen. Little tiny booties, a matching sweater and a bonnet. You should see the stitches, they're tiny. You know, everyone's knitting now. You think Bev would believe me if I told her I knit it myself?' Kate shook her head. 'I showed them to Billy and you should've seen the look on his face. I don't think he could believe a real person could be that small.'

'Why in the world would you show baby clothes to Billy?' Kate asked, and was surprised by the irritation in her voice. For heaven's sake, what was it to her? They reached the promenade and Kate looked around appreciatively. Bina didn't pay much attention. She chatted on about the shower and then suggested they walk back to Isobel's to eat.

Brooklyn Heights was not really part of Brooklyn, Kate had always thought. It was Manhattan once removed, and the view of the island from the promenade was breathtaking. They were quiet for a little while and then Bina broke the silence. 'All I've been doing is talking about myself. So,' she said with contrived casualness, 'where did you and Michael go last night?'

'We went to a movie,' Kate informed her friend and realized she had said it with about as much enthusiasm as if they had gone to a funeral.

'The new George Clooney?' Bina asked, her eyes lighting up. To Bina, George Clooney was a walking god. Kate often thought that part of Jack's appeal to Bina was the slight dimple in his chin that resembled the star's, although Bev and Barbie and the rest of the crew would agree that no other aspect of Jack's appearance was even the slightest bit Clooney-esque.

'Not exactly,' Kate began. How could she explain their visit to the Film Forum? 'We went to a documentary.'

'Oh . . .' Bina said. 'About what?'

'Afghan women and their struggle for literacy,' Kate said flatly.

Bina looked confused by the very thought. Kate wondered what the last documentary Bina had seen was. Something they had to watch in grade school about agriculture?

'That sounds . . . serious,' Bina stammered, apparently unsure how to respond. She paused a moment and looked across the bay at the Empire State Building whose red, white and blue lights had just been lit. The city was settling into the slowly darkening sky, its lights twinkling from the many buildings. 'So, are you two getting serious?'

Kate could hear Mrs Horowitz's voice channeled through Bina's lips. 'I'm not sure,' she said.

239

'There's not a serious bone in Billy's body . . . and what a body,' Bina added.

'Bina!' Kate exclaimed. She looked over at her friend, whose change since Jack's departure seemed to be a lot more than physical. 'You didn't . . . I mean you wouldn't . . .' The thought of Bina with Billy disturbed Kate deeply. She tried to decide whether it was fear for Bina or envy. She could hardly believe it, but there was some envy in her. Billy was better than George Clooney.

'Of course not. I still love Jack,' Bina said. Kate breathed a sigh of relief. 'But I've got eyes. And he's got hands,' Bina added, raising her brows playfully.

Kate was not sure this talk was as light-hearted as Bina was making it out to be. She herself had felt Billy's devastating, if shallow, charm and Bina was nothing if not inexperienced. 'Bina, remember you are not supposed to be getting attached to this guy. He's only a means to an end – at least according to you and Elliot.'

'I know. Believe me, I know. This whole plan is going to work. I just have a feeling,' Bina said. She paused. 'And there's something else. Billy makes me feel . . . well, it's like I feel prettier when I'm with him.' She looked away for a minute and her face reddened. 'I mean, I know people are probably looking at him, not me. But it makes me feel special, too.' She smiled as if remembering something. 'He always tells me how nice I look and he notices things, like if I wear a barrette.' She paused again. Then she lowered her voice as if what she had to say was fragile and could be broken easily. 'You know how much I love Jack.' Kate nodded. 'Well, I saw Max – you know, he's so nice. I don't understand why he isn't hooked up with someone. Anyway, he told me that Jack was sending him e-mails.' Kate managed not to gasp or show any emotion. A single one of those pictures would break Bina's heart. 'Anyway, I'm certain he misses me. And when he comes back I'm sure he'll ask me to marry him.'

The two of them walked down Henry Street. Kate was afraid to say a single word to her friend. She didn't want to encourage her about Jack and though she did want to discourage her about any attachment to Billy Nolan, she was not sure of her motives. They came to Henry's End restaurant, which was already bustling though it was early for dinner. Well, Kate reminded herself, people ate earlier on this side of the river. 'Are you hungry?' she asked. 'Shall we eat here instead of Isobel's?'

'Sure,' Bina told her. 'Just don't make me eat a Bambi – and don't you eat Thumper.' Henry's End was famous for wild game, though Kate would settle for steak.

'You can trust me on that,' Kate told Bina.

Her friend took her arm. 'I'll always trust you, Katie.' They paused for a moment. 'Hey, maybe you and Michael will get married and we could have a double wedding. My parents would love that.'

Kate had a flash-forward of an overdone ceremony with both her and Bina walking down the aisle on Dr Horowitz's arm, followed by a life full of documentaries, talks of anthropological discoveries and Texas cocktail parties. 'Please, Bina,' Kate said. 'Not when we are on a very high bridge with a lot of cold water underneath it.'

29

'There's a possibility you're actually going to get engaged?'
Elliot asked Kate, his face pruning up with disapproval.
They were sitting in the Starbucks located exactly halfway
between his apartment and hers. There were two others
in the neighborhood, but one was slightly closer to Elliot's
and the other was slightly closer to Kate's, so they always
compromised on this smaller, somewhat shabbier one.

'You better stop disliking him,' Kate told Elliot. 'If I *do*
marry him, and you stay snotty, I won't be able to see you
anymore.'

'Wedding bells are breaking up that old gang of mine,' Elliot
warbled. Kate shook her head. It was a corny old song, and
while Elliot didn't live up to most gay stereotypes he knew
the lyrics to every show tune and pop standard of the previous
century (with an emphasis on World War I and Barry Manilow
tunes). Elliot put down his mocha coconut frappé and tidied
up the little table between them using three napkins, then
picked his frappé up again. 'Like I'm really threatened that
you'd give up our friendship,' Elliot said, and took another
swig. 'Who else do you have to talk about every detail of your
emotional seismograph and Barbara Pym to?'

Kate had to smile. It was true she described every tremor

242

to Elliot and – like a geophysicist – he predicted when the earthquakes were coming to rock her world. And Barbara Pym was one of her secret addictions – an English author she and Elliot both reread frequently. Kate found the books soothing because almost nothing happened in them; no one's feelings were hurt and very little changed. A big event was a visit from the vicar and most chapters ended with someone having a hot, milky drink. Which reminded Kate about Elliot's beverage.

'Did you know that there are more calories in that coconut frappachino than three Big Macs?' Kate asked.

'Speaking of Max,' Elliot said, ignoring her concern, 'is he still sniffing around? And is he sniffing around you or Bina?'

Kate made a dismissive gesture. Like a good mom, Elliot always thought every man was in love with Kate, and if they weren't he was offended. 'He seems to be busy carrying news about Jack to anyone who'll listen. I think he still feels guilty because he introduced Bina to him. Anyway, he's harmless. Bina doesn't have time for anyone but Billy,' Kate continued, and only after the words were out of her mouth did she notice the slight bitterness in her tone. Luckily, Elliot – who had radar for things like that – didn't pick it up because of the loud noise he was making as his straw sucked up the liquid at the very bottom of his cup.

'That's disgusting,' Kate said.

'Well, I promise not to do it in front of your friends at the shower.'

'Bev's shower?' Kate asked, her voice rising at least an octave. The realization hit her hard but she knew it was going to be true. 'You're invited to Bev's shower?'

'You sound surprised,' Elliot said. Then, in a mocking tone, he added, 'You know Bev and Brice and I are *very* close.' Kate merely rolled her eyes. 'Hey, I saw Brian Conroy at lunch today and he was actually laughing with two other little bandits,' he continued. 'I think they were slinging tuna fish

243

at the girls' table but I didn't catch them at it.' Elliot smiled at her. 'You might actually be doing some good work,' he said. They looked at each other for a long moment, Elliot smiling at her, his brown eyes warm and wet as a Labrador's, and Kate basked in his approval. Then, as was their custom, they simultaneously shook their heads and bleated, 'Nah!'

'I wish you could do something about the Reilly twins,' Elliot grumbled. 'Yesterday, I gave Joseph the test on fractions that James was supposed to take, so James failed, and now his mother is complaining to me because his grade will suffer. Like it will stop him from getting into Harvard. Can't you give them an anti-duping drug or something?'

'If only. I think she's the one who needs therapy,' Kate said.

'That's a big surprise,' Elliot huffed. 'All of these type A parent bastards need Prozac or a big smack.'

'Don't worry. Most of them *are* on Prozac,' Kate laughed. The pressure the parents lived under and too often exerted on their children was always palpable in the halls of Andrew Country Day. 'So what is it with you and Michael?' Kate asked. 'He's the kind of stable, nice guy you've wanted for me. And he likes me.'

She looked down at the bracelet hanging from her wrist and her cell phone rang. She was expecting a call from her friend Rita about drinks after Rita got out of work, which wasn't usually until six or seven o'clock. She pulled out her cell phone and, without even glancing at the caller ID, hit the green button.

'Hi,' she said cheerfully, fully expecting Rita's nasal voice.

'Hi back atchaya,' Steven's voice said.

Kate felt her stomach crumple and drop, like a soccer ball that had collapsed in the air near the goal. Suddenly there wasn't enough oxygen in her chest cavity.

'Oh. Steven. Hello.' She opened her eyes wide, but not as wide as Elliot's, who moved in on her almost immediately, a

244

look of horror on his face. Silently he mouthed, 'Steven? *The* Steven?'

Kate, already rattled, looked away. She didn't need to be observed. She was over Steven. She was *long* over Steven, but that didn't stop the color from rising into her cheeks. She could feel her throat tighten.

'Am I getting you at a bad time?' Steven asked.

She wanted to say, 'No. The bad time was the six months after you stopped calling,' but, needless to say, she didn't. Any time was a bad time to talk to Steven, as far as she was concerned, and Elliot was making it abundantly clear that he shared that opinion. 'No,' she said. 'I'm just having coffee with Elliot.' Then she could have bitten her tongue, or slapped herself, or both. Why couldn't she be oblique – or even lie and say she was with someone else?

'Good old Elliot,' Steven said, which made Kate even more annoyed with herself. 'I miss him.' His voice dropped a half-register. 'I miss *you*, too,' he said. Kate felt the flush spread to her neck and chest. Meanwhile, Elliot was crouching in front of her, gesturing wildly. He kept pulling his index finger across his throat, telling her to cut the conversation.

She turned her head to the right, but Elliot, still crouching, jumped like some kind of dwarfish character from *The Lord of the Rings* back into view.

Kate didn't need to be reminded of how dangerous Steven was. She had really loved him, and he had encouraged her to. Long ago, Kate had made a rule to never care for any man more than he cared for her. But Steven had cared for her – at least as long as the early lust stage had lasted. Then, after eighteen months, his ardor and his commitment had dropped off. Kate hadn't felt it at first, and by the time she had realized that he was not still focused on her she had run into him, walking with the woman to whom his focus had shifted. When Kate, humiliated, had confronted him, he had been reluctant to admit the truth and had reassured her that

245

nothing had happened between him and Sabrina, but after Kate broke up with him, a miserable six weeks later, he and Sabrina had hooked up. Now, the question Kate longed to ask was 'What's happened to Sabrina?' But she wouldn't let her curiosity overwhelm her common sense and pride.

'Look, I thought we might meet for a coffee or something,' Steven said.

'I don't think so,' Kate said. 'I'm having coffee right now.' In front of her Elliot was mouthing, 'No. No. No,' like a demented toddler beginning a tantrum.

'You're not making this easy,' Steven said, and the depth of feeling in his voice gave Kate a little thrill. All at once she realized what she had felt was missing in Michael – access to deeper feelings, or the ability to express them.

But Steven's feelings – deep, or not – had not been dependable. He was either an excellent actor (Elliot's opinion) or a man afraid of his own emotions, longing for connection and then backing away from it (Kate's theory). Kate still believed that Steven had loved her, but had been afraid.

'Was it my job to make it easy?' Kate asked while Elliot rolled his eyes. He put a hand over his own mouth to indicate that she should shut up – as if she didn't know that already. She swatted at him. More than half a dozen of the other patrons were looking at them by now.

'Kate, you have every right to be pissed off at me. But I swear that a day hasn't gone by that I haven't thought of you, or missed you, or even tried to get up the courage to phone you.'

'It must have been a tough year,' Kate said.

'Don't tell me you haven't thought of me,' Steven said, and all the miserable nights, the lonely weekends, the mornings she woke up alone and missing him came rushing back.

'I've been pretty busy,' she said. 'And I'm about to get engaged . . .'

Elliot shot up from his crouch, gave her a thumb's-up

246

with both hands and then sank down in his chair as if exhausted.

There was silence at the other end of the phone and Kate was torn between two emotions: she wanted Steven to give up and feel just a little bit of pain on her account. She also wanted him to try harder, and she was ashamed and embarrassed by that.

'Would that stop you from just having a drink with me?' Steven asked. 'I really feel as if I need to tell you what happened. I mean, I'm in therapy now and . . . I just understand a few things that I didn't know before.'

Kate wasn't sure she wanted to know what Steven had learned about himself. And she knew it wasn't a good idea to see him. But she felt an irresistible pull toward him. 'How about next Monday?' she said. 'About four o'clock.'

'That would be great,' Steven said. 'O'Nieal's?' It was a restaurant on Grand Street, a cool but lush bar and dining room. It had been a place they often went to, not far from his loft.

'No,' she said. She didn't want to be seduced into drinks followed by dinner followed by anything else. It was out of the question.

She thought as quickly as she could about a more neutral site. 'How about Starbucks?' And after he agreed she hung up and threw her phone into her purse.

'You are not going!' Elliot said. 'You know why you're not going? Because I cannot hear one more word about that stupid fucking assfuck. Do you know how much Steven I had to live with last year? How many times can a man – even a gay man – sing "I Will Survive" with you?'

Kate didn't know if she should laugh or cry. They did actually sing Gloria Gaynor's song a few times, but only at Elliot's demand and because it always made her laugh.

'We wore out three CDs, and speaking of wearing out, you might be self-destructive but I have a life. I can't go through another Steven bout. Maybe you don't remember what it did to you but I do. And I just can't take it. Neither can you.'

'I'm not going to go through another Steven "bout",' Kate snapped. 'But he's in therapy and he probably needs some closure.'

'What he probably needs is some pussy,' Elliot said. 'And that's fine with me as long as it isn't yours.'

'Elliot!' Kate was about to continue but Elliot wasn't done yet.

'I can't believe he calls you for the first time in a year in the middle of the afternoon on your cell phone and you make a date with him. Have you no pride?' Elliot asked. 'You're a disgrace to your sex. It's because of you that women need to read *The Rules* and those other stupid self-help books.' He moved his arms in a spasm of disgust and completely upset his drink. 'Oh, shit,' he said, and Kate wasn't sure if he was referring to the spill or her mistake.

Because it was a mistake. Wasn't it?

30

It was crowded in Bunny and Arnie's new apartment; everyone sat or stood in perfect silence in the dark. Which was quite a trick when Kate considered the compulsive talkers she was with. Bunny, Barbie, Mrs Horowitz, Bina, two of Bev's cousins, Bev's mom and two aunts, assorted friends from work, her astrologist, not to mention Elliot and Brice, were all there and quiet. But only for a moment.

'Surprise!' the entire crowd shouted as the door opened. The lights went on and pink and blue balloons – big, but not as big as Bev's third-trimester belly, though as stretched as hers seemed to be – fell from the ceiling. Flashbulbs went off all around the room recording her as she screamed and jumped. Guests screamed and jumped as well. Dunkirk must have felt a little like this, Kate thought. After the explosions were over, Kate, afraid of a miscarriage, watched as a palpitating Bev leaned on her mother's arm.

She was taken toward a seat, from where she surveyed the scene of laughing friends and relatives. She clutched her face and screamed. 'Aah, you guys,' she said as soon as she could speak. 'I swear my water almost broke! You shouldn't have.' She'd been told to 'drop over at Bunny's new apartment for a look-see'.

Kate agreed with that – there was something sadistic in

surprise frights, but 'Yes, we should have and we did,' Barbie told Bev, joining her on the hideous blue sofa.

In fact virtually all of Bunny's new apartment was in blue, and most of it was hideous. Kate had forgotten that nobody in Brooklyn south of Prospect Park believed in antiques – things were either new or junk. Kate considered the royal-blue rayon damask upholstered furniture in the living room new *and* junk, but everyone else had oohed and aahed over Bunny's new marital home on the obligatory tour before Bev's arrival. Even Elliot, not only color-blind but largely tasteless, had raised his eyebrows at the smoked mirror framed with golden cherubs and the Museum Shop lamps with fake busts of antiquity mounted under the shades. Brice, however, was in ecstasy. 'Just like Picasso,' he had murmured to Kate and Elliot. 'She's having her blue period.'

The wall-to-wall carpet was a peacock blue in the living room, a Madonna blue in the master bedroom, and a royal blue in the second bedroom. The bathrooms, one full and one half, were also, needless to say, blue. One was papered in periwinkle with green vines and had matching green towels – 'as the essential accent,' Bunny had explained. The other was done in navy foil – 'I wanted something masculine for Arnie,' she'd told them, though why shiny dark walls were manly was something Kate couldn't fathom.

'I didn't know they still made foil,' Brice had said, marveling.

'I know. I had to go on-line to find it,' Bunny confided.

'You could have this place published in *Nest* in a New York minute,' Brice told her. Of course, he then had to explain what the magazine *Nest* was, leaving out the part that it was a sort of *House and Garden* for the over-the-top louche and bizarre. Just as well, Kate had figured.

But Kate wasn't only looking around at the apartment, she was also looking at her friends. Each one was committed to a life that would almost inevitably include children, PTA meetings, family holidays, trips to Disney World and all the

250

trimmings that came not only on the Christmas tree (or Hanukah bush) but also with the comfy order of family life. She looked around and wondered if she would ever leave the little nest she had carved out for herself in Manhattan and, if she did, what she would trade it for. Somehow the prospect of doing it in Austin without either her Manhattan or her Brooklyn friends to support or encourage her seemed grim. At least when she had been with Steven she knew that her future – if there was one – would be in New York.

Here in Brooklyn once Bev got over her surprise, all of the guests felt free to tear into the incredibly plentiful food. That, set out on the dining table and credenza (both covered with sky-blue cloths with napkins to match), was a truly impressive spread. Everything from bagels accessorized with four varieties of cream cheese to pasta salads, Thai satay, canapés, and canollis was arrayed in absolutely overwhelming profusion. Elliot picked up a plate and heaved a big sigh of happiness. 'I love it here,' he said.

'Oops. He's up another waist size,' Brice said and patted Elliot lovingly.

Everyone seemed to be enjoying themselves enormously, except Bina. Kate didn't want another recitation of Billy Nolan's charms so she had avoided Bina just a little but it didn't seem necessary: Kate realized that Bina was avoiding her. She was sitting, her plate heaped high, next to one of Bev's cousins but she wasn't talking or eating. Only Bev's nephew, a four-year-old who sat on the floor dutifully chewing whatever his grandma or mother put in his mouth, seemed capable of bringing a smile to her lips.

'Okay. Let's get down to business,' Barbie told everyone once the food frenzy had subsided. 'Open the presents! Open the presents!'

Everyone cheered and agreed, except Bina. Kate kept an eye on her as box after box was unwrapped.

*　　*　　*

All the gifts had been opened and Bev's mother was wrestling in the wrapping paper as if it were a pile of leaves that had been raked up in the fall. Bev was holding up a little sweater and examining the knitted bonnet that went with it.

Kate touched the piece of hand-knit material and, all at once, she was almost overcome by a wave of feeling so unexpected and so strong that she had to sit down. Up to now, for some inexplicable reason, Bev's pregnancy had only been that – a swelling stomach, a few inappropriate outfits and some complaints. Holding the tiny sweater, Kate realized that very soon Bev – and Johnnie, of course – would have a new person, as tiny as the little bit of wool, to hold and love and care about for the rest of their lives. Kate felt so very far away from that reality that tears of envy and despair filmed her eyes. She had to turn her head away so no one would notice her sudden rush of emotion.

I want a baby of my own, she thought and realized at the same time that she was further away from that possibility than she had been for a long time. Because she suddenly knew, absolutely knew, as she held the little sweater, that she wouldn't want to be putting it on Michael's child. The very idea was . . . well, it just wasn't possible.

'Have some rugella, Katie,' Mrs Horowitz offered, and Kate looked up. She must have appeared as dazed as she felt because Mrs Horowitz exclaimed, 'You're so pale. Are you all right, darling?'

The answer, of course, was 'no' but how could she explain that to kind, concerned and simple Myra Horowitz?

'It doesn't matter if he's not a real doctor,' she said to Kate, her voice low. 'As long as you love him.' Kate managed a smile and took a pastry.

The women were all trying to balance their second helping of over-filled paper plates on their laps and simultaneously manage plastic cups of juice, margaritas or New York State champagne.

The Bitches, Brice and Elliot had gathered in a small group in the corner near the easy chair that Bev had settled into.

'So, is it a girl or a boy?' Barbie asked.

Bev looked at her mother, then shrugged her shoulders. 'Johnnie and I want a surprise,' she said, but Kate saw their complicity.

'I think you should name him William,' Elliot said.

'After the prince?' Bev asked.

'No. After Billy Nolan. The man who made all this possible,' Elliot told her.

'See, Elliot's theory works. Just think. You're next,' Brice told Bina with frightening assurance.

'That's right, Bina,' Bunny agreed.

'Jack'll come around,' Bev's mother told Bina in a comforting tone. 'Remember how long it took her Johnnie to propose? I'm glad you stayed local, Bina, and didn't go into Manhattan like Katie.'

'Yeah,' Barbie echoed. 'It's even harder to get them to commit.'

'I don't think that location has . . .' Kate started to say. But before she went any further her Manhattan team came in for the rescue.

'Kate's doing okay,' Elliot said defensively.

'Yeah,' Brice chimed in. 'She's getting a proposal from this doctor guy.'

Kate felt the blood leave her face.

'Get outta town!' Barbie cried.

'You sneak! You didn't say a word,' Bunny squawked.

'What's his sign?' Bev demanded.

Kate was kissed and pummeled for a few minutes, until she could raise her voice over the cries of 'you go, girl' and 'mazel tov' to object. 'I'm not "getting a proposal",' she told them all, then gave Brice a dirty look. He shrugged an apology. Kate tried to find words to describe her situation with Michael and put out the blazing fire of curiosity around her. 'We're talking about options.'

'Options-schmopshins,' Mrs Horowitz said. 'So what kind of doctor? Not a surgeon,' she warned. 'Surgeons are cold, Katie.'

'He's not a medical doctor,' Kate said, then heard all the sighs of disappointment that moved through the room like a summer breeze. She shot Elliot and Brice a murderous look. 'They don't know what they're saying. Anyway, we were talking about Bina.'

'Maybe we shouldn't,' Bina said. 'I saw Max and . . .' Bina saw Max? Since when? And why? Kate thought of all the e-mails Max had forwarded to her. She hoped that Max hadn't shared them with Bina.

'Oh, everything is going to work out fine,' Bunny said, and she put her arm around Elliot. It seemed to Kate that the group had adopted Elliot and Brice as girlfriends in drag.

'She's got Dumping Billy on her side,' Barbie said.

'He hasn't dumped you yet though, has he?' Bev asked Bina.

'No. Not yet. But I'm really looking forward to it,' Bina said, obviously uncomfortable.

'Well, it's been a long time – for him,' Barbie pointed out.

'According to Elliot's theory, that makes sense,' Barbie said.

'No. Actually, it doesn't. This whole thing doesn't make sense and it's making me crazy,' Kate told the women. She was feeling more and more upset. Somehow everything seemed wrong: her with Michael, Bina with Billy, Jack with a bevy of foreign beauties, Steven calling her from out of the blue. It seemed at that moment as if it was more than a French farce. It seemed as if life itself was being wicked and unmanageable. Looking at Bina and feeling for herself, tears sprang to Kate's eyes.

Kate took a piece of the shower cake to comfort herself.

'Oh, well, it has to be at least two months or else it doesn't work, but I am a little uncomfortable,' Bina admitted.

Bev put her hand on the back of the chair in order to help herself up. 'Honey, you've got to go on about as long as I do. And you don't have any idea what uncomfortable is until you are pregnant in the summer. You CANNOT give up now,' Bev said matter-of-factly.

'Stay the course,' Barbie advised Bina.

'A million points of light,' Bev added, though why or what the reference meant in this case seemed very obscure.

'I think it was only a thousand, and Bina's on nine hundred and ninety-nine,' Kate said.

'Right, Billy can't last much longer,' Barbie said. 'You're not his type.'

'Oh no? He's asked me to the Hamptons this weekend,' Bina said without enthusiasm.

Kate could tell her friend was in a strange mood, but even Mrs Horowitz didn't seem to notice.

The Bitches squealed with delight, wisecracked, elbowed and laughed to each other.

'What's so funny?' Bina demanded.

'What you don't know about men could fill a library,' Bev said.

'A big one. A Manhattan one,' Bunny added.

'What don't I know?' Bina asked.

'Bina, honey, this will be the end. Men like Billy freak out after a weekend alone with a woman,' Barbie said. 'He's sure to drop you after that.'

'But then why would he ask me?' Bina did look really upset. Kate wondered again if Bina was falling for that self-centered idiot. 'It wasn't my idea.'

'That's the point,' Bunny told her.

'They like the idea of intimacy . . .' Bev began.

'. . . But the reality is they freak out because of all the one-on-one time,' Barbie continued.

'Really, Bina. Go to the Hamptons and you are as good as dumped,' Bunny assured Bina.

'I don't know, it seems like false pretense,' Bina told them.

'Maybe it is but you can't turn back now,' Bev said as she walked to the table of refreshments.

Bina had been juggling her plate of food on her lap and suddenly lost control of it. The entire thing fell down her dress and onto the floor. The Bitches fell silent and stared at her.

Kate had felt something was wrong with Bina's behavior since they'd arrived, and now, as if to confirm that instead of clearing up the mess, Bina took Kate's hand and began to pull her down the hall. 'I have to talk to you,' she whispered loudly.

'Wait a minute,' Kate said and put down her glass of red wine, afraid that a spill would turn the carpet an irrevocable purple. Bina pulled her into the guest bedroom and sat down on the sofa bed piled high with coats.

'I can't believe it, Katie,' Bina said, and her whisper had a sob in it now. 'I'm so ashamed. I never thought . . . I could never believe that I . . . Ohmigod, Jack.'

Kate had no idea what Bina was going on about but she was upset to see her so upset. And in a different way from her usual innocent hysteria. 'What *is* it, Bina?' she demanded.

'If my mother knew . . . oh Katie! I cheated on Jack.'

'Bina, a few dates doesn't mean . . .'

'No. I mean I really did. I had sex. I mean the whole thing. And it was . . . wonderful.' As Bina burst into tears Kate felt the room and the noise of the party receding.

This new information, this sexual misadventure of Bina's, was exactly what Kate had been afraid of. She felt herself becoming angry but wasn't sure who she was angry at or with. Elliot should never have proposed this, Kate should never have allowed it, Bina shouldn't have fallen for Billy's empty charm, and, Kate admitted to herself, she was most angry that Billy in true Lothario fashion had taken advantage

256

of Bina's inexperience. What had she done? She and Elliot and the Bitches had interfered in Bina's life, and the results were this: a girl awash in guilt and tears and confusion. Hadn't they all succeeded in ruining Bina's loyalty and single-minded devotion? Perhaps it was a bad thing, to count on one man to come through for you and to believe that there was nobody else. Still, Bina should have been left to make her own choices; setting her up with a man like Billy Nolan was sure to be her undoing. And now, what if she decided she loved him? What if after the heartbreak of Jack's desertion she was dumped again, as was inevitable? It would destroy her self-confidence. Kate didn't even want to imagine what Bina might do.

She took her friend by the shoulders and stared into her red, teary eyes. Bina looked like nothing so much as a cocker spaniel puppy with an eye infection. 'Listen to me, Bina, whatever you did is all right. Jack has been off sleeping around and if you had a slip, so . . .'

'But I don't feel like it was a slip,' Bina said and began crying anew. 'I feel as if he appreciates me. He says that since he saw me he's felt that not grabbing me up was a mistake.'

Kate repressed the idea of rolling her eyes, remembering how she had to challenge Billy to even consider Bina as date material. 'Bina, you can't believe everything men say,' Kate began to explain. She felt a fury that she had to tamp down. It was rage at Jack for leaving Bina, and at Elliot and the Bitches for concocting this manipulative scheme, and at herself for helping to make it happen. But beneath all of that, there was another feeling.

'Katie, I never doubted my love for Jack. I mean, I do love Jack. It's just that now that I've had some more experience, well, I just can't explain it. He's so understanding. And it's like we never run out of things to talk about.' She paused.

'Look, Bina, you have not been disloyal. Just don't confuse this, well, this little adventure with real love.'

Bina looked at Kate solemnly. 'You're right,' she said and

257

nodded. 'I won't let it happen again. Because I really, really do love Jack.'

'Good girl,' Kate told her. 'Now, just don't think about it anymore.' As if. Kate imagined that it would be hard to think of anything else but sleeping with Billy Nolan once you had done so. It was a godsend that Bina still preferred Jack. 'You just forget about it,' Kate said. 'You don't have to do what you don't want to do.'

Bina nodded. Then she wiped her eyes. 'But he was so very, very good in bed.' Bina blushed. And Kate felt her own face color because she realized what the other feeling was. She was envious.

Kate left the shower before Brice and Elliot. She was too despondent to take the subway so, as an indulgence, she looked for a taxi. It wasn't easy in Brooklyn – another reason to stay in Manhattan, Kate reflected sourly. But at last she flagged down an off-duty taxi who was merely avoiding a fare that would take him deeper into Brooklyn.

Kate sat in the back seat, grateful for the time alone. Though she loved both Brice and Elliot she simply wasn't up for their chatter. She had a lot of thinking to do and though she had put off dealing with her reality until now, she would have to come to terms with it. What was it that she really wanted? Of course, that was easy to answer: a perfect life with a rewarding job, a loving, dependable and passionate husband, healthy children and good friends. Good fucking luck, she told herself. She couldn't see any indications that her future would promise all of the above. If you got one part you wouldn't get the other. Yet Kate had promised herself for all these years that she wouldn't compromise.

As they crossed the Brooklyn Bridge, she stared at the city. The skyline, as always, moved her deeply. But now she had to admit that she was even more deeply moved by Bina's revelation. How could she go on with Michael when she felt such a draw to someone as useless as Billy Nolan? His behavior with Bina had only further convinced her of his heartlessness, and the fact that a part of her – not the good part – still desired him was shameful. One thing she was certain of, she wouldn't become confused and reassess Steven's actions in light of Billy's. What did it matter which of them was worse? Kate looked out the taxi window and wished that she could forever stay suspended on the bridge between the two boroughs in her life.

31

Kate sat at a window table in the Chelsea Kitchen and played with her fork, laying it down, picking it up, tapping the bottom and then touching the tines to her water glass, her plate, and even the folded napkin. She was uncomfortable in the restaurant but she had decided that she would do this in a public place. That's what men do, she thought, and remembered Steven. Probably it was because they were afraid of scenes. Kate knew that wasn't a realistic threat with Michael, but she couldn't imagine having this talk and then moving through his apartment on her way to the door or, worse, asking him to leave her own place.

Since the afternoon of the shower Kate had known with blinding clarity that Michael was not for her. She'd talked it over with Elliot who must have told Brice. She'd also told Bina who must have told Mrs Horowitz and Bev, who surely told everybody. It seemed cruel that only Michael himself didn't know.

Beside her on the floor was a Big Brown Bag from Bloomingdale's. When she forced herself to put down the fork she used the same hand to check again that the bag was there – as if anyone would want to steal second-hand folded shorts and athletic socks, a razor, half-used-up toiletries and an old tie Michael had left behind at her house. She wiped her palms on the napkin, surprised to find how sweaty they were. The truth was that Kate had little experience in being the initiator of a break-up.

When the waiter came over she asked for vodka on the rocks. She didn't usually drink hard liquor, and when she did it was usually a Cosmopolitan, a drink that had come in and gone out of fashion but one she liked. Today, however, she needed a jolt of something. She remembered a phrase her father used to use – 'Dutch courage' – and for the first time she really appreciated what that meant. She did need courage, Dutch or otherwise.

When the waiter returned with her order she downed it in two long gulps with only a breath between them. She realized only then that she didn't want Michael to see her drinking, and she also didn't want him to smell alcohol on her breath. Why? That had always been a strained part of their relationship. Somehow, though he had never tried to intimidate her or force her to be different from how she was, Kate realized she had often walked on eggshells with Michael. She wondered now if she had ever really been herself with him. She wasn't sure if it was his personality that had imposed restraints on her. Perhaps that wasn't fair. Perhaps his academic credentials and his comfortable suburban background had created a sense of inferiority in her. Maybe they both had a classic fear of intimacy. But whatever it was, Kate knew there was something not right, something not fixable in it.

She waved to the waiter and handed him the evidence. 'Can I get you another?' he asked, no doubt taking her for a heavy drinker, but she shook her head. Then she picked up a piece of the garlic bread from the basket on the table. Better to smell of garlic than vodka. People mistakenly thought you couldn't detect vodka on a person's breath, but Kate always could – maybe because of her father.

She munched on the bread and looked out the window. In the late afternoon there weren't many people on West Eighteenth Street. She wondered where the man with the red tips at the ends of his black hair was going, and whether the woman who looked like a real estate broker in her fake Chanel suit actually was one. Kate sighed. She'd probably never be able to afford to buy an apartment or to own her own home. As a couple it was difficult enough here in Manhattan. As a single person it was impossible.

She had no home of her own, no summer plans and soon she'd have no man in her life.

Kate's thirty-second birthday was less than three months away. She hoped that Elliot, now that he seemed glued to the Bitches, wouldn't decide on a stroke-inducing surprise party for her. After today she certainly wouldn't be in the mood to celebrate.

Kate took a sip of her water and looked out at the traffic. It was a wet day and though the drizzle had stopped for the moment, it had put a sheen on the macadam, the trucks and taxis and even the sidewalks and the buildings across the way. She loved New York, Manhattan to be specific, and this simple silvery scene outside the restaurant window calmed her. How could Michael assume, without any discussion, that she would simply pick up and leave? What did it say about the rest of his presumptions, his innate arrogance and insensitivity? She'd never even been to Austin. Kate shook her head.

On the other hand, she could be completely crazy. Aside from the Arnies, Johnnies, Eddies and the rest of the Brooklyn world, it seemed there were no marriageable men. Rita and every other one of her Manhattan girlfriends complained about how the men here were players or neurotics or commitment-phobes. She thought back to Steven and the pain she had gone through after he left her. She wasn't going to have this talk with Michael just because of her upcoming date with Steven. Steven was out of her life, although she couldn't help feeling a bit of excitement, the old buzz, when she thought of a meeting with him. It would be nice to see him and feel nothing. She hoped she could manage it. She looked down and the fork in her hand was actually trembling. Could she hurt Michael like that? Could she bear to be alone, start dating again and risk ever being hurt that way again?

The waiter returned with a pitcher of water. Her glass was half empty, or half full. She supposed, as he poured out the water, that it was all in the eye of the beholder. If she discussed what she was about to do with Barbie, Bev or even Mrs Horowitz they would tell her she was crazy. Her glass was half full. Still, while she knew that Steven was dangerous and not for her, simply hearing from him had reminded her of how much she had felt for him when they were together. The disparity between that feeling and the pale echo of it that she felt for Michael frightened her. She just didn't think that she could bear to go through life without stronger feelings for her companion.

Kate couldn't suppress the surge of feeling she was experiencing not only from Steven's call but also from the overwhelming envy she'd felt when Bina told her about her affair with Billy. Kate knew she couldn't stay with Michael. It wasn't even the way he had simply assumed she'd drop everything and follow him to Austin. It wasn't the prissy way he walked or the rigidity he showed. Michael was a safe, dependable partner and, she admitted to herself, he'd make a responsible father. But for someone else's children, not hers.

Even if she was ruining her last chance of settling down, Kate couldn't settle for him. She placed the fork she'd been holding back down in its proper place. She noticed a woman, possibly an au pair, walk by with a little girl who looked about four. They were both wearing yellow raincoats. Kate smiled and thought of the children she was working with at Andrew Country Day. Everything about her job, from her little office to Elliot down the hall, to the easy commute from home, to the children she worked with, seemed precious to her. Now, at the thought of losing it, she could feel just how precious it was. Even Mr McKay seemed loveable in his ridiculous way. And Michael believed it was nothing to her? Did he know her at all?

When Michael walked in Kate was still staring out the window and jumped when he put his hand on her shoulder. 'I got caught in the rain,' he said as he shook his umbrella and took the seat across from her.

Kate looked at him. His jaw was still strong, his nose was still regular, his eyes a warm brown. But Kate, as if a spell had been broken, no longer found him the slightest bit attractive. As he set his briefcase on the empty chair she wondered whether this kind of reversal had happened to Steven: whether one day he just looked at her and felt nothing but . . . a mild distaste. The idea made her skin crawl. The mixture of the drink and what she was about to have to do made her stomach and the rest of her feel creepy as well.

'Would you like something to drink?' Michael asked her and she managed a weak smile. She certainly wasn't going to tell him that she'd already had plenty.

'No, thank you,' she told him soberly, though she wasn't entirely sure that she was sober now.

The solicitous waiter appeared, unbidden, and Kate had to hope he didn't blow her cover by asking if she wanted *another* vodka rocks. Not that it really mattered.

'A cup of tea,' Michael requested. 'Earl Grey if you have it.'

'Nothing for me,' Kate said, and the statement seemed to be too true. After the waiter moved off, Michael looked out the window as Kate had been doing. 'Well, we won't have to put up with this kind of weather in Austin.'

'Why?' Kate asked. 'Doesn't it rain there?' But she didn't pursue it. Why be unpleasant? She didn't know how to begin and so she just launched herself into her prepared speech. 'Michael, I can't go to Austin. First because I don't want to; I like it here. Secondly, because you didn't ask me. You *assumed* I would come with you. We had no discussion. It was as if you were granting me some kind of favor. You just thought I would jump at the chance.'

Michael blinked and put down the cup that he had halfway to his lips. Kate saw some of the tea splash over the lip and onto the tablecloth but Michael didn't seem to notice. 'Kate. Kate, I just felt . . .'

'I'm not sure what you felt,' Kate said. 'But it isn't what *I* felt. And you didn't know it.'

Michael sat absolutely still and the table – no more than twenty-six inches wide – seemed to Kate to be expanding to tundra proportions. She could almost see Michael receding into the distance, his face blueish in the reflected light from the white cloth that stretched between them. 'Kate, I never meant to be presumptuous. I just thought, well, I thought you wanted what I wanted.'

'That may be true, but since we never actually spoke about what we wanted how was I to know?' Michael sat still and looked at her as if he was seeing her for the first time. Perhaps, for all she knew, he was. Had she been guilty of trying too hard to please? Had she kept her feelings and fears from him? Somehow it didn't seem to matter anymore. Even if Michael now told her he was willing to give up the Austin job and make a home with her here, Kate was no longer interested. Am I fickle? she thought. She couldn't answer the question but she knew that a single life, alone and with no children, would be better than a half-life with Michael. And that was all it would ever be because, though he looked good on paper, Michael simply wasn't the man for her.

'Kate, I can't tell you how floored I am by this. I mean,

it's coming out of nowhere. I've been busy making plans assuming . . .'

'Never assume, Michael,' Kate said. 'Never presume. My life is just as important to me as yours is to you. I'm not sure you ever recognized that.'

'Of course I did,' Michael said. 'But you could make new friends and set up a practice in Austin. You could visit back here whenever you wanted. And it's not as if you have family here.'

'Oh yes, I do,' Kate said. She thought of Elliot, and Brice and Bina and the Horowitzes. Even the Bitches meant a lot to her. 'They might not be DNA-related, but I have family all the same.' She paused. 'I don't know whose fault it is, Michael; let's not talk about fault and let's not blame one another. It isn't as if I've felt this way for months and withheld the knowledge from you. It's just that once you told me about Austin and made your decision unilaterally, I guess I made mine. I'm very sorry.' She reached her hand across the tablecloth to touch his but he pulled his own back, spilling the tea in the process. It spread, like a brown blot, across the pure white space between them. And for a moment she was reminded of the bowling alley and her spilled beer. 'I'm sorry,' she repeated, 'because there's nothing else to say.' She stood up, holding the shopping bag. 'Here are your things,' she said. 'If I've forgotten some of them, let me know.'

Oddly, she didn't feel sad and she didn't feel free. She felt nothing. Michael was still looking at her, his face torn between what looked like disbelief and anger. 'Good luck in Austin,' she said. And walked out of the restaurant and into the drizzle that had begun again.

Kate walked in the rain for a while, at least until she was wet enough to feel punished for hurting someone's feelings. Then she tried to bring herself back around by taking out her cell phone. Although he hadn't, there was always a chance that Steven would call. Of course, once she checked her messages she'd realized he hadn't and knew that he wouldn't but she would keep checking anyway.

Steven had hurt her, she had hurt Michael. The pain went around and around and it seemed insane. She felt she'd be miserable for the rest of her life but she couldn't imagine Michael feeling too bad for too long, though. It wasn't his style. The very reason she left him was because he didn't feel things.

After about half an hour she found herself in front of the gym. She walked in in time to see Elliot just finishing up his cardio on the StairMaster. He was almost as wet as she was, but once he caught sight of her he was concerned. 'What have you done? You're supposed to take your clothes off before you shower.' He took her over to one of the leather banquettes and took her sodden raincoat off her shoulders. 'You're wet right through,' he said, and fussed for a few minutes with towels. When Kate's wet hair had been wrapped in a turban and the towel hugged her neck, Elliot was ready for conversation.

'I broke up with Michael,' Kate said.

'Good.' Elliot nodded. Then he put his arm round her. 'It was only a matter of time. And this saves you a ticket to Austin, which you could spend on a share in our house this summer.'

Kate, who had expected more surprise and a lot more sympathy, shook her head. 'I don't think being the only woman in a house full of gay men in Cherry Grove would be the thing for me right now.'

'Oh, come on. You'd have more fun than you would with any of your straight boyfriends. When did Michael make you laugh the way Brice does? When did Steven *ever* make you laugh?' Elliot stopped, leaned back against the banquette and Kate knew she was in trouble. He leaned forward, his elbows

267

on his knees, his nose an inch away from hers. 'You're not still going to meet up with Steven, are you?'

And, of course, Kate was.

32

Kate expected nothing from the meeting with Steven but her pride made her primp. She was vain enough to want to look her best, and she put on extra mascara and French braided her hair. Steven had always liked it like that.

As she was leaving her apartment and pulling the door shut behind her, she stopped, intensely looking out into space, remembering too vividly the last time she'd seen Steven and the way they had parted at this door.

'Forget something?' Max asked from behind her.

She was startled and spun around. 'Oh, no, just thinking is all. What's up with you lately?'

'Not much. How about you?' He lounged against the hall wall.

Now was not the time to explain what she was doing or going to do, and Max certainly wasn't the person she should spill to. 'I'm actually going to be late for a meeting,' she said and tried to step by him. Max wasn't exactly a nuisance: he was a nice guy but she didn't have time for him.

But Max wouldn't let her go. He reached out and touched her arm. Again, she was startled by him. Since when did Max want to make small talk? He was usually wrapped up in Max. 'I've heard from Jack again!' he said, and shifted from foot to foot. 'Or should I say I've gotten e-mails. He sent me more pictures.'

Kate sighed. It was bad news that didn't have to be shared.

As if he could read her mind, Max then looked away and said, 'I still don't think I should show them to Bina.'

'Absolutely not!' Kate told him. Now was not the time to discuss Bina's mental state when she was trying to figure out her own. 'I really don't think so, Max. You know she's pretty tight with Billy now and I don't want her to get upset about Jack again.'

'Billy? Who's Billy?' Max asked, his forehead wrinkled.

'Oh, that's a long story you don't have the time to . . .'

'I'll listen. Try me. I've got the time.' He sounded more anxious than casual.

God, he was such a gossip. 'Unfortunately, I don't,' Kate told him. 'I'm going to be late.' She made her way to the stairs at the end of the hall. She looked back to see Max sliding down the wall to sit on the floor. Since when was Max so compassionate about her friends? Sure, Jack was his cousin and he might feel some responsibility for Bina, but not to this extent.

'You know, I worry about Bina,' Max said. 'I need to talk to Jack.'

'No, you don't,' Kate called to him as she ran down the stairs. 'Leave well enough alone.'

Steven looked terrific. Well, Kate reflected, Steven had always looked terrific to her. As he stood up his length unfolded, reminding Kate of one of those hinged yardsticks. He smiled, and his smile broke the parenthesis – the lines on each side of his mouth that looked so attractive in men. 'Hi,' he said. 'What can I get you?'

Kate was glad she hadn't committed to dinner. Though he lived in the East Village, Kate had selected the Starbucks near her apartment. It was safe: Steven wouldn't expect her to have a meal with him and Elliot never frequented the place. Steven had what looked like a café latte grande in front of him, half of it gone. He must have arrived early. 'An iced tea,' she said, in answer to his question, and took the seat across from him at his tiny table in the corner. He nodded and was at the counter in a moment. It gave Kate a chance to smooth her hair and look at him from behind.

He was still long and lean – at six foot three it was easy to be long, but perhaps he wasn't quite as thin as he had been. His hair, however, was still as beautiful: a thick black waterfall that gleamed like a crow's wing. Kate remembered too vividly how she had loved to stroke his hair. He turned and came back to her, the iced tea and a paper plate of biscotti in his hands. They were the anise ones that she liked. She was touched and surprised that he remembered, but when he picked one up himself, she thought that perhaps it was just because he himself had come to like them.

It was the time of day when few people dropped in for coffee: after the rush that came after lunch but before the rush that came after dinner. There were no clients lingering except for the inevitable madman writing in something that looked like a journal, and an older gentleman – obviously retired – who sat in a plush chair near the window and read a rumpled copy of the *New York Times* in the waning light.

She took a sip of her tea and they sat for a moment in silence. Kate had promised herself that she wasn't going to do much talking. She felt him looking at her and returned his gaze passively.

'You look terrific,' he said.

Kate smiled, and hoped the smile was what art critics and novelists called 'enigmatic'. 'I'm glad you could meet me,' he added. He paused. Kate maintained her silence. Perhaps, she thought, completely irrelevantly, she could someday become an analyst and be paid to say nothing for hours. 'Well, enough about you,' Steven said, 'how do I look?'

271

'I think you've grown,' Kate said, tongue-in-cheek. 'Do men have growth spurts?'

'Sure, but only emotional ones. And it's pretty rare.' He stopped smiling and his face took on the lean and hungry look that Kate remembered from their love-making and his talk about his ambitions. He wore it, she knew, when he wanted things. She remained silent, waiting to hear what it was that he wanted now.

'Kate, do you ever think about how it was . . . I mean how it was between us?'

She was grateful that Elliot wasn't there to smack his forehead and whine about the months she had relived every detail of her time with Steven. 'I've been busy,' she said. Steven nodded.

'I deserved that,' he said. 'But I've been thinking about you. Actually, I can't stop thinking about you. I do it all the time.'

'That isn't good,' Kate said, in exactly the same tone of voice Elliot would have used. God, was she going to sound more and more like a gay man?

Steven didn't seem to notice. 'Kate, I'm here to tell you, I was an asshole. I would say cad, but it's too archaic. Asshole covers a lot of territory, but you know what I mean.'

Kate nodded and took another sip of her tea. 'I think lying asshole would be more accurate,' she said. She turned her head toward the window so that she wouldn't display any visible emotion to him.

To her horror, out of the very corner of her eye she thought she saw Max walking by. Was he with a woman? She couldn't see them as they turned the corner but she prayed they wouldn't step into the shop. Max had met Steven more than once and would definitely agree with Steven's current self-assessment. Lately, Max had seemed so protective on Bina's behalf that on her own behalf he would probably do his best to beat Steven to a pulp. Though Kate abhorred violence, she could take a certain pleasure in imagining Steven punished. Still, she preferred to handle it in her own emotional rather than physical way. Luckily, nobody entered the coffee shop and Kate could focus again on Steven.

'I don't know what to say, exactly,' Steven told her. 'Except that I've been reading Piaget and I think I'm a case of arrested development. I was emotionally somewhere between seven and nine years old when we were going out.' Kate raised her eyebrows. She expected an apology but not such a complete and accurate one.

'Kate, I don't regret anything in my life as much as I regret letting you go.' Kate tried not to let these words sink in. There had been so many weeks, months that she had hoped to hear them. Now she told herself to stay cool and calm. Steven looked around. 'God, this place is murder,' he told her. 'Please, Kate, let me take you out for a drink and dinner. Just give me a chance to explain everything.'

Kate meant to say no. She meant to shake her head. She had gotten the satisfaction and closure that she craved and now she only had to be cold and polite and negative. Just one shake of the head.

'My job is very demanding right now,' she told him.

'When will it let up?'

'Oh, not for the next month or so.'

'So if I call you in four weeks could we see one another?'

When she found herself nodding she was as surprised, but not as delighted as Steven appeared to be.

33

Kate had barely had time to shower and get into bed, totally exhausted from her scene with Michael and the subsequent meeting with Steven, when the phone rang. She shrank from it as if it were a snakehead fish instead of just a telephone receiver. Rather than talk to Michael she would put a snakehead fish up to her ear. She screwed up her courage and took a look at the caller ID. When she saw that it was only Bina's number she heaved a sigh of relief and answered the ring.

'I can't believe it!' Bina almost yelled. 'It's working! It's working almost too good! And I haven't even broken up with him yet.'

Kate was totally confused. 'What are you talking about?' she asked, her voice more resigned than irritated.

'He called! He's going to ask me to marry him!'

Kate felt a jolt of jealousy mixed with complete surprise. 'Billy is proposing?' she asked, incredulous. She knew that Bina and Billy had been having fun, but she could hardly believe . . . with her break-up from Michael so fresh, the idea of Bina settled was unsettling, especially when it involved Billy Nolan. If he had proposed to Bina, it must have been precipitated by the sex. Kate cringed thinking about it – it

274

was always odd to imagine a friend in the throes of physical passion – but Bina, unlikely as it appeared, must have been great in bed.

'Not Billy! Jack! Jack called from Hong Kong,' Bina was almost shouting. 'He said he's flying home the day after tomorrow and he's doing it to see me. Kate, don't you get it? Elliot's plan worked. Jack is coming back to me.'

Kate, tired as she was, had trouble digesting this news. Her head was a jumble of Max's e-mails, Elliot's numbers and graphs, Bina's gossip about her dates, the recent shocking news from the baby shower. All of it seemed to converge on Kate, literally making her dizzy. 'Jack called and proposed?' she asked, as soon as she could figure out what had happened.

'Well, yes and no.' Bina's voice was slightly less joyous, slowed a bit by reluctance to admit the truth.

'Okay. Tell me exactly what happened,' Kate said, and wished that she hadn't given up smoking years ago. This was going to be the kind of long, involved description that only a cigarette could help get you through. 'And tell me it in order from beginning to end.'

She heard Bina take a deep breath. 'Well, first the phone rang.'

Kate realized it was just as well she'd given up cigarettes: she'd probably need a whole carton for this. 'Yeah. Then what?'

'Then I picked it up. No, actually my mother picked it up. Then she handed it to me and said "It's for you."'

'Did she know it was Jack?'

'Not then. Not until I screamed. Well, maybe she did, do you want me to ask her?'

'No.' Kate pushed an extra throw pillow behind her head and wished she had a glass of beer. 'Just tell me what he said and what you said, Bina.'

'Okay, so he said, "Bina, is that you?" So I said who wants

275

to know, but I knew it was him because I knew his voice right away. You know, it sounded like he was calling from Coney Island or something, not from the other side of the world.'

Kate marveled again at her friend's ability to insert a cliché into the most extraordinary situation. 'Then what did he say?' Kate sighed.

'He says, "Bina, I got to talk to you" and I say I'm listening and he goes, "I've made a big mistake, Bina." And I go, well, how is that my business?'

Kate was astounded that Jack and Bina's dialogue continued in the exact same way it always had despite the trauma of their separation. She couldn't help but compare it to her uncomfortable conversation with Steven.

'So he says "This is Jack." And I say – you're gonna like this, Katie. I say Jack who? Wasn't that good?'

'Great,' Kate said.

'So he says "Jack Weintraub." And I go, oh, I was confused. I thought it was Jack Marco Polo. And he's like "What?" And I'm like "You know, the single guy that discovered a whole new world in the orient."'

Kate thought for a moment of correcting Bina and telling her that she was talking about Asia, but decided against it. If she gave lessons in geography and political correctness she'd be on the phone all night.

'So he says, "Bina, don't mock me. Have you been going out with someone else?" And I say, "What's it to you?" And he says, "Now I know you are." And I say, "Think what you want, but I know the truth." And then he's like, "Bina, I really have to talk to you." And I say, "Whatever." And he's like, "I know you're probably angry at me and everything . . ." And I interrupt him and I say, "Think again, because I hardly remember you." Hey, Katie, do you think he heard gossip all the way in Japan?'

'He's in Hong Kong, Bina.'

'Isn't that a part of Japan?'

276

Kate just shook her head. 'So what happened then?' she asked.

'Now it gets really good. He goes, "I have to talk to you." And I say, "Isn't that what you're doing now?" And he says, "I've got to talk to you face to face." So I go, "That will probably be difficult since you're so two-faced." And he says, "Meet me at the airport on Thursday, Bina. I'm flying into JFK just to see you. Please don't say no."'

Kate waited. There was silence at the other end of the phone. 'So what did you say?' Kate asked, hesitating, remembering how Elliot had warned her not to see Steven. But, of course, this situation was very different.

'I said yes!' Bina almost yodeled into the phone. 'And he says, "I have something I want to ask you and something I want to give you." Isn't that great? So do you think it's too late to call Elliot and Brice and tell them or should I wait until tomorrow morning? I mean, if it wasn't for Elliot's statistics I never . . .' She paused. 'Ohmigod, Katie! Ohmigod! I have to get Billy to dump me for this to work, right?'

'Come on, Bina, that's all nonsense, Jack called you because he loves you and misses you.'

'Forget that. This is because of Elliot. If I didn't go out with Billy . . .'

Kate flung the blankets off and stood up. 'Don't be ridiculous,' she said. 'You don't have to do anything now but show up at the airport.'

'I'm calling Elliot,' Bina said. 'I have to find out how long I have to date Billy, and then you and Elliot have to figure out how we break up.'

'Oh, come on,' Kate said. 'You can just tell him it's over.'

'Nahuh,' Bina said while Kate stomped into the hall and across to her tiny kitchen, phone in hand. She prayed there was just one beer left somewhere in the back of the refrigerator. 'He has to break up with me, remember?' Kate opened the refrigerator door. It made that lonely light that illuminates

277

single women at one a.m. after they've had some horrible disappointment. 'I have to figure out a way for him to dump me, Katie,' Bina continued. 'And I have to do it by Thursday, otherwise . . .'

Behind the mayonnaise jar Kate caught a glimpse of the brown neck of a Samuel Adams. She uttered a silent prayer to the god of alcohol and grabbed it. 'Look, Bina, you don't have to believe me,' Kate told her friend as she poured the beer into a glass. She never drank from the bottle. It reminded her too much of her father. 'Jack has just about proposed. I don't know if you should accept him but if that's what you want, that's what you're doing Thursday night.'

'I'm calling Elliot,' Bina said. 'I'm calling him and then I'm calling Barbie and then . . .'

Oh, God. After the baby shower, Kate didn't think she could do one more function with the Bitches. 'Fine,' Kate said. 'Call them all, but leave me out of it.' She hung up the phone and chugged all the beer. Then she put down the glass and left it alone on the counter while she went, alone, to her bed.

34

Thursday morning dawned beautifully. Kate knew because she was awake – as she had been, on and off – for most of the night. The window in her bedroom faced east and she saw the murky brown that passed as darkness turn first beige, then pink and, lastly, salmon as the sun rose. It was close to the summer solstice, and the light would last till eight thirty that evening, but there was no light in Kate's heart. Though this brief period between the beginning of spring and the deep heat of summer was Kate's favorite time of year, she woke with a heaviness in her chest and a gray despair that no dawn could affect. She had been working and eating – though without an appetite – and walking to and from school but she felt barely conscious of any of it. Although she didn't regret breaking up with Michael and she didn't expect anything from Steven, she felt lonely and hopeless. Like many women in Manhattan, she would go without a partner because either she was good enough or they weren't. Her Brooklyn friends had exhausted her, and like a sore spot on her gums that she couldn't keep her tongue away from, there was something annoying and painful about Billy Nolan and Bina's affair with him that she preferred not to think about, but that her mind kept going back to. Perhaps worst of all, she couldn't talk to Rita or her other Manhattan friends about it because they would never understand, and she couldn't talk to Elliot about it because he was the instigator, and the truth was she didn't want him, like a dentist with a fine instrument, picking at this sensitive spot.

It was a quarter after six and Kate had just drifted into a light sleep when the phone rang. She couldn't imagine who it would be. She picked up the phone to hear Bina's imploring voice at the other end. 'Please Kate, help me! I have to go to the airport. I went out with Billy last night and I acted as snotty as I could but he just laughed. I flirted with another guy, but he didn't seem to mind. Kate, I tried everything everyone suggested. You have to help me. Jack lands in an hour and a half and . . .' Bina began to cry. And while Kate had heard Bina cry through almost every phase of their lives, there was an element to this that was new. Kate made shushing noises while she tried to wake up to define what was different. And then it came to her. For the first time, Bina was crying like an adult. Gone was the open-hearted hysteria that allowed Bina to be so infuriating and yet sweet. Instead, Kate heard overlays of guilt, and shame, and anxiety.

'I made a mistake, Kate. But I don't want to have to tell Jack and if Billy doesn't dump me, Jack won't propose and I've ruined my life.' Bina's sobs were muffled, but Kate couldn't help but think that she too was afraid she had ruined her own life.

'It's all going to be all right,' Kate assured her. 'I'll get a limo and pick you up in thirty minutes. I'll drop you at the airport, just look good. I'll take care of everything. I promise you, it's all going to be all right.'

'Cross your heart and hope to die?' Bina asked, and before she assured her, Kate thought same old Bina at the other end of the line.

*   *   *

280

Dressed, made-up, coiffed and scented, Bina sat beside Kate in the limo. Kate had pulled herself together, called the car service, picked up Bina in Brooklyn and had swept her into the back seat. Impressed with the car, Bina was still nervous.

'But what are you going to do?' Bina asked.

'That's for me to know, and for you to never find out,' Kate said and leaned forward. 'Take the BQE,' she told the driver, who seemed to be taking the scenic route – as if there was one – to JFK. 'Do you know which terminal he is coming into?'

'International?'

'There is more than one international terminal,' Kate began to explain; although she wasn't absolutely sure that was true. She leaned forward again. 'International arrivals,' she told the driver. 'Follow the signs.' She leaned back into the leather of the seats. The limo was a bit of a luxury. But she didn't want to have to argue with the driver once they reached the airport. She turned to her friend and looked into her eyes. 'Listen to me,' Kate said.

'I am,' Bina told her.

'Okay, really listen to me. You have nothing to tell Jack. You have nothing to confess.' Kate had to pause and take a breath. The idea of Bina and Billy together, the idea of him, of her . . . She repressed her jealousy as unworthy. 'It only happened that once.'

'Well, no. Last week I saw him and we got caught in the rain and he took me to his apartment to towel me off and . . .'

Kate imagined the scene too vividly. The eroticism of Billy gently drying her hair and face was disturbing and arousing. She could see why Bina would fall from grace again. 'It doesn't matter. You and Jack broke up. He's been a free agent, and so have you. Remember the army had that policy: Don't ask. Don't tell?' Bina nodded. 'Well, follow it. And if you're asked anything by Jack, remind him that you love him. Ask him if he loves you.'

'But I slept with . . .'

281

'There are no "buts".'

'But even if I don't tell him about the sex . . . Okay, I won't tell Jack anything.'

'You promise?'

'I promise. But to make this work I have to get Billy to dump me.'

'I'm going to take care of that,' Kate said. 'Now, fix your makeup.' Obediently, Bina rooted around her huge purse and pulled out a cosmetics case. Kate helped her with her primping and then turned the mirror on herself. She looked a little pale, and there was bruised-looking skin under her eyes because of her lack of sleep, but she would do her own toilette later.

'Okay,' she said, as they pulled up to the sidewalk at the airport. 'You look great, you should feel great, and Jack is coming here just for you. Because he loves you.'

'But I'm not sure . . .' Bina began.

'I'm sure,' Kate said. 'Now go to the rope where passengers get out of customs. He'll probably be out of there in less than ten minutes.'

'Aren't you going to wait with me?' Bina asked, her eyes opening wide.

'No. I have something else to do,' Kate said and gave Bina a hug. 'Keep your cell phone on and your powder dry. Call me the moment anything happens.'

Bina got out of the car and walked through the sliding glass door entrance, then she turned and waved and gave Kate the thumbs-up sign. As soon as Bina disappeared, merging with the crowd inside the terminal, Kate leaned forward to speak to the driver one more time. 'Take me back to Brooklyn,' she told him.

35

It was just a few minutes to eight in the morning when Kate rang Billy Nolan's bell. It took several minutes before his sleep-blurred voice responded. Kate put her hands over the intercom and murmured something, pitching her voice higher than normal. Surely, this wasn't the first time that Billy Nolan had had an unexpected visit from a woman at an inappropriate time. The more realistic worry was that some other woman was there first. But, as she'd hoped, the door buzzed and Kate pushed into the hallway. I'm only doing this for Bina, she told herself, but she knew it was a lie.

Since Bina's confession at the shower, Kate had felt herself possessed by her desire for Billy Nolan. No matter how hard she had tried to deny it, she had been jealous and intrigued by Bina's flirtation with Billy. To be brutally honest, from the first moment she had met him on the terrace, Kate had felt an almost irresistible pull toward Billy. She had tried to fight it, and she knew that he, like Steven, was not 'relationship material', but if she did this for Bina maybe she would also be able to get Billy Nolan – his smile, his charm, and his easy physical grace – out of her system once and for all. Kate wasn't going to waste time in a meaningless relationship, but if this would precipitate a break-up with Bina and that would give her confidence then . . .

Kate stopped to look in the mirror at the stair landing. She wasn't wild about what she saw. Her face was pale, and there were circles of darkness under her eyes. She hadn't been able to sleep last night and it showed. Well, it would have to do. She pulled out a brush from her purse and puffed up her hair. She wondered, once again, if she should have had a haircut when Bina had. Too late now. Her lipstick was still holding up but she did a full-face smile to see if there was any on her teeth. She could use a bit of shine but she didn't have any gloss so as she walked up the stairs Kate caught herself licking her lips. Then she remembered Elliot's absolutely ridiculous acronym and regretted it. Well, she told herself, I'll regret more than that after this morning is over. She got to Billy's door and, with her heart knocking in her chest, knocked on the door as well.

Billy, his hair tousled and a loose cotton robe drawn around him, opened the door. 'What . . . ?'

His physical presence was almost a blow to her. She could smell sleep on him. It was better than any cologne.

Kate pushed in past him. It was a good thing she was getting him early, before he had coffee and his brain might become operative. Based on her experience, most men were easy. It wasn't hard to get them to sleep with you. It was harder to get them to listen to you, to know who you were, or to commit to you. But none of those challenges lay ahead of her. She walked across the room, put down her purse, sat at the edge of his bed and crossed her legs.

'Sit down. Make yourself at home,' Billy said with as much sarcasm as it seemed he could muster at eight a.m. He closed the door behind him. 'To what do I owe . . .' He gave up trying to be urbane. 'You want a cup of coffee?' he asked and, scratching his head, began to move toward the kitchen.

'No thank you,' Kate said, trying not to lick her lips. 'I didn't come here for your coffee.'

Billy stopped at the sink, his hand midway between the coffee-maker and the faucet. She had not gotten an opportunity to look at his hands since the dreadful bowling evening. Kate had always been interested in men's hands. She considered herself a sort of connoisseur, disliking short, stubby or hairy-backed hands, yet equally turned off by overly slender almost feminine ones. Now she was transfixed by Billy's. If she had tried to design the perfect ones, strong yet sensitive, the hands of competence and sensual knowledge . . . She blushed.

He walked toward her slowly, pulled a chair opposite her and sat down. 'What did you come here for, Doctor?' he asked. 'Is this another consultation?'

Okay. She deserved that. And probably more. If he was going to make her eat humble pie, she would. But couldn't he feel her almost ridiculous longing? She was grateful that it wasn't palpable to him since it suffused her being. 'Look, I was wrong,' she admitted, then paused. She'd rehearsed this coming from the airport but all that she had prepared seemed to have evaporated. 'The thing with Bina isn't working, is it?' she blurted.

Billy looked at her. 'Have I missed something? Are we still in high school?' he asked. 'And even if we are, is this a question that has to be answered at seven in the morning?'

'It's five after eight,' Kate said, sounding almost prim. Shit! Jack should be walking toward customs at this very moment. 'Just tell me the truth,' she said. 'Bina means nothing to you, does she?'

'Bina is a very nice girl,' Billy told her.

'I know that, but that isn't the question I asked you.' She looked down at her exposed toes and the pre-Raphaelite painting of *King Cophetua and the Beggar Maid* appeared before her eyes. She'd always found it erotically charged. 'Look,' she

285

said, 'I came over here to admit that I made a terrible mistake. Bina is beginning to be really attached to you and it isn't fair. She's going to get hurt and it's going to be my fault as much as it is yours.'

For the first time since she had arrived, Billy actually looked awake. He sat there in silence, his elbows on his knees and his long hands at rest between his legs. He looked down at them for a long moment, then looked back at her. 'Look, I never meant to hurt her. I go out with women who know how to take care of themselves.'

'Well, Bina isn't a woman like that.'

'I know. That's why I never slept with her. Not that it's any of your business.'

Kate looked away from his beautiful face. So he was a liar as well as a flirt and a serial dater.

'Don't waste my time with lies,' she told him.

'Hey!' He stood up. 'I don't lie. I've never dated more than one woman at a time, and I break up with one before I start in with anyone else. I never promise what I don't deliver. I'm a bartender, for God's sake. They know I'm . . . well, not serious right now. And if that is a repetition compulsion, well, that's my problem. Meanwhile, I make them feel good about themselves.'

'It's time to break up with Bina,' Kate said firmly. The fact was she felt anything but firm. She was more frightened than she could ever remember being. What if he was disinterested or, worse, what if he laughed at her and threw her out? At that moment she felt it would be unbearable. Yet she couldn't show her fear. She looked at him, his hair still messy from bed but as adorable as ever, his brow wrinkled in incredulity. 'It's time,' she repeated.

'What are you? Her social secretary or her mother? And how do you know how I feel?'

Kate stood up. She was so much shorter than he was. She leaned forward and looked into his eyes. She felt the heat from his chest and she could have melted. There was a place beyond words where honesty and intention is felt. Kate did more than apologize. She bared herself and let him in through her eyes. Silently, she kept her eyes on his and let him feel her intentions. All of the sexual heat, all of the longing that she had repressed was there, visible to him if he would look. She allowed herself to move from herself to him through her eyes. It was a lot more effective than two Palm Pilots linked up. Billy actually pulled back for a moment, then leaned forward.

'Doctor, are you . . . ?' His expression changed from confusion to incredulity to . . . well, it looked like delight.

Kate took the sweater off her shoulders and tossed it onto the chair behind her. Then she sat back down on the bed and unbuttoned the top button of her blouse. 'I think you should call Bina,' she said. 'She won't be home now, but you can leave a message.'

'That seems pretty cold,' Billy ventured.

'Her old boyfriend is in town. She won't mind if you break up with her right now.'

'B-b-but over the phone?' he stammered.

Kate looked him full in the face. She felt surprised at his sense of honor and guilt at her own manipulativeness. But she put both of those out of her mind. 'I promise this way is best. I wouldn't hurt her for the world.'

And, as if hypnotized, Billy did just that. He picked up the phone and Kate had the delicacy to leave the room while he left the message that Bina felt was so crucial.

Kate excused herself. In the bathroom, she called in sick – only the second time she had missed a day of work – then had a moment to look at herself in the mirror. What are you doing? she silently asked her reflection. She couldn't convince herself that she was giving her body to this man simply to perform the ending to a crack-brain scheme that she certainly had never believed in. She wanted to sleep with Billy, but she was already afraid that she wanted more. And

287

she knew his record with women. Could she afford to spend more of her time in a relationship that would lead to nothing in the end?

She looked away from her own pale-blue eyes. She knew she didn't really have a choice. She wanted Billy Nolan more than she had ever wanted anyone. But this has to mean nothing, she told herself. There is no future, only the present. I won't make the mistakes I made with Steven and Michael. This isn't a relationship, she told herself firmly. This is what other people call 'fun'.

Fun was not exactly the word Kate would use for coupling with Billy.

'I've wanted you since the first time I saw you on the terrace,' he said.

Kate felt something within her tighten. They were the words she wanted to hear but didn't dare believe. They were true for her, though she had not admitted it to herself and she certainly wouldn't admit it to Billy. That way lay madness. She just smiled, enigmatically, and tried to put all thought out of her mind. That was easy to do because no one had ever made love to her the way Billy did. She wasn't surprised by his strength or his skill, but his tenderness had taken her aback. He cradled her head with both of his hands and held her face to his as he kissed her. He stroked her hair. 'It's so beautiful,' he murmured. 'I love your hair.' He buried his face in it, just beside her ear. 'I love how it smells and how it feels. I wanted to touch it but I didn't think I'd get the chance.'

Kate turned to him and he put his mouth on hers. She couldn't decide what she liked better: when he used his mouth to kiss her or when he used it to speak to her. Because his hands spoke to her as well. They moved miraculously from her breasts to her thighs and up again to her mouth, each time going further, becoming more probing, more intimate and even more responsive to her. Kate had always found the first few times she made love with someone to be a little awkward, and ultimately unsatisfying. She had to be able to relax and Michael, or Steven, or the other men in her past had to become familiar with her timing and her responses, just as she had to grow to know theirs.

But with Billy it was different. He heard and registered every intake of her breath, the slightest movement of her hips or shifting of her body. She felt she could ask him for anything without speaking a word. But she didn't have to ask. He was slow and practiced and skillful, but she also felt such a flood of feeling, such an exchange of emotion that she lost herself. As they made love, Billy kept his mouth on hers, and it seemed as if he had a hundred variations of kissing, all of which were in sync with his movements and her own. He only took his mouth off hers when he paused to look at her or when he moved his mouth to her nipples and then lower.

He brought her to the brink with his hand and with his mouth and then moving against her and then again with his hand, until Kate felt her body trembling all over. She almost couldn't catch her breath, but the feeling was wonderful, not frightening. And when she put her hand on him his gasp was so deep that she felt an almost greater pleasure in touching him than she felt when he moved on her body. Kate had no idea what time it was when he finally slipped inside her for the last time, and when both of them fell asleep, exhausted and satisfied, he kept his arms wrapped around her waist, holding her to him even as they slept.

36

Kate opened her eyes. She had one of those moments of waking dislocation. Where was she? It wasn't her ceiling, or Michael's. Then she turned her head and saw Billy, still sleeping. The previous day and night and all of its sensual memories flooded back. Kate smiled and felt her cheeks flushing but, unobserved, for once she didn't mind.

While they had slept, her hair had fanned out and now a red tendril was curled around Billy's upper arm. Simply looking at his arm, lying on the sheet, bathed in the sunshine that spread from the window across the upper part of the bed made her feel . . . extremely happy. It was a feeling she wasn't used to – it combined satisfaction with expectation, as if she were a child and there were two Christmases – she had just had one but was about to have another.

Kate stretched and luxuriated in the feeling. Happiness, this deep joy, was something you could not hold on to and she was wise enough not to try. She only drank in the sunlight, the clean white sheets rumpled around them, and cherished the moment. She wasn't thinking about the sex, though it had been exquisite. It was simply looking at him, and the feeling of warmth, comfort and protectiveness that started in her chest and radiated through her as she lay there, staring at the hairs so perfectly aligned on his forearm, that was joy.

Slowly, so as not to wake him, she lifted her head to look at his sleeping face. Even without animation, his features had a beauty and liveliness that Kate wondered at. But from their conversation the previous night she felt Billy Nolan was not just another pretty face. After all, in his own way, Steven had been very handsome. But unlike Steven, to Kate's complete surprise, Billy seemed to have a depth of feeling, a compassion and understanding of others that had been blocked in Steven by his narcissism.

As she looked at him, Billy – as if feeling himself observed – opened his eyes. 'Hello,' he said, his voice dipping somehow in the middle of the word, making it sound like a self-assured and very happy greeting. Kate felt herself blush again and this time it did embarrass her. She fell back on her pillow. Billy raised himself on one elbow, bent over her and kissed her. His kisses were so sensitive, so searching and gentle. That reminded her of the way they had made love, his lips almost never leaving her own – except when he was kissing some other part of her. He lifted his head.

'Good morning,' Kate said and tucked the sheet in on either side of her.

'Now you're my prisoner. Stuck in my bed for life.' Kate thought that that sounded like a delicious idea, but only smiled.

'What time is it?' Billy asked, then fell back and yawned.

Kate hadn't a clue. She didn't even know what day it was and that also felt delicious. Lying in his bed, she felt suspended in time and if she could have asked for one place and feeling to have for all eternity, this moment would be a good choice. Then she forced herself to turn and look at the clock on the bedside table. 'Oh, God,' she gasped. 'It's Friday! And almost nine. I have to call the school!' she told him, and fell back onto the bedclothes in horror. She

291

couldn't go running out of his apartment, scuttling like a bug to gather up her belongings, because she was way too late to get to school. Kate *never* missed work – when she'd had the stomach virus that had torn through the school she'd still managed to come in. And she'd already taken yesterday off. The children had to be able to count on her. But it was the end of the term, a half-day, and she had her reports to write up and the summaries that would go to the administration and the children's parents. She ought to be there, going through her notes, but for once, she was tempted to think of herself first. Mr McKay, on the other hand, would have to be told and he wouldn't like it. She knew her contract was being considered for renewal right now and it was not a time to screw up. Still, she couldn't leave. Billy was looking at her, his eyebrows raised in question.

'My job,' she said. 'I have to make a call.'

He picked his phone up and handed it to her. 'Feel free,' he said. 'As long as you don't call another man, my minutes are yours.'

'He isn't exactly a man, he's a principal,' Kate told him.

'Well, I'm glad you've got at least one principle,' he said and kissed her again as she was punching in the Andrew number. 'When you arrived I wasn't sure.' She made a face and pushed him away. He lay down holding a curl of her hair between his fingers and playing with it.

When Vera, Mr McKay's secretary, answered the phone, Kate was relieved. She asked for Mr McKay, but hoped he might not be available so that she could just leave a message.

Unfortunately, Vera put her right through. Kate heard his nasal voice at the other end of the phone. 'McKay,' he said. 'Yes?'

'This is Kate Jameson. I'm very sorry but I won't be able to come in again today.' There was a pause at the other end. It was amazing how powerful silence could be. She

292

wanted to fill it, to blurt out excuses but didn't let herself.

'Are you ill?' McKay finally asked.

Kate hated to lie. 'No,' she said, 'but I have a personal emergency.' She looked over at Billy, under the sheet and clearly aroused. 'Something's just come up.' Billy gave her a look. He rolled onto his side and put his arm around her waist. Kate would have smiled but she felt McKay's silent curiosity move like a snake through the telephone lines. Stalwart, she kept silence at her end. She watched Billy, who picked up the ends of her hair and held them to his mouth in a kiss.

'I'm sorry to hear that,' McKay intoned, and Kate wasn't sure whether the regret she heard was because he thought she had a personal problem or because she wouldn't be in.

'Because it's half a day, I'll be able to catch up easily. Most of my reports on the children are done.'

They discussed scheduling for a few moments and then Kate, with a sigh of relief, was able to hang up. Billy grinned at her. 'Playing hookey?' he asked. Kate nodded. 'I'd like to play something else as well,' he said. 'And if you don't agree, I'm afraid I'll have to call the truant officer and report you.'

Kate giggled. 'I'm not in school anymore,' she said.

'Oh, we'll see about that,' Billy told her.

She supposed if she thought about it, she'd get crazy. After all, here was a man who had slept with half of the women in Brooklyn, including her best friend. The idea did make her a little bit queasy so, like some of her young patients, she compartmentalized – she simply put it in a mental box that she closed tightly and put aside. It wasn't possible that Billy Nolan could be faking all of these feelings or was it? His vast experience showed in the skill he displayed when they made love. Every touch, every movement felt wonderful, perfect almost. If it got any better it would be frightening. As it was, it was almost spooky. He seemed to know, almost before she

293

did, where to put his hands, how hard to press, where to put his mouth, when to be playful and when to be intense. If she compared his love-making to Michael's – which she was trying with little success not to do, she felt as if Michael was only a sandwich and Billy was a Thanksgiving feast. Kate was grateful. If there was no pumpkin pie, there was plenty of other sweetness to make up for it.

The two of them spent the morning making love. Then Billy made breakfast. He was a good cook, and Kate was hungry. She looked around the sunny living room. 'This is a really nice place,' she said as she finished the last of her bacon.

Billy laughed. 'You sound surprised,' he said.

Kate blushed. 'Have you lived here long?' she asked.

'My dad moved in when he got sick. Emphysema. He didn't like being alone in our old house after my mom died. He couldn't work as a fireman anymore, so he began working full-time in the bar and I helped him turn this into an apartment.'

'So you can cook and do carpentry?' Kate asked as she brought the dirty dishes to the sink.

'Yeah,' he said. He paused and looked away from her. 'It was fun to work with my dad, but we barely got the place finished before he died.'

'Was it from the emphysema?' Kate asked.

Billy nodded and grimaced. 'It's a terrible way to die. Terrible to watch.'

'I'm sorry,' Kate said.

Billy shrugged and began to scrape a plate. 'You shouldn't be a fireman and smoke,' he said.

'My father was a policeman who drank, and you shouldn't do that either,' Kate said.

Billy nodded, filled the sink with hot water and put the dishes in to soak. He looked around. 'Anyway, I liked this apartment, and when I took over the bar it seemed handy to live here. This place still reminds me of him.' He turned

294

back to the sink and added some dish detergent. Then he wiped his hands on a paper towel and turned back to her. 'Funny thing,' he said. 'We just had breakfast but I'm hungry again.' He raised his brows suggestively, put his arms around her waist and nuzzled her neck. Kate felt herself responding to the pressure behind her and, with his arms still around her waist, they went back to bed.

It was after their matinée and when Billy had gone off to the shower that Kate's cell phone began to ring. She saw that it was Bina and picked it up.

'Katie? Katie?'

Kate could never get over the fact that Bina believed anyone might answer one's personal cell phone. 'Yes, of course, it's me,' Kate said.

'Ohmigod, Katie! He proposed. Just like Elliot said. I couldn't believe it, but Jack proposed.' Kate was flooded with a kind of horror as she remembered – for the first time since she had gotten to Billy's place here in Brooklyn – that she had originally come to facilitate Bina's long-delayed engagement. Was she a selfish or selfless friend?

'That's great! That's really, really great!'

'And you won't believe this,' Bina continued. 'This is how I know Elliot was right. You won't believe it.'

'Try me,' Kate said, dryly, knowing what was coming. Just then her phone starting beeping for a call waiting. She glanced at the caller ID and didn't recognize the number so she let it go to voice mail.

'Well, I had a message from Billy breaking up with me just in time. And Jack asked me to marry him at nine-o-four, right after the call! I know exactly because the taxi driver had WINS on and they tell you the time almost every minute. And I know the time of Billy's message because my machine . . .'

'Congratulations. Or best wishes. Or mazel tov,' Kate said. 'Your mother must be thrilled, and your father. And me. I'm thrilled for you.'

'I'm thrilled, too. And the best part is that he apologized for what happened, you know, about him not, well, you know. He said he just panicked. He got frightened and couldn't get the words out.' She paused. 'Do you think that's true?' she asked Kate.

'I'm sure that was part of it,' Kate said, remembering his request for exploration. It seemed Bina hadn't forgotten it either.

'And he said he wanted just a little more time to, well, you know . . . we've been going out so long and he's never cheated on me, and he just wanted to be sure. I don't blame him for that. Would you?'

'No.'

'Yeah, but . . .' Bina paused, she lowered her voice. 'But I can't forget what happened. You know, about . . . well, you can't imagine how fantastic it was with . . .'

'I think I can,' Kate said as she glanced over toward the bathroom. 'Look, I gotta go. I'll talk to you tonight.'

Kate had just stepped out of the shower herself when her cell phone rang again. She looked at the caller ID and knew she was in trouble. She thought for a moment that she would just ignore it but she knew Elliot would never give up. 'Where are you?' he asked without any preamble. 'You're not here at work and you're not at home. You're out, so you're not sick. Unless you're at the doctor's, are you at the doctor's?'

'No,' Kate said. 'And I can't talk right now.' She was self-conscious. She felt Billy listening, even though she wasn't sure that he was.

'Okay, so where are you?'

'I'll tell you later,' Kate said, lowering her voice.

'What?'

'I'll tell you later.'

'Oh, God. You're in bed with Steven.'

'Not exactly,' Kate said.

'What is that supposed to mean?' Elliot asked. 'Oh, I knew it. This is really terrible. So you are with Steven.'

'No.'

Elliot paused, doing the math. 'But you're in bed with someone else.'

'Yes, Einstein.'

'I can't tell you how relieved I am,' Elliot said. 'At first I was going to call all the hospitals, then, when I thought of Steven, I was going to call all the mental hospitals. But instead of getting neurotic, you just got lucky.'

'This may not qualify as luck,' Kate said.

'Well, girlfriend, I want to hear all of the details the minute you get home.'

37

'We're coming to a rise. You ready?' Kate nodded. It was hot, and the heat was already radiating up from the macadam they were skimming over. Kate had roller-bladed before, but had never felt really secure. Now everything seemed easy. In the week in which she had spent every free moment with Billy, she had had a strange and varied array of feelings. The weekend had been deliciously idle. After work the next day he had made her dinner. She stayed at his place but the following evening – traditionally a slow night – he had come to her house and they ate take-out pizza and one of her great salads. She had seen Elliot at school but had ducked him, her friend Rita, and the entire Brooklyn cadre. Now, on a warm afternoon, the two of them had 'come out' though not in the Elliot and Brice sense of the word. She had been hesitant to roller-blade but Billy, a surprisingly good and patient teacher, had coached her until she felt where her center of gravity was and was confident enough to lean into her strokes. But the fun was doing it with Billy. They were roller-blading in Prospect Park, their hands intertwined behind their backs. Billy held her with the gentlest pressure, but his support gave her confidence. He warned her of every hill and curve before it came up and tightened his grip when they swooped down an incline. It was exhilarating. Kate believed their skating was almost as sensual as their sex.

'You skate so well,' Kate murmured as they glided into the tree-shaded part of the road.

'Six years on the hockey team and only one chipped tooth to show for it,' Billy told her. Kate looked up and smiled at him. She had wondered about the tooth. It was the imperfection that made the rest of his perfection bearable. She thought of a Brad Pitt film where he had played a boxer. Special makeup had transformed his nose and given it a broken jauntiness. Kate had read somewhere that more women found him attractive in that movie than any other. 'I like that chipped tooth,' was all Kate said and then felt his arm push her slightly. She thought for a moment it was a reaction to her compliment, but 'Eyes forward,' Billy said as he avoided a stumbling skater and then moved Kate smoothly through a crowd of children crossing the road ahead of them. Out of the shaded alley, the sun beat down fiercely, but their gathering speed created a pleasant breeze. Once they were on the flat open stretch, they really began to move.

'I can see you've had a lot of practice,' she noted while she kept her face forward as instructed.

'Hey,' Billy said, 'you're no virgin yourself.'

'I wasn't any good,' she told him truthfully. 'It's because of you.'

Everything was different because of him. It had been just over a week since Jack's return and Kate's morning visit to Billy's, but they had seen each other every night since and spent the two weekends together. Kate was amazed by a lot of the things that they shared. It wasn't only the French. He had also lost his mother early, although he never spoke about her death. He had spent his teenage years being raised by his father. They were both only children, and both orphans.

Kate had to admit she had been prejudiced about him; he wasn't a dunce, and he didn't just get by on his good looks. In

299

fact, if she could put aside his appalling record of conquests, he was the most compatible male companion she had ever spent time with. Kate's work for the semester was ending, and, with more time for shopping and cooking, she found that she enjoyed having Billy to her place for little dinners.

When it was Billy's turn to close the bar, she went to his place early, and worked or read until he was through. He'd come up intermittently for quick kisses, usually bringing a treat or a drink. On nights he got off early, he made the trip to Manhattan, driving into what he referred to as 'the City'. Kate remembered when she used to call Manhattan that and it made her smile every time he said it.

'Another hill,' Billy told her now. 'Let's put our backs into it.' Kate did. It wasn't just his skating that was impressive. There was almost nothing about Billy Nolan that Kate was not impressed by. He wasn't at all what she had thought; he didn't seem glib, or shallow, or arrogant. Not once you knew him. And his affection for her seemed so warm and real. Could he be acting? Kate hated to doubt him.

He seemed so sensitive, not only to his own vulnerabilities – as Steven had been – but also to the feelings of others.

The only thing that clouded her feelings was the nagging thought of the host of women he had previously conquered. Kate, in the time she spent away from him, sometimes wondered if all the women he had known had felt like this and – more importantly – if he had felt just the same about them as he seemed to feel about her. It was hardly the kind of question you could ask, and even if you did, it was not the kind of question that could be answered honestly.

They crested the hill and the long slide down actually made Kate scream, partly with pleasure and partly with fear. Not so different from the way she felt about this relationship. At the bottom of the hill, Billy released one of her hands and coasted over to a bench beside an ice cream vendor. Just behind them was a field for roller-hockey and beyond it a park exit. Kate was grateful for the sit-down. 'I'm exhausted,' she admitted.

'So am I,' Billy told her though she doubted that was true. There didn't seem to be an ounce of body fat on him, and Kate knew that under his clothes he was lean and powerful without any extra bulk. Thinking of his body gave her a momentary frisson. 'Thirsty?' Billy asked and she nodded. 'Let's go.' They took off their skates, put on their shoes, and bundled their gear into his backpack.

They were just leaving the park when her cell phone rang. She pulled it out and saw that it was Elliot. For the last week she had been ducking his calls when she could and had been equally evasive when she saw him at school. She had talked about Bina's engagement, the shower they were going to throw for her, Elliot and Brice's plans for the summer; everything but the identity of her new boyfriend. She hadn't wanted to lie to him but she knew how strongly he would disapprove of the truth.

'Are you going to pick it up? Or is it another boyfriend?' Billy asked. Just then the phone stopped ringing.

'He's a boy, and he's a friend, but he's gay,' Kate told Billy. 'Does that count?'

Kate and Billy made their way to Jo's Sweet Shop for some ice cream. It was an institution, the old-time confectionary where parents brought their kids for hot chocolate after winter skating and where the sundaes were enormous and good. Kate had always envied the kids who got taken to Jo's. A game broke and behind them an after-the-skating/roller-hockey crowd complete with blades, skates, and Prospect Park parents swarmed in to get drinks and ice cream to cool off. With the usual bullying, the bigger kids elbowed the smaller, some parents pushed ahead of other parents, and chaos reigned. Billy and Kate, buoyed forward on the tide of people, watched as a seven- or eight-year-old boy was virtually trampled. He began to cry.

'Oh, God!' Kate cried. She worked her way over to him,

301

knelt and put her arm around him. 'Oh, sweetie. Are you hurt?' she asked. It was so pleasant not to have to be professional with him.

'He stepped on me!' the boy exclaimed, pointing upward. Kate looked up at a big hulk of a teen hockey guy still in his gear. From her (and the little boy's) low point of view the guy looked like a giant. But Billy grabbed him by the back of his hockey shirt and tugged him away.

'See? He's gone now.' Kate comforted the child.

People began screaming their orders. 'Two cookies and cream sugar cones with sprinkles!'

'A vanilla Coke!'

'Three large chocolate cones and an ice tea!'

The shouted orders were almost drowned by the kids' excited yelling and by loud complaints about people pushing ahead and whose turn it was. The adolescent working behind the counter was clearly overwhelmed by the crowd. Kate reunited her little boy with his dad while the poor soda jerk tried and failed to gain control. With more park-goers pushing in from the back, those in the front got even more rowdy. 'Please form a line!' the teen shouted desperately. No one was listening.

Billy returned to Kate's side. He stood her at the entrance to the workspace behind the counter. 'This is madness,' he said. Then he leapt over the counter and moved to the center, facing out to the crowd.

'All right,' Billy began in a voice loud enough to be heard not only throughout Jo's, but all the way into the park. 'All right now! Kids with hockey sticks on the left. Kids with skates on the right.'

There was silence for a moment and then pushing and shoving began as the crowd tried to part.

'KEEP IT DOWN! I MEAN IT!'

As if he were Moses and the crowd was the Red Sea, his will was done. Kate smiled as the two lines formed. Billy leaned toward the poor, overwhelmed kid in the apron. 'You take the so-called adults and I'll do the Mighty Ducks.'

The teen nodded and began taking orders from the line on the right. Billy looked at the children and gestured to the eight-year-old who had been crying. 'Service first to the player who was body checked.'

His dad brought the little boy up to the counter. Kate couldn't help but glow. Billy leaned to the little boy. 'What position do you play?' he asked him.

'Goalie,' he replied, and looked at his father as if he wasn't completely sure.

'Your lucky day!' Billy exclaimed. 'Goalies get free cones! Wanna double scoop?'

The teenager behind the counter gave him a look of 'no way'. Billy ignored him, took out his wallet and placed it beside the ice cream tubs. 'What's it gonna be?' The little boy asked for a vanilla cone with sprinkles and hooted with joy when he saw the double dipping he received. Billy moved to the next in the line.

'What's it gonna be?' he asked.

'A cup of chocolate with nuts and whip cream,' the next kid said.

'You got it. And it's on me.' Billy sprayed some of the aerosol cream on his shirt. 'Get it? It's on me.'

The portion of the crowd that was up front laughed. Kate watched Billy with a combination of astonishment, awe and delight. When he took his next order, he smiled at the kid. 'Position?' Billy asked him.

'Guard,' the boy said proudly.

'Whoa!' Billy pretended to be taken aback. 'Guards get free toppings.'

'Wow!' the boy cried. 'Hey, Mom! I get a free topping.'

Billy leaned over to Kate and gave her a quick kiss right below the ear.

'What do I get?' she asked him coyly.

303

Billy was already busy making up a cone, but he looked up at her.

'Depends on what position you play,' Billy said and smiled.

The thing about him, Kate thought, was that he knew the way things worked. He wasn't a macho guy, but he was strong enough and confident enough to be willing to take chances.

When the manager of the shop came from the back, leaving the booths and table behind, he took over from Billy. Thanking him, he insisted on giving Billy and Kate free cones. They were ridiculously large; Kate thought they each had four scoops, but Billy's might have been five. As they finally made their way out of the sweet shop, Kate looked at Billy. 'That was quite a scene, Mr Nolan,' she said. 'You're a take-charge kinda guy.'

'Hey, not much to expect from a bartender who's dealt with bachelor parties,' Billy said.

'Well, you really managed that crowd.'

Billy looked down at his cone, melting over his hand in the heat. 'Yeah. If only I could manage my own ice cream.'

'Okay. This I know how to do,' Kate said and moved him over to a trash bin. She knocked two scoops off his cone and into the bin, did the same with her own, pulled a wet-nap out of her pocket, wiped his hand and then, with her finger, the last trace of whipped cream from his neck.

'Hey, no fair,' Billy said. 'That was mine.' Kate just smiled and put her cream-covered finger in her mouth. Billy gently took her hand and put her finger into his own mouth. Then he gently pushed her against the wall of the sweet shop and, keeping her left hand in his, lifted his arm and leaned into the wall, pressing his weight against her. Kate thought of Victorian heroines and how they 'swooned'. She was feeling pretty swoony.

'What do you call this position?' he asked her, his voice low.

At that moment the door of Jo's opened and a bunch of kids

streamed out. When a couple of them saw Billy they began making an incredible noise.

'Exhibitionists,' Kate told him and smiled.

On the subway, the unruly park crowd pushed as the train doors opened. Kate was about to be crushed against a pole until Billy corralled her, placing her in the corner of the car against the front window. He protected her with his body but the intense crowding had the two of them pushed against one another. She was shocked when his hands disappeared under the back of the waistband of her jeans. He leaned forward to whisper in her ear. 'What do you call this position?'

'Tight. Very tight,' she said.

Back at Kate's apartment, Billy slowly undressed her. She was surprised and touched by his tenderness: he took off her sandals as if she were a very young child. But as he worked his way up she felt that he considered her grown-up by the time he had unbuttoned her blouse. Then he was on top of her, kissing her neck and making his way to her breasts. He took each of her hands in his and held them beside her face on the pillow. He stopped to look at her. 'And what do you call this position?'

'Perfect,' Kate whispered.

38

Despite his nose for news and Kate's constant exposure to Elliot at school, she had managed not to raise his suspicions or start him questioning her on why her mood was so light. If he wrote it off to relief at her break-up with Michael, it was just as well. Kate and Elliot often fought and sometimes didn't speak for a day or two, but they had never lied to one another and Kate did not want to set a precedent now. A sin of omission, however, was less than a fib. But Kate was afraid it was only a matter of time before Elliot sniffed her out. He was a Hound of the Baskervilles when it came to uncovering and bringing back his prey. Sooner or later, Elliot would discover the reason for her sunny disposition and, when he did, thunderclouds would gather.

Kate stood in a patch of sunshine and watched the kids all around her. She reflected how lucky the children at Andrew Country Day were. Of course, they were lucky to have their material needs so well taken care of and parents rich enough to send them to a private school. But looking around her, Kate knew it was more than that. Andrew Country Day was one of the few city schools that had been able to maintain an almost campus-like setting. The two original old brick buildings formed an 'L' along the street and avenue sides of the block and the new extension – not nearly as architecturally interesting but covered in ivy and somewhat in keeping with the general look of the earlier buildings – formed a 'U' that allowed what would have been the individual buildings' backyards to be joined in a large common garden. Part of it, of course, had been paved, but old trees, including a giant willow, and a beautiful border of manicured lawn gave the enclave the beauty and dignity of a New England college quad.

She felt her first year had been successful, but wasn't quite certain that Mr McKay and the board shared her view. When Michael had assumed she would drop her job it had made her realize her deep pleasure in it. The scene around her was so lovely and her work with the children so meaningful that she felt she couldn't part with them. A small but dark voice within her whispered that she couldn't be this happy in her private life without losing something in her professional one. Of course, she recognized it as superstitious nonsense, an old fear from her childhood that would probably always haunt her when things went well. She put the dark thought away.

Kate was grateful to be part of it – the rambunctious children, the concerned staff, the involved parents. If Mr McKay was somewhat obsessive about the lawn and plantings, rather than the welfare of some of his charges, at least the staff recognized it and worked around it. No one was allowed to step on 'his' grass, though everyone ignored the rule except in his presence.

The daffodils were long over, but roses and azaleas bloomed against the green of the ivy that covered two of the three walls that encircled the play area. A breeze made the glossy leaves move in a wave up and down the wall, almost like hundreds of green Rockettes doing a synchronized kick. Kate took a wisp of hair from her face and drew it back into her barrette. A group of fifth-grade girls sat on the grass in the sun, as languid and colorful as the women in a Monet painting. 'Hi, Miss Jameson!' Brian Conroy yelled as he – illegally – ran across the lawn. Kate didn't have the heart to scold him. He looked, at least for the moment, happy as he ran, chasing two older boys who were leading a group of younger ones on a race, blowing off excess energy.

The breeze died down and the sun grew warmer. Kate took her sweater off, tied it around her shoulders and surveyed the schoolyard. Although she, as a psychologist rather than a teacher, rarely had playground duty and while it was usually despised, Kate was actually grateful for it today. The weather was beautiful and she felt too happy to sit indoors. It was also true that she was afraid to have lunch with Elliot because, knowing her as well as he did, he would easily be able to see her mood: why was it changed and immensely uplifted?

Of course, infatuation would do that and she was definitely infatuated with Billy Nolan. If she wasn't as mature as she was, she might have used another word instead of 'infatuated'. But she wasn't that much of a fool. It was simultaneously hard to believe that Billy cared about her as much as he seemed to or that he was merely acting. His string of relationships – if you could call them that – certainly didn't bode well for anything serious with him, but the intensity and depth of their conversations and the even deeper intensity of their love-making made her believe there was something special going on. Of course, if she allowed herself to think about it too much, doubts and questions crept in. Was she deluding herself about Billy being the right sort of man for her? Was she in fact slumming? How could she go back to her roots, to everything she had run from? Brooklyn, alcohol, Irish men, dysfunctional families.

She admitted now that she had been attracted to Billy from the moment she met him on the terrace at the wedding. All through the spring she had tried to ignore the strength of that feeling as well as the conviction that it was mutual and, though she did not like to think about his relationship with Bina, not to mention the Bitches, everything had turned out well. Jack's proposal had come. Bina was convinced that it was because of Billy, but Kate knew that Jack must have missed her sweetness and their shared history. And perhaps Max had put in a word or two about Bina's 'explorations'. Whatever it was, Bina was so busy with wedding preparations that she wouldn't discover Kate's secret liaison.

Kate didn't know whether Elliot really believed that any woman who dated Billy Nolan would, once dumped, receive a proposal of marriage, but what she did know was that she neither wanted to be dumped by him nor proposed to by anybody else.

The school year was coming to a close and while it had been uncomfortably hot earlier in the week, the weather had cooled down and today was as perfect as the weather ever got in Manhattan. Kate kept watch over the children, running and playing in front of her, and smiled. It was almost like watching sea water eddy in tide pools – the children's allegiances, posses and games changed at different rates, making swirls of motion that were faster in one corner, slower in the middle, and stagnant at one side. Kate actually raised her brows at that. Whenever the children stayed clustered in one place, Kate knew from experience, there was the possibility of trouble. Last week they had found a dead pigeon and only Elliot's intervention had prevented the fourth-grade boys from flinging it at the girls. She walked toward the gathering but before she got close, the group, who had been arranging some game, dispersed and the children ran off in twos and threes. All was well. No decomposing pigeon.

Again her hair escaped from its mooring and blew across her face. As she grabbed it, her fingers brushed her jaw line in exactly the way Billy's had stroked it just hours ago. A little shiver ran down her back and she felt a flutter in her stomach. Sleeping with him had been so extraordinary, so passionate but tender, that thinking about it seemed dangerous – Kate was afraid that she might remember that

309

it was all a dream and have to awake to a much colder reality.

But it wasn't a dream. Her time with Billy seemed to get better and deeper with every encounter. Kate, a survivor of plenty of adversity, not only empathized with the way Billy had coped and overcome his own difficulties, especially his speech disability, but also admired him for it. Underneath the fun and the joking, Kate felt sure Billy was courageous and good-hearted. He had cleverly summoned up or learned the skills needed to survive, but he didn't seem to have been hardened or made cynical by his experiences. She wasn't slumming, she told herself, ashamed she had ever thought that. She wasn't a snob. Billy Nolan was educated, well-read, bilingual and owned and ran a business. Who was she to judge him harshly?

Kate walked over to the willow, but didn't take a seat on the bench beside it. It was well known that Mr McKay frowned on staff sitting down when on playground duty. So, instead, she leaned one hand against the bench, picked up a tendril of the willow in the other and again lifted her face to the sun. It amazed her how life could change in such sudden profound ways. She felt, for once, like one of the lucky ones, one of the people in the world that things work out for, a being who could simply exist and breathe warm, summer air without struggling. She felt as if everything she wanted would come to her.

Although she wasn't sure she wanted Mr McKay, when Kate turned her head she saw him scuttling toward her on the flagstone path across the lawn. Kate straightened and the bit of the willow wand still in her hand broke off. She hadn't talked to him since she'd called in her absence that morning she woke in Billy's bed. The thought made her blush.

'Dr Jameson,' Mr McKay began, 'I've been wanting to talk to you.' Kate felt another flutter, but this one was not nearly so pleasant. Was he going to criticize her for daydreaming, or

310

for neglecting to scold the girls who were sitting on the lawn despite the interdict against it? Worse yet, was he about to reject her contract renewal? Was the small, dark voice the voice of truth?

But Mr McKay looked at her with something approaching a smile and, to her relief, ignored his precious sod. 'I'm glad I caught you here,' he said and for a moment his voice sounded almost cordial. 'Your contract is up for renewal and the board and I would like to extend it.' He paused. 'We feel that you are becoming an important part of the Andrew Country Day School tradition.'

Kate wasn't sure about any tradition she fulfilled but she was sincerely delighted by the offer. 'Thank you,' she said. 'I'm very happy here and I hope I'm making a contribution.'

McKay nodded, his face once again poker-straight as if he had lost all his cordiality chips. 'Good. Vera will have your renewal contract.' As he walked away, Kate watched his narrow back and managed to feel some affection for him, even when he waved the fifth-grade girls off the lawn.

The bell rang, the children began to line up and Kate was freed to go back to her office. But on the way down the hall, Elliot appeared at his classroom door.

'Are you trying to avoid me?' he asked.

'No, of course not.' She lied like a rug.

'Look, I figured it out. I know who your mystery man is and why you're embarrassed to tell me.'

'Shh,' Kate said. For God's sake. They were in the hallway of the school. Anyone could hear. 'Come into my office,' she told him, but she was filled with dread. She was going to be busted and Elliot would tell everyone, and Brooklyn would be abuzz with the news that she, Dr Katherine Sean Jameson, had stooped to a Brooklyn bartender. Worse, that she was taking him seriously. Once in the office, Elliot closed the door and she turned to face him.

'I figured it out,' Elliot repeated, complacently. 'It's Max.

You're sleeping with Max and you're embarrassed. But there's nothing wrong with him. I've always thought he was kinda hot, myself. It might be a little awkward after you end it since he lives just upstairs, but any port in the storm.'

For a moment Kate was tempted to agree with him. But she simply couldn't lie to a friend as close as Elliot was to her.

'Okay. What is it?' Elliot asked.

'Mr McKay wants to renew my contract,' Kate told him.

'That's not what I'm talking about.' Elliot stopped her and looked her over. 'You're seeing *him*, aren't you?' he said accusingly.

Once again Kate felt her complexion betray her. As the blush flooded her cheeks, she turned her eyes away from her best friend's. 'Yes,' she said.

'Oh, for God's sake. You really are a masochist,' he cried. 'Kate, is it like childbirth or something? Don't you remember the pain Steven put you through? Don't tell me you're sleeping with him again. You promised me it wasn't him.'

Kate looked him straight in the eye. 'It isn't,' she said. 'I wouldn't dream of it. I'm sleeping with Billy Nolan.'

For a minute, Elliot was stunned into silence. Then he shook his head. 'You little sneak. I should have known you were up to something,' he said. 'I thought, well, I suspected you might be thinking of that idiot, Steven. But no, you have to sniff out worse trouble. And I didn't think there could be worse trouble than Steven Kaplan.'

Kate, who thought she was prepared for Elliot's anger, was taken aback. 'You don't even know Billy,' she said. 'To you he's some kind of magic charm, some statistical improbability.'

'And what is he to you? A good bonk? Because that would be all he is good for.'

Kate felt herself go livid, and the blood that, for once, drained from her face actually made her almost dizzy with anger. 'I appreciate your concern,' she said, her voice cold. 'But I don't think you know what you're talking about.'

'Right! I haven't been around for the last ten years to witness and dissect every bump and curve in your so-called love life. You forget who you're talking to, Kate.' He pointed to the drawings on her walls. Many of them new – farewell gifts from children who would not see her until the autumn. 'You want to mess up your life?' Elliot asked, his voice lowered. 'I've watched you grow in the last year. Michael might not be right for you but he was stable and a professional and probably a good father-to-be.' He moved closer to her but Kate pulled away. If he touched her, she was afraid she might slap his hand away.

'You're being unfair and horrible,' she said and realized she sounded like a child. She took a deep breath. She knew she owed a lot to Elliot: his loyalty, his friendship, his help in graduate school and his assistance in getting her this job that she loved. But it didn't give him the right to judge her and judge Billy in this way. 'You don't understand,' she said.

'Oh, yes, I do. I know masochism when I see it. And I'm staring at it right now.'

'Shut up,' Kate told him, her voice lowered to a hiss.

Elliot shrugged. He turned and walked to the door. Then, before he left, he turned back to her. 'Out of the frying pan and into the furnace. This is going on your permanent record, Missy.'

39

Kate looked at the pan bubbling on Billy's burner. It certainly didn't look appetizing, but it smelled pretty good, though she couldn't honestly say she was hungry. Her argument with Elliot that afternoon had not only upset her (and her stomach) but had also made her nervous. What was she doing here? Elliot had told her this was only a get-over-Michael fling but it didn't feel like one. It felt . . . well, Kate needed to hear that this feeling she had for Billy, who was poking at the contents of the pan with a fork, was mutual.

Billy was cooking dinner for the two of them and Kate was keeping out of his way while he worked over the shallow pan in which he seemed to be simmering a lot of tomato sauce, meat, and capers. 'What is it?' she had asked him, looking at it doubtfully.

'An old Nolan family recipe. Hey, don't judge it until you've tried it. And why don't we go out for lunch on Saturday? I'll have to work Saturday night.'

Kate shook her head. 'I have a previous engagement,' she said. 'Bina's bridal shower.'

'Boy, that sounds like fun,' he said. Then he shrugged. 'We've got the bar booked for her fiancé's bachelor party. Let me tell you, I'm not looking forward to that.'

Kate looked down at the pan again and thought about Bina and how upset she seemed. Between the end of school and her time with Billy, Kate hadn't had much time for her friend, and couldn't bear to hear about the ongoing wedding preparation minutiae. Bina was obviously bewildered about why.

Billy, seeing the look on Kate's face, patted her shoulder. 'Don't you worry, everybody likes it. It's a guaranteed way to tenderize the toughest meat. My mom used to make it.' Billy had never spoken of his mother before, except to say she was dead. For a moment Kate considered asking about her but decided that discretion was the better part of valor.

Kate took the glass of red wine Billy had poured her, left the scene of the culinary crimes and wandered over to the window. After her fight with Elliot he had called to make up. He asked her to meet him for a drink but she'd been forced to admit that she was spending the night with Billy and he had made his disapproval obvious and vocal. Kate had tried to ignore all of the calmer, more logical things he had said to dissuade her: about how Billy was a playboy and how she was barking up the wrong tree, and how Elliot loved her but didn't want to have to 'pick up the pieces'. Then he had stopped short. 'You're not just doing this to get a proposal, are you?' he'd asked. 'After all, you turned Michael down and you don't know what the cat might drag in after Billy dumps you.'

The words had chilled her. 'I never believed that ridiculous theory,' she had snapped.

Elliot had stopped being protective only to get offended. 'How can you say that?' he'd asked. 'It got Bina engaged. Proof positive.'

Kate, with a lot of effort and side-stepping, had managed to convince him that she was not taking this affair seriously – no matter what Elliot believed, there would be no proposals. Now, as she stared out the window at the rain, she admitted to herself that both were lies. She was taking Billy seriously, and she was beginning to hope that his feelings for her were totally sincere. Elliot's assured assumption that Billy would, of course, dump her had shaken her more than she liked to admit. Was it possible that she was nothing to him but another notch on his belt? She looked over at him, busily throwing far too much pepper into the pan. He wasn't even wearing a belt for God's sake and his Levi's rode his hips in the most provocative way. Kate turned away. She'd never looked at Michael with this kind of carnal longing.

She looked around the room. It wasn't the way other men she'd known lived. Steven's West Side apartment had always looked like a student's place with its sprung sofa and the books he still had in cartons, while Michael's place, neater and furnished with new IKEA pieces, looked temporary. Michael, like one of Bonaparte's generals, knew how to set up house temporarily until he moved on to the next – in his case academic – battle. But Billy's three big rooms indicated that he had put down deep roots. Beneath her feet the very worn Persian rug in faded blue and maroon looked as if his grandmother might have walked on it. The Chesterfield sofa didn't look as if it was bought from a catalogue – the oxblood leather didn't appear to have been professionally 'distressed' at the factory before it was shipped. But there were new things, too: on one wall there was a big art piece – Kate couldn't call it a painting or a collage because it was something in between – which seemed to be torn bits of white paper glued to a white canvas. On the wall between the windows there was a small abstract of a woman lying under what looked like a very fluffy duvet.

And a series of lithographs hung in a row over the sofa. Kate took the time to look at them. 'What do you think?' Billy asked her. He had come out of the kitchen. 'Are they art or did the artist who owed me a big tab rip me off?'

She smiled at him. 'I like them,' she said.

Billy took an appraising look. 'I think I do,' he said. He indicated the art on the walls with a flourish of the meat fork

still in his hand. 'Valuable art or bad debts. You be the judge.'
He smiled. 'Dinner's almost ready.'

Kate nodded and Billy disappeared back into the kitchen. If
she was completely honest with herself, she had to admit that
Billy Nolan was the first man she had felt this kind of desire for.
It was too comfortable to be infatuation, but too passionate to
be completely comfortable. It would, most likely, end in tears.
And the rain against the window seemed appropriate.

'Hey! How about a little help here?' Billy asked, coming out
of the kitchen again, this time with plates and flatware. 'You
set the table.' He went to the mantelpiece and took down two
candlesticks, the candles in them stubby and of two different
heights. 'Spare no expense,' Billy said. 'Candlelight. Paper
napkins. The works.'

Kate smiled and set the table. She fetched a wine glass for
him and put out the salt and pepper. A matchbook from the
bar lay on the coffee table and she lit the two black wicks. As
she did it, the thought occurred to her that the last time Billy
had used these candles it might have been to dine – and sleep
with – Bina. She stood absolutely still until the match burned
down, almost to her fingernail. She dropped it, just the way
she dropped the idea of Billy with Bina or anyone else and
moved away from the table.

To distract herself, Kate looked around at all of the French
volumes lined up neatly on Billy's bookshelves. She reminded
herself not to be too inquisitive, not to bring up the past or
the future, but she couldn't help being curious, and it seemed
harmless enough. 'What's with the French?' she asked.

'Oh. I like it. It's not as rich a language as English, but it
has subtleties that we lack.' She sat down at his table, where
he had placed her dish, and he carried his own over.

'Did you learn it in school?' she asked and picked up
the knife to cut into the meat. She found the knife wasn't
necessary because the beef was so tender it fell to pieces. It
was also delicious.

317

'A little,' he said as he picked up a forkful from his plate.

Kate smiled at him. 'You must have been a terror,' she said. 'A real class clown.'

He shook his head, his mouth full. He had to swallow before he could answer. 'No. I didn't even talk in class. I had a stutter so bad that I was really self-conscious. I didn't want to talk to anyone.'

Kate put down her own fork and stared at him. She had almost forgotten his slight stammer. But stuttering, she knew, was almost impossible to cure completely and many of the treatments had only a temporary effect. 'How did you . . . when did you lose the . . .'

'Oh, I went all through high school with it. But when I was a junior, I had a good French teacher and I noticed that in French I didn't stutter. It was strange, to be able to say whatever I wanted to without worrying about certain words and letters I always got stuck on. I felt like I was being let out of a prison, so I learned every word I possibly could in French. Senior year I really didn't study anything else. And I didn't care about the grade. I just wanted to be able to speak when I wanted to.'

Sitting across from him, Kate was amazed by what he was telling her. 'What happened then?' she asked, not like a psychologist, but like a child being told a bedtime story.

'My teacher introduced me to some of her French friends, and even though my grades weren't good enough to get me a full scholarship to college, she helped me get into *l'Ecole des Beaux Arts*. I was supposed to be studying French history, but what I was really doing was reinventing myself. I felt like I was reborn. I wasn't the kid who stuttered. I was the American who spoke French as well as any Parisian. Sometimes people I met wouldn't believe I was American.'

'And what happened to your stutter? In English, I mean?' Kate asked, touched and amazed by this story.

Billy shrugged. 'When I had to come back because of my

318

father, it just seemed to be gone. Sometimes when I'm tired or under a lot of stress I stammer a little bit.'

Kate remembered his speech at the wedding. He had stammered a little then, and perhaps he had when they had first met. She refrained from mentioning it except to ask, 'How do you control it?'

Billy shrugged again. 'I just relax and it goes away.'

'You never had speech therapy? No one ever tried to help when you were younger?'

'Oh, there was some attempt at grammar school. You know, a speech therapist. She used to come and take me out of class. I was mortified.' He looked down at the plate. Kate thought he might be ashamed again but he looked up. 'Does this need salt?' he asked.

Kate shook her head. 'It's delicious,' she told him truthfully, remembering her manners. But she was too fascinated by his story to pay much attention to the food. 'Didn't your parents try to help? I mean was there any other . . .'

'Well, both of them were very concerned. Every time there was an article about stuttering with some new cure they got excited. But it was expensive and nothing really worked for long and by the time I got to junior high I just told them to forget it.'

'And you found a way to cure it yourself,' Kate said. His resourcefulness amazed her.

'Well, I kind of fell into it, didn't I? I wasn't so stupid that I ignored the possibility.'

'And what did you study in Paris if not history?'

'Girls. I mean I could talk to them. And I studied cheap train tickets. I got to Berlin and Bruges, and Bologna.'

'Only places that began with "B"?' Kate asked with a smile.

Billy stared at her. 'B was the letter I had the most trouble with,' he said. 'I wonder if that was just a coincidence.'

Kate shrugged. 'Jung would say no,' she told him, 'but I'm not sure.'

319

'What did Jung say about repetition compulsion?' Billy teased and Kate didn't know if she should laugh or cry. She didn't have to do either because he rose and cupped one hand round her neck, then combed his fingers down through her hair. 'I have ice cream,' he told her, 'but I can think of a much more delicious dessert.' Kate smiled up at him.

40

'My God! These girls and showers! They are the cleanest people in the city of New York. Not to mention the ones with the most gifts.'

Brice, despite his sharp tongue, was smiling. He sat between Elliot and Kate in the cab, a big, beautifully wrapped gift sitting on his lap. Kate wasn't sure she could face everyone in Brooklyn but Bina's bridal shower couldn't be missed and afterwards she was seeing Billy. They were going to Sheepshead Bay for a seafood dinner.

Elliot was silent. She knew he was angry at her but there was nothing she could do. She thought of the Pascal line: '*Le cœur a ses raisons que la raison ne connaît point.*' The heart has its reasons which reason knows nothing of.

The story of Billy's French lingered on in Kate's mind. She tried to imagine what a silent, humiliated young Billy Nolan had been like. She couldn't. It was either a failure of imagination or too sad to visualize. Somehow, his history changed her view of him in the present. Instead of cocky and too self-assured she saw his outgoing personality as a celebration of his freedom. It made her feel far more tender toward him, as if he needed protection. That was, of course, ridiculous, since the days when he was a vulnerable child and

321

adolescent were long over. Billy Nolan could certainly take care of himself, but despite her intentions to keep a lid on her feelings, she found herself feeling more and more for him.

They were crowded in the back of the taxi and Kate was relieved when the cab pulled up in front of the Horowitz house.

Before they even reached the front door it was flung open by Mrs Horowitz. 'Come on,' she called. 'Hurry up or you'll spoil the surprise.' Kate would never tell her that she had 'spoiled' the surprise by telling Bina in advance about the party. The two of them had made a pact long ago that they would never allow either one of them to show up badly dressed and be scared out of their wits by a 'wonderful surprise'.

Kate and the guys walked in and joined the others. There were kisses and hugs and introductions. Kate added her gift to the big colorful pile already stacked on a card table. Then Mrs Horowitz called out, 'Sha! Sha! They're coming!' Kate sighed while everyone else in the room seemed to suck in their breath so they could shout loudly. Dr Horowitz flung open the door and made way for Bina. Kate thought she did a miserable imitation of a surprised person, when everybody yelled, but no one seemed to notice and when Bina gave Kate a special look Kate smiled at her.

The party went through each of its traditional segments: the 'weren't-you-surprised-yes-I-was' part. The 'no-you-shouldn't-have-this-wasn't-necessary' section. On to the 'oh-let's-eat-isn't-this-delicious' portion (and they were big portions) and culminating in the traditional oohing and aahing over gifts. Kate knew she was watching an important female rite of passage but she just wasn't in the mood. She regretted giving up the day with Billy, she was annoyed by all of the Horowitz extended family and their questions about when it was her turn, she was bored by the chatter and old jokes. Not to mention resentful of the way Brice and Elliot seemed to relish it all.

322

Kate wondered why Bina kept throwing looks at her and hoped that Elliot hadn't told her about what Kate and Elliot were starting to refer to as 'the Billy thing'. Several times Bina seemed to try to get next to Kate and talk to her, but Kate managed to slide away. Elliot wouldn't have – couldn't have – broken the confidentiality of Kate's private situation without her permission.

When the cake was cut and being passed around, Kate, who could take no more, went into the bathroom to tidy herself up. She looked about as lousy as she felt. She put on some lipstick and a little blush but it didn't seem to do much. She decided it didn't matter. She had been so happy for weeks that her discomfort seemed especially painful. Why was seeing her friends such an onerous task? She thought about it for a little while. Kate believed she wasn't like her friends. She had a career and loved her work. She hadn't been out looking for a husband from the time she was twenty. She didn't feel as if she needed a man to protect her or to support her. But somehow because of breaking up with Michael or seeing Steven or because of this . . . thing with Billy Nolan, she felt as insecure and lonely as she used to feel back in high school.

Since her talk with Elliot she had been feeling more and more doubt. Somehow being here with Bina and all her married Brooklyn friends made it seem more unlikely that she would ever get to share their experience. Billy wasn't 'a safe bet'. He was not the kind of man that women got to marry or that men threw bachelor parties for. Kate imagined his whole life had been a kind of bachelor party and Elliot was right, there was no reason for her to think that would change. Kate began to feel extremely sorry for herself and realized it was best to leave the bathroom now before she had to leave it in tears.

As she walked into the hallway, Bina sidled up to her. 'I have to talk to you,' she hissed. 'Quick before anyone notices.' Bina took Kate's hand and drew her down the narrow hallway to her bedroom.

Nothing had changed in there in years. The same flowered pink curtains hung at the window, the same matching wallpaper covered the walls and the print repeated itself on Bina's bedspread. The dressing table with the pink skirt that Kate had envied so when they were in seventh grade still sat between the two windows. Kate herself sat on the bench in front of it. 'What is it?' she asked.

'Oh, Katie, I just can't keep this lie going,' Bina said.

Kate took a deep breath. She loved her friend's simplicity but sometimes it was just too much. 'Oh, Bina. Nobody cares. If you just act normal now and carry on everyone will be thrilled.'

Bina's face registered horror. 'I can't believe that you would tell me to do that,' she cried.

'Bina, it's just a party. It's not a lifetime.'

Bina's mouth dropped open. 'I'm sorry,' she said. 'I beg to differ with you. I think a marriage is supposed to last a lifetime.'

Kate stopped examining the pictures and mementos on the dressing table. 'Bina, what are you talking about?' she said. 'Just because you pretended to be surprised doesn't mean you're starting your marriage with a lie. For God's sake, have a sense of proportion.'

Bina took a step backward as if Kate had physically attacked her. Then her lip began to tremble. 'Is it really you saying this?' she said. 'Max thought you would understand, but even if you don't, I can't go through with it. I can't marry Jack. It's not like he really loves me. I know what he was up to in Hong Kong. Max showed me.'

Kate sighed angrily. After all that Bina had gone through to finally get Jack it seemed a little late in the day to find a misplaced sense of pride. 'Well, that was very wrong of Max. Remember, you were dating too.'

'Yeah but I didn't want to.'

'Oh, come on, you had a lot of fun with Billy.'

'But that was just fun.'

Kate raised her brows. 'And why are you feeling guilty about that little sexual escapade?'

'Because it wasn't an escapade,' Bina said. 'I keep comparing it to being with Jack and . . .'

Kate certainly doubted that Jack could be anywhere near as erotic and imaginative and warm in bed. But she certainly couldn't tell Bina why she suspected that. And it was hopeless for Bina to think about Billy as an alternative to Jack. Kate truly believed Bina loved Jack and with a little time she would get over this guilt and unhealthy comparison and settle down. Kate believed with her whole being that she wasn't counseling Bina about this because of her own incredible yearning for Billy. Billy would, no doubt, drop her as he had dropped Bina and all of the women before them. 'Bina,' Kate said, rising from the bench and taking her friend by both of her shoulders. 'You have to get over this guilt. You have to move on. This is what you have wanted your whole life.'

'But I was wrong,' Bina wailed.

'No, you weren't,' Kate told her. 'You're wrong now. So just calm down. Enjoy all this.'

Just then the door opened. 'Oh, here they are,' Mrs Horowitz sang out. 'The best friends are at it in here,' she called and lifted her camera to take what would develop into a hideously unflattering picture of both of them.

41

Sunday afternoon was lovely: warm in the sun but cool in the shade of the buildings with a breeze that kept a slightly humid city air from being uncomfortable. 'Let's take a walk,' Billy suggested. 'I'll show you some parts of Brooklyn you might not know.'

Luckily, Kate had worn her Nikes and felt energetic. 'I'm sorry that we can't spend the night together,' Billy told her as they left his apartment. He pointed to the bar. 'Bachelor party tonight. Bina's husband-to-be. I'm glad things worked out for her. Anyway, it's my watch. I'm always on watch during bachelor parties.'

Kate nodded. Billy seemed completely accepting of Bina's nuptials. Had their relationship meant absolutely nothing to him? She shivered, though the weather was perfect. Surely what she felt for him was not unrequited. Billy, always sensitive to her movements, put his arm around her. 'Yeah,' he said, 'those bachelor parties make me shiver too, but I just close my eyes and think of England.'

Kate hadn't even considered the kind of raunchy goings-on that were typical. She didn't want to ask if Jack would have lap dancers or strippers or – even worse. The sun and the cloudless sky were so lovely that she decided to put the whole idea out of her mind and do her best to live in the present. The present was perfect.

They walked faster than just ambling, but slower than power walking. Billy took her hand, and although it was sentimental and wrong of her, Kate felt protected and loved just because he cradled her hand so safely in his own.

'This is Windsor Park,' he said as they turned a corner and walked along a block of small houses, each with a garden in front of it. 'Mostly Italian,' Billy said. 'Cops. Plumbers. A nice family neighborhood, but the yuppies are moving in from the north.'

Kate enjoyed the gardens, some of which were planted with so many colorful flowers that they were almost in bad taste. In some front yards, as if the flowers weren't enough, garden statues of everything from Bambi to the Blessed Virgin added what home magazines called 'interest'. They walked past a big Catholic high school and crossed a walkway over the Brooklyn–Queens Expressway. 'This is the edge of Park Slope,' Billy told her. 'You can't touch a house here for less than eight hundred thousand dollars anymore.'

Kate looked from side to side at the brownstone and brick facades. Billy pointed to one where, unlike the others, the paint was peeling off the front door and the windows were old metal casements instead of the elegant flat expanses on the other houses. 'You can always tell a hold-out from the old days,' he said. 'The old lady who probably owns that place hasn't even painted her kitchen in a decade.'

They came to a corner where a tavern had set a few tables outside. 'Not quite a café yet,' Billy said with a smile. 'Wanna drink?'

Kate nodded. They shared a beer and sat on a bench, watching women with strollers and kids with bikes and dads move past them. 'So you drink?' Kate asked, though it was now obvious that he sometimes did. She had feared that he

327

might be a sober alcoholic, and didn't drink at all. She was relieved to learn that she had been wrong.

'My father told me there were two kinds of people not to trust: the ones who drank too much and the ones who didn't drink at all.' He stood up. 'You okay?' he asked, and Kate was, although she had to write off one more assumption she had made about him.

They walked for another half-hour until they reached a building that was neither as perfect as the gentrified ones, nor as run-down as the one he had shown her. He stopped and searched in his pocket for a moment. 'Come over here,' he said as he ran down the three steps and stood in the doorway. For a moment Kate thought he was only looking for a slightly private place to kiss her but before she reached him he had inserted a key into the door. He took her hand and led her down the hallway of the brownstone, which had been divided into apartments. At the back he used another key to open another door. Inside there was an empty white room. 'Come through this way,' Billy said and led her across the gleaming wood floor to a back door.

Once through it, Kate felt as if she had entered another world. It was a backyard garden, but what a garden. A small lawn was perfectly tended. It made Mr McKay's patch of grass look bald by comparison. The lawn had bluestone placed in it as islands in a green sea. They led in a curving path to a bower of trees – Kate thought they were pear trees. Behind them there was a small – no, a tiny – pond surrounded by iris and fern. Kate could see goldfish darting under the lily pads and duckweed. Two chairs, their wood weathered to a silvery gray, sat beside the pool. Behind them ivy crawled up the brick wall that divided the yard from whatever lay on the other side.

But Kate didn't care what was on the other side or anywhere else. It was the most serene, most beautifully groomed city garden she had ever seen. She didn't want to be anywhere

328

but here. She looked at Billy, who had stopped in the sunshine on the lawn and was watching her. She walked back to him. 'How did you know about this place?' she asked.

'It's mine,' he said.

'What do you mean?'

'Well, when I was a kid we lived here. It was my grandmother's house. She lived on the ground floor and we had the top. But my mother took care of the garden. She taught me, and then I started to like it.' He took her hand and led her to one of the chairs. 'Do you like it?' he asked.

'It's breathtaking,' Kate told him. She thought of *The Secret Garden*, her favorite book when she was growing up. 'You've kept it up? Do the people who own the house now . . .'

'I own the house now,' Billy told her.

'But you live . . .'

'Yeah, I live over the bar because it's convenient and it's the right amount of space and it reminds me of my dad. I've been renting out this place but I keep the bottom floor empty so that I get the garden. I renovated the house – I mean not by myself but with a carpenter friend and a plumber who used to work with my father. Anyway, it's apartments now but easy to turn back into a family house maybe someday.'

Kate sat trying not to show her amazement.

'*Ça te plaît?*' he asked.

Did she like it? '*Je l'adore*,' she told him. '*C'est un vrai paradis.*' She didn't want Billy to see just how impressed she was because it would embarrass her, and possibly embarrass him. She was a psychologist, and supposed to be aware of people's psychological depths, but she had judged Billy as a pool more shallow than the one they sat beside. The idea of him tending the grass, planting flowers and raking leaves just had never occurred to her. Why should it? She wasn't sure what this garden said about Billy, but she could see how much it meant to him. And she knew what it meant to her. A man

329

who could create and tend a garden like this was very special. But it hadn't been obvious to her at all. He seemed so casual, so carefree. But a garden like this took care and . . . diligence. It also took vision. Kate caught her breath. A man with such tenderness as this could surely be a good father, husband, best friend.

She dared to look at him. He shrugged. '*Il faut cultiver notre jardin,*' he said, quoting Voltaire. 'I used to work here with my mother.'

Billy had told her about his father's death, but she hadn't asked him about his mother's. Now she did. 'Pancreatic cancer,' Billy told her, and Kate winced. She knew it was a particularly ugly and painful death.

'I'm so sorry,' she said. 'When?'

'Quite some time ago. The day before Thanksgiving. It still makes the holidays tough.' Kate nodded. Although she didn't miss her father, and she was always included at the Horowitz table, she felt like the orphan she was from Thanksgiving to New Year's. They sat for a while, both silent but it wasn't an uncomfortable silence. Kate felt that by bringing her here Billy had shown her more than his landscaping skills. She took his hand and the two of them watched the fish move in golden darts under the surface of the water.

42

Kate fumbled with the lock to her door and pushed in. The lights were on and she gasped and almost jumped when she realized that her living room was filled with people. For a moment she was terrified that Elliot, Barbie, Bina and the rest would scream, 'Surprise!' and she had become a fatal shower victim. But no one yelled, 'Surprise'. In fact, no one said anything.

She couldn't believe that Elliot – whom she had trusted with a key – would invade her nest, bringing a flock of raptors with him. She would get her keys back, and she would get him back some other way. Before she had a chance to ask what the hell was going on, Elliot, who was perched on a windowsill, spoke. 'Some of you might ask why we are gathered here today,' he said in a pretty good imitation of Mr McKay's pompous tone.

'What's going on?' Kate asked. Her stomach sank as if she was in an elevator gone bad. But at the same time she felt her rage ready to choke her. She didn't even have a place to sit or put her bag down.

'We're worried about you,' Bina said. She was the only one there who looked apologetic.

'Katie, look you're allowed to go out with him, and you're

even allowed to sleep with him, but you're not allowed to fall in love with him,' Barbie added.

'What are you talking about?' Kate asked. But of course she knew. Elliot must have told everyone and now they were trying to do some kind of . . . intervention, or something, as if she were a drunk who needed to be confronted with her self-destructive behavior.

'Time to go now. Party's over,' Kate told them, using Billy's phrase that closed the bar. She turned into her little hallway to get to the bedroom and away from all of these so-called friends. Unfortunately, Brice was standing there, leaning against the wall.

'Sorry, girlfriend, you have to hear this,' he said, and gently turned her around and marched her into the middle of her living room. Bina got up out of the wicker chair and Brice maneuvered Kate over to it. Bev leaned forward – well as forward as she could lean given the state of her belly – and took Kate's hand.

'I know how it is, Katie,' she said. 'You want a home of your own. You want a wedding and a husband and a baby,' she added as if anyone could forget. Kate snatched her hand away.

'I have a home,' she said. 'It's right here and I would like you all to do me a favor and get out of it. Please,' she added so that she didn't sound quite so rude. After all, they probably meant well.

Elliot came up behind her and put his hands on her shoulders. His face was beside her own. 'I wouldn't have done this if I didn't think it was really serious,' he said.

'I want my keys back,' Kate told him and extended her hand. 'I mean now.' It was better to be locked out permanently she thought than ever to walk into a scene like this.

'Look, you moved out of the neighborhood. You might not remember what players in Brooklyn are like, but you have

332

wasted enough time. You're not getting younger this week,' Bunny said.

'Yeah. A fling is okay, but once you're thirty your flings are flung,' Barbie told her. 'And even if the guy dresses well, don't get confused. Whatdoyathink? A blow job's a commitment?'

'Shut up, Barbie,' Kate told her. 'None of this is your business.' She turned and looked at them all. She couldn't defend herself with logic. And a part of her knew they were probably right. But that was a part she didn't want to be in touch with.

Elliot looked around the room. 'I told you this wouldn't be easy,' he said to the assembled bunch of gossips, nosy bodies, yentas and morons that, up to now, Kate had considered her friends. He leaned toward her again. 'Kate, I'm not saying you did the wrong thing in turning Michael down.'

'I am,' Bev interrupted. 'He was a doctor and a Pisces. Perfect.'

Brice silenced her with a look. 'I think what Elliot is trying to say is that you can waste a lot of time with men like Steven and Billy but you get propositions, not proposals, from them.'

Kate could feel her face getting warm with anger and embarrassment. 'We only want what's best for you,' Elliot said.

'We're worried about you,' Barbie added. Then she looked down at Kate's feet. 'Where did you get those shoes?' she asked. 'Are they Ferragamo?'

'Not now, Barbie,' Brice admonished. 'This isn't Full Frontal Fashion.'

'No. It's Full Frontal Confrontation and it's over.' Kate took a deep breath. She looked at Bina, who had been quietest. 'How was the bachelor party last night?' she asked.

'Didn't you hear?' Bev asked.

'There was a fist fight.'

'You're kidding?' Brice said. 'Why haven't I heard about this?'

'My Arnie said it was incredible. Max and Jack really went at each other.'

'Yeah, my Johnnie said Jack's black eye probably won't heal before the wedding. And if Billy hadn't of broken it up . . .'

Once again Kate felt her stomach lurch, this time over the scene in a Brooklyn bar during a bachelor party. She knew Billy kept a baseball bat beside the cash register, but she wondered if he had been hurt. This, however, was not the time to ask.

'So what happened?' Elliot wanted to know.

'Oh, Max called Jack names and he got mad and took a swing at Max but then Max got wild and jumped him. Whadaya expect? They were all drunk.'

Kate stood up. She wanted to call Billy and find out if he was okay. She also needed all of these so-called friends of hers to leave her in peace. But Elliot had other plans. 'Kate, you have to promise us all that you'll break off this thing with Billy,' he said. 'I mean, what's the point? After he dumps you you don't want to get proposed to by a stranger.'

'Will you stop that!' Kate told him. 'What makes you so sure he'll dump me? And if you believe that garbage about proposals . . .'

The room filled with half a dozen 'ooooooh's. 'Jesus,' Barbie said. 'Do you actually think he's serious about you?'

'Kate, this is a guy who has made fear of commitment a permanent lifestyle,' Bev said. She stood up with difficulty. 'You know,' she said, a strange look on her face, 'I feel a little twinge.' She put a hand onto her belly and as she did her water broke.

43

It was the last day of school and Kate was straightening out her files, packing her two plants and saying goodbye for the summer to the children who dropped in. Once she was finished, she knew she should go to Bev's to see her baby. Though she was curious to see it, her resentment of the Bitches still lingered and, if she was brutally honest with herself, she was afraid she'd feel some envy.

Not that she was unhappy. She had the children at the school. Overall, she was very pleased with her work at Andrew. Though she hadn't made any progress with the Reilly twins, she had convinced their parents to dress them in different clothes. It hadn't stopped them from continuing to pull the switcheroo, but at least now they had to go into the bathroom or gym and swap their outfits to do it. If there was a darker side to their masquerading, she would have to find it in September. But most of her other work had gone well. Tina Foster was no longer taking dares or launching herself out into space. Though she was still a tomboy and preferred to chase boys than sit with the girls, she didn't seem at all self-destructive.

As Kate put some papers into her backpack, Jennifer Whalen appeared in the doorway. Jennifer had stopped her exaggerated lying, and Kate smiled at the little girl. 'Coming to say goodbye?' she asked. Jennifer nodded. 'You know, I'll see you in September.' Jennifer nodded again and then rushed into the room and hugged Kate.

'Thank you for helping me with my shelf esteem,' Jennifer said. Kate looked down at her but withheld a smile.

'You're very welcome,' she told her. Jennifer nodded wisely and gestured to all of the empty shelves in the office.

'Do you have shelf esteem, too?' she asked. Kate allowed herself to smile.

'Plenty,' she told the little girl and Jennifer smiled too, turned and skipped out of the room. 'See ya next year,' she called.

Kate had just knelt down to straighten the dollhouse when she felt someone else's presence behind her. Still on her knees, she turned and was totally surprised to find that Billy was standing in the doorway. He took a step into the room and closed the door behind him. His face was bruised, with a swollen patch on one cheek and a scratch over his eye. She jumped to her feet. 'Are you all right?' she asked and moved toward him. He must have been hurt in the imbroglio at Jack's party as she had feared. She wanted to hold him and touch his face but he put a hand up to stop her.

'So who do you expect a proposal from?' he asked. His face was pale, and the bruise seemed even darker against his livid skin.

'What do you mean?' she asked.

'What kind of game were you playing with me?' he demanded. 'Don't try to deny it because I heard all about it at the bachelor party. Those assholes called me "Dumping Billy" for most of the evening. And when one of them finally told me the score, I couldn't believe it.' Kate realized she was holding her breath but couldn't seem to do anything about it. 'Bina got that jerk-off Jack. Who are you expecting to get?'

For a moment Kate considered saying, 'You. I want you,'

but knew this certainly wasn't the time for an admission like that. She moved toward him and tried to take his hand but again he extended his arm as if to be sure she wouldn't get close to him. She could see the anger on his face, but beyond that she thought she could see real pain in his eyes. He must really care for me, she thought. This, however, was not a way she had ever imagined finding that out.

'It's not what you think,' Kate began and then tried to figure out how she could possibly explain all of the machinations and manipulations that had gone on since the fateful day of Bunny's wedding. Before she could launch into an explanation, Billy started.

'Did you all do research? You know, to find out about the women I'd dated in the past and what happened to them after we broke up?'

'I didn't,' Kate said.

'Don't become a lawyer,' Billy snapped. 'If it wasn't you it was someone in your posse.'

Kate looked away. She should have seen this day coming, but somehow she had just thought things would continue as they were going, or that he would tire of her the way he had with so many other women. She wanted to wiggle out of this, but she couldn't lie. The problem was she also didn't want to tell the truth.

'My friend Elliot . . .' she began.

'Is he the one you expect to propose to you after we break up?'

'Billy, he's gay, hooked up, and my best friend. He's a mathematician and, well, he noticed . . . he discovered that after you left girls they immediately got married. He thought there was a cause and effect. And he convinced Bina that . . .'

'And you convinced me to go out with her. Repetition compulsion my ass. The whole thing was a set-up. And I have no goddamn idea why it worked, but Bina is marrying Jack and I figure you've got someone on the hook . . .'

'Billy, you really have this wrong.'

'Oh? I had three hours of bullshit from every guy at the party, all of them blaming me for their marriages.'

Kate felt herself begin to lose her own temper. 'I think you made a reputation for yourself long before I came on the scene,' she snapped. 'I just didn't know when you were planning to dump me.'

'How about right now?' he asked. 'And best wishes on your upcoming nuptials. I hope whoever your victim is richly deserves you.' He spun around, opened the door and virtually smashed into Mr McKay.

'Am I interrupting something?' Mr McKay asked, his eyebrows raised and his eyes darting back and forth between Kate and Billy.

'No,' Billy told him. 'We're finished.' And Kate could only see his back as he strode down the hallway.

44

Kate cried for an hour in her office. Then, when Elliot found her and bundled her in his arms to take her home, she cried in the taxi all the way back to his apartment. She cried when Brice got in, and she cried over the dinner he made. At last Elliot took her to the sofa, sat her down and put his arm around her. 'Kate,' he said, his voice warm and compassionate. 'I know how you hurt. And I hurt for you. But are you sure this isn't just a Bina Horowitz impersonation you're doing?'

Kate, despite her pain, almost laughed and choked, snorting tears up her nose.

'You also have to consider my rug,' Brice added, sitting beside them. 'It's a faux antique Tabriz.'

Kate took a shuddering breath. She couldn't go on crying forever, though she felt as if she wanted to. But what was the point? She'd ruined her life. She'd hurt the man she loved and now he despised her. She had an empty summer yawning ahead of her. Still, she might as well stop crying. She managed a wet grin. 'There's my good girl,' Elliot told her.

'Why don't you try to pull yourself together?' Brice suggested. 'Go on into the bathroom and clean up your face?'

Kate nodded and stood up.

'Do you want me to help?' Elliot asked but Kate shook her head.

'I'll brew up some teabags for your eyes,' Brice told her and patted her arm in a comforting way. 'It will take down the swelling. Believe me, I know.'

Looking at herself in the bathroom mirror, Kate couldn't help it: she began to cry again. Her face was a ruin, her eyes red and minuscule in the puff pastry around them. Her nose, especially around the nostrils, almost perfectly matched the color of her hair. God, she was ugly! She filled the sink with cold water, took a deep breath and lowered her face into it. The shock felt good and she stood, bent at the waist, her face in the sink for what seemed like a long time. Maybe, she thought, she could drown this way.

She thought of Billy in bed, his arms around her. She thought of him from the back, moving, shirtless, as he cooked breakfast. She remembered every book and picture in his apartment, their walks around Brooklyn and his garden. Without ever admitting it to herself, she had hoped that garden, that house, would be one they shared and that they'd fill it with children – children of their own.

Kate's body shuddered for air and she lifted her face out of the sink. She looked back at herself in the mirror as she gasped for breath. She knew this, this breakdown was more than just about Billy. She had been crying because she hurt him, and because she herself was hurt. But she hadn't cried for a long time, and she felt she had also been crying for her past as well as her future. All the tears she had held back in grammar school, on lonely holidays, in high school, through the struggle of college and graduate school, all of the unshed tears seemed to be leaking out of her now. She filled the sink again and immersed herself. She opened her eyes under the water.

She could see now that Billy had been a chance to regain the good part of her background, to heal a lot of her wounds. She had, perhaps, changed her style, but despite the education and the move to Manhattan, her roots were showing. She blinked. Only underwater, her eyes painful from crying, could she see that Billy had been a unique opportunity to love and be loved by an equal, by a partner who would truly know her.

Kate burst up out of the water like a submarine exploding onto the surface of the sea. She still looked dreadful, perhaps more so since some of her hair was now in long wet strands, but she might as well give up. She was about to begin crying again when she heard her cell phone ring. She ran out of the bathroom.

Brice framed her with two hands. 'Ophelia. Drowned for Love and Answering a Phone,' he said. 'Pre-Raphaelite school,' he added.

'Want to stop running the marathon and help clean up dinner?' Elliot asked.

She paid no attention. She got to her purse and began frantically scrabbling through it. Her phone was still ringing. Billy had changed his mind. Somehow he had realized that it had all been a mistake, that she loved him and wanted him and everything else that had happened was nonsense.

She was on her knees, her makeup bag and change purse and wallet spread all around her on Brice's carpet. But when she finally managed to find the phone, the caller had hung up. She quickly punched in the request for received calls, but she didn't recognize the number. It was a two-one-two area code, not the seven-one-eight of Brooklyn. It didn't matter. It had to be Billy. He had come looking for her. She pressed the call button and waited, literally holding her breath. It would all be all right, she told herself. It *had* to be all right. In a moment someone answered the phone.

'Hello, Kate?' It was a man's voice, but her stomach lurched when she realized it wasn't Billy.

'Yes?' Kate said, though she wanted to hang up and throw

the phone not just into her purse but into the sink of cold water. If Billy didn't call, what did she need a phone for?

'Kate, it's me. Steven.'

'Steven!' At the sound of his name both Elliot and Brice nearly dropped the plates and silverware they were clearing from the table.

'*That* Steven?' Brice whispered.

'Drop the phone into this soup right now,' Elliot said, holding out a full bowl. 'I mean it, Missy.'

Kate motioned for them both to shut up.

'Did I get you at a bad time?' Steven asked.

Kate almost laughed aloud. She couldn't remember ever crying for this long in her whole life. 'The wrong time' was a massive understatement but, 'No,' she said. 'I can talk.'

Elliot shook his head wildly, but Kate paid no attention. She wasn't particularly interested in Steven's reason for calling but the deadness she felt talking to him was new and curious. She remembered how she had lived for his calls. Maybe in two years I could feel this way talking to Billy, she thought. Maybe she could learn eventually not to care about anyone. But where was the benefit of that?

'Look, if you're not busy, would you consider meeting me for a drink?'

'Now?' Kate asked. She looked down at her watch. It felt like midnight but it was only eight fifteen. Typical Steven move: calling with no warning and expecting her to jump. But she felt no resentment. 'I don't think so,' she said.

'It's really important,' Steven told her. 'I'm sure you have other things to do, but I have something I have to tell you.'

Kate couldn't think of a single thing that Steven could tell her that would be of any interest, unless he had taken a job distributing Publishers Clearinghouse lottery checks and she was a winner. And even then, what would she do with the money? Buy a big apartment to be alone in? Thinking of her empty apartment made her say yes. 'Where?'

342

she asked, while Elliot shook both his head and his finger at her.

'Can you come downtown?' Steven asked.

Typical. He wanted a favor but she had to go out of her way. She looked like shit and she felt like shit and she told him yes. What did she care? He gave her an address and she hung up.

'Kate, don't tell me that you're going,' Elliot said.

'I am,' Kate told him. She fumbled through her makeup bag, took out a mirror and smeared more concealer under her eyes.

'Rebound therapy is not a legitimate approach to this,' Elliot told her.

Kate stood up, threw her scattered things back into her bag and looked at Brice and Elliot. 'I'm not going to rebound. I'm not a damn basketball.' She walked to the door, then turned back to them, a happy couple in a world of couples. 'I've already ruined my life,' she said. 'You don't have to worry anymore.'

Kate sat beside Steven, her purse on her lap, her legs crossed. One foot was perched on the bar rail. She was actually grateful he had asked to meet at Temple Bar because it was probably the darkest boîte in Manhattan. It was so cool that the entrance, on Lafayette Street, didn't even have a name. It was the kind of place that Steven would know about and go to. It was all dark velvet, elegant up-lighting, murmured conversation and seven-dollar Cosmopolitans. Nothing at all like the Barber Bar. It was pure Manhattan.

Steven hadn't seemed to notice her disarray or, if he did, he had the good grace not to mention it. But as she sat there and looked at him, she realized that he was more about being noticed than noticing other people. There was something about the way he flipped the dark wing of his hair away from his face, the way he held his head, even the way he gestured that made Kate think he was always performing for an audience, real or imagined. Had she always thought that? She couldn't remember. Now she simply sat there, tired and sad, and tried, as best she could, to listen to him. It was a long harangue and had gone on for some time now.

'. . . and I deserved it. I really did,' he was saying. 'I know I hurt you and I know now that I was a fool. I guess I just wanted to prolong my childhood.' He looked away from her but she could see his expression in the mirror behind the bar. She wondered, in a kind of disinterested way, why he was bothering to go through this again. Elliot didn't have to worry. The good news was there was no way she was going to sleep with this player, no way she was going to let herself be hurt again. The bad news was she was so numb that nothing could ever hurt her again.

'I've done a lot of soul-searching,' Steven continued. 'I didn't really like what I found.' Join the club, Kate thought, but only nodded. 'I've been irresponsible,' he said. 'The fact is, I've behaved like a boy, not a man.'

You and five hundred thousand other single men in Manhattan, Kate thought. But again she just nodded. How could she have put up with him? The idea of beginning to date again, of having to meet new men and sit in bars like this and listen to their ruminations and take them seriously seemed not just more trouble than it was worth but a kind of torture that no one should be subjected to. Where was Amnesty International when you needed them? Kate supposed she could get used to going out again or she could simply give up, wait until the rest of her friends had babies and make a career of being a dedicated aunt.

Surprisingly, Steven reached out then and took her hand. Kate jumped a little but managed to keep her purse on her lap and her perch on the bar stool. 'I know you're not listening, and I don't blame you,' he said. That brought Kate's attention back to him. Perhaps Steven was more aware of others than she'd given him credit for. 'Kate, what I'm trying to say is that when we were dating we had different goals. At least I thought we did. But I've had a long time to think about it, and I spent most of that time regretting losing you.'

Kate looked at him, face to face, for the first time. What was he doing?

Steven sighed. 'I can't believe how stupid I was when we met for coffee,' he said. 'It was arrogant of me to think that an apology would be enough to put us back where we left off.' He looked away for a moment. 'Sometimes I lack . . . well, there's probably a lot that I lack. But because I lack you I'd like to try, slowly, to prove I've changed.'

Kate, despite her pain, tried to remember if he'd been more stupid than usual. She supposed asking her out at all had been a little arrogant, but nothing she would not have expected from him. The problem with Steven, she realized, was that he had always had everything easy. He had never had to suffer or work to get anything he wanted so it was only to be expected that he believed he could get whatever he wanted simply by asking for it. Kate took her hand back from his. He looked down at the bar for a moment as if he had recognized a rebuke.

'Kate, you shouldn't waste your time on any man who doesn't value you. Who isn't willing to commit to you.'

Tell me about it, Kate thought, and idly wondered whether Steven had decided to become a counselor for single women. Maybe he wanted her as a client. But, once again, he took her hand in his. Kate felt nothing. But because of her purse and her unsteady seat she couldn't easily pull back.

'Kate, I'm asking for your hand.'

'You have it,' she said.

'No. I mean . . . I mean I'm asking for your hand in marriage.'

Kate couldn't – didn't – believe what she'd just heard. Was she having an aural hallucination, projecting this onto

345

Steven or was he making some bad taste joke? But, to her utter amazement, he reached into his pocket and took out a ring. Before she had a chance to do anything, he slipped it onto her finger. Kate stared at the diamond, flanked by two smaller emeralds, her favorite stone. 'Do you like it?' Steven asked.

She stared up at him. What in the world was he thinking of? His audacity, his presumption, was enough to infuriate her, but then she stared down at her hand. The diamond seemed to wink at her in the reflected light of the hundreds of bottles behind the bar. And then she began to laugh. Once she started she couldn't stop. Her foot slipped and her purse fell to the floor but she couldn't silence herself. She wasn't trying to be cruel – she had lost control.

At first, as she began to laugh, Steven looked at her with a smile. Then, as her laughter continued, he stopped smiling. Other patrons' heads began to turn and look in their direction. She didn't want to humiliate him, but he had already done it for himself. Why is life like this? Kate thought. Whatever you wanted was wrong for you, and you didn't get it anyway. Then when you did, you didn't want it anymore.

With a tremendous effort she got herself under control. She stopped laughing and even stopped smiling. Even Steven deserved at least that. She thought about all the things she could say, all the things she could tell him but decided his education and therapy was none of her business. She simply took her hand from his, pulled the ring off and handed it back to him. 'I'm afraid not, Steven,' she said. 'It wouldn't be good for either one of us.'

His face immediately took on the stricken look she knew all too well. But that wasn't her business, either. In a few days he'd find some other woman who would comfort him, trying to get that look to change. Good fucking luck to her, Kate thought. Then she stood up and patted Steven on the shoulder. 'I have to go,' she told him. Her empty apartment seemed more like a haven now. 'Be well,' she told him. Then she turned and walked down the long bar to the door. It wasn't the best exit line, but it would certainly do.

45

Kate lay on her bed. The oppressive heat had closed down on New York and although it was only June the temperature and stagnant air felt more like August. Kate was unprepared for the heat. She felt unprepared for everything in her life right now; she had an air conditioner stored in the basement but hadn't asked Max to help her bring it up to her window; she hadn't folded and put away her school clothes and refilled her tiny closet with her light summer things; she hadn't made plans for the July Fourth weekend. In fact, summer had come and Kate felt as unprepared for her whole life as she did for her vacation. Somehow without planning any of it she had wasted too much time with Michael, revisited a ridiculous relationship with Steven, inappropriately fallen for and been blown off by Billy. Meanwhile, everyone she knew was moving forward with their lives. Brice had gotten a promotion, Elliot was teaching a course at the New School, the two of them had rented a share in Fire Island, Bina was preparing for her wedding, Bev's baby was keeping her busy, and the latest news flash was that Barbie was pregnant. It seemed as if everyone had a direction – good or bad – but she was rudderless.

The sun, usually welcome, slanted across her bed and,

falling on her legs, made her more uncomfortable. She pulled the rumpled top sheet over her, but her nightgown was damp with sweat and her hair felt matted. She sighed. Each summer she thought about cutting it off. Perhaps this was the summer she'd do it.

Kate thought about the reasons she should get up. She had laundry piling up, she hadn't been to the gym in more than two weeks. She ought to try to get the air conditioner in somehow. There was a pile of books she had been saving to read over the summer. The plants in the living room needed watering. Still, she couldn't force herself to move. She tried to think of something she had to look forward to and failed miserably.

What came to her mind instead were thoughts that didn't bear thinking about: both her parents were dead, she had no sisters, no brothers. Elliot would be gone for the whole summer. Her friends were married. She'd cut off Michael and was glad of it, but the proposal from Steven had thrown her. She didn't want Steven – but she had once. And she didn't want Michael but she thought she might have. She obviously didn't know what – or who – she wanted. Maybe she never would. All she knew was that she ached for Billy, and that of all her friends only she was alone. She was becoming more and more convinced that she would always be alone. Something must be wrong with her, something deep, caused, no doubt, by the traumas of her childhood. Her mother had died, her father was emotionally unavailable and then he died. She had chosen abandonment or abandoning as a way of life.

She threw the sheet off of her and was exhausted by the effort. Why had she moved to Manhattan? Why had she struggled through school? Even her work with the children, over now for the summer, seemed hopeless, useless and second-rate.

But it was the scene with Billy that had made her inconsolable. Thinking about it was almost unbearable, but she played the scene over and over in her mind. Now she thought of the day they had gone roller-blading in the park, and his easy leadership when the crowd became unruly. She wondered if his garden was still so cool despite the day's heat. Thinking of the grass, the fish glimmering in the water, the canopy of leaves, she felt again how special Billy was, and what a perfect idiot she had been. She had sent him two notes: one was a simple apology and the other a longer explanation. She hadn't gotten a reply. It wasn't possible to know if he had really loved her, if he'd read her letters or if – regardless of the nastiness – he would have dumped her anyway, but falling in with Bina's crazy superstition and Elliot's plan had been madness. She thought again of his face when he had confronted her at Andrew. She had seen real pain there and couldn't bear knowing that she had caused it. And she had hurt Michael. And she had hurt Steven, though he had deserved it. Still, she had never meant to hurt any of them, and certainly didn't want this pain she was in.

Her loneliness was too big for her little bedroom. She felt it expand out the door and into the living room until the place felt like a vacuum of love. Kate turned on her side and thought of Billy. It was always Billy. She began to cry and the tears were absorbed by her already-damp pillow.

When the bell rang Kate awoke with a start. She felt sticky and disoriented but managed to rise from the crumpled bedclothes and move toward the door. Who would be visiting her, unannounced, at one o'clock on a weekday?

She opened the door and Max stood there with Bina beside him. Both should be at work. It was Monday, wasn't it? Her terrible weekend had seemed endless, but it couldn't possibly still be Sunday.

'Katie, we have to see you,' Bina said.

'Can we come in or did we get you at a bad time?' Max asked.

Kate was too sad, dispirited and confused to tell him that all time was bad time for her. She just stood aside and let them walk past her into the living room.

'God, it's hot,' Bina, still mistress of the obvious, said and took a seat on the sofa.

'Oh. I should have remembered to bring up your air conditioner,' Max said. 'Why didn't you ask me?'

'I've been busy,' Kate told him, but the sarcasm was lost on both of them. She must look awful, but neither of them seemed to notice. Instead of looking at her, they seemed to either be exchanging looks or avoiding her glance. She thought of the Reilly twins and their bad behavior, but what did Max and Bina have to be guilty about and what naughtiness could these two possibly be up to together? Kate sank into her wicker chair. 'What's up?' she asked.

'It's just that . . . well, I can't . . .' Bina's mouth began to tremble. Kate, perhaps for the first time in their friendship, simply wasn't sure that she could sit through one more of Bina's cloudbursts. After all, she was getting everything she wanted and needed. She'd have the Vera Wang knock-off dress, the bridesmaids, a wedding with all her family there, the down payment on a house, a husband who might now appreciate her and, no doubt, babies on the way. And, as always, after the flood of tears Bina would be cheerful and sunny again. It was Kate who would be drained.

Just as she expected, the waterworks began. Before she could manage to say anything or get up from her chair, Max put his arm around Bina. 'It will all be okay,' Max said. 'I promise. It will all be okay.' He looked up at Kate. 'Tell her it will be okay.'

'What will be okay?' Kate demanded. 'Bina, stop crying and tell me what's wrong.' It was probably a problem with the specially ordered satin pumps she would be wearing, or a mistake on the part of the florist.

'Everything. Everything is wrong,' Bina sobbed. 'I don't want to marry Jack. I can't marry him. But I have to.'

'No, you don't,' Max told her.

'Ohmigod!' Bina said. 'What will people think?'

Kate tried to keep her mouth from dropping open. Why in the world would Bina be unable to marry Jack? Then the hideous thought occurred to her. Could she be pregnant? Pregnant by Billy? 'Bina, you have been using birth control, haven't you?'

Bina looked up for a moment and wiped her eyes. 'Yeah. Sure. Why? Do I look like I'm bloated?' Max handed her his handkerchief and she wiped her eyes. 'My mother sent out three hundred invitations,' she said. 'A calligrapher wrote the addresses.'

Kate could hardly believe that Bina would still feel guilty about her 'indiscretion' with Billy. She leaned forward and took one of Bina's damp hands in her own. 'You shouldn't feel guilty. Just because you slept with somebody else doesn't mean you can't marry Jack. It's not like you had a real relationship. Or that you loved him.'

'It is a relationship,' Max said. 'A serious one.'

'And I do love him,' Bina said and began sobbing again. 'I love him with all my heart.' Now Max took Bina's other hand, which left her none to wipe her nose with. Kate turned away. If she could possibly feel worse than she had, this was the one thing that could do it. It wasn't only Kate herself who was hopelessly in love with Billy Nolan. Now Bina Horowitz was as well. Both of them were ridiculous. Then the thought occurred to her that the terrible scene with Billy might not have been precipitated by Jack's bachelor party but because Billy had decided to reunite with Bina. Would he lie like that to her? Kate couldn't bear the idea of Bina as a rival, not even if she was the one who succeeded where Kate failed. But Bina had to see reason.

'Look, it's just an infatuation. It's a physical thing. It isn't real love,' Kate said, sick to her stomach as she tried to convince herself as well as her friend.

352

'It is real love,' Bina said and looked at Max. 'It's real, isn't it, Max?'

'Of course it is,' Max said.

Kate wanted to know where the hell Max got off encouraging Bina's delusional behavior when, to her utter amazement, Max leaned forward and gave Bina what looked like the biggest, wettest, sloppiest tongue kiss Kate had ever had the shock of witnessing. Then he looked at Kate.

'It isn't just an infatuation, Kate. We're sure of it. I love Bina and she loves me. We didn't mean to do anything behind Jack's back. I mean, after all he's my cousin. But he was, well, playing around and telling me all about it and . . .'

'Wait!' Kate wasn't sure she was hearing this correctly. 'You slept with Billy Nolan and now you're sleeping with Max?' she asked Bina.

'Billy Nolan? Why would I sleep with Billy Nolan?' Bina asked. 'I just needed him to dump me. Then he did and Jack proposed, and I said yes, and you said it was all right even though I slept with Max but . . .'

Kate tried to think back. When Bina had told her about her 'indiscretion' she hadn't been talking about Billy. Kate had misunderstood. And she had spent all of this time tormenting herself about Billy's promiscuity while he and Bina had never . . . 'Oh my God!' Kate said.

'See. I told you. Ohmigod!' Bina echoed. Max smoothed Bina's hair and kissed her on the top of her head.

'Look,' he said, 'I don't mind telling Jack and I don't mind telling Bina's parents, but she's afraid that it will cause a big to-do and that they'll hate me.'

Kate felt so hot and so confused that she was actually dizzy. The room was airless but her mind kept working while she struggled for a breath. If she could possibly feel more regret about the end of her affair with Billy she felt it now and it seemed as if the room was closing in on her and the air was being squeezed out of her lungs. Billy had never slept with

353

Bina. Her doubts about his character, her suspicions, had to be set against the fact that Billy had gone out with innocent Bina and had seen and respected her innocence. She could barely take it in. 'But the towels. The night in the rain when he dried you off.'

'Bina told you about that?' Max asked. 'Did you tell her what we did afterwards?'

'That was you and Max?'

'That's the point,' Bina said. 'I want it to be me and Max, not me and Jack. But I have Jack's ring and the rabbi is scheduled and we picked out the flowers and hired the band.' She began to cry again.

'Do you two want to get married to one another?' Kate asked.

'Of course,' Max and Bina said almost simultaneously.

Kate took a deep breath. She looked at the two of them and remembered the way Max had looked at Bina after her makeover, and the time she had met them sitting together on her stoop, and the night she met Steven and saw Max with a woman, and even the noises she had heard upstairs. 'How long has this been going on?' she asked the two of them.

'Almost three months,' Max told her.

Kate tried to work backwards. She realized that all the time that Bina was dating Billy she had been interested in Max, and Kate had been jealous and . . . oh, the whole thing was too ridiculous. She looked across at her friend. 'Not the same old Bina.'

Bina shook her head.

'Okay,' Kate continued as the reality sank in. The truth was she had never liked Jack. She had never thought he was good enough for Bina. And Max was perfect. All of this was a good thing, and if it had also proved to her that she had been even more unfair in her assessment of Billy Nolan, she probably deserved the extra punishment, though she wasn't sure she could withstand any more. Just because she had totally fucked

354

up her life didn't mean that Bina had to follow in her footsteps. 'Max, you take care of your family. I'll take care of Bina's side. And it's best to do it right away.' She looked at Bina. 'But you're the one who'll have to tell Jack and you'll have to give him back the ring.'

Bina nodded.

'I'll get you a bigger ring,' Max told Bina.

'I don't want a ring. I just want you,' Bina told him, and then they kissed again.

Kate reached over to her phone and picked it up. She dialed the number she knew so well. 'Mrs Horowitz.' Kate looked at Max and Bina sitting so close to one another on her sofa that they took up the room of one. She nodded to them. 'Mrs Horowitz, it's Kate.' Kate was greeted with the usual effusive hellos, invitations to come over for a meal and questions about her health, her job, and her dating life all without a pause or the opportunity to answer. 'I'm just fine,' she said. 'But I have some news for you.'

46

'God, it's hot,' Elliot said, as if they didn't already know that. He and Brice were in formal dress again, and once again they were in Brooklyn. But this time both of them were tanned, and the contrast of their sun-burnished skin and the blazing white of their shirt fronts made them both even more attractive than usual. Kate, wearing a lilac silk strapless gown, was roasting, but they must be melting inside their jackets.

Outside the Brooklyn Synagogue dozens of friends and relatives milled around greeting guests in voices as shrill as the call of mynah birds.

'Howahya?'

'Waddaya doin'? We haven't seen ya in three Passovers.'

'So she's finally getting married. I tell ya her mother was plotzing.'

'Are the Weintraubs here? You know the story, don't you?'

The crowd began to move up the steps and into the building. Kate hung back while Brice moved with the crowd. 'I'll get us good seats,' Brice told them.

Kate stood alone with Elliot. She took a deep breath. 'Another wedding,' she said and tried to keep her voice cheery. 'At least this is the last. I'll never have to buy an ugly bridesmaid's gown again.'

'Hey, you're not a bridesmaid,' Elliot told her. 'You're an old maid of honor.'

'Thanks for reminding me. You're the first of a long and distinguished list.'

'Long and distinguished?' Elliot repeated. 'Are you talking about a part of my anatomy?'

Kate just sighed again. She knew that both Elliot and Brice were trying to keep her cheerful but this was really hard. She was still unable to pull herself together about Billy. Although she knew that there was no such thing as just one person for any other person, she felt as if she would compare Billy to every man she ever met. And the others would suffer by comparison. She had been stupid and she was being punished and there was nothing she could do about it except pretend she didn't hurt as much as she did and wait for time to take the sting out. Having to participate in this wedding, however, certainly wasn't helping her to have a sense of proportion.

As if he knew just what she was thinking – and he usually did – Elliot took her arm. 'Okay, Katie,' Elliot said and made her grimace at the name. 'It's show time.' They began to move up the steps together. 'Look on the bright side,' Elliot told her. 'It's not a three-hour Catholic mass.' He lowered his voice as they entered the sanctuary. 'It actually looks more like a Jewish mess. Check out the outfit on the old lady with the walker.'

Kate glanced in the direction Elliot indicated and saw the old woman with a fur piece draped around her neck. 'Is it living or dead?' Elliot continued. 'And I mean the lady, not the fur.'

'Shut up,' Kate hissed. 'That's Grandma Groppie. She's Mrs Horowitz's mother and bakes the best mondlebroit in Brooklyn. She used to send me a box when I was away at school.'

'And for that you're grateful?' Elliot asked.

Brice called out to Elliot before Kate had a chance to smack him. People were talking, waving to one another and having mild disagreements over where they should sit. Behind her two old yentas were busy gossiping. '. . . So, takka, he changes his mind but he doesn't know she's going to change hers.' The woman, her hair fifty years older than Heather Locklear's but the exact same shade, nodded her head. Her companion, short and dumpy but wearing a regal beaded dress, shook her head and tisked.

'After all those years you would think Jack Weintraub knew what he wanted.'

'Oh, the Weintraubs. For them it's a crisis to pick towel colors.'

'These kids today. What a shanda.' Heavily, she took her seat. But the elderly blonde wasn't finished.

'Don't judge like that, Doris. I lost Melvin after forty-one years of marriage and if I had to do it over again, better I should have eloped with Bernie Silverman like he asked.'

'Bernie asked you, too?' the Doris woman asked in a shocked voice.

Kate was fascinated but she, of course, was part of the wedding party and had to join the rest. 'Can I leave you here?' she asked Brice and Elliot. 'Or will you misbehave?'

'You can trust us,' Elliot said.

Brice nodded. 'I've never seen a Jewish wedding, except in *Crossing Delancey*. Will they really hold Bina in a chair in the air and dance around her?'

'This isn't *Fiddler on the Roof*,' Kate snapped and left the two of them. When she found Bina and her mother the hysteria was already more intense than she expected – and she'd expected plenty. Somehow Bina had forgotten one shoe. 'I must have left it on the dressing table,' she was telling her mother.

'Ohmigod! What are we going to do?' Mrs Horowitz said.

'Myra, it's not a tragedy,' Dr Horowitz said. 'If it was a foot she lost, it might be a tragedy.'

'Norm, what is she going to do? Hobble down the aisle

358

like a cripple? And do you know how much we paid for these shoes? You have to go back to the apartment and get the other one.'

Kate looked at Bina and figured she was about to begin crying. But today Kate saw a different Bina from the one she had known. It was a cliché to say that the bride was glowing, but between Bina's obvious joy and the heat, her face looked beautiful and incandescent, almost as if a candle burned within her. 'Forget about it,' Bina said. 'I'll just go barefoot.'

'Are you meshuga?' Mrs Horowitz asked. She turned to Kate. 'My daughter, the bride, has gone crazy. Talk to her, Katie.'

'I think it's a great idea,' Kate said. 'After all, Julia Roberts did it.'

'Another meshugana,' Mrs Horowitz said. She looked at Kate. 'You look beautiful, darling,' she said and kissed Kate on the cheek. Just then a sweating man in a shirt open at the neck came in.

'We're ready to go,' he said. 'The cameras are set up and we've put the lights on. You better start before the congregation melts.'

'Where are the girls?' Mrs Horowitz asked.

'They're in the ladies' room. Where else?' Dr Horowitz answered.

'Go get them and I'll get the flowers. Katie, you keep an eye on Bina so she doesn't decide to marry a third guy.'

Kate and Bina were left alone. 'You look beautiful,' Kate told her friend. 'Are you as happy as you look?'

'Ohmigod! I'm so happy. And it never would have happened without you. Thank you, Katie.' Bina's eyes filled with tears. 'I love Max so much. I didn't know it could be like this.' Kate knew exactly what she meant, but said nothing.

Just then the girls arrived, looking like a bunch of tangerines that had rolled out of a broken bag. 'Katie!' they called.

'Shh,' Mrs Horowitz said. 'They'll hear you. With decorum.'

'And the bouquets,' Dr Horowitz called. 'Refrigerator fresh.' All the bridesmaids received the same nosegay of orange orchids with glossy lemon leaves. Then Kate got a larger bouquet of lilacs, dianthus and white roses.

'That's not the only thing that's fresh,' Mrs Horowitz whispered into Kate's ear. 'I made kugel just for you. Just don't tell the caterers.' She fluffed up Kate's dress and then looked up at Bina. 'Time to go,' she said.

'Exactly,' Dr Horowitz told her. 'Now go sit down where you're supposed to, Myra. I walk her down the aisle.'

'See you at the bima, Bina,' Mrs Horowitz said and cackled. 'I waited thirty years to use that line,' she told them as she went to take her place.

Kate stood under the traditional canopy in front of the whole congregation with the Bitches arrayed behind her. There wasn't a lot of room and the brims of their picture hats were bumping into one another as well as into the back of Kate's neck. She had her hair up and was actually grateful for the tickling because it kept her distracted. Max and Bina stood on either side of the rabbi. Kate couldn't take her eyes off Bina. She looked so happy and stared adoringly at Max. He was a little bit pale, but he returned the passion of Bina's looks. In fact, it seemed to Kate as if they were unaware of the rabbi, the wedding party or the couple of hundred guests before them. Kate looked out at the rows of faces. She wondered how many of the couples sitting in the pews loved one another. She also wondered if Jack, who, along with his family, had boycotted the wedding, felt desolate. Elliot gave her a little wave, and it helped her feel less lonely.

Most of the ceremony was in Hebrew and Kate was clueless as to what it meant. But she did know that it meant that Bina had gotten the man she loved, and that Max was a kind, loving and dependable man. Kate supposed that she would never find

360

a man she could look at the way Bina was now looking at Max. When the wedding vows, first pronounced in Hebrew, were repeated in English, Kate couldn't keep the sadness at bay any longer. She loved Bina and was really happy for her but Bina would now join the sisterhood of young wives and mothers. It was ironic that just at a time Kate had merged her old friends with her newer ones she would lose Bina to housekeeping, motherhood, and preschool.

'Do you, Max, take Bina to be your lawfully wedded wife . . .'

Kate heard the words and this time it was not Bina's but Kate's own lips that trembled. As tears rose to her eyes, she raised her bouquet as if in self-defense. She thought of Billy, now lost to her, and the way he looked at her when her face had been beside his on the pillow. Had it been with as much warmth as Max now displayed?

'I do,' Max said.

'So do I,' said Bina, inappropriately jumping the gun. People throughout the temple laughed and Kate, who had been on the edge of tears, had to laugh as well. Same old Bina.

The heat and the noise at the reception were almost overwhelming. It didn't help Kate's mood that it was being held at the same banquet hall where Bunny had been married and where all of the Billy Nolan nonsense had begun.

Elliot and Brice were doing their best to keep her diverted but it wasn't an easy assignment.

'When do the Elders of Zion do the blood ritual with a little Christian baby?' Brice asked.

'That's *after* the appetizer,' Kate told him.

Unfortunately, the two of them couldn't keep up the bodyguard act because Kate had to sit on the dais with the wedding party. That left her open to the women who kept accosting her, wanting to know 'When is it going to be your turn?' Kate wanted to tell them she was a lesbian and had already had a civil union performed in Vermont, but she wasn't sure there was oxygen and an EMS team nearby. When the announcement that the dancing was starting was made, she stood up because she couldn't bear to sit there like a target any longer.

'And now, ladies and gentlemen, for the first time on the dance floor, let us put our hands together for Mr and Mrs Max Cepek.'

The room was filled with the sound of applause, shouts of 'mazel tov', the dinging of forks against glasses and the squeals of children who were running from table to table. Max stood up, put his arm around Bina's waist and swept her onto the dance floor, where the two of them began to waltz. Kate applauded along with the rest despite the tears in her eyes. Over Max's shoulder, Bina threw a kiss to Kate and mouthed 'thank you' to her. Kate nodded and felt she could bear no more. As quickly as she could without calling attention to herself or tripping on the hem of the damn dress, she stepped off the dais and, as unobtrusively as possible, opened a door to the terrace.

47

Kate slipped out onto the terrace unnoticed and leaned against the closing door. She was dizzy and having trouble catching her breath. She knew that most likely she was having what psychologists would term 'an acute panic attack' but at the moment she was more woman, less psychologist. She took a moment or two to calm herself. Behind her in the hall, she heard the band begin to play 'If I Loved You'. Kate walked through the heat to the end of the terrace, but there was no escape. It was a corny song and she didn't like ballads from musicals. That was more in Brice's department. But there was something undeniably poignant about the unexpressed fear and longing in the song. She felt her own loneliness welling up inside her.

She'd never get married, and even if she did she had no parents to throw her a wedding. Not, she admitted, that she wanted a wedding thrown at her any more than she wanted the damn bridal bouquet that Bina and the Bitches were conniving to have her catch. She sighed, a catch in her throat.

Then, just a few feet away, there was a shaking of the ivy along the balustrade. At first it was just a shiver, but without the slightest breeze. Kate stepped away, expecting

363

a squirrel or even a chipmunk to emerge. But, instead, the trembling became wilder and the vines beneath the ivy actually jumped back and forth. Kate watched, fascinated, until a hand grabbed the railing. It was followed by a second hand and then Billy Nolan's head and shoulders appeared. Kate nearly screamed, but luckily found herself without a voice. Billy lifted himself by his arms then threw his long legs over the balustrade.

Kate was certain he hadn't been invited, or had he? She couldn't tear her eyes away from him as he stood there, breathing heavily, recovering. He was wearing jeans, a white shirt and loafers – obviously not attire for a wedding.

Had Bina and Elliot been at it again? Were they plotting behind her back? But she'd already broken up with him and gotten her proposal. Surely he wasn't invited. And if he had been, why was he dressed so inappropriately? And why had he chosen to arrive in such an unusual – not to say dangerous – way?

Kate's face registered dismay and she turned around, walking to the end of the terrace. Whatever the answer was, Billy surely wouldn't want to see her. She was embarrassed to be caught out here by him.

Meanwhile, Billy had caught his breath. He looked up and caught her gaze. 'No wonder my dad preferred ladders,' he said.

Kate was speechless for a moment. Then she had to ask, 'What are you doing here?'

'I might ask you the same question,' he said.

She blushed. 'I'm here to see Bina celebrate.'

'Out here on the terrace?' Billy asked.

It was too much. She didn't need to be teased by the man she'd loved and lost.

'I just . . . I have to go back now,' she told him. 'Nice seeing you,' she said.

She got as far as the door, her hand actually on the knob,

when his arms came around her and his hand rested over hers. 'Don't touch the dial,' he said.

Kate watched, her face reflected in the glass of the terrace door. She was flushed and her lips were trembling. It wasn't a pretty picture. Behind it everyone was on the dance floor, celebrating with Max and Bina. Why was Billy torturing her like this?

In the mirror of the door she saw him lean forward. She felt his face beside hers. 'Kate,' Billy whispered in her ear, 'want to dance with me?' Without turning around, Kate shook her head. 'Oh come on,' he said, the familiar coaxing tease in his voice. 'You know you want to.'

Kate turned to look at him. They were face to face, an inch or two between them. She could feel the stream of air from his nose on her forehead. She might not be able to have him, but for now she could have the same air he breathed inside her. Then he took her in his arms and held her to him. They began to move to the music, as close as two people with their clothes on could manage.

Kate was stiff at first but soon couldn't help but relax into his body. God, she missed his smell, his skin, his clean heat. This was breaking whatever was left of her heart but she couldn't help it: she moved her arms up so that they draped over his shoulders.

'Kate,' Billy said, pulling back slightly, 'tell me you missed me.'

'Missed you?' Kate echoed. Could she – or should she – describe the ache and emptiness and regret she'd felt since . . .

'Look, I don't know how the whole thing started, or whose idea it was, or whether it started as a joke,' Billy began, 'but I heard about your proposal.'

She looked up at him. How did he know about Steven? She'd only told Elliot. But then, she reflected, he'd probably told Bina and she'd told . . . well, everybody. 'It was ridiculous,' she said. 'It had nothing to do with you.'

His shoulders, under her arms, shrugged. 'Maybe yes, maybe no,' he told her. 'You know what happens after you date "Dumping Billy".'

'Stop,' Kate told him. 'I never dated you because of that. It's a stupid nickname.'

Billy shrugged again. 'Everyone called me that. And everyone knew its truth but me.'

'You don't think you've got some kind of . . . power, do you? I mean to get people married?'

Billy laughed. 'Don't worry. I'm not delusional. At least not in that way. I watched as, one by one, all the guys I knew got married. And I wondered what was I waiting for? What was wrong with me?' He looked down at her. 'I had a prolonged adolescence. And I knew how much my dad loved my mom. I . . . I had fun, but I didn't want to settle. You know what I mean?'

Kate nodded up at him.

'You were different. You had the courage to leave, to raise yourself above what you came from. You, well, you're accomplished.' He paused. 'And I probably shouldn't say this but I think we have a lot in common. I'm not saying I have your education or anything. But we both overcame a lot of early loss. You know what I mean?'

Kate nodded again, speechless, listening. His body against hers, moving to the music through the heat, felt like some kind of delicious dream. Kate didn't want to think of waking up.

'I think people who haven't suffered, well, good for them, but they're different from those of us who have,' he said. 'I don't know all the psychology, the way you do, but I know that people like us, we're always going to be scared that we're going to screw up, that we're going to make the wrong decision and wind up where we started. You know?'

Kate nodded. She knew too well. She felt her heart begin to beat faster. Was it possible that he wasn't just forgiving her but . . . she couldn't think. The heat and her excitement seemed to close in on her.

'I don't know why I had higher ambitions than the guys I know. Or why I went to France. I don't know why when I came back I wouldn't settle for a job working for someone else. Why I took over the bar and changed the clientele. I just wanted to be . . .' He paused. 'It seemed like I wanted something more than Arnie and Johnnie did, not that . . .' He took a deep breath. 'I mean, how do you pick a partner not just for a few months but for life?'

Kate nodded. Steven had done for months and so had Michael, but for life? How did one know?

Billy continued. 'It's not like I'm a snob, or I look down on the guys I know or the women I dated. We had fun. When we broke up I didn't hurt them. I liked them.'

'I know you didn't,' Kate said. 'They all like you.'

'Good. And it seemed to help them resolve things.' He smiled. 'I mean they did all get married. My magic touch?'

Kate felt her face get hot again. 'You know I never believed that nonsense . . .'

'Until it happened to you . . .'

'It didn't happen to me. I had known Steven for years. And I wasn't interested in him anymore.'

'Really,' Billy said. And at that moment the band inside began to play the 'Hokey Pokey'.

Kate pulled herself away from him to look. 'How did you do that?' she asked.

Billy just looked at her and smiled. 'Coincidence.'

Kate wouldn't accept that. Had he timed this all out? Did he know the band – he seemed to know everyone. She continued to stare at him. 'How did you get them to play that just now?'

Billy shrugged. 'Magic?'

Billy leaned forward and nuzzled her ear. '"You put your left foot in, you put your left foot out. You put your left foot in and you shake it all about,"' he murmured. '"You do the Hokey Pokey and you turn yourself around."'

He swung Kate out, away from him but held her hand tightly. Then he pulled her back in to him, this time closer than ever. He stopped dancing and put his arms around her. He kissed her, and she let him. She kissed him back even if this was the last kiss he gave her, if he was about to disappear to punish her for her deceptions. 'This is what it's all about, Kate,' he said. Tears came to her eyes. Billy kissed her again.

'You're not angry at me?' she asked.

'Well, of course I was angry with you. I was furious.' He paused. 'You know how it is. The truth hurts. But I figured the entire thing out, and the parts I didn't know Barbie and Bev were happy to fill in.'

'They were?'

'Sure. And you know what the French say: *Tout comprendre c'est tout pardonner.*'

To understand all was to forgive all. Kate, for the first time, began to feel hope flood her. 'But we, well, we tried to use you for Bina and I, well, I . . .' Kate looked at his clear eyes and felt a stab of grief as sharp as a staple gun to the heart. How could she have been a party to the whole ridiculous scheme? How could she have used him, loved him and lost him? 'I didn't mean to hurt you, it was just . . .' Kate didn't get to finish. Billy put his hand over her mouth and then kissed her again.

Kate looked through the terrace door to see a large crowd of women gathering around a barely visible Bina and Max. She knew the couple planned an early escape to get the last-minute flight they'd booked for their honeymoon.

'Kate,' Billy said, and she turned back to him. 'I know I just own a bar in Brooklyn, that I'm not as educated as you are, but I can't stop thinking about you. From the first time I saw you I . . .' He was interrupted by a hubbub below them. The wedding crowd was pouring out of the front doors. Billy and Kate watched Max from above as he covered Bina's face. The

368

two of them were pelted with confetti and flower petals. (Mrs Horowitz had not allowed rice. She said it was too dangerous and could put somebody's eye out.) The driver of the wedding limo was holding the door open, but the guests and family were shouting and blocking the couple's way. Billy looked down and grinned. 'Ah. The usual gauntlet.'

Kate watched her friend. Bina was laughing and struggling to get into the car. 'Throw the bouquet! Don't forget the bouquet . . .' yelled Barbie.

Bina looked around wildly. 'Where's Katie? Where's Katie?' She yelled back. '*She* has to catch it.'

Same old Bina, Kate thought. She knew she should be there but she couldn't tear herself away from Billy now.

'Let's go, Bina,' Kate heard Max urge. 'We'll miss the plane.'

'Not until Katie gets my flowers,' Bina cried.

Meanwhile the crowd was turning into a mob. Arnie and Johnnie were 'decorating' the limo with shaving cream and streamers. Mrs Horowitz was giving a bag – probably full of kugel – to the driver while Dr Horowitz tried to confiscate the aerosol cans.

'Throw the bouquet! The bouquet!' Bev screamed.

'Katie!' Bina shrieked. At that Max took the flowers from her hand. With all his strength he wound up to the pitch and tossed them in a wide arc, soaring into the blue, blue sky as all eyes followed them.

With a somewhat violent whoosh Bina's bridal bouquet hurtled through the air toward the terrace. Kate stepped back in time to avoid being seen by the crowd below. To her amazement, the bouquet fell with a splat at her feet. Startled, she and Billy stared at it silently. She felt paralyzed with embarrassment and . . . fear. Her longing was almost too much to bear. Then Billy broke the moment by stooping gracefully, picking them up and offering the flowers to her. Kate accepted them as if in a dream. She stared down at the bouquet in her hands, then at Billy then back to the bouquet. She said a silent prayer that this moment wasn't just a coincidence. That it meant something real and lasting. She knew she was blushing, but she forced herself to look at Billy Nolan, even if it gave her away.

'How did you manage that?' Billy asked. 'Was it magic?'

Kate, no matter what the cost, nodded because it was.

'Kate, will you marry me?' Billy asked.